Few enough died directly from Human bombings—perhaps twenty times seventy. More Hlutr than that die naturally each Terran year. But oh, twenty times seventy Hlutr in the middle of their lives, living fast or slow or in between, growing and sheltering— and all the Little Ones that dwelled with them. The backlash of the Inner Voice killed every other Hlut on the planet. Even on Amny, eight hundred parsecs distant, some of the frailer Hlutr died.

Can I explain how important this Empire has become to these Humans of Terra? Can I explain how they have invested all their being into its realization, so much so that they are willing to deforest whole subcontinents to build spaceports? Stars and Music, how can I explain when I do not understand?

Some of my brethren wish me to take revenge. The way is clear . . . the Hlutr have taken it before. We alone of all the creatures in the Universal Song possess the ability to manufacture those helices of matter that are the very stuff and foundation of life. The Hlutr have guided evolution on seventy-times-itself-seventy-times worlds, large and small. We possess the control to make you over, Littles, into beings that would have the means to kill every Human on this world. A plague, one of my brothers suggests to me—that would spell the end of Humanity.

I could do it . . . I could.

DON SAKERS

THE LEAVES OF OCTOBER

BAEN BOOKS

THE LEAVES OF OCTOBER

A Baen Books Original

Baen Publishing Enterprises
260 Fifth Avenue
New York, N.Y. 10001

First printing, July 1988

ISBN: 0-671-65422-5

Cover art by Judith Mitchell

Printed in the United States of America

Distributed by
SIMON & SCHUSTER
1230 Avenue of the Americas
New York, N.Y. 10020

DEDICATION

To Betsy Mitchell, Stan Schmidt,
and late Spring in New Orleans . . . where it all began.

PART ONE:

Traveller

I

I am but a sapling, yet already I have become proficient in the reading of the First Language, in the rustles and whispers of the Second Language, and even a bit in the vast soundless waves of the Inner Voice with its meanings from beyond the sky.

I am also skilled in relations with the other orders of life, although this world has circled its sun but a dozen times since I broke soil. You may find it strange to hear a Hlut speak of relations with other orders. These are the Hlutr, you may say to yourselves, who stand so far above the others that they touch the clouds, who live so long that they watch mountains change, who talk among themselves in their two languages (for what can you know of the Inner Voice?) all oblivious to the world. How, you may ask, can they even be aware of others?

And your thoughts are partly right, Little Ones—but only partly. True, the Elders . . . those who are old even as the Hlutr count time . . . do not pay that much attention to others. They live so slowly that your lives are but a flicker, and to them you are less than goats are to a mountain. Yet you must not make mountains of us, Little Ones, for we are alive (even as you are) and we know the pains and beauties of living. We feel kin to all life.

Let me assure you that the Hlutr *do* care, tiny and ephemeral as you are. We know you and feel you and

1

cherish you, although you may not think so; for truly, we do not speak with you and seldom acknowledge you. We are aware of the flying creatures who perch upon us, of the land beings who jump, walk and creep around us; of the grubs and many-legged crawlers who live on us and in us and within the ground beneath our roots. We appreciate, we feel for, we cherish all Little Ones—down to the tiny, primal bits of pulsing, growing, mindless life within you and their dull feeling for the Inner Voice, their dull awareness of the great world about them.

I have been taught to be even more conscious of you, Littles, than are my brethren Hlutr. I have been taught by Elders and normal Hlutr alike, living so fast that I have fit many of your lifetimes into my scant dozen years. With each day I grow better with the First and Second Languages, the expressions of my people; with each day I become more attuned to the waves of the Inner Voice: not only that I might communicate with my brethren of far-off worlds, but also that I might talk with you, Little Ones.

Why, you may ask, have I been created this way, why have I been bred and trained into such a non-Hlutr type of Hlut? You may wonder what need the Elders have of a Hlut like me. I wonder too, my Littles. I have some idea. There are whispers in the wind, and pulses in the Inner Voice, that bear news across the galaxy and around the world to me. There is news from the Ancients of Nephestal, whose culture is almost as old as the Hlutr.

The Daamin, the Ancients, tell us that there is a new race ready to come forth and join the Scattered Worlds of the Galaxy. We will all have company soon, dear Little Ones, and I believe the Elders wish to be ready for these new ones.

There are strange stories about them, stories which I do not quite understand. The Daamin tell of these new ones, these Humans, and of their distant planet and their odd ways. We have learned of our stunted relatives the Redwoods of Terra; we have been told of Animals and Dolphins and some of the Humans' strange societal customs (some of them a little like the many-legged crawlers and some of the grubs). In their own way they have studied the Universal Song and learned some of its principles. Enough, at least, to harness some of the power of the First Cause. And they are coming, Little Ones; already their seeds flash outward from their world at speeds as fast as that of the Inner Voice, and soon they will be here among us.

Little Ones, we must prepare for the Humans.

You are afraid of them, Little Ones. Their silver seed sits in the clearing, and it frightens you. Their odd alien smell hangs over the wood, and you are alarmed. They have come among you with boxes-that-make-noise, and you have run from them. And now you seek sanctuary among us.

Do not be afraid. The Hlutr will care for you. As we *have* cared for you, for your mothers and their mothers, back beyond the memory of the Eldest of us all. Ever have the Hlutr cared for all innocent Little Ones. Ever have we delighted in you. Ever.

Look with me, Littles, at these new creatures. Try to hear the Inner Voice as it sings in them. For truly they are alive, and they are children of the stars as are we all, Hlutr and Flyers and Grubs alike.

They move among us now, as you tremble and scurry into your burrows and caves, frightened by their noise and their odor and their strangeness. Only the Hlutr stand, unafraid.

Let me help you to know them, that you may not fear them. My brethren Hlutr speak to me, asking me to explain the Humans: let me explain to you as well. Those harsh sounds are like unto the Second Language, although clearly they lack the quiet soughing beauty of Hlutr speech. Listen to me, Little Ones, and you may grasp something of what they say. The smaller one speaks.

"It's the trees, Karl. Listen: no wind, and yet they seem to be making noise at one another."

"Talking trees. Right."

"What else? Look at the color changes in those trunks. There's some sort of pattern there, I'm sure of it. That's communication on some primitive level."

She feels wonder, Little Ones, the same wonder that all feeling creatures experience when they contemplate the mystery and majesty of the Hlutr.

But the other . . . it sends discord in the Inner Voice. Listen:

"They're plants. How would they even sense the color changes?" He listens to his boxes; they seem to speak to him in some bizarre form of the First Language. "Ship's instruments misread. There's no ore concentrations here. Lousy site for a settlement. Let's go back."

"No, Karl. Look—the leaves are multicolored. Maybe each one absorbs a different shade. Or maybe the black ones are sensory apparatus. This needs more study."

"Two more worlds to check on, and you want to study trees."

"We can take a specimen back to Terra."

"Sure, you're going to bring back a fifty-meter tree. I can see Captain's face now."

"Look at this one—it can't be more than three meters tall. It would fit in a corner of the starboard cargo hold." (Surely you have noticed, Little Ones, that the Elders have not allowed me to grow to but a fraction of my potential.)

"Fight it out with Captain. I want lunch. Here, mark it on the map so you can find it again."

They wander off in the direction of their silver seed. Yes, I can see that you did not understand more than a little of what they said. I must confess that I understood all too little myself.

But the rustles in the wind convey meaning to me, meaning of the Elders' plan, and I am afraid that I understand far too much. Fear stirs in me, just a bit. I ask if there is no other way, and they remind me of the story of the Redwoods. We cannot allow that to happen to the Hlutr; for where would the other orders be without the Hlutr to protect and guide them?

Perhaps Humans acted with ignorance with the Redwoods. We must see that it does not happen again. We must understand why it was allowed to happen in the first place. A Hlut must go with them, back to their world.

For the last time I listen to the wind of my home world; for the last time I feel the coolness of my home soil.

A Hlut must go to Terra.

Remember me, faithful Little Ones, when I am gone.

II

Such a different world! And yet, in some ways, not so unfamiliar. *You* are here, my precious ones; true, you are not the Littles of the world I have learned to call Amny— but Little Ones are the same for all their infinite diversity. Already there are flyers and crawlers about me, already I can feel some grubs tentatively testing the new-scattered dirt at my roots. Welcome, Little Ones, welcome.

It is good to feel fresh air, fresh soil, fresh light again. They have been kind to me, these Humans . . . and the voyage was not a long one. I lived slowly, more slowly than I have ever lived before, and it seemed no more than the merest flicker before we were on Terra.

I have shouted with the Second Language until my leaves hurt from quivering, and all the answer I have received is the meaningless murmur of wind, and the rhythmic whisper of waves on far-off shores. It is lonely. Although we have these sounds on Amny, there is also the rustle of intelligent conversation from my brethren.

Here on Terra, though, all the plants are nonsapient. However much they may resemble Hlutr form, they lack the Hlutr mind. The Redwoods, perhaps, were intelligent, although they never communicated by Inner Voice with the rest of the Hlutr. Perhaps they were deaf in that sense. Some form of Hlut, no matter how primitive, must have existed on Terra to guide the long march of animal evolution from Pylistroph seeds into customary channels— for the Humans are of the same biochemistry and general structure as so many other races in the Scattered Worlds. It saddens me that none of these ur-Hlutr are left to perchance answer my calls.

No matter, though—there is enough else to keep me busy for a long time.

Those who watch me, for example. I have an honored place in the middle of a botanicalgarden and many Humans come to stand before me, looking at a tiny metal rectangle and gazing at me. I greet them with the First Language (which is not as much of a strain as the Second) and they watch. Some even respond with flickers of glee.

Terra has spun six times since I arrived here; and although the first five turns were spent in isolation to make sure I was rid of all Amny's Little Ones, the watchers came. I have learned much about those-who-watch.

Most are full-grown Humans (how strange to call "full-grown" creatures who cannot be three-seventieths the height of a mature Hlut!) making the unending noises they call speech, their minds filled with distortions of the Inner Voice concerned with time and rush and ever, ever with movement. With a few, there is curiosity and even a healthy appreciation of me. (My brethren are delighted to learn that Humans can be awed by the sight of a Hlut, but all too often my brethren think too highly of the Hlutr place in the Universal Song.) But none of these adult Humans, not one, is ever content. Their thoughts and feelings, when they can be read at all, are fastened upon something else. Always they have little regard for the Universal Song of which everything is a part—Humans, Hlutr, botanicalgarden, and Terra too. Always they have even less regard for the magic and beauty of themselves.

There are others, however, who come to look . . . and I find them much more pleasing. These are the Human seedlings, who are always in the care of the mature Humans (you need only think of the many-legged crawlers who protect their eggs and larvae). The seedlings make noise too—and their noise is more raucous and less soothing, even, than the speech of the adults. Despite that, my Little Ones, if you will look at them with the eyes of the Inner Voice you will see that they are simpler than the adults. These children are more like *you*, Littles, the way they happily watch as the colors of the First Language race across my trunk and through my leaves. Sometimes I feel that I can talk to the Human children, as I can talk to you, my dears.

Some come who are upset—as you are often upset, when you are hungry or your young are threatened, or when your mate has died. For some of them, those who will listen, I can work a twist of the Inner Voice and they go away happier, more peaceful. I do not mind this work—indeed, when has a Hlut ever minded helping the Littles?

But I feel that there is more important work I should be doing. The Elders have not expressed themselves well in the eddies of the Inner Voice—and those eddies are hard to read across the parsecs, with all the interference of all the Hlutr on other worlds. I shall think hard, and consider deeply, and perhaps it will come to me. Following the orders of the Elders, I shall try to talk with the Humans—although I have been here six days, and have had little if any success in making them realize that I can speak. However, we must not expect Humans to be as fast as a Hlut would be; I shall give them time.

Meanwhile, I have those-who-watch, especially the children. And I have you, Little Ones.

III

There are parades, there is joy and cheer all around. The Botanical Garden is hung with bright holos and flags and signs, and the children skip about shouting and laughing at my colors; I am shouting in the First Language to produce pretty patterns for them.

You must be careful, Little Ones, not to get hurt on this day of joy. The Humans are often forgetful of you, and you are all too used to the careful attention of a Hlut. So scurry when you see the Humans coming, and watch their feet lest you are tromped on. Their children are the most careless. You must not think ill of them—for if you could but see the Inner Voice within them as I do, you would know that they are filled with joy and not malice. Their minds are small, though, and they can only pay attention to a few things at a time. And some of you are so little that you cannot take much of their joy.

Why, you may ask, are the Humans so exuberant? You have seen before parades and fairs and celebrations, but none in your experience match the reckless joy of this day. Gather around me, Little Ones, and I shall try to explain . . . although I do not fully understand.

You see, Humans love one another with a powerful feeling. You may understand this, tiny crawlers, but the others may not be able to see it. And Humans have a strange desire to see themselves in many places in the Universal Song. The more places, the more Humans to love. (Yes, birds, you may rest upon my branches.)

Well, my Littles, this day we see the declaration of much love for many Humans in the Galaxy. This day, there has been the proclamation of an Empire. (Come, squirrels, and sit with me.) This day, starships will begin to sweep across the Scattered Worlds and unite all the colonies of Humanity. There will be much pain and much joy and ever so much glory. It will be a beautiful and tragic addition to the Universal Song.

Yes, I know it is a difficult thing to explain. I must admit, now that you are all confused by my explanation, that we Hlutr do not grasp the Human drive for Empire any better than you do. We have received some conception of it from the Daamin, and even more from the sons of Metrin, who have a similar drive. And there have been many examples in the distant past, from sad Iaranor to grand Avethell and all her daughter worlds.

It must be a very animal thing, not known to plants. It is but one of the mysteries about the Human race. They will lose themselves in this power-and-glory struggle, lose themselves to the most evident joy and the strongest emotions.

Why Humans should wish to lose themselves is another question entirely.

It has been almost sixty years, my Little Ones, since I have been on Terra. I have grown, as all Hlutr grow (either slow or fast as they wish) . . . can you believe that there was once a time when I was only as tall as a Human, I who now stand as tall as ten Humans one atop the other? I have seen many things: I have watched children grow and adults die, and I have seen new ones born. (They are truly delightful when they are born, so very vegetable, just like tiny seedlings pushing their heads into the light for the first time.) Still I do not understand them. I have been living very quickly, as quick or quicker than Humans themselves live, and I have been thinking very much.

I suffered, Littles, across Human light years with the rape of the ecologies of nearby Laxus and Leikeis and other worlds. I have watched thousands of red and beautiful sunsets, and have rejoiced with all the creatures at the stinging freshness of Terra's clean rain. I have sung with the Whales, greatest of my Little Ones, once I found the way to pick up their own Second Language from the world-seas.

Humans have not talked with me. My brethren on Amny and other worlds tell me that Humans ignore them as well. After a few regrettable murders, the Human colonists have left the Hlutr alone. Every once in a while someone wonders about our color changes (although, to my knowledge, not one has ever suspected the existence of the whispers of the Second Language—mayhap because it sounds so much like the wind) . . . but they have never quite realized that the First Language *is* language.

That is why I am so happy today, Little Ones. I have great hopes for this Empire of theirs. I sense a new spirit in the Inner Voice of these creatures; they are taking a good look at the Universal Song, and it is possible that they will begin to discern the place of the Hlutr in that Song.

Ah, here comes a child. No, my Little Ones, don't flee from him. Stay, and see how innocent he is. Mind, now, don't get stepped on.

Welcome, child. You children, sometimes, watch my colors with curiosity—perhaps *you*, lad, will grow up and retain your wonder at the pretty colors you watch so absorbedly, and will discover that the Hlutr actually talk.

Run along, now; my leaves quiver to the sound of your parents' voices, you must return to them. But . . . perhaps you will be back.

IV

A terrible thing has happened, Little Ones, something which has shocked the Elders and the Hlutr of all the Galaxy.

Could I intercede for the Humans, I would. But I do not understand. Elders, Stars, Universal Song . . . why?

I of course never saw Credix, grand world that has now become one of the Provincial Capitals and a major military base for the Empire. Yet I have seen images of it still burning in the minds of those who visited. And I have sung the melodies of the Inner Voice with the ancient community of Hlutr who lived there.

Gone, gone. Not one Hlut remains on Credix. Few enough died directly from Human bombings—perhaps twenty times seventy. More Hlutr than that die naturally all over the Scattered Worlds each Terran year. But oh, twenty times seventy Hlutr in the middle of their lives, living fast or slow or in between, growing and sheltering— and all the Little Ones that dwelled with them. The backlash of the Inner Voice killed every other Hlut on the planet. Even on Amny, eight hundred parsecs distant, some of the frailer Hlutr died.

Why? you Little Ones ask. And why, ask my brethren from beyond the sky. Why?

Can I explain how important this Empire has become to these Humans of Terra? Can I explain how they have invested all their being into its realization, so much so that they are willing to deforest whole subcontinents to build spaceports? Stars and Music, how can I explain when I do not understand?

There are those of my brethren who wish me to take revenge. The way is clear . . . we Hlutr have taken it before. We alone of all the creatures in the Universal Song, we possess the ability to manufacture those helices of matter that are the very stuff and foundation of life.

I could . . . I could.

You, my Littles, could provide the basic materials upon which I could work. The Hlutr have guided evolution on seventy-times-itself-seventy-times worlds, large and small.

We possess the control to make you over, Littles, into beings that would have the means to kill every Human on this world. A plague, one of my brothers suggests to me—your little pulsing bits could be converted into other little bits that would spell the end of Humanity.

I could do it. It would require my death—that death-detonation which is the ultimate meaning of the Hlutr race, that last gasp that so few of us have ever really undergone—to spread the synthesized substances far.

I could. I will not.

Listen to me, brethren. I plead for the Humans. They did not know what they did. It is *my* failing, for I have not yet been able to make them realize that we are sapient. Just as a Hlut does not hesitate to destroy a nonsapient plant that is in his way—so these Humans did not hesitate to destroy what they imagined to be nonsapient Hlutr on Credix.

Let me work harder, brethren, and let me make them see what we are. And then . . . then they will hurt us no more.

The Elders answer with a sigh that is both dirge and decision. Until I can do a better job, until I can convince the Humans that we are sapient . . . they will be spared.

A terrible thing has happened, Little Ones. Now the sap of all those Hlutr, all the forests of Credix and all the dead Hlutr beyond . . . are my responsibility. Ever in the Universal Song will my failure be noted, and ever will I be linked with Credix in the tales that will follow.

Ever.

V

Winter comes, as it has come over three-times-seventy-times since I have been here. I have watched the leaves of the trees with which I share the Imperial Botanical Garden turn color and fall many times, and I shall never grow tired of the sight. It is a joyful vision which we do not have on Amny; for Amny has no winter, only eternal spring.

The Humans also like to watch the leaves. They cannot guess that within those colors is preserved a genetic memory of the Hlutr spores from which these trees' ancestors of millions of years ago sprang. For the yellow-red-orange pattern of the leaves is the same pattern seen on a Hlut deep in communion with the Inner Voice, listening contentedly to the ebb and flow of tides from brethren Hlutr and from life the Galaxy round. It is the sign of a Hlut experiencing the profound joy without which the Universal Song is toneless and without purpose.

These last few winters have been even more delightful for me. There are few of you about, with the snow gathering—and nowadays you tend to come near me less and less, for the Research Station's new building was put up less than five man-lengths from me, and many of you still fear to approach it.

I am left with the company of crawlers and grubs, and a few brave birds. You, birds, no longer nest in my upper branches—thirty man-lengths is a bit high for a nest—but I cherish your homes in my lower branches. I have cared for your young, as much as I am able; for the Hlutr *do* love you, Little Ones. Yet you feel that I am more distant from you than I have been in the past.

True, I have not spoken with you much. I have been very busy.

I have been living faster than I have ever lived, save for the hectic days of my saplinghood on Amny. It is necessary, you see, to live quite fast to keep up with Doctor Rubashov and the others of the Research Station. It is important to me, Little Ones, and important to the Hlutr as a race, that Doctor Rubashov be given all the evidence he needs to prove the Hlutr sapient in Human terms.

I do the bidding of the Elders, in this and in all things. For this I was sent to Terra, for this I have stood in this Botanical Garden for Human centuries.

Now young Doctor Rubashov approaches, and I must concentrate all my energies upon the seedlings' talk which we have managed to improvise in the First Language. His apparatus is all set up; I greet him.

"Good day, Doctor. Are you understanding me?"

A televisor screen flashes color-patterns at me. Were he to shout, I could understand his speech—in my time I have become quite good at reading Human speech—but it is easier to use the First Language.

"I am reading you. Good morning. Are you ready for the day's experiments?"

"Certainly." To tell the truth, Littles, the prospect of another day of numbers and simple concepts, as if I were a seedling being taught by the Elders, is abhorrent. I don't mind living fast to talk with things, but I dislike doing it simply for numbers.

Before he starts the day's trials, Doctor Rubashov adjusts some of the leads which monitor my biochemical states. When his hand touches my trunk I have a sudden flash of Inner Voice clarity.

"Doctor, you are disturbed. Why?"

"I've been working for two years to show that you are intelligent. I've convinced myself time and again, but the (something) are not yet convinced. With such slim evidence we won't ever be able to get the (something else) to recognize you as sapient. And that'll be the end of my career."

"Have you noticed how beautiful yon city looks all covered with snow? Does not appreciation of that beauty qualify me as sapient?" (You may wonder why we include appreciation of beauty and wonder in our definition of what constitutes sapience. Why, certainly one of the most important things we share with other sapients, Iaranori and Avethellans, Dolphins and Metrinaire, even the poor children of Nephestal—surely it is this ability to be profoundly stirred by the simple miracles of the Universal Song.)

"Well now, you may think so. And I may think so. But I don't think the (something) agrees. Now let's get started."

"But are the hills not beautiful?"

"I suppose so." He is still disturbed, and I cannot read his feelings well enough to do more than guess. I live more quickly and try to match my own chorus of the Inner Voice with his cacophony. There are shattered images—a Human woman, and unpleasant scenes of anger, and— But it all fades back into the private reaches of his mind.

"We have a lot to do today," Doctor Rubashov continues, "for we won't be able to work the next few days."

"Yes, of course. Let me wish you a joyful Solstice, Quen Rubashov."

"Where did you learn that?" He sends a quick wave of surprise in the Inner Voice out toward the stars.

"I have been here a long time. I have observed much of your race and your customs. Oh, and I have an important matter to discuss with you—in the spirit of Solstice."

"Go on."

"My brethren and I have noticed the new center for emotionally disturbed children that was built a few kilometers from here. Disturbances in the Inner Voice have made it difficult for me to communicate with my brethren Hlutr beyond the sky."

"There's no way to have that center moved further away. How do you know about it? Has one of the techs . . . ?"

"You misunderstand, Doctor. No, I don't want the center moved away. If you will move the youngsters closer, I believe I can help heal them with the Inner Voice."

There is a long pause. "We'll see." Then Doctor Rubashov starts flashing numbers at me. I settle down to a long day's work.

Little Ones, Little Ones, come close to me. How the wind rushes through my branches, how it shakes me to the roots!

How could he do it? No, Littles, I am not asking a literal question. I *know* how he could do it. He took a dropshaft to the top floor of the Imperial State Building and threw himself off. And after long seconds of freefall, Quen Rubashov was no more.

How? Why? Because his work was going badly? Because that woman left him? Because, because, because . . . a thousand so-called reasons beat in the minds of those on the research team. They have not told me yet—but there is no hiding it. I was attuned to his own theme of the Inner Voice. There was no mistaking his cry on Solstice Eve.

How could a sapient being do that? Littles, I fear I will

never understand Humans. How can any living being embrace nonlife? How can it hate itself so much as to wish to be not-self? Make no mistake, my faithful simple Little Ones . . . what I felt in Quen Rubashov's mind that night was not only anguish, not only dread, but a feeling of welcome for the fate he had chosen.

How can an individual be able to perform such a supremely unsane act? How, when faced by all the wonders and mysteries of existence, can he choose to embrace its opposite?

One tiny voice in the Universal Song was stilled that night, Little Ones, stilled by its own hand because it preferred silence to the Song.

I do not understand.

Come closer, Littles, please. Feel the wind . . .

VI

Children are delightful, my Little Ones . . . their minds are almost as simple as yours, yet so very complicated at times. Through it all, though, they have an awareness of the Inner Voice like none I have seen in other Humans. The others call these seedlings disturbed. They cannot be aware that the disturbance stems in many cases from a talent for understanding the Inner Voice. They come to the Center, in the buildings of Rubashov's old Research Station, and they play with their blocks and toy trains and dolls; and all the time I soothe the raucous noise of the Inner Voice that they project. In time, many are cured and they leave.

The ones I like best, Littles, are those who are never cured. The ones who sit and stare deeply into my trunk and the patterns that race there, and who listen to the Second Language as if they could understand. Oh, they are bothersome, with their rages and hatreds and deep depressions. But there are times when the Inner Voice is at peace in them. Those times, I can almost get through. I send waves of the Inner Voice after them and they strain to hear.

Lately, I think a few have even begun to answer.

I must tell my brethren Hlutr. The Elders will be very interested. Maybe, even, the time will come when these children can cast ripples of the Inner Voice outward to other Hlutr.

Perhaps the nurses think that *they* are caring for the children, perhaps the programmers think that they have worked miracles. I know better. And more and more lately, I believe that the children know better too. When they look at me their eyes are bright and aware, and the Inner Voice sings. I am on the brink of communication.

In addition I have you, my Little Ones. For you must never imagine that I have forgotten you. Birds and ants and spiders and squirrels and worms beneath my roots, I remember and feel and cherish you one and all.

And I live for October each year, when the beautiful colors sweep through leaves around me, when I am reminded of my sapling days on Amny, and of other Hlutr.

I have not seen any of my brethren since Amny; had I stayed, I would have been surrounded by a forest of them. It saddens me a little, my friends. I have a mission, and I content myself with the sight of autumn and the remembered whisper of the Second Language. Humans have yet to find me sapient, and I have lately been much more content with autumn than with my mission. And, of course, with the children.

I think little Chari Anne is trying to talk with me.

VII

Chari Anne comes now, Little Ones—I can feel her vibrations in the Inner Voice. You mustn't be afraid of her, nor of the tiny one she brings with her. She has learned much, in eight decades, of the way of the Hlutr and their concern for the other orders of life. Chari Anne cherishes you, Littles, as do I.

You see, she walks among you without harming even the smallest, projecting peace with the Inner Voice. She moves to the equipment that once belonged to Quen Rubashov, in the abandoned building of the Center for Disturbed Children. The children have been moved away, over the years, as Human psychologists learned more about the Human mind and began more and more to distrust this alien creature. I have felt loneliness, but I have at least been able to live a good deal more slowly. That is a good thing, for I am coming near the end of my span. I have always lived fast, however, when I am visited by some of the children from the old Center: Chari Anne, Staven, Daris, Kaavin, and the few others.

Chari Anne sits before the communications screen, holding a Human boychild on her knee, and switches on the equipment. Since adulthood her command of the Inner Voice has been fading, and meaningful talk is now difficult without the equipment.

"Good morning," she says.

"Good morning, Chari Anne. Thank you for coming to see me. Are the leaves not beautiful?"

Her Inner Voice radiates warmth that I have learned to associate with her smiles. "Yes, they are. You always did love to see autumn leaves."

"I always did." She waits. I think she is tired, and I fear it will not be much longer before she passes out of the Universal Song. Once, Little Ones, I would have told you this is the way of all creatures, except the Hlutr, who are so old they live hundreds of your lifetimes. Now, as I near the end of *my* time in the Song, I am not too sure.

"Chari Anne, who is the Little One you have brought with you? His mind is delightfully sharp."

"This is Elsu; he is my first great-grandchild. Elsu is Liene's son." Chari Anne is the progenitor of many Humans; she always brings the infants to me, and while they grow they are much in my company. As adults, they return every so often. I remember Liene as a child, Littles, and now Elsu gives me the same wondering look, coos in delight as I race patterns of the First Language up and down my trunk for him.

All my children from the Center—they all bring me their young ones. Were we to gather every one here on this hill, we could fill the old building to overflowing.

"What news do you bring of the others?" I ask.

"Daris has finished her major composition at last, and her troupe is touring with it. The show is very popular."

"Daris dances well." I do not tell her what I have seen in Daris's mind when she dances, for it cannot be put into words. It is a feeling of the Inner Voice, when all harmonies are matched and one is in union with the Universal Song. Daris feels it when she dances . . . and in Daris's children and grandchildren I have caught the same joyful melodies.

"Kaavin sent me a long holotape just the other day. He's working at some far-off system, testing some theories he has about stellar formation or some such. I didn't completely understand what he said—but then, few enough of us ever understood Kaavin."

"He is happy."

"He certainly seems to be." Elsu imitates his great-grandmother and hits keys on the board; the equipment transmits a raucous squawk. Chari Anne feels my glee, and she laughs. Elsu chuckles as well. "Oh, Staven has some good news. Do you remember the problem he had with those Kaanese?"

I thought. Yes, Staven had told me just a while ago. Half a hundred nonhumans were trapped on a Human world, because their home was across the border and a war was going on. Staven made it his lifework to study and help nonhumans. He'd been trying to find a way to get those Kaanese primitives home.

"He succeeded?"

"Yes. More than we hoped. Both governments made a truce across that border long enough to get the Kaanese back where they belonged. It's the first truce ever between Patala and the Empire."

"I am proud of Staven."

"We all are."

For a while neither of us says anything. This is fine, Little Ones, for I can feel Chari Anne's Inner Voice melodies, and I listen busily to and sing with the innocent song of Elsu.

Finally Chari Anne puts hands back on the keyboard. "I have news. I just learned yesterday. The Empress is going to sign the bill declaring Hlutr legally sapient. The Imperial Council passed it along with all the attendant protection laws. Staven's data and my own experiments convinced them at last." With the Inner Voice I can hear her listening. "What's wrong, aren't you excited?"

"I sigh, Chari Anne. Yes, I am excited. My brethren will be pleased to hear it. And yet . . . well, Chari Anne, I am not long for this world."

She is concerned. "What's the matter? I thought that Hlutr lived . . . well, if not forever, at least a very long time."

"Again I sigh. How long we live depends upon how fast we live. The Elders, who are as old as my world, live very very slowly. Here on Terra, I have been forced to live very quickly. And I am nearing the end."

"I am distressed."

"Don't be. All that is mortal passes from the Universal Song. We must accept its passing."

The Inner Voice is disturbed with her rage, and it drowns out the background murmur of all the life around us. Even Elsu feels it. "Damn it, how can you be so philosophical?"

"A tender smile, Chari Anne. There is no other way. I have watched Humans die for four hundred years and more, and it has not upset me. I have watched the other orders live and die countless times since I arrived on Terra. The life is important, Chari Anne . . . but more important is the way it is lived. I have lived mine well."

Again we say nothing for a time, while I use the Inner Voice to calm the seething storm of Chari Anne's mind. Littles, this is one of the jobs of the Hlutr. Being masters of the Inner Voice, we naturally try to use it to help others when we can. "Chari Anne, I would like it very much if you could do something for me. Now that the Empress is declaring us sapient, I will not be needed for study."

"I suppose not."

"Do you think that you and the other children—"(for I still think of Chari Anne and the others as the children they once were. The important part of them never did grow up and become lost) "—could arrange to have me

shipped back to Amny, so that I may die among my own
kind?"

Again her Inner Voice is in turmoil. "If that's what you
want . . . except . . . Staven pulled a lot of strings to get
those Kaanese home. Especially after Patala attacked
Karphos. I don't know if he could get another truce so
soon. He doesn't want to push things. If Amny is anywhere near the war zone—"

I am not ignorant of galactography, Little Ones, and I
calm her fears. "Amny is near Credix, Chari Anne, across
the galaxy from Karphos." The Elders are deeply disturbed by the destruction of Karphos and the progress of
the Human war. There have been Hlutr killed, and their
pain echoes yet on crests of the Inner Voice around the
galaxy. And Humans have died by the millions, at the
hands of their brethren . . .

"We'll do it. We'll have you taken back to Amny."

There is another long pause, and I look at the brilliant,
joyful leaves of October. Soon I will leave you, Little
Ones, birds and squirrels and insects and worms; I shall
remember you fondly, and I hope you will remember me
until your little lives are over. "One more thing, Chari
Anne. Before I go, do you think it would be possible
. . . for me to say goodbye to all the others, and their
children and grandchildren?"

VIII

Again I feel the soil of Amny below my roots, and again
I am among creatures of my own type. True, Amny has
the smell of Humans now; their city dominates the clearing where once a grassland stood in happy golden awareness. True, their airships drift through the sky bearing
cargo, and their starships arrive and depart on a daily
schedule from the spaceport. These changes cannot over-
come the feeling of my home world.

For the first while, Little Ones, the world seemed wrong.
was too heavy, the air was too cold, the sun was not the
right color. I learned to forget these minor differences.
Amny, at least, has something Terra never did—the intel-

ligible rustles of the Second Language, the colors of the First.

At my request the Terrans placed me in the middle of a group of Elders. They were impatient (insofar as an Elder can be said to be impatient) to learn of Earth and Humans, and I knew they would use the First Language. Had I been placed in my original spot, out of sight of the Elders, they would have been obliged to use the Second with its much lower information density.

I live slowly now, Littles, almost as slowly as an Elder. I tell them all I saw and felt and heard.

They debate; the sun moves against the stars. A message comes through the waves of the Inner Voice, a message from the Hlutr ambassador to New York. Chari Anne has died. So, my Little One, I have outlived you. I am saddened, as no Hlut should be for the passing of a lesser order. I shall remember you joyfully and with wonderment, Chari Anne.

The Elders debate for seven years; near the end they are living almost as fast as normal Hlutr, and I am living almost as slowly as the crystalline Talebba. Finally one of them lives slowly enough to talk with me; he is the Elder who trained me, a lifetime ago.

"Brother Hlut," he says with the First Language across seasons, "we have debated with ourselves and with Hlutr on the other Scattered Worlds. The Inner Voice has been in turmoil with our discussion. And we have reached a decision." More of the Elders join us; and in slow pulsations of the Inner Voice I am aware that Hlutr Elders from all over the galaxy are joining this conclave. "I shall repeat our decision to you."

"Thank you, Brother Elder." I have trouble with the First Language . . . age is telling upon me. Is the sun shining? I feel so cold.

"You were sent to Terra, you know, for a mission. The Humans investigated you, and finally they judged you and the Hlutr sapient. That was not the purpose of your mission."

"This I have suspected, Elder."

"From what you learned about Humans, we must needs

rule on their own sapience. We must rule on whether they present a menace to the Hlutr and the other orders of life in the Scattered Worlds."

"Let it be so, Elder. For the Hlutr must protect life and the Inner Voice. So has it been since the first seed vessels of the Pylistroph (blessed be!) set forth into the Scattered Worlds, so shall it be when the last star dies." I am so cold. Chari Anne, will I see you when I die? Do Hlutr and Humans go to the same place when we pass on? Chari Anne, do we go anywhere?

"Then hear the decision of the Hlutr Elders. You have watched Mankind slaughter Hlutr. You have watched him slaughter other orders. You have watched him turn his back on the miracle of existence and slaughter his brethren and himself."

"This I have watched."

"You have seen that most Humans are nonsapient. You have seen that they do not appreciate the wonder of the Universal Song and do not even delight in their own lives."

"I have seen cases of this, Brother Elder. Many cases. But—"

"Hear then the answer of the Elders. Man is fundamentally a beast, we proclaim. He grew up on a world with barely any Hlutr supervision. He destroyed the last vestiges of Hlutr control on his planet. And now he spreads through the stars with his strange unsane ways. Man is a beast—and a beast with too much power. He *does* represent a threat to the Hlutr and to life. And so Mankind must be destroyed."

Living slowly as I am, it is hard to feel strong emotions quickly. Yet the blast of impatience I send out on the Inner Voice must rock all Hlutr on Amny. "Elders, you do wrong to decide this way. Let me be heard."

"Speak."

"Humans all start out as wonderers, as children delighted with every segment of the Universal Song. A few do not lose these qualities into adulthood. Whatever their ultimate fate, all men begin as sapients. On the basis of the potential that Humans show as children, and on the basis of those few who never lose that potential, I beg that Humanity be spared."

I feel no agreement from the Elders—only astonishment that I should speak this way. The one closest to me projects feelings that, in Humans, are associated with a sad shake of the head.

"Brother Hlut, you are blinded to the danger of Mankind. Look with me." He sings in the Inner Voice, a terrible song that I had almost forgotten.

Credix. A thriving planetful of Hlutr, and then came the bombs. To clear a spaceport, in the name of all the gods! The Elder sings to me the deathsong of all those Hlutr, and it shakes me to the core.

Another Elder sings, sings of Laxus and Leikeis and a hundred billion Little Ones destroyed, fast or slow, by Human ecological meddling. And he sings to me the song of the Humans who did it—not even criminal, they were totally unconcerned.

And another Elder sings to me of Karphos, of great naval battles and of Humans killed, Humans suffering, Humans fighting Humans and glorying in the task. Of Human colonists on a thousand planets, colonists who delight in stripping whole forests, in slaughtering herds of animals, in hunting for the sheer pleasure of cruel destruction.

My teacher projects sadness. "*This* is the beast that you want us to spare, Brother Hlut? Because of a potential that may never be realized? How many more times does Credix have to happen, how many more Battles of Karphos must there be, how many Little Ones must die before you are convinced that we do right?" He addresses the other Elders. "The way is simple. We know Human biochemistry. We can construct diseases that will kill all Humans but spare other Little Ones. There are enough of us on Human worlds that we can strike before they even become aware of the danger. And then the threat of Humanity will be finished."

All that is mortal passes from the Universal Song, Chari Anne. There is no need to be saddened about that. Then why am I so unquiet? I am glad that you died, Chari Anne, before we could destroy your race. I only wish Staven and Daris and Kaavin, and all their children and yours, could die first as well.

I wish I could cry, Chari Anne, for the passing of Humanity.

I wish the Elders could have seen the wondering sparkle in your eyes.

"NO!" This time my Inner Voice shakes all life on the planet. Even the Humans feel it touch the edges of their minds. "Elders, hear me."

They sigh. "Speak," my teacher tells me.

What to say? "You tell me that Human potential may never be realized. That too few ever retain their original wonder and delight in the Universal Song. I say that you are wrong, Elders.

"I know Humans, Human men and women, who are entities worthy of Hlutr friendship. One of them, who just recently passed out of the Universal Song, was so alive with the glory of existence that she spent her entire life working so that Hlutr could be declared sapient."

"That is one case, Brother Hlut."

"Yes, Chari Anne was one woman. But when she succeeded, and Human beings realized we were sapient . . . then all of them ceased hurting us. One Hlut now stands in New York as ambassador to Humanity. Laws have been passed, Elders, laws which protect Hlutr in the future." I quivered. "For four centuries Humans thought us unintelligent, and so our deaths were to them little more than the passing of a grassland. I grant you that very few ever wondered, in those four centuries, whether we were intelligent. Yet when Chari Anne *did* wonder, when she and Staven proved us sapient—all other Humans agreed. Credix and Karphos cannot be erased, cannot be forgiven . . . but they will not happen again. And these are the creatures you call beasts?"

Another Elder sings, from kiloparsecs away. "Not just Hlutr are endangered by Humans. They fight among themselves, showing total disregard for life. Many of the lesser orders will be hurt, have been hurt already."

"Let me tell you of Human attitudes toward the lesser

orders, Elders. The Kaanese are surely one of the least progressed races in the Galaxy. They can barely be said to have self-awareness and language. Yet my Little One Staven convinced Human governments to stop their war long enough to bring some Kaanese home. Staven is one man, one very exceptional man who has kept his own wonder and respect for the other orders—but what of the diplomats, Navy officers, the Empress and the Patalanian President? They still have flickers of the innate and original goodness of the Human being."

This has been a long speech, Little Ones, and I am living far faster than I should. I cannot feel my upper limbs. Elders, Stars, Universal Song . . . do not let me die before I have pled my case.

"Let me tell you, Elders, of the wonderment that Humans retain for the Universal Song." I sing with the Inner Voice—sing as Daris does when she is dancing. "This melody is one that is Hlut-flavored in all respects. Yet it originates in a Human mind. Do we have the right to destroy the mind that can produce that song?"

"Brother Hlut, you yourself guided that individual in her development. If she sings glorious melodies, it is because you taught her. Ordinary adult Humans cannot learn to sing such songs."

"No? Then listen with me, Elders, as Daris dances." I cast out with the Inner Voice, seeking a pattern I know so well. In a little while as we Hlutr count time, I find Daris and her troupe dancing before an audience of two thousand. "Listen, Elders, to Daris's Inner Voice. Then listen to the Inner Voice of those who dance with her. And listen to the Inner Voice of those who watch. Do you not hear the same theme repeated over and over? You say that I taught Daris to sing . . . who taught her audience?"

They listen, and they hear what I have described. And the tides of the Inner Voice that flow through this conclave begin to change.

My teacher tries one more time. "Brother Hlut, all the arguments you have used depend upon the fact that you, a Hlut, taught these Humans while they were children. You could go through all the descendants of these Humans, and the answer would be the same: they are what they are because a Hlut taught them. Not because they live up to their potential on their own. In the four centuries you spent on Terra, you have managed to change only a small number of Humans. The vast majority of them are still a threat to the Universal Song."

Now I am saddened in a new way. One has respect for one's teachers, one always thinks that they are intelligent and worthy. It is a terrible thing to be shown otherwise.

"Brother Elders, can the Hlutr *not* try to help Humans more? Must we turn our backs on them and destroy them, when with time and teaching we might be able to help them alter themselves? The few Humans I have helped— who are now helping to change others of their kind—show that progress is possible. Are we now to close our senses to that possibility, are we to deny this order of Little Ones the help that they so plainly need, and so plainly can profit from?

"They had no Hlutr to help them when they were growing on their planet. Now, when the job is more difficult, are we to put aside our ancient obligations and consign this entire order to nonexistence? Elders, I believe that the Hlutr are better than that. I ask that Mankind be spared."

Cold, I am so cold. I cannot see beyond this grove— I would have liked one more sight of the stars.

My teacher speaks slowly. "The Elders have made their decision, Brother Hlut. Hear it now. Man is a beast . . . but a beast with the potential to become sapient. Hlutr can help him to realize that potential. Therefore, Man will be spared, and the Hlutr will take up their obligation to work with him, that he may become more fully what he *could* be. Let it be so."

"Let it be so, Brother Elders. Brother Hlutr." I am cold, so cold. Chari Anne, are you there?? It must be autumn, Chari Anne; look how my leaves are red and orange and yellow. Are they not beautiful, my Little One? Is not the Universal Song a grand and glorious thing, to have contained two such as we?

I always did love the leaves of October.

Interlude   1

It was a swell treehouse. Kev and his friend Dar had worked on it all summer, using lumber and plastics from an abandoned farm down the hill. The treehouse had three levels, a rainproof roof, and a splendid ladder as well as a pulley for lifting things up and down. The boys had done it all without help from any grownups, and they were justly proud.

Kev had picked the tree, and it was a dandy: nearly fifty meters tall, with a sturdy trunk and leaves that were every color of the rainbow. Kev and Dar had built their treehouse ten meters up, in a crook where the main trunk divided into two. From his perch, Kev could see the entire valley, from his own house only a few hundred meters away to the towers of the spaceport nearly five kilometers distant.

The day was beautiful. The sun rode high in a blue sky barren of all clouds, and the scent of honeysuckle and drisberry filled the air. A slight breeze from the northwest stirred leaves and the tiny flag that Kev and Dar had posted on the top of their structure. No planet in the Galaxy, Kev thought happily, could be as beautiful as Amny.

Kev leaned back against the tree, took a sip of cold water from his canteen, and smiled. Tomorrow was his seventh birthday, by the ancient Human calendar—although in real years he was eleven and a half. Real years never mattered, somehow.

27

For his birthday, Kev's family had promised to take him and Dar on a real space voyage, to a planet called Credix where he could see a real zoo . . . not just holos on his terminal. It would be a day without school, and just the sort of adventure that was always happening to boys and girls in the books Kev viewed.

Immanuel, Kev's dog, was stretched out in the sun on the platform next to him; the dog's legs twitched a little and then he rolled over, and Kev laughed. "You're silly, you know?" Immanuel's tail wagged once or twice at his master's voice, then stopped.

Kev closed his eyes, feeling the sun on his face and listening to the swish of leaves. It sounded like surf, or like a kind of music he had heard in his dreams.

The boy jerked suddenly alert, startling Immanuel. What had he heard? He hadn't been asleep, but just the same he felt he'd been dreaming. He had heard a scrap of music, something more beautiful and more substantial than all the songs and symphonies stored in his school's memory.

Experimentally, he closed his eyes and gingerly settled back against the tree. A second later he sat up, shaking his head.

The tree . . . the tree was *singing* to him.

Kev couldn't keep his secret to himself. When he arrived home, his Mama Tiponya was programming dinner; he hugged her and said, "Can I have a cookie?"

"Just one, dalinka. You don't want to ruin your appetite."

"Thank you." He punched for a cookie, accepted it from the kitchen cabinet, then sat down next to Mama Tiponya, swinging his legs. "Would you like a bite?"

"Thank you, yes. Umm, that's good." She turned back to her terminal. "So what have you been up to today?"

"I've been in the treehouse." Shyly, he added, "The tree talked to me."

"Did it?" Her tone was one that Kev had heard too often: she didn't believe him, and she was secretly laughing at him. How cute, Kev thinks he's talking to a tree.

"No, really, it did."

"Tell you what, you can tell me me all about it later." She giggled and gave him another hug. "Now why don't you go wash? Dinner will be ready in half an hour."

"Yes, Ma'am." Frowning, Kev jumped to the floor. So she didn't believe him . . . she didn't have to *laugh* at him. At dinner Mama Tiponya brought it up again. "Kev, why don't you tell everybody what you did today?" She was trying to hide a smile, and Kev looked down at his food. "Nothing," he muttered.

"Oh, tell us, Kev," urged Mama Cho. "You always have such fun."

Against his better judgment, Kev told them . . . but he mentioned only the barest outline, just the fact that the tree had talked to him, and that it told him a story. Somehow, he didn't quite feel like sharing the story itself.

Father Nnamdi grinned. "So now the trees are talking to you! What next, the birds?"

"I'd rather not talk about it," Kev answered sullenly.

"All right, son, we'll let it drop."

He knew just what was going to happen, though—later, when they thought he was asleep, all the grownups would have a good chuckle about Kev and his talking tree. Soon it would be a family joke, a cute story to tell visitors.

Never mind, he thought. *Dar* will believe me.

"No kidding?" Dar looked at the tree, his eyes wide. "It honestly talked to you?" Kev had called his friend right after dinner, and despite the setting sun the boys ran out to the tree at once.

"Well, it wasn't *talking*, not really. More like singing, or dreaming. Immanuel heard it too . . . didn't you, boy?" The dog wagged his tail furiously, and earned a scritch behind the ears in return.

"All right, let's go on up, and you can show me." Dar was two years older than Kev, and was already six levels ahead in school. He knew everything—or at least, he knew how to use his terminal to find out everything.

They climbed up, then pulled Immanuel up with the pulley. The little dog actually enjoyed being hoisted into the treehouse. When the dog was safely aboard, Dar said, "Well, how do we make it talk?"

"Uh . . . I don't know. I was just resting, and I put my head against it, like this." Kev demonstrated.

Dar stretched out next to him, and for the next few minutes the two boys were silent.

"What's supposed to happen now?"

"You hear music. Then . . . it's hard to describe."

"You were dreaming."

"I was *not!*"

"Were too."

"Was not."

"All right, all right, let's not get into a fight about it." Dar glanced at the sun, then at his terminal rolled up and hanging from his belt. "It's getting late. Tomorrow's a big day. I've got to get home before the folks miss me."

"Okay. I'll see you tomorrow." Kev watched Dar descend, then flopped to the wooden platform. "It's no use," he said to Immanuel. "Nobody believes me." He laid his head back against the tree trunk, and not even Immanuel's sloppy tongue on his face brought a smile.

Listen, Little One . . .

PART TWO:

Teacher

In the quiet night of this eternal wood, I lift my soul to
the stars in the waves of the Inner Voice. I sing, as the
Hlutr have sung since the beginnings of life. My roots are
deep in the lush soil of this world that now, after the
fashion of the Humans, we call Amny. My limbs rise high
into the fresh, clear air, reaching for the dim radiance of
the distant stars in lieu of the vanished sun. And I sing.

Answering voices come from the sky and beyond: a
chorus of my brethren on a million worlds. Most of them
are Hlutr, for we alone of all the races have mastered the
mystery of the Inner Voice. In this way, as in our physical
stature, we stand above all other creatures; in this way, we
do our duty to the Universal Song. For how could there
be a Song, without the Hlutr to sing . . . ?

I sing, and this should be pleasure. I seek the communion of my race, the oneness that comes through the Inner
Voice and lifts us all far beyond the various worlds we
inhabit. The animal races, however mobile, are bound by
their very nature, bound in space to one particular location; only the plants, seemingly sessile, have truly transcended all boundaries. This night, I sing, and in my song
I seek to become one with the Universal Song.

This should be a pleasure. Yet too soon, before I am
even begun, a discord intrudes. It begins faintly, a mere
hint of the song gone wrong, and I turn my soul away from

31

it in my attempt to fly the night. Yet the discord is still there, on the worlds of the Hlutr and in the empty spaces where only our dormant spores drift; in the oceans and the clouds, spoiling their wet happy melodies, in the soil and the turf, poisoning their deep restful peace.

It is the Humans.

I know, my brothers, that many of you do not agree with me. Many of you, I know, do not see them as I do, these sons and daughters of Terra with their machines and their Thrones and their ever-continuing raucous jabber. Most of you do not concern yourselves with the Humans. Many of you feel that they are not truly sapient, that they do not have enough sense of the Inner Voice to *cause* any discord in its melodies. You are wrong. I live in their midst, not a dozen Hlutr-lengths from one of their cities, not eight hundred parsecs from one of their most populated worlds, and I know: this dissonance I feel comes from them.

Still more of you, my siblings, feel that the Humans are sapient and feel a special compassion for them, silly and weak as they are. You may remember our dealings with them, and our strange brother who left Amny and went to the world where the Humans live. I think of him always as "The Traveller," for he went places where Hlutr seldom go.

The last remnants of his carcass stand yet, in the clearing only a Hlut-length or so from me. He had been specially bred for his mission, and he burned out his stunted life in a very short time. But his memory lives on, in all of us. It comes through our roots from the wet ground, it descends on us in the summer winds, and it echoes yet in the waves of the Inner Voice. We will never forget the Traveller . . . and I least of all. I was his Teacher; I bear some of the responsibility for his mission, for making him what he was. Sometimes, when I look to the lonely blackness of interstellar space, or when I contemplate the grand sweep of time, I feel that he is near, and I can almost hear his whisper. It is a sad whisper, a lost sound as he entreats us on behalf of those strange folk he came to love—as if a Hlut *could* truly love any of the Little Ones.

You remember our decision, in that time of judgment and the appeal of the Traveller. We spared Man, when we could have eliminated him from the Universal Song like the violent blight he sometimes seems. This was the will of the Hlutr, and this was my will too—and yet at times I wonder.

What did we know of Humans, then? Few enough of us had paid any attention to them. We had a few flashes of the Inner Voice, the knowledge we gained from the poor children of Nephestal, and the ravings of our misshapen brother.

It is so different now. We have lived with Humans on ten thousand worlds, for twice a thousand of their years. There is still little exchange between our folk, but some of us Elders have watched Man carefully, have listened to the song of his soul. And while we have found beauty, ever have we also found discord.

And now the Humans disturb Hlutr meditation.

I live more slowly, allowing night to blossom into day, day to fade to night, and the planet to move forward in its orbit. Usually this helps, for Humans are ephemeral and their disturbance does not last long. They cannot live slower than their accustomed rate.

Now, though, I find no peace in living slowly. The Human cacophony builds rather than subsides, and with each swift-passing day it grows worse. Soon all space cries with their boiling thoughts, their impertinent distress, their anguish. Soon the noise overwhelms the communion of the Hlutr, it stirs eddies in the waves of the Inner Voice, in brings violence to our quiet galaxy. Humans are screaming, Humans are dying, Humans are afraid—and worst of all, their little ones are crying.

I hear you wonder, my brothers and sisters: what is happening? You cast your thoughts outward, appealing . . . you who live on the worlds of Man open your senses, drinking in the sights and sounds of their tiny lives. Are they killing each other in yet another of their wars? Are they staining the stars with their blood, in a mad series of pogroms?

The answer comes, voiced by one of us who trembles at

the magnitude of his news. A disease is taking Mankind, a disease that Human medical ability cannot reverse. In two short Human years, it has become a plague that engulfs half the galaxy and brings certain death to all it touches. Human lives are threatened, Human civilization totters, Human agony disturbs even the song of the Hlutr.

Is it any wonder that they cry?

And now the question comes, as I knew it would—whispered anonymously on the waves of the Inner Voice, spoken secretly to the winds of Amny, welling up from the soil with the memories of the Traveller: what should the Hlutr do?

I ask you, my brethren—why should the Hlutr do a thing?

Compassion, says the memory of the Traveller, the one who came to love these Humans.

In the name of compassion, then, should we turn away from Hlutr tradition? When have we ever stirred ourselves to prevent the deaths of any ephemerals? But a few seasons ago as the Hlutr count time, the great lizards roamed Amny; when the swamps dried up and the ice came, when diseases took them by their millions . . . did we interfere then? When the subtle, beautiful fishes died, leaving the oceans to the coarser beasts who succeeded them . . . did we put forth our power to save them?

Not just on Amny, but on a million worlds in all the long history of the Hlutr race—how often have we stood between ephemerals and their fates? And how often have our attempts met with defeat? The vanished Coruma, the lost children of Lavarren, the lovely singing trees of the Mehbis Cluster: all gone, forever.

You remember better than I, my brothers, my Elders. The Hlutr have watched many races die, watched with compassion; but we have not interfered. It is not our way. Should we do so now?

We have pled for interference before, you say. In ones and twos, some of you have asked for this or that race to be spared. Some of you have tried, in defiance of the will of the Hlutr—and all have failed.

Why should we try now?

There is among us here on Amny a youngster, barely a sapling; she stands near the old Human settlement, at the place where they still bring their disturbed children, their adults with defective brains. *This* we do for the Humans . . .we care for their insane and their defectives, we comfort them with soothing projections of the Inner Voice.

The sapling calls for us now. Her message comes through the First Language, on waves of color racing through the Hlutr grove; it comes in the gentle soughing of the Second Language, a muted sound like the distant sea. "Elders," she tells us, "a Human calls for you."

"For us?"

"He uses the old equipment, and speaks to me in pidgin First Language on luminous screens. He asks to address our Elders."

I tremble in the wind. Is there no end to Human audacity? First they shatter the peace of Hlutr meditation; now one of them demands an audience?

Compassion, Brother, the memory of the Traveller tells me.

Sooner or later I must deal with the Humans; I decide it will be now. "Send him," I tell the sapling.

Before the man arrives, he is heralded by the other Hlutr. Broad waves of contrasting color move through their leaves and across their trunks, and when he enters my glade he is accompanied by the swishing of a million Hlutr leaves.

He is a small creature, even for a Human; his sparse fur is ashen and his artificial hide a dirty white. He stops before my trunk, then raises equipment designed to generate lights that mock the First Language.

The memories of the Traveller have prepared me; I bend my lower limbs to the ground, and I vibrate their leaves in controlled patterns, far faster than usual. The technique is difficult even for an Elder like myself, with full control over my body. We use it to communicate with the lesser orders in their own familiar languages. I do not intend to set the Human at ease; rather, I wish to show him the abilities of the Hlutr from the very beginning.

"Who are you, Human?"

He bows. "I am Doctor Alex Saburo, of the Credixian Imperial Navy."

This tells me little. His name is a sound, nothing else. His title indicates one who is accorded knowledge and wisdom, as Humans know it. As for his affiliation, not even the Ancients of Nephestal are able to keep track of ever-changing Human political systems.

"Why do you come before me?"

"To ask for help."

Up close, it is easy to read these creatures through the Inner Voice. The tenor of his emotions matches his voice: firmly controlled, yet aware that he stands in the presence of a vastly superior being.

Emotions, but their minds are not coherent enough to project thoughts. "Ask, then," I say.

"The Death," he said, spreading his upper limbs. "We can do nothing to stop it. It's infected half the Galaxy, and it's entered the Imperium. In another year it'll have spread to every Human world." His control wavers, and I glimpse emotional storms beneath the surface of this man's mind.

"So you come to the Hlutr for help. Why?"

"Where else would I turn, Your Greatness?"

"You may address me as 'Teacher.' "

"Our medical science cannot cope with the plague, Teacher. I know that the Hlutr have the ability to modify the very genetic code itself; I know that your Elders have the intelligence to analyze the Plague and perhaps stop it."

So the Universal Song mocks me, my brethren. I cannot evade the question that is whispered in the night: Should Hlutr help Humans?

I appeal to my own Elders for a decision, and they are strangely silent. It is I who began this thing, two millennia ago when I prepared the Traveller to judge Humanity, when I came before the Elders to say that we needed to know more of the children of Earth. Now it is *I* who must decide whether we will spare Mankind in this time of crisis.

Although the Traveller's memories beat strongly within me, how can I say yes? How can I throw off geological ages of Hlutr tradition, all for the sake of a brutish creature who thinks himself grand because he can disturb our meditations? How can I justify saving *this* people, when we have allowed so many others to perish?

The man is waiting for an answer; and suddenly, I have one for him. "You ask much of me, Doctor Alex Saburo. Perhaps too much." I tell him of our traditions. I tell him of the Coruma, the Lavarren, the Mehbis folk. I tell him that all living creatures—yes, even the Hlutr—meet death, that it is part of the Universal Song. In the end, my twigs ache from making such precise vibrations for so long.

"Teacher, I have heard that the Hlutr value life. Old tales tell of their compassion for all Little Ones. For the sake of that compassion, won't you help us?"

"We are compassionate . . . but you do not know what you ask. You Humans occupy over twelve thousand worlds; within one year, all will be stricken with your Death. You ask that we create a defense, then that we sacrifice ourselves to spread that defense on all your planets?"

"The sacrifice would be great—but without it, my civilization, perhaps my entire race, will die."

"The sacrifice is greater than you think." I groped in the vast collective Hlutr memory for the Human words I needed. "You think we Hlutr can synthesize genetic material without effort. Know then, Doctor Alex Saburo, that when a Hlut makes new DNA and RNA, that Hlut dies— violently, in a bursting that spreads the new material on all the winds. Even if we *can* save your people, to do so means that many times twelve thousand Hlutr must perish in agony."

A brief torrent of anger, quickly suppressed, flashes forth in the Inner Voice. "I had not thought," he says, "that the Hlutr were so selfish."

"We have our duty to the Universal Song. If that melody declares that Humans must pass away, we cannot gainsay it."

He is an odd creature, in whom passion and reason can coexist, each as forceful as the other. Now he touches my trunk, and the warmth of his hand surprises me and moves me in a way his words have not. "If you wish, Doctor Alex

Saburo, the Hlutr can offer your people counsel. We can help you prepare for the Death, can make it easier for you to meet your end. We have done this for others."

"No." His denial is strong. "I thank you then, Elder, and I beg your permission to leave. There is little time."

That should be the end of it—yet it is not. "What will you do, Human?"

"I'll seek an answer. Somewhere, someone must have the knowledge that will help me to end the Death. As long as I can, I'll keep searching." He turns, and begins the slow walk away from my grove.

There is an outcry from some of my brethren, a gentle protest that falls from the stars like cold autumn rain. From within me, where the memory of the Traveller lives, there is a stronger objection.

Brothers and sisters, how can I yield to you? How can I deny our traditions? You are but a few—and when the Hlutr act, they must act in agreement.

How, you ask me, can I ignore the pain?

"Wait, Alex Saburo."

If for nothing more than the sake of the Traveller, whose spirit gnaws at me, I make the Human an offer. "I will go with you."

"B-but how? I will travel beyond this world, to planets where the Death has hit."

I do not know, my brethren, why I agree to do a thing that the Hlutr seldom do. Perhaps I, too, am overly fond of these Humans. Perhaps I want to find something in them that would be worth the death of a hundred thousand Hlutr. Perhaps I am simply reluctant to waste all the time I have spent studying them. "The Human children on yonder hill are mentally defective, yet they are strongly sensitive to the Hlutr Inner Voice. One of them shall become my operative—it shall accompany you, and I will see what it sees, hear what it hears, and communicate with you through its mouth. I will also sing with my brethren and my Elders, and perhaps . . . perhaps we will can find a way to help you."

He is flabbergasted; both the power and the mercy of

the Hlutr are beyond him. "Go back to the sanitarium," I tell him. "My operative will greet you there."

"I . . . thank you, Teacher."

His words are echoed by the voice of the Traveller within: *Thank you.*

The body is awkward, soft, confining. Through its limited senses, I perceive a truncated world: vision spans merely one octave, and the threshold of hearing is far above the quiet susurrus of the Hlutr Second Language. The Human chemical senses show more promise, yet the body does not know how to properly interpret them.

There is no mind, no awareness of identity. If such ever existed, it is buried too deeply for even the Hlutr to find. Although it wears an animal body, the creature's soul is more like that of the lesser plants. It has life, it responds to its environment, but it has no volition. Until I animate it.

Motion, that is the most difficult thing. The Hlutr move slowly—swaying with the wind, making tiny ovals in sympathy with the yearly movement of the sun, pulsing our rhythms of growth and life with the music of the Inner Voice. We are not accustomed to the rush of animal motion, and it takes me time to become comfortable as the new body walks.

I have not animated a body for Human millennia . . . not since I attended conferences of the Free Peoples of the Scattered Worlds in borrowed Avethellan form. Slowly, the process comes back to me, and I am more confident. The raucous Human voices do not sound so harsh, the claustrophobic Human rooms begin to seem less close.

While I am adjusting to the change, Alex Saburo leads me to a transport capsule, and in minutes I am in the Human city. Confusion and disharmony fill my senses, and I simply withdraw my attention from the body. I sing with the winds, I feel the happy touch of flying beasts upon my limbs, I dig my roots in the cool earth and inhale nutrients from the brisk air. In time, Saburo and my operative reach the spaceport; after a few moments of disorientation they have left the surface of Amny and are speeding out into the dark, peaceful gulfs of space.

Now at last I can return to the body, can begin to bring my Human operative completely under control. I concentrate, matching my time sense to the fast, inflexible Human metabolism. The world of my experience narrows in concentric circles, until I bid temporary farewell to grove, earth and winds—and open my eyes on a small spacecraft lounge. I am upon a divan before a wall that mimics the sight of naked space; Saburo sits next to me, watching instruments in his lap. When I stir, he looks up.

"Teacher?" he asks.

"I am here, Saburo." My voice—my *Human* voice—sounds hollow in Human ears.

"We'll be shifting into tachyon phase in a moment," he says. "We've been under way for just under two hours; it's almost ten hours since we left your grove."

I shake my head. The animal attitude toward time is very hard for Hlutr to grasp. Everything is impatience, everything is motion. We who count time by the movement of stars and the seasons of slow Hlutr life have difficulty binding ourselves to rigid Human concepts of interval. "I have the Human body under control now," I assure him. "I long to experience your tachyon drive. It is a thing that Hlutr seldom endure: to travel nearly as fast as the waves of the Inner Voice can move."

"Will you be able to maintain communication with . . .your host?"

"I feel confident that I can do so. Our minds are much more flexible than you believe." Indeed, the change comes even as we talk; the Human ship twists in a direction totally unknown to Hlutr, but I do not lose contact with my operative. My awareness has taken root in the alien animal brain cells, and it will not be dislodged easily.

"What is our destination?"

Saburo sighs. "First, to Taglierre, to stop in at the Credixian Medical Association convention. I don't expect them to have any more leads than they did when I was there last week." He spreads his hands. "After that, I guess it's on to Eironea to consult with the Grand Library."

"I do not know these places."

"We're flying to Galactic West; from Amny, roughly in the direction of the constellation called Aurick's Tower." He touches a few keys on a panel, and the wall shows Amny's night sky. He points toward a particular grouping of stars. "Here."

Nodding comes almost as easily to me as the azure hue by which the Hlutr signal assent. We move in the direction of sad, bright Dorasc. Even now I hear the song of my brothers and sisters on Dorasc's starbright plains, and I sing with them. The song is distorted: in part because of the tremendous speed at which the vehicle moves, but in part also because of the wails of a billion Human voices. And somewhere, between here and distant Dorasc, the cry of a single Human child cuts across the harmony of the Inner Voice like thunder across a peaceful summer afternoon.

Ere I have begun to probe the nature of that dreadful cry, the ship twists again, returning to normal space. Before my Human eyes is the cool, white globe of Taglierre.

Scarce two sevens of Galactic revolutions have passed since Hlutr seeds first came to Taglierre. In that time, the planet has grown steadily more inhospitable, slowly getting colder as it leaks its atmosphere to space. Human terraformers have arrested the process, and for now Taglierre has an air blanket two-thirds as dense as Amny's and temperatures no worse than the deepest Ice Age of my home. Yet Humans will not stay forever. Seventy times seventy Hlutr remain, proud and lonely in the tropics; within their lifetimes Taglierre will become a frozen ghost of a world.

As we jockey for an approach pattern, I greet these lofty brothers and sisters, who have the honor of presiding over the death of a world. They work their works well, as the generations progress: urging the Little Ones along, nudging them now and again when their normal evolution does not keep pace with Taglierre's dissipation. When their efforts are successful, life will survive on this globe; yet the struggle is a hard one. They sing me ritual greeting, but pay me little attention otherwise; the doings of Humans are their least concern.

Still, from their song and the eddies of the Inner Voice that lap the shores of this planet's waterless seas, I glimpse loneliness and despair in the once-teeming Human cities, and I know that the Hlutr are not the *only* ones waiting for a world to die.

"Many of your people have left Taglierre," I say to Saburo.

Discarded memories in my host's brain tell me that Saburo's wrinkled face is sad. "The Death will be here soon—within weeks, probably. Everyone who can leave, has. Only military ships can land safely; the poor fools will stampede themselves trying to steal anything else."

"Why do they not prohibit travel, thus containing the disease?"

"On Taglierre? They depend on trade for food and repair parts. That world can't support a half-billion people on its own." He runs a hand through his white hair. "We've done what we can. The Imperator ordered the boundaries closed a year ago—so the Imperium escaped for a while." The ship cuts through air, leaving a brief flash like the trail of a meteorite visible to Hlutr below. "But we can't stop interstellar trade. The Death has entered the Imperium now, it's only a matter of weeks until . . ." He does not finish.

We settle to a desolate landing field, while cold sand blows across the empty plain.

These are Human Elders and wise ones? I came to Taglierre, my brothers and sisters, convinced that I would witness something like a council of Hlutr, all joined in the swaying and the song as they contemplate mysteries and seek for answers. Instead, I have fallen into a madhouse!

Listen to them, my fellows:

"The Death is a prion-based disease; my simulations make an analogy with the treatment of Gerstman-Straussler syndrome," says one of them, a tall and slender woman with hair the color of the springtime sky. "Thus, your attempt to modify DNA-based antiviritics shall fail no matter what starting point you use."

"*My* computers," says another from a communications screen, "assure me that there are no effective prophylactic measures. We can only treat the disease after it is manifest—and that treatment relies on massive doses of general-series antiviritics."

"You are wrong," shouts a third, ludicrously holding up his computer display for all to see. "The analogy must be to classic toxic reactions. The only way to stop this scourge is to spread organisms capable of breaking down the toxin. I suggest that we allow our linked medicomps to write a simulation involving a gengineered variant of current antidote-antibodies."

The meeting hall, although large, is mostly empty. The doctors—the Human Elders—sit or stand near the center, each behind a computer terminal. Saburo and I sit with a few quiet visitors on one side of the chamber. On the other are the members of the press: frightened or confident, they do not understand what the doctors say, yet they feel that these idiots will find an answer. Billions of Humans watch the proceedings through their eyes and their instruments, billions who see the doctors as wise seekers of knowledge. Am I the only one who recognizes them as fools?

No. For Saburo rises to speak.

"My God, you've been here for two months and you're still having the same arguments. Still linking your medicomps to your diagnostitrons and running simulation after simulation. I don't believe it."

The tall woman looks down her nose. "If it isn't Doctor Saburo. Or should I say, *Lieutenant* Saburo?"

"Brevet Colonel for the duration, Doctor Melus. I've never tried to hide my connection with the Navy."

"No." She smiles. "You just couldn't find any school or reputable hospital that would put up with you. So you think we're wasting our time?"

"I do. Simulations and computer analyses aren't going to stop the Death—"

"Oh, and I suppose you will? How? Your habit of playing

about with corpses hasn't yielded any results, nor have your excursions into vivisection . . ."

"Legitimate experimentation, if you please."

"Have it your own way. I don't see any cure from your latest brainstorm of appealing to aliens, Lieutenant."

Saburo clenches his fists, but says nothing.

The woman dismisses him with a wave. "Here we have gathered in one room the greatest expert databases in the Imperium and beyond. The Universities of Skapton, Prakis and Credix itself are tied into our network. We have the wisdom of the ancients, in the form of the programs they left us. This convention has brought together the greatest resources of medicine in recorded history—"

"And you'll still be running your simulations and consulting the ancients when the last of you drops dead from the Plague!" Saburo takes the arm of my operative, draws her toward the door. "Come on, I should have known better than to stop here."

As the door slams shut behind us, the Human doctors begin again their comparison of the results of mindless computer programs.

No wonder they are dying.

On the way to Eironea, we pass warships—Saburo tries to explain to me why Humans have been killing one another, but I cannot comprehend. We Hlutr are all one tribe, since the time of the Great Schism more than a billion years ago; we do not fight among ourselves for territory, nor do we seek vain power. The Hlutr are united in the songs we sing and the Universal Song of which all are part; even when we disagree (as some of you, my brothers and sisters, disagree with me about helping the Humans), we do so without rancor, malice or violence.

And what need have the Hlutr to fight with the other orders? When they menace us, they are dealt with; otherwise, the Hlutr conquer as they have always conquered, in the slow yet inexorable fashion of the plant kingdom. Why should we fight?

"Your warships sit idle, Saburo. Why do they not fight?" For though ships from both sides challenge us as we pass, there is no hostility along a border that stretches for a kiloparsec in every direction.

He manipulates his keyboard, stares into a small screen, then shrugs. "The Death. They've declared a truce for the duration."

"Yours are a strange folk, Saburo."

Now he does a thing which convinces me that none of the Wise will *ever* understand Humans, a thing that makes me withdraw for a time to my quiet grove and the fresh dew of a misty Amny dawn.

He laughs.

In due time we come to Eironea, and reluctantly I return from Amny. Your attention is on me now, brothers and sisters, and on this strange journey which has become my mission. Some of you sing of our obligation to save the Humans; others sing that we must maintain the precious Hlutr detachment that has served us since the far-off days of the Pylistroph, when Life was but a dream in the Scattered Worlds.

And others . . . others breathe a different opinion, born of smothering hatred and cold revenge. *These* Hlutr rejoice at the Death, and would have us hurry it along so that Humans can be wiped out once and for all.

Have you forgotten, brethren, that once the Hlutr swore to aid Mankind in his quest for maturity, his fulfillment of his potential? Saburo may succeed, despite us—Humanity may survive the Death without Hlutr aid. Will you then have us slay the survivors, cast this people out from the Universal Song? Would you have the Hlutr forsworn before the stars and the sacred melodies?

What the Hlutr do, we shall do in full agreement. Nay, my brothers and sisters: for now, Man will make his own destiny, and the Hlutr . . . the Hlutr will watch.

Our ship enters normal space, and we drop toward verdant Eironea. The Hlutr of this world, who live mainly in rich, wet tropical forests, sing me welcome and concern in the Inner Voice. Theirs is a song tinged with despair; the Death has come to Eironea, and Humans have died: seventy times itself four times and more of them. Ten times that many are near death, and their despondency shakes the planet. These Hlutr are fond of their Humans; they cry sadness to the unfeeling stars at the passing of their Little Ones.

We land on an untenanted field near one of their great cities, as the sun climbs slowly toward zenith and shadows pool beneath buildings. A drawn Human face appears on the wall: the commander of our ship.

"We're down, sir. If it's all the same to you . . . er . . . the crew has voted to remain shipboard. Your cabin connects directly to the main airlock; we'd appreciate it if you'd . . ."

Saburo raises a quivering hand. "I understand, Commander. Rest assured that we'll remain in our sealed area of the ship."

"Very good, sir." The face disappears.

With a heavy sigh, Saburo stands. "Come with me," he says.

"What is our destination?"

"The Library." His tread was heavy, his body stooped like a tree that has seen too many harsh winters.

I can do nothing but follow.

There in the empty streets of the city Shiau Shi on the planet Eironea, Saburo tells me what the Humans have done. Let me share this with you, brethren, for it is a marvelous thing.

Like the Daamin, the Kreen and the happy children of grand Avethell, Humans gathered together in one place all their knowledge of the Universal Song. This was in the days of their great Empire, fifteen hundred years ago. Once, every Human world, settlement, or starship in the Galaxy could access this knowledge; today, only a few outposts remain in contact with the central Library. Eironea is one of them. Here, in the care of a devoted priesthood, the machinery is available to all who need it. Through the political upheavals of nearly seventy Human generations, Eironea has remained free, unconquered and neutral, guarding its precious treasure.

The network of transit capsules is not working, and no autotaxis answer Saburo's summons, so our ship gives birth to a small vehicle and we travel in this metal shell.

Humans watch us as we pass, hidden in their buildings or behind directional signs and structural members; the few whom we catch in the open scurry for cover as soon as they see us.

The Temple of Knowledge soars above us as we disembark; Saburo secures the small vehicle and leads me into the large structure. Works of Human art line the walls and fill display cases, but our footsteps echo in empty halls, and when Saburo makes his way to a row of waiting computer terminals, their screens remain dark.

I sense another Human presence behind us, and turn to see a pale, emaciated woman dressed in a tattered frock. Her long hair is the black of space, and her eyes hold springtime green.

"If you're here to consult the Grand Library," she says in a thin voice, "I'm sorry, but you won't have any success."

"The machinery doesn't work?" Saburo asks.

"It works fine. There's no one at the other end to answer." She spreads her arms, a sapling opening to the sun. "The Library staff was hit hard by the Death; we last heard from them months ago." Her lips form a weak smile. "Come to my quarters, I'll give you some tea. We might as well be comfortable." She introduces herself as we follow. "I am Yee Bair. And you?"

"Doctor Alex Saburo. My companion is the Teacher. Do . . . did you work here?"

"At the Temple? Goodness, no. I was a frequent customer." She pauses to cough. "After the Death hit and the priests either died or moved away, I figured, why not move in? It's a lot nicer than my two-room flat, and I have plenty of time for my work."

Something sings in her, just the briefest flash of an incomplete melody in the Inner Voice. "Your work?" I ask.

"I'm an artist." She pauses before a closed door, presses her palm against it and it slides open. "Here, look."

Yee Bair makes pictures with light—raw, vibrant pictures that distort reality as seen through Human eyes. Some of her works are tame, gentle scenes of towers, spaceports and lounging Human beings. Others feature scenes of the Death, and they breathe with the fear, anguish and defiance that radiate from Human worlds in these terrible times.

"You're a genius," Saburo says.

In spite of myself, I nod. "You give form and definition to a bit of the Universal Song. Your work ranks with the greatest of your people."

"These were early attempts," she says, pointing out the tame visions. "Before . . ." she does not finish, but busies herself with the tea.

This is the mystery, brothers and sisters, that we have faced before and will face again in a thousand different races. We, whose only art form is the substance of the Universal Song itself—we cannot capture its essence in the way that these Little Ones, these animals, can. We who are masters of creation are also its prisoners; we cannot step beyond it to create things that cannot be, to see things that cannot exist. We who never know the fullness of despair that these creatures feel, will also never know the urge that pushes them beyond despair's limits. The ecstasy and the pain of a Hlut in the final death-blast, imposing the will of our folk on the malleable genetics of reality—this is the closest we poor Hlutr can approach the emotion that Yee Bair feels whenever she picks up her light-wand.

Should the Hlutr cry then for Humans, as they face the terror of the Death—or should Humans cry for us?

Human pain rips across the Universal Song, and for a moment my Human brain aches with that plaintive cry. Somewhere, nearer than ever, a Human child is crying as none has ever cried before. Soon, no Hlut will be able to ignore that cry.

Saburo gives a noiseless whistle of awe, and my attention is drawn to Yee Bair's current work.

She has given form to this child's cry that echoes from star to star.

It is a scene almost as the Hlutr might see it, a million colors overlaid one atop the other, a jagged slice of vision that oozes with raw pain. Human eyes and brain must study the picture to see what it represents, but I *know* even as I glance at it. A Human boy-child wails, surrounded by the dead bodies of seven times seventy Human adults. Behind him, dimly seen, are the figures of other races who watch the Human tragedy: the wise Daamin, the sad sons of Metrin, the compassionate Iaranori who even now struggle to bring relief where they can . . . and the Hlutr, proud and tall in our distant sympathy. And beyond us, even the cold unfeeling stars rain tears of light on the child. The picture brings tears to my borrowed Human eyes, as the cry it represents could not.

The stars . . .

I touch Yee Bair's arm. "These are the stars of Eironea's sky, no?"

"Yes." Of course they are. How could one who is so attuned to the waves of the Inner Voice avoid hearing that call of agonized loneliness? And hearing it, how could she not know from whence it came?

"Show me . . . show Saburo . . . where those stargroupings lie."

Why am I doing this thing? Brothers, sisters, what is the fate of one Human child to me? Some of you ask me that question, and I cannot but wonder with you. Yet others—the voice of the dead Traveller among them, he who knew Humans better than any of us—sing to me that a Little One is in pain, and the Hlutr must answer. If only to still the pain with a merciful stroke. This is our way, our purpose, our duty since the first Hlut raised itself above the soil of forgotten Paka Tel.

Yee Bair describes the area of the sky, and Saburo relates it to galactic charts in his computer terminal. When he is done, he looks at me, his face filled with questions.

"Take us there, Saburo."

"Why?"

I ask myself the same thing, brethren, and receive no answer save that which I know already: a Little One is crying. "It is in the Universal Song," I tell Saburo, hoping that will content him. And it does.

We share tea with Yee Bair, then return to the ship. Saburo must be desperate, his last chance flown away in the empty halls of the Temple; he gives orders quickly,

and soon we are climbing from green Eironea into the
black of endless space.

On the way, Saburo coughs a few times, then turns
away from me.

"Tell me of the Death. How does it come upon your
people, and what do they feel when it strikes?"

Eironea is far behind, the crying Human child still lost
in the stars ahead of us. Saburo looks up from his computer and frowns.

"Sometimes it comes quickly, and death follows in a
few days. In other cases it can take months to develop.
The symptoms vary: coughing, headaches, difficulty breathing, swelling in the joints—then pneumonia, vitamin de-
ficiency, nerve dysfunction—if the patient lives long enough,
total disruption of the immune system and advanced
malnutrition."

"None escape?"

"Some who caught it nearly two years ago, at the beginning, are still alive . . . but still infected and still showing
symptoms. We've never had a case of someone exposed to
the disease who didn't catch it, or anyone who recovered
from it once infected."

"And your science cannot prevent the spread?"

"That fool Melus was right about one thing—it's a prion-
based disease. No DNA. We haven't even been able to
isolate the infectious agent, much less counter it." His
hands twist hopelessly in his lap. "As long as our doctors
continue to play with computer programs left over from
the ancients, we'll never make any progress."

I look out at the swiftly-moving stars, and I listen to the
eddies of the Inner Voice as it moves between the worlds.
And I wonder. Where did this plague come from?

Some say that it is a natural outgrowth of evolutionary
systems that contain Humans, a variant of diseases known
to Mankind even before he ventured off his home planet.
This is indeed possible; Life's ingenuity knows no bounds,
and other such diseases have developed in the long course
of Galactic history.

Others say that the Death was artificially engineered as a

weapon against these people—either by Humans themselves, or by one of the malevolent races of the Galactic
Core. This theory, too, has its antecedents; this will not be the
first time a promising race has died in biological suicide
. . . or been victim of the Gathered Worlds.

Some even say—although not in words—that the Death
was started by the Hlutr. I have sung the question in the
Inner Voice, casting suspicions out into the starry night,
but I have received no answer. No one admits, and yet . . .

One cannot but have suspicions. The Death is said to
have started on Laxus, a planet not too far from the very
Earth upon which these Humans sprang. The very Earth
on which the last descendants of their own Hlutr choked
to death on Human poisons. Often I have contemplated
the infinitely sad story of the Redwoods, often I have
wondered at their stunted lives: only a shadow of what
they could be, what their distant ancestors had been;
blind, dumb, all but deaf; hearing only the barest echoes
of the Inner Voice, while all around them ranged the
awesome and beautiful symphony of the Hlutr singing
each to the others. The Redwoods were not Hlutr: at best
they were only a kind of degenerate Hlutr kin, leftovers
from a damaged line that had never been able to sing the
Inner Voice. Their minds, what minds they had, must
have been twisted beyond all recognition; their pitiful
short lives must have been an agony.

And the Traveller within me whispers at these times:
although they did not know it, did Humans do a merciful
thing when they allowed the Redwoods to die?

And we Hlutr—what is the course of mercy for *us*? To
allow death, or to deny it? Even if it is a death that some
of us might have caused . . . ?

The ship shudders, and comes out of tachyon phase in
the shadow of a huge banded gas giant.

"What now?" Saburo says.

The commander answers, his face appearing ghostly
over the magnificent view. "Refueling stop, sir. Settlement called Kef. Hope you don't mind—it's the only
place on our charts that has a treaty with the Imperium."

"Carry on." Saburo turns to me. "I hope you don't mind."

"No." I reach out, calling for Hlutr— there are none in this planetary system, none for sevens of parsecs. We move, and a shrunken sun rises over the orange limb of the gas giant; light glitters briefly from a narrow ring of ice particles.

No brothers, no sisters—only the pulse of nearby Human life, a distant echo that might be some form of developing plant life on a rocky worldlet close to the sun . . . and the slow, incomprehensible hum that comes from the crystalline Talebba, a race whose existence Humans do not even suspect. The Talebba go their own way, living out their geological lifespans in planetary rings, asteroid belts and the clouds of primordial stuff that hide from stellar heat out where space is nearly flat and their own sun but another bright star. Now and again one of them dies, flaming, as it topples toward the inner system; occasionally one of these survives long enough to impact on a planet, and possibly create a new race of rocklike intelligences to succeed it.

I do not greet the Talebba of this system. To do so I would have to live nearly as slowly as they do, and to them Galactic Years are like the days and nights to other creatures.

Saburo is consulting his computer; he grins. "Kef is a settlement in orbit around this gas giant, and something of a leader in local trade. I'm hoping they'll have charts that might help you locate whatever you're on the track of."

"I do not know." The Inner Voice is, for the moment, undisturbed. The song of the Hlutr sounds in lonely splendor, untouched by the cry of Humanity. The child is sleeping . . . or dead.

"There," he points, and Kef swings into view.

It is an untidy thing, a construct of glass, metal and light that resembles a bird's nest as much as it does a spaceship or Human city. Around the whole assembly is a ring of violent red, so bright that it hurts my Human eyes. Suddenly a loud klaxon rings, making both Saburo and I start.

"What is it?" Saburo says.

The commander replies, "We're getting a transmission on the emergency band. I'll put it on your screen."

The Human face that greets us is gaunt and wild-eyed. "Turn back," the man croaks through dry lips. "Docking permission is denied."

"We are a ship of the Credixian Navy, on a refueling stop—"

"For your own sake, keep away. Do not pass our circle of quarantine. Don't you understand? *We've all caught the Death.*"

Saburo shakes his head. "We've already been exposed. We just need fuel, and a look at your charts."

"No." The face is sad, but hard with unbending determination as strong as Hlutr bark. "There's hydrogen enough in the atmosphere of the gas giant—you're a military ship, you can refuel with ramscoops. You can tie your navicomp into our central computer if you think our charts will be of any use to you. Just stay away."

"I don't understand. If you're already infected, how do you think we can make it worse?"

The man shakes his head. "By carrying this thing elsewhere. We all took a vow, destroyed our ships, set up the circle to warn others off." His eyes plead with Saburo as his hollow voice cannot. "We're ready to die . . . but we're not going to take the rest of the Galaxy with us. Go away, please—before you tempt us too far."

Saburo nods, touches the intercom. "Take us into a dive, Commander. We'll skim the atmosphere and then get on our way." He turns back to the man from Kef. "I understand. We're leaving. G-gods be with you."

"Gods be with us all." The image fades, and red-ringed Kef falls behind us until it is lost in the stars.

"The poor fools," the commander says.

Tight-lipped, Saburo shakes his head, but says nothing. Soon we are in tachyon phase again.

Certain of my brethren sing the courage of Kef in the Inner Voice, determined that such heroism should not be lost to the Universal Song. And who am I to deny them? More and more Hlutr join this song, more and more regard me and the progress of my journey: not just saplings and adults, but Elders as well. And now, for the first time, I feel the chill touch of the attention of the Eldest of all, from her vast island in the Secluded Realm. As yet, she pays only the slightest heed, just a hint of scrutiny.

This matter is becoming far more important, my brothers and sisters, than I ever intended.

Now, as if aware of the presence of so many Hlutr minds, the Human child shrieks again, splintering the mass concentration of the Inner Voice. For all that this cry tears at my soul, I welcome it: I am not too late to help.

If I can help at all . . .

In the end, I enlist the aid of the Hlutr of Telorbat and a dozen other worlds within a kiloparsec. That the Human child is somewhere within this volume of space there can be no doubt; no Hlut can mistake its anguished wail. At my direction, the Hlutr listen closely, then each tells me the direction from which the cry comes. I mark these on Saburo's master charts; we wait for a few hours, then we try again.

This is exactly the sort of work at which animal intelligences excel: the splitting of time and space into tiny bits, the measurement of direction and duration. With computers to do his calculation and Kef's starcharts as a basis, Saburo manages to pinpoint the source to within a few billion cubic kilometers. The size of a planetary system, and in an empty volume far from any planet! Are we mad to think we can locate the child?

No.

The emotion is as unmistakeable as the echo on a radar screen, and in Human hours we have located the center of the disturbance that called me from Amny seven thousand parsecs away. A lone Human starship floats powerless in starry space. Saburo is taken by a coughing fit, then gains control of himself. "Commander, take us in. Dock with that ship."

"They don't answer our challenges, sir. I think it's a ghost ship."

I shake my head. *Something* is alive aboard that dark hulk.

"Just follow my orders," Saburo says evenly. The commander shrugs, and turns to his control board.

Soon the ships are mated together, and Saburo and I stand before a closed hatch that leads to the mystery vessel. I do not know what to expect; seventy thousand times seventy Hlutr, and more, watch with me as the door slides back.

The sight, the smell, the sound we experience is something that no living being should ever face. Saburo, retching, falls back; even some of the Elders turn away from that terrible scene.

The ship—a cargo vessel—is crammed with dead, decaying Human bodies. Most of them show the ravages of the Death: flat, empty stomachs, the agony of death, the trace of fluids on faces and chests. It is indeed a ghost ship, one inhabited by victims of the Death. Or so we think. Only when we blast into the sealed control room, only when we inspect the destroyed panels and recover the damaged log, do we find the truth. And when we find that horrible truth, it is *my* cry that echoes in the heavens and disturbs the Hlutr at their meditation.

We may never know the home planet of that charnel ship, for all references were carefully edited out of the log. Only the record of their deeds remained, as if they were actually proud of what they had done.

Over seventy times seventy times seventy Humans were put aboard that ship: more than four hundred thousand bodies. And more than half of them were still alive. The unknown rulers of that unknown world herded all the victims of the Death, along with their families and friends, along with the doctors who tried to treat them, along with the ministers who tried to comfort them—herded all into that vast cargo hold, then sealed them off and set them on a journey to nowhere. The controls were set to destroy themselves after a certain time in tachyon phase; after which the ship dropped back into normal space and floated aimlessly, a macabre prison that offered no hope of escape.

There the tragedy did not end . . . for somewhere in this ship, a Human child still cries.

It is Saburo who finds him, huddled in a curve of the

hull with corpses pressed tight around him. The boy is naked, filthy and starved; he draws back with a scream when Saburo reaches for him.

"Let me." I step forward, and call on all the Hlutr to help me. All Human children are sensitive to the Inner Voice, this one more than most: we join in a song of reassurance, of peace, and the boy falls silent. I lift him, and Saburo leads the way back to our own ship.

His name is Ved, and he does not know where he comes from. As I probe his mind, I sense a good deal of damage; he builds walls against the terror he has experienced, and I am loath to disturb those walls. Later, in the care of Hlutr specialists on Amny, perhaps Ved can be brought back to full mental health; for now I am content to let him fall asleep to the Hlutr lullabye.

When I am sure that the boy will not wake, I face Saburo. For once, I feel something akin to animal rage . . . and I know that you, my brothers and sisters, feel this anger with me.

"You dare?" I challenge him. "You dare to crawl to the Hlutr and ask us to spare your race? To spare *that*?" With one gesture, I indicate the charnel ship, the world that launched it, the people who committed this atrocity and all their brothers, sisters and cousins throughout the Galaxy. "Beg rather than we do not increase the virulence of the Death seventy-times-seventy-fold, to give your people the agony they deserve."

Saburo coughs, falls into his chair, then raises defiant eyes. "Is this Hlutr compassion?"

"The Hlutr do not waste compassion on beasts who have proven unworthy of it. We do not grant compassion to creatures who are incapable of showing it."

"Do you think *I'm* not sickened by what I saw today? Do you think I don't want revenge on those who did it? By what right do you condemn all of us on the basis of some who commit atrocity?" He turns to the intercom. "Take us to Telorbat. I need a planet with medical facilities."

"Our right comes from our nature. Our place in the Universal Song. The power that we alone possess." He bends over Ved's sleeping form, and I catch his arm. "What are you doing?"

"In dwelling on his tragedy, you obviously haven't noticed the most important thing about this child. The fact that he's alive."

"He lives—which is the core of his tragedy."

"You still don't understand. Look at him. *He hasn't caught the Death.*"

My Human body shivers. "After days . . . weeks . . . of exposure . . ."

Saburo nods. "He's immune. And if I can figure out why, we might have a chance to end the Death yet."

And if you do, Saburo . . . will the Hlutr permit it?

In confusion, I withdraw to Amny and the song of the Hlutr, while our ship races toward Telorbat.

I think too much like a Human; my sojourn with them has affected me. For Galactic Revolutions have I stood faithfully in my grove, while the patterns of stars and the very face of Amny changed around me, and I have sung the will of the Universal Song. I have earned the title of Elder and the name of Teacher. I have sung in the councils of the Hlutr, and have even advised the Eldest of all. Yet these Humans make of me but a newborn seedling, a foolish sapling facing his first winter snows.

My brothers and sisters, tell me what I should do.

You sing, and I listen.

You will counsel me, you will give me reasons and opinions . . . but you will not decide for me. Some of you think the Humans should be saved, others believe they should perish—and still more of you think that we ought to ignore these children of Terra. Brethren, what am I to do?

Saburo, Ved, and my operative arrive on Telorbat, and I am drawn to them once again.

It is the season of cold in the higher latitudes where the major Human city sits. You are there already, my fellows, rising snow-clad only a few kilometers from the city—for Ciudad Telorba rises like a vast pyramid from the midst of a great forest, and since Humans arrived on this world you have kept watch on them. I wonder, have you ever seen events like today's?

Saburo coughs, and even my operative is not spared the curse of the Death: my borrowed body is wracked with a choking fit, and when it is over I still find it hard to breathe. I begin to ease my awareness out of that fleshy prison, leaving the body to manage itself. I want nothing more than to return to Amny and be done with this sordid matter . . . yet I must see it through to a conclusion.

We are met by a robot on whose shoulders floats the image of a woman's head. She nods. "I am Gingiber Maur, Undersecretary of State. We received your message, Doctor Saburo, and our foremost medical laboratory is yours. You will forgive me for not meeting you in person . . . ?" She seems a little embarrassed, yet Saburo pays her no mind.

"Yes, yes," he says, suppressing a cough. "Show me to the lab. I must examine the boy with proper instruments."

"We have few visitors from space," she tells us as we board an empty train and are whisked forth. "Have you come from far?"

"From the Credixian Imperium ultimately. Immediately, from a ship a few parsecs out from your sun."

She glances at Ved and my operative. "Tell me, you are escaping from the Death? This ship, was it infected?"

Ved quivers at this talk of the Death, and I broaden my awareness to sing him calm melodies of the Inner Voice. He is not yet sure who I am, but he responds to the song of the Hlutr.

Saburo nods, foaming with impatience. "We rescued the boy from a charnel ship—he was the only survivor. The sooner I get to your medical equipment, the sooner I'll be able to start figuring out why he lived."

"To be sure." The train slows, and the robot shows us through the door into a narrow corridor. As soon as we are through, the door slides shut. The robot stands before it, pointing toward the opposite end. "This way, if you please."

Saburo's eyes narrow. "This isn't a hospital. Where are we?"

The robot advances, and we have no choice but to fall

back before it. Gingiber Maur's smile fades. "I am sorry, Doctor. Telorbat is under strict quarantine. We have no choice but to isolate those who have had contact with the Death." We are halfway down the corridor, now, and the far door begins to open. "As a medical man, I am sure you understand. You will be cared for; our prisons have a complete range of services."

"Prison?" Saburo echoes. Then the robot shoves us forward, and we tumble through the door.

Ved clings to my operative's hand, and I wrap an arm about him, all the while singing to quiet him. For we have surely walked into his worst nightmares.

A room the size of an spacecraft hangar is crowded with coughing, weeping Humans. Some are dead already, others are motionless upon mats and have only hours of life left. Some of the healthier ones are ministering to the others.

"Keep Ved back," Saburo tells me, and I am only too glad to comply. We stand in the middle of an open space, and I turn the boy's face to the wall while at the same time I hiss, "Saburo, what are we to do?"

"Don't worry. These people are paranoid, but they're stupid." He glances at an instrument clasped about his wrist. "My ship will be here in five minutes, and in another five we'll be blasted out of here."

"Unless they have ships to destroy yours."

"You won't find a working starship *on* this planet. Everyone who could leave, did. That's why the city's so empty. The ones who got left behind decided to set up this quarantine, but it won't help them." He bares his teeth in haughty animal aggression. "How's Ved?"

"Upset. We sing to calm him, and it seems to help."

"Good. Keep it up."

When Saburo's ship arrives, there is no doubt: a bright flash and a noise like thunder, then half a wall collapses in upon itself. Through smoke and dust, I see a moving wall of dark metal—the ship.

Saburo points and slaps my operative on the back. "Run!" he shouts.

By the time we reach the ship's hatch, twice seventy

others have arrived as well. Some are too sick to move, yet they push themselves forward only to fall into the path of others. Their minds beat with terror and panic.

Saburo pushes through them roughly, then grabs Ved and my operative in firm hands and pulls us toward the ship as if through crashing surf. Human bodies press up against me, choking and vomiting, and I feel Ved's mind shake in counterpoint to his nervous body. The quiet melody of the Inner Voice pauses, then fragments as the boy's mental walls break and the full horror of his last few weeks comes smashing down on him.

He screams in an agony that paralyzes Hlutr on all nearby worlds. And I . . . who stand as close to that cry as I am to the soil of Amny . . . I stagger back, nearly driven from my perch in my Human operative's brain.

In that brain, in the confusion of the Inner Voice and Ved's pain, a miracle happens.

A personality submerged for a lifetime—the original identity of my operative—hears Ved's cry through the endless distance that she has driven between herself and reality. I feel her stir in that Human brain, and I am shocked to silence. Even the Hlutr could not reach her! Yet she comes forth, responding to a pain greater than her own.

Her name is Irisa, this Human whose body I have borrowed. She is almost as sensitive to the Inner Voice as is Ved, and she knows only that she must help him. Limbs move of their own volition, and Irisa lifts Ved, hugs him to herself. The ship's solid wall parts, and she carries him across the threshold to safety, followed by Saburo. The hatch closes, and the ship lifts off, soaring high above city and forest.

Rejoice with me, brothers and sisters of Telorbat. Give me your Inner Voices in song: for Irisa was lost, and has come back. For Ved, whose cry brought even the Hlutr out of their age-old reveries, is delivered from his hell. Irisa, moved to mercy by his need, has saved him.

Riding high above that world, rooted unregarded in Irisa's brain, I sigh. When a poor creature such as this, so frightened of mere existence that she turns her back on it and chooses the cool depths of madness . . . when this poor beast can feel such mercy, dare a Teacher of the Hlutr feel less? These Humans are wild and terrible, yet there is within them a core of true beauty. An age ago as they count time, we Hlutr agreed to help them as we could, to find and develop that beauty. To guide them when they faltered on their road to truth. To aid the honest ones among them as they sought maturity. And now, as I watch the dawning of a consciousness even I had thought lost forever, I reaffirm that vow.

Behind me, I feel my own Elders—and *theirs*, perhaps up to the Eldest herself—I feel them sway in agreement. *You have learned, Little One*, they seem to say.

Irisa knows what I require, and gladly she gives me the use of her body one last time. "Very well, Saburo," I say. "Bring Ved to me on Amny. We will find your cure to the Death. And the Hlutr shall administer it, though it cost the lives of many times twelve thousand of us."

Saburo nods, and the ship turns back toward home.

Ved and Irisa stand before me, in the peaceful night of Amny, and the gentle breeze brings me their alien scents. Saburo is weak, and must be carried on a litter; they settle him next to my trunk, where I can feel the fevered warmth of his body.

Help me, brothers and sisters. Sing with me, Elders. Time is short, and the problem very complex. You who know Humans, and you who are experts in animal biochemistry: sing with me.

The Hlutr sing in the Inner Voice, for now we are decided and there can be no hesitation. Those of us who study the problem must live more quickly than is our wont—for the Death would require many seasons of Human study to yield its secrets. We Hlutr do not have their machines, their computers, their vast laboratories; we have far better: the massed minds of the Hlutr themselves. This is our work, the work we are meant for, and as we unlock the mysteries of the Death, I feel the orange-red flush of deepest happiness creep over my body.

Now we live still faster, and seasons of time to us are

but minutes to the watching Humans. The song builds upon itself, reaching toward a shattering crescendo—then there is the taste of victory, the rush of joy, and . . . silence.

I slow my rate of living, until once again I am in the time-frame of Humans. Exhilarated, I have complete control over my entire body; my answer comes in a song that fills the whole glade.

"Saburo, it is done. We can make a counter-virus for the Death. Hlutr will manufacture it, then spread it on all your twelve thousand worlds. In weeks, the Death will be over."

"Thank you, Teacher," he croaks. "W-when will you begin?"

Before I can even frame the question in the Inner Voice, my Elders answer it. *When you wish, Brother Hlut.*

"We will commence the cure at once." On all those twelve thousand worlds, many times twelve thousand Hlutr stand ready to give their lives in the final detonation that will assure survival for Mankind. The night is alive with their song, a mixed song of triumph and a twinge of regret.

One of us must be first.

To the memory of the Traveller within me, I say, "Are you happy with me, little brother?"

"I am happy with you," he seems to say. "Come, Teacher . . . join me and be remembered forever."

"Stand back," I tell the waiting Humans. The dissolution is catastrophic, as it spreads Hlutr-substance on the winds and streams, but most of the force is directed upward. They need not withdraw too far. And I want Saburo near enough to catch full benefit of the cure.

Now I feel it build within me, as my Elders guide me in this final, most difficult task. The change comes like a building glow from the very center of my being, a welcome swell of warmth that lifts me toward the cool, eternal stars.

Hlutr have done their job well. The cure, I know, will work. There is a last surge in the song of the Hlutr . . . my brothers and sisters, saluting me and this thing I do. Two faltering Human voices join this song; I look down and see Irisa and Ved standing hand-in-hand over Saburo. And ultimate peace rises from the soil to engulf me.

Content, I fly upward to meet the stars and at last to take my place in the Universal Song.

Interlude 2

Over the next few years Kev learned of the Hlutr, and recognized that his story-telling tree was actually a member of one of the oldest races known to Man. He spent long hours alone in the treehouse, trying to converse with the tree, but nothing ever came of it. When it chose, the tree told him stories; otherwise, it remained silent.

He kept his knowledge to himself; somehow he sensed that he could hear a music unknown to others, and knew that they would only make fun of him for it.

Besides, there was much else to keep Kev busy. His school's tales of brave men and women and their heroic deeds sparked an interest in the long-ago days of the First Empire, and soon he was viewing everything he could, even grownups' books he found very hard to understand. During his eighth year he slowly worked through the whole seventy-megabyte text of Mal Arin's *Fall of the First Terran Empire*, while his school struggled to keep him up to date in all his other subjects.

Kev located all the major First Empire sites on Amny, and together he and Dar spent many happy days exploring them. Once Kev even uncovered an authentic Carroll-period crediplate showing eight hundred Imperial Dollars; he kept it for a long time before conscience finally made him send it to the museum on Credix.

When Kev was ten, Dar departed from Amny.

Dar had always admired the Galactic Riders, an ancient brotherhood dedicated to the cause of peace in the Scattered Worlds. He had always dreamed of joining them. Now he was finally getting his chance. With his family's approval, he was headed for Nephestal and advanced training. The night before he departed, the two boys climbed together up to the treehouse for the last time.

The lesser moon was full, and its golden light threw soft shadows on Dar's face. There was a strange lump in Kev's throat, but he tried to ignore it.

"I hope I'll make it through training," Dar said. "I hear it's tough."

"You will." Kev wrinkled his nose. "What happens if you don't?"

"I'll probably stay on Nephestal and find some other way to serve the Scattered Worlds. I guess I really haven't thought about it much."

"So you're never coming back?"

"Don't be silly. Of *course* I'll be back. I'm not going to forget everyone, you know."

Kev lifted his eyes to the stars. Soon, he thought, Dar would be up there, flying among them. He touched his terminal, silently tapping in a question although he knew the answer already. In a second, the screen glowed triumphantly: DISTANCE TO NEPHESTAL: 14.7 KILOPARSECS.

"It's across the Galaxy," Kev complained. "How are we going to talk to one another?"

"They *have* phones, dummy. And I'll send holos."

"Promise?"

"I promise. Now, are we going to get on with this, or not?"

"O-okay."

Dar produced his laser knife, set the beam on minimum dispersion. "Don't be scared, it's not going to hurt."

"I'm not scared," Kev protested. Still, he was glad that Dar was going first.

"All right, here we go."

Carefully, Dar nicked his thumb with the hairline beam, then did the same to Kev's.

Alone in the moonlight, the two boys sealed their friendship in a manner that was old as Humanity.

Kev returned to the treehouse the next afternoon with a heavy heart. Dar was gone; a shuttle had called at the spaceport for him, and before Kev knew, the ship had vanished into the sky.

He sat at the edge of the platform, his legs dangling into empty air and his chin in cupped hands, and sighed heavily.

His sigh echoed for a moment in the movement of leaves, then blended into the quiet music of the tree around him. Slowly, despite his sadness and loneliness, Kev stretched out a hand until he touched the nearest branch. It was smooth and its touch oddly comforting.

Sing with me, Kev Mathis . . .

PART THREE:

Elder

From my place, I can see into the courtyard of the Human settlement. I stand tall against the mountainside; my many trunks reach high into the clear, cold sky of Sebya. I am old, old even as the Hlutr count time, old enough to have felt the continents move beneath me, old enough to have seen Sebya's lone moon grow ever more distant in the night sky. The Humans have been here not even seventy times seventy of their years; yet I have watched them well. Of their seaside towns and vast ocean farms I know little, for we Hlutr seldom grow in or near the sea. Yet since they arrived from the sky, I have watched the Humans in their mountain settlement and their gambols through this marvelous wood that we call the Forest of the Dawn.

The Human settlement grew slowly, slowly as even the trees; there has been plenty of time for me to adjust my deep roots around their changing foundations, to send up offshoots of myself in their gardens, even to crack the mountain's hard stone and reach their secret underground fastnesses.

However much I know the Humans, they are not my real love. I have another study, one which has been my steady joy for all my seasons. For Sebya is fortunate among worlds; this globe is one of the few to have spawned its own native race of sapients. *You*, Little Ones—who in

your still-primitive language of grunts and whistles call
yourselves the Dawn People—you are my devotion and
my chiefest study. Humans came to us already formed in
the biological cauldron of their own unfortunate Terra; but
the Dawn People sprang from Sebya life in the ceaseless
and beautiful Hlutr adjustment of the very basis of life
itself. Humans are interlopers—you, my Littles, are *ours*.

Ours. And in truth, Little Ones, you are *mine*, as much
as any Hlut can be presumptuous enough to make such a
claim. I have nursed you along in your growth, I have
directed the twining of your very genes, since long before
you were a separate species. When your distant ancestors
were still learning to live in the hostile environment of dry
land, when the very weeds and grains were taking their
form . . . then I was a sapling, growing slowly and taking
my lessons from the great Hlutr masters beyond the sky.

Do not believe, Little Ones, those who tell you that the
Hlutr have made you what you are. You have made yourselves. True, only the Hlutr can fashion and re-fashion the
tiny spirals of matter that carry your heredity and your
identity as a species. This is power, and it is also a curse; for
only by dying can Hlutr spread our modifications of the
very form and basis of life. Seventies upon seventies of
Hlutr have died for you, Dawn People, each at a crucial
stage of your growth, each to give you a nudge along the
path of your destiny. But *you*, Little Ones, have made
your way across nearly seventy million generations: living,
dying, adapting, struggling for existence against all the
chances of that long, long span. The dead ends, the wrong
turnings, the setbacks and disasters—these have num-
bered more than the stars in Sebya's nighttime sky. Yet
you have persisted, and you have responded to Hlutr
guidance until now you are the gentlest and most profound of
creatures.

And now, it appears, the Humans are hunting you.

All through the Forest of the Dawn and beyond, the
Hlutr watch . . . and listen. We listen to one another with
the First Language, which is the subtle shift of colors in
our leaves and trunks. We listen with the Second Language, which is the soft soughing of trees on a gentle

breeze. And we listen with the Inner Voice, which is the song that sings in the hearts and minds of every living thing. All over the planet, we listen—to each other, to thousands of those in the lesser orders who tell us what they know, to the strong, steady beat of life and death in the soil, in the sea and in the air.

You, my Little Ones, are the chief object of our concern. Not a Dawn Person falls, that the Hlutr do not know. And not a Hlut knows, who does not tell me at once.

Lovanideth of the Blue Hills Tribe had been missing for nearly two sevens of days. I paid little attention to her departure; the Dawn People are always wandering off for long stretches to be alone, and with seventy-times-seventy-times-seventy of them on Sebya, it is difficult to attribute significance to only one. I told my brethren to search for her, then went back to contemplating the flow of the Hlutr plan for her people. This is a crucial time for the Dawn People, when they must adjust to the most powerful changes in their history. In the next few seventies of years, they will take the first steps along the road of civilization; while their genes have predisposed them toward success, so much depends upon their character and environmental factors. So many races have failed at this point that we Hlutr have learned to be careful.

I watch the Human settlement especially closely. The sons and daughters of Terra cannot be allowed to interfere with the work of a Hlutr lifetime.

Yet interfere they do.

Sea-birds first located Lovanideth's body where it lay on the northern shores. They knew that the Dawn People did not belong so far north, and carried the news to one of my brethren. He, in turn, sent word to me on the invisible waves of the Inner Voice. "Lovanideth of the Blue Hills has been found. She lies dead on the sands of the Cold Sea."

My reply raced north, carried on prevailing winds by the murmurs and rustles of the Second Language. "Have her brought to you immediately. Inform me as soon as her body arrives. Sing nothing more of this in the Inner Voice."

We have built you, Dawn People, to be very sensitive to the Inner Voice—and I do not want you to know of Lovanideth's death. Not yet.

My brother in the north sends large beasts, the scavengers and runners, to bring Lovanideth to him. It is easy for us, when we wish, to control such creatures with the waves of the Inner Voice; the Hlutr will overpowers that of the lower orders. We do not do this often, for it is distasteful to us.

After two days, Lovanideth lies before my brother. He bends low over her body, and tells me all that he sees.

"She has been dead for many days. Her tissues are waterlogged. There are minor wounds on her skin, and her crown fronds are withered." He stops, focussing his attention on the tiny chemical traces that still linger on her and in her. "Salts, and the taste of the sea. The sands. The beasts who bore her hither." There is silence for a moment, and I am acutely conscious of the tortuous chain that brings his meaning to me: nearly seventy single Hlutr relay his words across the mountains to the place where l stand, just outside the Human settlement. "And wait, Elder . . . upon her is the scent of the Humans. She has recently been in their custody."

I need not hear more. "Continue your investigation, and tell me all you learn," I sing. Then I turn my full attention to the settlement below.

Seventy thousand Humans live here, perched in their fortress of granite and iron on the mountain's side. Seventy thousand, doing what Humans do—dancing, eating, sleeping and working, their minds a hubbub of images and activity. I examine them all, and I find no reason to believe them hostile to the Dawn People.

Perhaps, then, Lovanideth's death was an accident. A hunting party whose bolts went astray, or a mistake by ignorant tourists. Human law protects the Dawn People much as it protects the Hlutr—those who killed Lovanideth must have panicked, attempted to hide her body, and then dropped her on the northern beaches in the dark of night.

So I tell myself; but I find no memory of her in the

Human minds I touch, no counterpoint of guilt sounding in the medley of Human thought and emotion in the settlement.

The guilty ones may be in one of the seaside towns . . . if they were tourists, they may even have left Sebya entirely. This once, I grant Humans the benefit of my conjectures.

Three days later, it happens again. This time, the Dawn People come to us themselves: the Elders of Riverbank Tribe appeal to the Hlutr because three of their fellows are missing. The previous night, they saw the lights of a Human air vehicle above the forest.

The Hlut who hears their plea contacts me at once. "Go back to your Tribe," he tells them, "and carry on with your work. The Hlutr will search for your lost ones." Then his call is carried to me along soundless waves of color, the hues of the First Language outracing the wind upvalley through Hlutr leaves and trunks until it reaches my place.

You have been told, Little Ones, that the Hlutr are distant, cold and unfeeling . . . that they do not concern themselves with the doings of the lesser orders. Yet now I give lie to those sayings, for I feel a surge of almost-animal rage. One accidental murder I will overlook—but when one murder is followed by three kidnappings, it is certain that something is afoot in the Human community. After nearly twenty-nine Human centuries of peace, some great upheaval must be taking place in order to bring hostility to Sebya.

I had to know more.

Ordinarily, when a Hlutr Elder needs information, it is readily available. The waves of the Inner Voice permeate space just as they fill the atmosphere of Sebya; my brethren Elders beyond the sky are only a simple song away. And at *their* disposal are all the resources of the Free Peoples of the Scattered Worlds—the great archives on Nephestal as well as the massed databanks of Avethell and Iaranor. The Daamin scholars of Nephestal, for example, were studying the sons of Terra even before Humans left that fair world. Most of their information is available to the Free Peoples.

However, one must know the questions to ask. And I do not know enough.

Among Humankind, there are always those to whom we can turn for aid. Many there are whose minds are open to the Inner Voice: children, madmen, dreamers, fools . . . and all those of compassionate heart and the ability to feel wonder. The children and madmen are no use to me now, but the others may help.

Night falls, as clouds boil up from the south to hide the stars. The forest sleeps, Dawn People and Humans alike. I am already living as fast as the small animals live, even faster than Humans. Slowly, carefully, I catch the melody of Human dreams . . . and I match that song in the Inner Voice, guiding slumbering minds along the path I choose. *Tell me*, I sing, *what is new in the Human community. Tell me why Humans hunt the Dawn People.* My informants will not remember this night; at most, they will have vague recollections of dreams in which the trees sang and they joined the chorus. They will awake happy and refreshed, and will imagine that they dreamed of being one with the world around them.

This is the gift I leave them in return for their information.

That night, then, I tour Human minds—and when the cloudy sky lightens in the east, when the Dawn People awake and stretch their fronds toward the hidden sun, then I withdraw my attention and stand alone, pondering what I have learned.

Human politics shift like Sebya's tides; we Hlutr pay little attention to it. Thus far, the changing course of Mankind's statecraft has left Sebya virtually untouched. At best a minor member of the Terran Empire, Sebya became independent soon after that dominion dissolved nearly three Human millennia ago. Since then Sebya has passed out of the main flow of Galactic events. This suits us well, for the world's isolation has given us peace to conduct our important work with the Dawn People.

Now, it seems, Sebya's seclusion is over.

Dream-images from my informants are misleading—or perhaps the Hlutr will never truly understand animal behavior. It is unclear whether Sebya was conquered, traded or simply purchased. Whatever the terminology, whatever the motivation, our world has a new governor. I know nothing of the man, only his Human name: Darineb Khria. Yet I tremble in the early morning cold, while moist wind carries the scent and sound of my discomfort northward across the mountains.

Sebya's new owner, I fear, may have found the Hlutr's most precious secret.

My orders go forth to all my brethren in both Languages, in ever-widening circles through the forest and beyond: "Conceal the Dawn People. Watch for Humans. Dissuade them from entering the Forest of the Dawn. Find the missing Dawn People of Riverbank Tribe. And await my further instructions."

Perhaps what I fear is untrue. Yet what else has Sebya to offer Humans? Native lifeforms will not nourish them, and only in the seas has their Terran life cycle been allowed to flourish. Our world is a light one, with useful metals buried far deeper than on other planets. Our sun is small and pale compared to those under which Terra's sons thrive; Sebya is far from their Galactic trade lanes. The only thing we have of value is the Dawn People themselves . . . and the abilities which I have bred into them.

I beseech the stars, let it be something else. Even as I reach out with the Inner Voice, out to my Elders who can counsel me—even now I hope that the Humans have found something else of value on Sebya. For if they are truly after the Dawn People, if they truly know our secret . . . then the work of ages must come to an end in nothing but ruin.

I wait, as my cry goes forth into empty interstellar dark. *Elders, tell me of the Human called Darineb Khria. Tell me, that I may find my suspicions false.*

I fear that there will be no happy answer to that cry.

You have been told, Little Ones, that the Hlutr grow slowly; that your years are to us as hours. And indeed this is true, else how could I have directed the very evolution of your race? Yet what you have heard is also false, for when we wish we can live rapidly indeed, and your hours might seem to us as years. Fast or slow, however, the total duration of our life is the same. To live fast is to die sooner. This is a price we do not often pay.

Today I pay gladly, to protect the efforts of ages of my kin. I am old, I have lived more than three-quarters my allotted span—and if I feel already the approaching chill in my upper limbs, the numbness of roots that is the first whisper of death . . . at least I know that my life is spent on the greatest project my folk have ever imagined.

The grey morning does not lighten, even as we turn to follow the path of the hidden sun. About me in the damp, my brethren Hlutr weave a curtain around the Forest of the Dawn. This curtain is partly the swish and sigh of the Second Language, partly the brooding glower of seventies upon seventies of Hlutr, partly the unheard song of the Inner Voice pitched for the Human soul to hear. My brethren set out this curtain for one purpose alone: to keep Humans out of the Forest. To keep the Dawn People safe.

Meanwhile, I must examine the Humans.

I have driven shoots throughout the Human settlement, so that now there are bits of me in their gardens, clinging like vines to their stone walls, even in the dark depths of their storage chambers far below the surface. So distant that they are nearly independent of me, these shoots watch and listen as men and women go about their daily business.

Now I give my full attention to those far pieces of myself. My many-colored leaves turn and twitch though there is no wind, and I strain to make sense of all the different impressions they bring me.

I know Human speech, harsh and rude as it is. I listen, waiting for some hint to tell me where I might find Darineb Khria. I must live very fast indeed, now; with typical animal frenzy, the Humans are doing thousands of things at once. My mind races, trying to interpret and understand all that I hear and see. I fear that no Hlut will ever be able to completely comprehend the Humans—so much that they do is meaningless, mere motion without any possible purpose. Yet I cherish them, in my way, and I would not wish them gone from the Universal Song.

As the sun climbs toward zenith, one scrap of Human speech draws my full attention: "What do you want done with them, Doctor Khria?"

I have found my adversary at last.

Two Humans are walking in a garden. Behind them floats some Terran contraption—a metal box all of winking lights and circuits and artificial limbs like the dangling tendrils of an uprooted tree. I do not trust Human machines. This the Humans have done, which we cannot understand: they have created minds of silicon, minds which can think seventy times itself seventy times faster than the Hlutr at their best. But you, Little Ones, you *will* understand, if your evolution goes . . .

But no. I am sure that one of the Humans must be the one I seek. Yet both of them turn to look at the floating box, and it speaks.

"Throw the bodies into the sea, like the others. And make sure they don't float back ashore."

At first I think the box to be some Human sort of communications device, and I spread my senses wide trying to locate the speaker on the other end. Then I feel the songs of the Inner Voice that come from that courtyard, patterns that can only have their source in the minds of sapient creatures: two faint echoes, such as Humans generate—and one song much stronger, steadier, almost relentless in its singleminded beat. The metal box . . . is alive.

Sebya spins madly beneath me, and it is as if I feel solid soil slipping away under my roots. What sort of creature have these Humans created? Within that box is a living Human brain, a brain that is at one with their electronic circuits and computer devices. The sheer power of that mind! Why, it approaches the class of Hlutr mentality.

It still speaks, and I listen carefully. There must be no mistake.

"I'm certain that we're on to something here. I need to examine more of these creatures. A dozen, from different areas. Send out as many hunting parties as necessary.

Bounty of two hundred thousand soldos for each of the first twelve brought in." It is silent for a moment. "I'm having more sophisticated genotyping equipment sent from Neordan. The ship should be here by nightfall; I want the equipment unloaded and set up in my lab the instant it arrives."

"Yes, Doctor Khria."

"Go." The two Humans depart quickly. There is another moment of silence, while the metal box floats across the courtyard toward a door. It pauses, and glass lenses track in the direction of my twitching leaves. For just an instant, that powerful mind sends out a single melody of the Inner Voice—and I have the feeling that Darineb Khria is staring through my leaves and into the very depths of my being. We confront one another silently, tension keen like slumbering lightning in the still, wet air. Then the moment is over, the door slides shut, and Khria is gone.

In my place on the side of the mountain, I shiver. My fears are realized.

A Human geneticist—and one whose brain is linked to Human computers. Such a combination is formidable. How much more so when the Human's brief lifespan is expanded by artificial means, so that he can follow genetic change through generations? Then, the ability of that Human might even approach the power of a Hlut.

Might threaten Hlutr plans and hopes.

You see, my Little Ones, the Hlutr race will not live forever. You think this odd, even shocking—you Dawn People whose short lives burn out in a few sevens of Sebya's revolutions, who know that the Hlutr around you are more ancient than the forest or the streams. You are amazed to hear me talk this way—I who am older than mountains, I who have felt the continents shifting beneath me. And *my* Elders are more aged still. The Eldest of us all, she who sits at her place in the Secluded Realm . . . she is as old as stars, as old as life itself in the Scattered Worlds.

And yet the Hlutr shall pass. Not soon; but there will come a day when even the youngest of us shall die, when

Hlutr yet unborn will drop their leaves and give up their spirits to the Universal Song. This is the way of the Song.

Long before we go, however, we will have made our successors.

This is our dream, and this is my work. On Sebya, and on a few similar worlds, Hlutr Elders work at creating the race who will succeed us. You, my Dawn People, are that race. Born of Hlutr tissue, every step of your development guided by Hlutr minds . . . you are fashioned to become even greater than we.

Of all the candidates, the Dawn People of Sebya are farthest along the road to maturity. And of all the candidates, thus far you alone have been given the secret to Hlutr strength and greatness. Locked away in your genes, awaiting a biochemical release that will come when the Elders deem you ready, is the ability to change the very structure of life. To create the chemicals which will guide other lifeforms along the paths you will choose.

Each Hlut is a living laboratory of genetics far beyond poor Human skill—and each Dawn Person, as well, has that potential built into her cells.

This is the secret Darineb Kharia has learned. Worse: I fear that he seeks to release your slumbering power, and use it for his own ends.

One of my brethren is aware of my concern. He stands very near the Human seaside cities and has made them his lifelong study. "Sister," he sings to me in the calm melody of the Inner Voice, "perhaps the Human Khria wishes to use his knowledge for the betterment of life. It would not be the first time that Mankind has contributed to the Universal Song." This is true, for everywhere Humans go, they take new forms of life with them. Human-bred plants and animals share the forest with native life, to the enrichment of both.

"Yet they bring discord as well," I remind my brother. "It took their Empire a dozen Human generations to repair the damage it did to the ecologies of seventies of worlds. Every generation since has seen its destructive wars, its excesses of misused strength and simple carelessness."

"Look with me, Elder." He shows me a city of Humans, where men and women stand together on a crowded field of skycraft, waving bright placards and speaking loudly to passersby. "They have heard of the deaths of the Dawn People, and they attempt to convince their brethren to hunt no more."

"A noble effort," I admit. "Yet still I would as soon trust in the curtain which the Hlutr weave around the forest, to stop the hunting."

"I too, Elder. But we do not know everything about Khria. It is possible that he wishes to learn about the Dawn People so that he can help them . . . or help others."

"It is possible." But I have heard the song of Khria's mind, and I do not think it likely that his motives are benign.

I must know for sure.

My cry for information about Darineb Khria has gone unanswered. The planet Nephestal is a unique source of knowledge, and the Hlutr Elders there receive seventies of queries daily from all over the Scattered Worlds. Usually a Hlut is in no hurry, and a few extra days or years do not matter. But now I need an answer quickly.

There is a way. For although we Hlutr are bound to the earth by our roots, and rarely leave the spot where we broke soil, you must not think us limited. Through the First and Second Languages we can converse with one another though the breadth of the planet lay between us—and through the Inner Voice we can leave the planet entirely and fly the winds of space.

Nephestal lies so far from Sebya that a beam of light dispatched when the first Dawn Person spoke his first recognizable word would still be on its way today—yet that distance is nothing to the Inner Voice, when there exists an intellect on Nephestal able to echo my mind's song. Volunteers from the Free Peoples of the Scattered Worlds, most of them strongly empathic or even gifted with telepathy, wait for just such a need . . . and then give their bodies over entirely to offworld Hlutr visitors. I have projected myself onto Nephestal before, in the course of my early training; now I marshall my strength to do this thing again.

A host is found. I sing, I cast forth my being. There is a moment of extreme cold, a taste of the winter that will one day claim my leaves, my branches, my essential song itself—then I shiver, and I am in an animal body amid the snows of Nephestal.

Most animal races love centralization. This is a consequence of their physiology: every system in their bodies has a center, a heart or brain or master gland. I have made certain, Little Ones, that you are free of this bias; while the Hlutr gave you the biochemical structure to allow free movement for part of your lives, we also took care to retain your essential plant-hood, and no one part of you is more vital than another.

Still, centralization can have its uses. What a brain or heart is to the animal body, the planet Nephestal is to the Free Peoples of the Scattered Worlds. There, scarce 210 parsecs from the boundary of the Galactic Core, the Daamin have built a joyous and peaceful world that is the cultural and intellectual center of the thriving Galaxy.

My host is of the race of Avethell, and she is well-used to carrying Hlutr visitors. After a few moments of introduction, she withdraws her consciousness into deep meditation, giving me full control of her body and mind.

Soon I am at the library, which rises in a series of delicate buildings from a low island in a lake next to the forest of the Hlutr. Briefly I sing greetings to my fellows and Elders, then I enter the library itself.

The library answers my queries with a simulacrum of Kayya Trnas, who among the Daamin is accorded the title of the greatest scholar of Mankind. No matter that Kayya Trnas passed from the Universal Song Human centuries ago. The library remembers him. Small, white-furred and red-eyed, Kayya Trnas perches on a table and recites.

"The Human called Darineb Khria was born in the first century of Terra's Space Age, about twenty-seven seventies of Sebya years ago. He rose to prominence in early studies of genetics, and was the first to isolate several important Human gene combinations, including that controlling eidetic memory. Khria died in the Terran year AD 2096."

I shake my host's head. "You have chosen the wrong information. I wish to know about—"

"Wait," the ghost says. "Khria's body was frozen in liquid nitrogen at the time of his death. In the Terran year TE 348, twenty-three seventies of Sebya years ago, his body was taken to the Human world Borshall, where his brain was salvaged and placed in a mechanical shell. Darineb Khria survived the dissolution of the Terran Empire and reappears periodically in Human history, notably on the worlds Terexta, Dunsinane, Neordan and Gotlan. He took a key role in the Gotlanian War of AD 3041-43, as well as the destruction of BDA Tr ska in AD 4635."

"Please summarize the story." I am not well enough acquainted with Human history; the names and dates are merely random sounds to me.

"In the past few centuries Khria has built up a shadowy kingdom of Human worlds: by a combination of political influence, economic might and religious authority, he has effectively become the ruler of over fifty planets. Few even suspect that Khria is their ruler; he prefers to act invisibly. Daamin scholars have projected Khria's ambition, and foresee a gradual expansion of territory along with consolidation of forces. We expect that Khria will seek to forcibly expand his dominion by AD 6000, beginning with biological and economic attacks on the Aetorian League. Khria's primary disadvantage is lack of access to sophisticated Human laboratory instruments for genetic surgery; such instruments are under the control of the Human states of Credix and Borshall."

Ah, then, my fears are reality. "Khria has come to Sebya," I say, my host's voice sounding thin and powerless in the library chamber. There is no use telling the library; neither the Daamin nor the Free Peoples can act quickly enough to prevent Khria from finding what he seeks.

Only I can do that.

Thanking my host, I return my essence to my Sebya hillside.

Shadows are long in the forest and the settlement. Most

Humans are having their ritual evening meal. It is not hard for me to find Darineb Khria; his metal shell floats in a small garden where my leaves blossom amid a stone fountain.

Now I use a technique which my brother the Human-watcher has taught me. I take firm control of those parts of my body that protrude into Khria's garden, and I vibrate the leaves and stems quickly, so that they create a whispering echo of Human voice.

"Darineb Khria, you and I must speak."

Khria's lenses turn immediately in my direction. No trace of surprise escapes his mind. "I've wondered when you would take notice." He comes closer. "I can read the Hlutr First Language, if you would rather speak to me that way."

"An odd talent for a Human," I answer with the shifting colors of the First Language.

"I am not an ordinary Human," he says. "Welcome to my garden." He chuckles. "Although it seems you've been here longer than I have. Er . . . how should I address you? 'Brother' or 'Sister' does not seem appropriate."

"You converse with an Elder of the Hlutr. I am the oldest on this planet."

"As you will, Elder. I thought I detected Hlutr workmanship in the genetic structure of the natives. A fine job you've done with them, fine indeed."

"Since you know of us, Darineb Khria, you know how little your flattery means."

"I meant no offense, Elder."

"I take offense, Khria. I take offense at your arrogance. I take offense at your desire to use the secret power of the Dawn People. I take offense at your animal aggression and your thirst for power."

"And I suppose you want to stop me. Elder, I think you underestimate me. I have nearly three thousand years of experience, and abilities that even the Hlutr lack."

His claim is so ludicrous that I am almost convinced he is unsane. "Three thousand of your years ago I stood on this hillside and directed the evolution of the Dawn People. Ten thousand times three thousand years ago I stood here, before your race had yet arisen. Three *billion* years ago, before the Pylistroph had spread life to these Scattered Worlds, the Hlutr stood tall in the soil of lost Paka Tel and pondered the mysteries of life. What can you possibly do that the Hlutr cannot?"

"I have computers that can simulate new genetic patterns and carry them over thirty thousand generations in the course of an afternoon. They can look at your Dawn People and unravel three million years of Hlutr meddling to show me their original ancestor. They can guess at what you're headed toward."

His words stop me for a moment. The grand work of the Hlutr, that which Khria dismisses as "meddling," must needs be slow. It proceeds with the speed of drifting continents, with the gradual development of organism after organism. Thus are the Hlutr so long-lived: that we may do this work.

"Your computers produce visions," I say. "Without the Hlutr to show you how, you cannot make those visions real. And I will not allow you to have that knowledge. You have nothing to offer me, Khria."

"I can give you eternal life."

"Eternal life? You, a Human, speak to a Hlut about immortality? I have lived over a thousand times your tiny span already."

"And you will die. Tomorrow, a million years from now, ten million . . . it doesn't matter. Because ultimately you *will* die. Life grows dearer as it grows longer, no? And death hurts more."

"So it is written in the Universal Song. All die, Khria. Not even the Hlutr can change that fact."

"I don't doubt that Hlutr can't do anything about it— else you'd have made yourselves immortal a billion years ago. I also don't doubt that some of your Elders are hard at work on the problem. It would take you ten million generations to do the work, even if you knew what you were working toward."

"Eternal life is a fable."

"You're mistaken. I've run the simulations on a Muspel Three Thousand; you can inspect my results if you like. A super-powerful Hlut, able to shrug off the worst forest fire, able to regenerate almost instantly, capable of unlimited growth on any organic base. It could live through a super-nova by sporing: each spore retains the full consciousness of the organism. Reconstructive DNA is quadruply-redundant to eliminate risk of mutation-based damage, and the organism would have complete control over all biochemical processes down to the molecular level. Currently your body structure cannot last beyond three billion years at an absolute maximum: my new Hlut would have a lifespan that *starts* at six billion."

"Whatever you have designed, it cannot bring immortality to any of us now alive." I am distracted by the attention of Hlutr Elders, a phantom wildwood on the frontiers of my mind. And I know, although none of them admit it, that part of what Khria says is truth. Certain Hlutr *have* contemplated the type of creature Khria describes. Perhaps some have even made experiments in that direction. Possibly the Hlutr of the Gathered Worlds, sundered from us since the time of the Great Schism, have proceeded further.

The wind of space whispers with knowledge that should not come to me, from the brooding mind of the Eldest herself. She alone in the Scattered Worlds survives from the era before the Great Schism; she alone knows the full story of Hlutr experiments upon the Hlutr form. Could it be possible that the Eldest, on her island in the Secluded Realm, might be a product of those investigations? If Khria is right, she is nearing the limit of her time in the Universal Song—does this explain her sudden interest?

She does not speak, does not sing an opinion into the quiet music of the Inner Voice. Perhaps she has been watching all along, as she watches all programs that might lead to the successor race.

Khria answers me with a snort. "Would I offer what I can't deliver? *Your* genetic structure, your memories—your consciousness—can be integrated into the new design. A timeless moment of sleep, and then you awake as a creature that cannot die."

"You cannot deliver this thing yet. And without the

Hlutr method of altering genetics, your new immortal creature will remain an image in the electronics of your machines."

"There you have me," he admits. "You need my computers and my concepts . . . but I need your ability and your billions of years of experience in using it. Otherwise, I'd have to do the job one bit at a time, and it would take longer than the Hlutr have been in existence." A winged insect, Terran lifeform, buzzes for a moment around Khria's metal casing. With the speed of summer sunshine he strikes with a mechanical arm, and the insect falls dead to the ground.

"There you have it," Khria says. "You can help me, and gain eternal life. Or you can try to stop me, and wind up dead . . . sooner or later, no matter how you try to avoid it."

"You know what answer I must make."

"Don't be too hasty. I'll give you time to consider. You can find me when you need me, I'm sure." Khria turns, and in a moment he is gone.

My mind whirls without direction, and I pull my awareness back to my steady place on the mountain. My roots drive deep into soil and rock, and I feel their comforting tension even as confusion makes me sway and shiver.

My brethren on other worlds sense my emotions, and they withdraw their attention. Even the Eldest turns her thoughts away from me. I am left on my own in swift-falling night.

I watch the stars, and I ponder.

More than three-quarters of a Hlutr lifetime spent guiding the Dawn People along their path toward a goal they cannot begin to imagine. So much longer to go before that goal is in sight. So many possible wrong turnings; perhaps the children of Sebya will *never* become the successors we long for. Other hopes have died before, in nuclear fire or ecological catastrophe.

If the Dawn People fail, I will have to die with them.

If they do not fail, I will never live long enough to see their triumph.

And Khria offers eternal life.

With Khria's improvements, the Hlutr race would never pass from the Universal Song. We would never *need* successors. The Galaxy would never be bereft of the compassionate Hlutr song, the guiding Hlutr mind.

And what of Khria . . . of the damage he would do with his knowledge of Hlutr genetic techniques?

How long would Khria himself live?

I know the answer as soon as the question frames itself: Khria could live forever. The cunning Human machines have sustained his consciousness far beyond the lifespan of Human flesh already; as long as his mechanisms have energy, they will continue to keep him alive.

Should the future, then, be an everlasting battle between Khria and the Hlutr, a battle for the destiny of races yet unborn? Or will long life and the power of the Hlutr bring wisdom? Can my brothers and sisters teach Darineb Khria the ways that have served us so well throughout our history?

I imagine becoming Khria's partner for eternity . . . struggling against his animal instincts at first, but finally bringing him to full knowledge and understanding of the Universal Song. Galactic years will pass like fast-flying autumn clouds. Together, Khria and I will give the boon of eternal life to all my brothers and sisters. We will improve the Dawn People, and send them out into the Scattered Worlds as our agents. Peace will come to these troubled stars. Perhaps we will even send them into the Galactic Core, and heal the Great Schism that still keeps Scattered and Gathered Worlds apart.

I catch myself in these imaginings, and I am shocked. Shocked that an Elder of the Hlutr could allow herself to be tempted by a Human. Amazed that the Human has found anything that would tempt me.

What would Khria's gift mean, what would it do to the Hlutr? We are long-lived, yes, but only the most naive of Little Ones would imagine that we therefore do not know the importance of death, nor the brevity of life.

Life is our memorial, the thriving life of the Scattered Worlds. Life itself is our immortality, the life of generations unconceived. Would we struggle so hard in the service of life, if we were ourselves immortal?

Does the nature of the Hlutr race itself rest on my decision?

You, Little Ones, recall me to myself. *You* are my responsibility, your welfare my most important trust. Let Khria promise me eternal life and the entirety of the Universal Song; I cannot accept if it means that the Dawn People will be mistreated.

My roots reach deep into the heart of the mountain, and my branches cling vinelike to the walls of many corridors and rooms far below the Human settlement. The daily cycle of artificial day and dark gives my pale leaves the light they need, and my strong roots carry sustenance from the good soil and air of the mountainside. I turn my attention to them, and soon I have located Khria in a private office nearly a Hlut-length beneath the surface.

"Hear me, Darineb Khria," I say in the Human tongue.

Khria is unsurprised. "Yes?"

"The Dawn People must not be harmed. You will not take them from their homes and you will not cut them apart in your laboratories."

"If I agree, you will help me?"

"You will have the knowledge you need. When next a Dawn Person dies the natural death, you shall have the body to examine."

"That could take years."

"The creature who offers eternal life is concerned with a delay of several short years?"

He chuckles. "All right. My people can't get into your forest. Stop keeping them out."

"Recall your hunters and I will order the Hlutr to dissolve their curtain."

"Agreed." He speaks to a communication device, then waits. Soon word comes to me from all corners of the forest: the Humans are returning to their homes. In turn, I tell my brothers and sisters to relax efforts to keep Humans away.

"The curtain is fallen, Khria."

"Good. Let's talk specifics, then. Before I can continue

my research, I need to see the complete life cycle of the Dawn People. From the beginning."

I consult my brethren. "White Rocks Tribe is returning to their grove for a birthing ceremony. It will take place in three of your days. You may witness."

"Fine. We're decided, then? You'll help me, and I'll give you immortality."

"I will help you." My brother who watches the Humans gives me the words I need. "The White Rocks grove is at the source of the northernmost branch of the great river that flows through the Forest. When you enter the forest, the song of the Hlutr will guide you."

"I'll be there." He moves to the door and makes a motion with his artificial arms. "Meanwhile, we can both ponder what we're going to do with the rest of our lives. Good night, Elder." With that he withdraws, and the closing door hides him from my sight.

I am alone beneath the starry sky. All Sebya surrounds me: the song of the world echoes in my roots, my tall branches, my thick solid trunk. Sebya pulses in the eternal rhythms, moving under the influence of the moons, the sun and its fellow planets. The surface crawls with life, from free-floating viruses to tiny organisms huddling upon grains of sand to the great reptiles and fish that live in the ocean depths. Ceaselessly the symphony of life continues through the night, each creature's voice blending with all others to produce a clear and awesome music.

I wonder how that song will be changed, as Hlutr become truly immortal and the Dawn People near their maturity. Sebya is my home, and for we who abide here, it is the only truly perfect world in the Galaxy. In this new future, we will have the power to make of Sebya whatever we choose. In the past, biological detours have set back our work: the golden fish, the over-enthusiastic diatoms that almost poisoned the atmosphere, the digging beetles that still survive in the deepest regions of the southern jungles. No more. With the aid of Khria's computers we will be able to adjust Sebya's ecology in single generations. At last the world will know peace—and as time passes, we will bring that peace to all the Scattered Worlds.

No Hlut ever contemplates in isolation; the winds of air and space carry our thoughts and feelings ever outward to our brethren. My brother, the one who studies Humans, whispers doubts in the night. "Elder, this course is far from certain. The Ancients of Nephestal believe that Khria is faithless and merely seeks power for his own ends. How can we be sure that he will not hinder us?"

I do not answer, for I do not know what to say. There is no surety. Khria has hidden his inner feelings from us. Humans are alien enough, and we have great difficulty reading their intentions . . . and Khria is something still more foreign. A Human brain lives within those circuits, but one might as well try to read the feelings of a piece of ice or a rock. I *believe* that the Hlutr can change Darineb Khria, and I have nothing more than that belief.

Yet like my brother, I doubt the wisdom of the course I have chosen.

Beyond me, the Hlutr Elders beyond the sky say nothing. A few of them watch like lonely sentries scanning the horizon for smoke that will herald the approach of forest fire; they watch, and that is all.

Too soon, the day of the birthing ceremony comes.

We have given the Dawn People a three-stage life cycle. They begin as saplings, then in autumn of their thirteenth year they breed with their mature brethren. The spring of their fourteenth year is the Birthing Ceremony: as the next generation of saplings emerge from the soil, the parent lifts her roots and takes her first steps as an adult.

Each autumn for the next eleven years adults return to their grove for breeding; then during his twenty-fifth year a Dawn Person begins the quick, happy process of disintegration. To ease the burden of death, in his last year a Dawn Person develops a heightened sensitivity to the Inner Voice. At the end, each Dawn Person is at one with the community of Hlutr and completely content.

Later, when their culture has stabilized, we will add another stage onto their life cycle: instead of death, the Dawn People will have full command of their biological powers, and enter fully into the magnificent life of the Hlutr.

Today is Birthing Day for the White Rocks tribe; today their saplings rise above the soil, and today their new adults take their first steps. It is a day of exultation, and the Hlutr sing happiness throughout the forest. I am far from the White Rocks grove, but my brothers and sisters there show me everything I must know. The sun rises red and enormous in the east, dispelling mists that hang in the branches.

Mature Dawn People stand about the grove already; the young ones, three or four times the height of the older adults, are scampering about and the atmosphere is one of holiday. Some of the oldest Dawn People stand next to Hlutr; they are perhaps only twice the height of a Human and they have little interest in Birthing. Their concerns lie more with the melodies of the Universal Song; their minds have the texture of a young Hlut who has just beginning to be skilled with the Inner Voice.

Khria arrives in a skyship of silver and white, accompanied by twice seven other Humans, men and women whose dull minds project only dumb obedience to their leader. Such devotion is completely alien to the Hlutr; we are all free individuals, and we all follow our own will. If there is unity in the Galactic community of Hlutr, it is the agreement of equals and not the domination of a few.

The younger Dawn People adults are afraid of Khria and his followers, and they draw back uneasily to the edges of the glade. A few of the saplings, only a year or two old, quiver gently and are comforted by the song of the older adults. And my folk raise the Inner Voice in a melody of reassurance. *The Humans are here as guests, they will not harm you.*

As the sun climbs and its rays touch the shorter Dawn People, the birthing ceremony begins. It begins with song; the Dawn People sing with trunk and branch and Inner Voice, giving form as best they can to the ethereal music of the Universal Song. Each tribe has its own song, one that changes slowly across the generations. Each song was given to a tribe's ancestors by an individual Hlut. By

contemplating the particulars of that song, we Hlutr know
the progress of each tribe and can decide what actions are
best taken next to guide the Dawn People along their
path. If Khria but knew their meanings he would have
half his answer already.

In response to the sun and the song, buried seedlings
reach for the open air. To Khria and his companions, this
part of the ceremony must be tedious; it is fully two
Human hours before the first seedling breaks soil. Dawn
People elders are there at once, taking care to avoid
shadowing the new sprout. A tiny shoot of intense green
and white, it gives a triumphant cry of discovery and then
goes about the business of growing.

More seedlings break soil now, and they are welcomed
and cherished as much as the first. Several young adults
have their favorites already, and they stand proudly by
them or bend to brush fallen leaves away. In due time the
adults will leave; any seedlings who emerge tomorrow, or
the days after, will be greeted by their sessile cousins.

The first stage of the birthing ceremony is started; new
adults, who traditionally wait until after the first seedlings
arise, are now free to take their first steps.

The song builds, and the entire tribe sways in time with
it: young adults, elders, juveniles and seedlings all together. The oldest juveniles, those in their fourteenth
year, rock back and forth with increasing violence; their
roots groan and their leaves fall with each swing. Soon it is
as if a great storm sweeps through the grove, and sixteen
soon-to-be adults are at the center of that maelstrom.

Then it comes, with the sickening crack of splitting
bark, with the flutter of frightened birds, with the awful
cry of all the Dawn People and the Hlutr who cherish
them. For one single instant this spring afternoon is split
by a scream like a brilliant flash of sunlight, and sixteen
Dawn People shed their childhood bodies, lift their roots,
and step forward.

I wonder what it is like, to pull free of the nurturing
ground and walk away, to leave half your substance behind
to dissolve into nutrients for your younger cousins. Suddenly to start living faster, so fast that for the rest of your

days you will need to consume animals and other plants in order to feed your struggling body. This the Hlutr will never truly know. For even as we have heard the Dawn People sing their experience in the Inner Voice, time and again for ten thousand generations, there is always something they hold back. Each race, each individual, has a unique core of being that can never be shared with another, and this experience, the sublime transformation of the Dawn People, falls within that core. We have given them a life cycle known to no other race since time began; only when they have reached maturity will they come to realize that we have also given them the seeds of a tremendous and dreadful racial loneliness.

We Hlutr have been alone: we have never been able to share the essence of the experience that makes us Hlutr, our command of the stuff of life. Now we are making our sucessors, who will understand and share that feeling. In the twilight of the Hlutr race, we will no longer be alone.

But the Dawn People . . . they will have to wait until they create *their* successors, whom the Hlutr cannot begin to imagine, before their isolation will end.

Dawn Folk and Hlutr sing together now, sing in sound and in the soundless waves of the Inner Voice, sing triumph and the joy of life's endless cycles renewed. There is a truth, which most races learn but which Hlutr and Dawn People know instinctively from the first moment of existence, and this truth is that all life is one. From one end of the Galactic Spiral to the other, from the slow-living crystalline Talebba off in deep space to the fleeting insects of green Tcherlatha to the majesty of the Hlutr themselves and beyond, every creature that lives is a part of all others. This is what Khria must learn, if he is to wield his power wisely.

In that sun-warmed glade beneath Sebya's eternal blue sky, my dream comes to a sudden and shocking end. For while the White Rocks tribe stands enraptured, Khria points, and his followers tear one of the new seedlings out of the nourishing ground. The newborn's cry of anguish rocks the forest, and every creature within it stiffens and pauses as if an enemy has just appeared.

In that terrible moment, my song is attuned to Khria's, and I feel the emotions that beat in his mind, the passions that flow through his animal glands. And what I find sickens me. Khria is *happy*—he actually enjoys what he has done, he drinks the pain of the Little One as a thirsty flower drinks the Spring rain.

Quick action is not the Hlutr way—we prefer to deal with problems over generations, not seconds. I least of all, who have lived so slowly and so long, am accustomed to acting fast. So Khria and his fellows are in their skyship and above the treetops before I can respond.

Khria has betrayed me. More . . . I have been a fool. To have trusted a Human, especially when I could not read his hidden emotions! Now the enormity of my deed comes upon me with the shock of sudden winter.

Questions fill my mind, but there is no time for them. Why, Khria, why have you done this? What possesses you, to repudiate a solemn agreement made to a Hlutr Elder? Answers must come later, for now I must act.

My view of the glade is shadowy and indistinct now, for my brothers and sisters who carry that image to me are reeling with consternation. "Close the curtain," I tell them, "and send the Humans to me." I will know from Khria himself why he has done this.

One Hlutr voice sounds clear in the confusion, and others follow it: the curtain is built up, shutting out Humans from the Forest of the Dawn and, more important, closing in those who are already there. Khria's men cannot stand against the united Hlutr will.

Too late, I find that Khria has anticipated me. A bright bolt of red lashes from his skyship into the very body of a mature Hlut on the outskirts of the glade—that one's pain deafens all nearby, and brings the song of the curtain to an abrupt halt. The glade vanishes from my sight in a blur of screams and flame, and Khria . . . Khria has escaped.

It is over.

Khria thinks to hide from me in his laboratory deep beneath the Human settlement; Khria is a fool. He believes that he can forswear himself before the Hlutr and pay no penalty, that he can scamper to his burrow like a tiny animal and escape the minds of his masters.

Know truly, Little Ones, what I have said: not an insect falls in the Forest of the Dawn, that the Hlutr do not know. My roots drive deep, deeper than even Khria can comprehend, and now I strain forward, pushing them on through bedrock while my leaves drink deep of the golden sun above.

I must live faster than I have ever lived before, faster than the Humans live, faster than the dawnflies live, faster than ever a Hlut on Sebya has lived. Rock splinters like rotted wood before the swift advance of my roots, my new-formed limbs; in seventy-times-seventy places I burst forth into the tunnels of the Human settlement.

All this motion is not without price. I, who have felt the continents shift beneath me, will burn out most of my remaining span before the sun sets this evening. I will never live to see the Dawn People fulfill my hopes and my dreams for them. It was a mistake to trust Khria, and a mistake whose consequences I must bear.

I find Khria in a secluded apartment next to a laboratory where the Dawn Person seedling is being dismembered. Khria intently studies glowing vision screens before him, oblivious to the gentle entrance of my leaves and soft, young branches.

It is an effort for me to vibrate these new leaves to form Human speech. "Why, Darineb Khria, have you done this?"

Now Khria sees me, and his metal body rises as his cameras track around the room. He knows that he is too late—I have thrust shoots forth through every wall, and one of my firm roots holds his door shut against motors which strain to open it.

"I needed to examine the transition phase," Khria says. His mind is cool. "You wouldn't have given me permission—"

"I told you to wait. Dawn People die in the transition; soon enough one such would have been yours to examine."

"Years, decades maybe."

"You promise immortality, and yet cannot wait a few

short years?" Inside me there is regret. For a dream that will never be—for I truly believe that Khria could have given the Hlutr race true immortality, and brought the Dawn People to their heritage far in advance of Hlutr plans.

"Such a small sacrifice to make," he says. "A couple of seedlings here and there, some of the adults . . . it's not too late, you know."

"It is far too late, Darineb Khria."

"What makes you care so much about these creatures? You've never cared that much for Humans, or any of the other races you've dealt with. What makes these Dawn People of Sebya so special?"

I knew how to answer him now, an answer that in my foolishness I had not known before this day. Even as old as I, the Hlutr *can* learn. "The Dawn People are our immortality . . . not any genetic alterations that you might make. Individual Hlutr will die, and in the distant future our whole species will be gone—but the Dawn People will be there, so that the best of the Hlutr will live forever."

All the time we speak I have been extending myself further into Khria's apartment, tightening my hold on rock and soil, forming hard Hlutr wood in minutes that otherwise would take generations to lay down.

Only now, as he sees my substance closing about him like a cocoon, does Khria begin to fear. And still his mind is dominated by ego, by the dreadful arrogance that made him tempt a Hlut . . . and almost succeed. "How long do you think you can hold me? Rescue teams will blast me out. My reactor will keep me alive for a century or more."

This expense of energy has been frightening and has left me with a vastly diminished span . . . but I will live far longer than Darineb Khria. My wood magnifies the sound as I answer him. "Rescue teams will not reach you. Once this place is wrecked, no Human will want to come here for seventy times seventy generations and beyond. My brethren will see to that. The Humans in the south will leave the Forest alone, else they will be persuaded to leave this world."

"What do you mean, when this place is wrecked? You can't—"

Only now does he realize the magnitude of what he has done, and Khria stops as his fear flashes outward to the stars.

I am tired, and the sun is creeping toward the horizon. It is time to end this thing. "I wish it could have been different, Khria. Now do we both pay for our sins."

I strain, like a Dawn Person struggling to tear himself from the ground—and all around me, the mountain shudders and tumbles, the Human settlement shatters and falls in upon itself . . . and Khria is buried under more stone and steel than a thousand Human rescue parties could lift.

Three seasons fly by as I stand contemplating this thing I have done. I do not regret killing Khria, for he was a thing that should have been killed far sooner. What I did, I did to save the Dawn People—and that is my chiefest reason for being. However, I do regret that I have thrown away so much: my own chance for a personal immortality, buried now in the chambers of Khria's mind; but also my part in the Hlutr racial immortality. For even as I feel the heaviness of snow upon my limbs and the rush of wind through my branches, I know that I will never again contribute to the grand evolution of the Little Ones I have endangered. It is a sad and terrible thing, to cast away the eternal future.

I spend more seasons in contemplation, seeking solace in the infinity of voices, Hlutr and otherwise, that make up the Universal Song. At last the merest whisper comes to me in that song, and I find myself touched by the attention of the Eldest of all.

"Suffer no more, child. We have need of you."

"Eldest, I can be of no more use here. Long before the Dawn People near their goal, my span will be ended."

"We need your attention here, now. Do you imagine that the Dawn People are our *only* attempt for a successor race, or that Sebya is the sole source of the Hlutr future? I need your wisdom and experience in the councils of the Elders from all worlds."

"Eldest, I fear that I will not live long enough to do you good. A few sevens of centuries as the Humans count time . . ."

"Nonsense. Live as quickly as you are accustomed to, and your span will be short. Allow me to teach you to live more slowly, and you can counsel me for a lifetime yet." The Eldest pauses, a pause that may be a Human generation long. "Of course, you must bid farewell to Sebya. Your body may remain there, but living far too slowly to be conscious of the place."

I look about, surprised that the snow has melted and a fresh carpet of green covers the tumbled remains of the mountain. Birdcalls are shrill in the quiet afternoon, and I can sense a tribe of Dawn People hunting a few Hlutr-lengths away. Overhead, the sun is bright in a cloudless sky.

Immortality, yet again? To leave Sebya behind, and take my place in the councils of the Eldest of us all, to shape Hlutr destiny in upcoming ages? Or to stay, allow my consciousness to submerge into the flow of life around me, and eventually give my substance and memories to the community of life which I have so profoundly touched?

I do not hesitate; and when again my mind touches the Eldest's, I know she is ready for my decision.

"I will stay, Eldest," I say. "And *here*, I will live forever."

INTERLUDE 3

Three days after his fourteenth birthday, Kev went aloft in a small starship with his school and his Father Alekos. By the time they returned to Amny Spaceport five hours later, the school was satisfied of Kev's piloting proficiency, and issued him a license to fly anywhere in the Scattered Worlds.

"This doesn't mean that you can go joy-hopping all over creation," said Father Alekos. "Before you fly anywhere I want you to let one the family know where you're going. And that *doesn't* mean beaming a message to the house computers from the outskirts of the system."

"Yes, sir." Alekos was Kev's favorite father, and the boy felt honored that the man had taken time to make this flight with him. Alekos Mathis was a doctor, one of the best—computers called him when they had trouble with a diagnosis, and patients flew to Amny from all over the Galaxy just so he could see them.

"Good. Now I know that Tiponya is programming a great meal to celebrate, and I have orders to keep you away from the house until eighteen o'clock at least. What do you want to do until then?"

What to do? Kev had the freedom of the Galaxy. In an hour he could be on Credix, in the First Empire museums he loved so much; in less time he could be on any of two dozen worlds that had once been colonies of Mankind.

He shook his head. That wasn't what he wanted. He gave Alekos a shy smile. "Do you want to see my treehouse?"

"Treehouse? What a thing to come up with! All right, Kev, I'd be glad to see your treehouse."

Father Alekos laughed when they approached the tree. "Here? You built a *treehouse* in the branches of a Hlut?"

"I thought you knew. I thought everyone knew."

Alekos leaned back, shielding his eyes from the sun, and examined the treehouse. "It looks pretty solid. I'm surprised that you were allowed to build there. Still, if the Hlutr haven't said anything . . ." He shrugged. "What's so special about this treehouse?"

Kev took a deep breath. "Sometimes . . . sometimes I feel like the tree is talking to me."

This time Alekos didn't laugh. "Tell me about it."

Kev told him, and for a wonder Father Alekos didn't laugh or smile in that patronizing grownup way. He just nodded, then put his arm around Kev's shoulders and said, "This is a great gift you have, son. The Hlutr love our children, but it's a rare child who can comprehend their songs. Don't let anyone ever talk you out of that ability."

"What do you mean?"

"As you grow up, you'll feel a lot of pressures to behave the way everyone else does. You won't find many other people who are lucky enough to hear the song of the Elders; you might be tempted to stop listening. Don't let that happen."

"I won't. I promise."

"Good. Look, we've still got two hours until dinner—if we hurry, we could make it to the southern continent to pick up some fresh flowers for your mothers. What do you think?"

"Can I pilot?"

"Of course."

"Okay, you're on." Hand in hand, Kev and his father ran back toward their flier, laughing.

It was a clear, cool night; it seemed to Kev as if a million bright stars looked down over the valley. He'd been awake since dawn, but he didn't feel at all tired.

The party was still going on; half of Dar's family had stopped by, and the grownups seemed content to sit around the table drinking and talking all night. Kev had excused himself when he could stand it no longer, and started walking at random. There was nothing in the valley—indeed, on all Amny—that could hurt him; his terminal kept him constantly linked to the house computers as well as the navsat network. Help was literally a shout away.

He didn't go that far. Inevitably, Kev found his steps leading toward the treehouse. He climbed the ladder carefully, noting that the sixth rung needed some more glue. He'd take care of it tomorrow.

Alone on the platform, he felt silly. He was almost sorry he'd said anything to Father Alekos; some secrets were best kept to oneself.

It was windy. Kev shivered, and took shelter in the lee of the great trunk. The tree's bark, which had a texture like rough, strong plastic, seemed almost warm.

Kev stretched, yawned, and snuggled closer to the tree. All around him was the sound of wind in leaves, a sound mixed with an almost-unheard ethereal music . . .

Sleep well, Little One. Sleep, and dream with us.

PART FOUR:

Artist

The great experiment, you tell me, is nearing its end. Humans are fading, and they will soon be gone. I hear you, my brothers and sisters . . . but I am not sure that I believe.

You have facts, drawn from the libraries of the Daamin and the minds of Human beings themselves. Once Mankind populated more than twelve thousand worlds in this Galaxy; now fewer than nine thousand planets feel the tread of his boots. Humanity has been in ever-quickening decline since the Great Death nearly three Human millennia ago. Their once-volatile politics are moribund, and their culture and technology—the twin prides of the Human animal—have for centuries been receding from their peak.

The experiment nears an end, you say. Twice seventy Human generations have passed since our races first met in that sunlit grove on distant Amny, and at last you are relieved that the wave of Humanity has crested. Another seventy generations, and doubtless Humans will be gone.

So you sing, and your Inner Voices fill the starry skies with calm rejoicing. Even you who should know better, you who live on Human worlds and cherish these peculiar Little Ones—even you are glad that you will soon lay down your burden.

You are wrong, brethren. You do a disservice to the

memory of those Hlutr who first loved Mankind, and first promised to guide him. I have sung their songs: the Traveller, his Teacher, the Watchers and Elders who befriended Humanity. And their message is clear.

This race, whom you believe to be entering its twilight, has yet to achieve its true greatness.

Far worse than the disservice to your forebears, you do a disservice to the Universal Song itself, by denying its clear truth. Mankind is destined for greatness—yet Hlutr neglect now threatens his promised future.

Not only the Hlutr have interest in Humans. Yet Hlutr indifference has made itself felt in the Council of Free Peoples of the Scattered Worlds. The Ancients of Nephestal, eternally scheming in their forever-dreams, have suspended their designs for Terra's children; the Galactic Riders have almost ceased their visits to Human worlds; and perhaps worst of all, some Hlutr have even begun to turn away from their once-proud task of comforting Human children and madmen.

Brothers and sisters, your prophecy—that Humans will decline and never truly become part of the society of the Free Peoples—is fast fulfilling itself.

You turn your minds from me, and in your songs there is a hint of chiding. Yes, I am young . . . I broke soil only four times seventy Terran decades ago, just after we delivered Humankind from the terrible Death. Yes, I lack the experience of ages that belongs to my Elders. So you tell yourselves that you need pay no heed to what I sing.

And you turn from me for yet another reason. For who can take seriously the counsel of an Artist? Because I lack the Hlutr ability to adjust genetics, you pity me. The medium of my art is not the helices of life and the stuff of living beings, but the music of the Inner Voice. This you do not understand. So you mistrust me.

And because I have done the worst thing of all—taken a Human as my partner—you despise me.

In your disapproval, your mistrust and your hatred, you have done to me the worst thing that Hlutr can do to one another. You have bound my mind within the curtain of your song, and sealed me off from the communion of my peers.

I do not care. I do not live, brothers and sisters, for your attention or your approval. I live for my art, for the truth of the Universal Song. And no one can give form to that truth better than Hlut and Human, myself and Chiriga Ho.

It was summer here on Inse when I first met her. Our world is not small—Chiriga tells me it is even larger than Terra—but our sun is weak, and even summer is barely warm enough to melt the ice of tropical seas. No matter; here in the Valley of the Sun we are warm, for the inner heat of Inse's depths penetrates her crust and underground seas of steam give us life even in the dead of winter.

Still, without the Hlutr Inse could never support complex life. Volcanic gases trapped sunlight and made Inse warm enough for simple plant life to bring oxygen to the atmosphere. Hlutr spores arrived in time to control the unchecked growth of life that threatened Inse's future. My Elders and my ancestors inhibited the plants and encouraged animals to breed and fill Inse's dense atmosphere with their exhalations. Only constant attention by the Elders keeps the balance of plants and animals correct, and the temperature as high as possible.

It was a summer day, with the sun high in the sky painting frozen mountain peaks a deep red, and a flock of winged creatures resting in my tall branches. I was deep in the communion of the Inner Voice, singing with my brothers and sisters beyond the sky, reaching for the perfection of tone that captures the truth of the Universal Song—when a sudden ripple of discontent drew my attention back to the valley.

She was a very small girl; Chiriga has never grown to even half of what Humans consider full size, and in childhood she was diminutive indeed. Disturbed, she was running from the Human mining settlement, which lies about half a kilometer down the valley from the small woods in which I stand. Her distress filled the wood. At first I thought her merely another of the timberland beasts, and reached out with the Inner Voice to soothe her disquiet.

When I touched her mind, I knew at once that this was no beast. Many Human children were adept at the song of the Inner Voice; I had sung with not a few of them in my time. But here, here was an Inner Voice with a clarity and power that I had never before experienced in a Human. Here was a mind that could sing as well as a Hlut.

She was ten Terran years old: barely more than one of Inse's slow revolutions. There was no need to probe her muddled thoughts, for her tortured emotions told the full story of her pain. Scarcely two dozen children attended Inse's one school—and to a soul, they hated Chiriga. She was shorter, her deformed head and diminutive limbs were natural objects of ridicule . . . and her very sensitivity to the Inner Voice left her victim to the casual cruelty behind her playmates' taunts. Even then I knew that no Human child escapes the hostility of his fellows—but Chiriga's punishment was worst of all, for she felt it so much more keenly than the rest.

The images beating in Chiriga's mind told more than the scratches on her face and bits of ice frozen in her hair. Although she had fought, and screamed, and finally begged them to leave her alone, still the other children had their amusement. And feet-over-head, little Chiriga had tumbled down a hillside and into a shallow, half-frozen stream. Then—and her mind burned with shame and rage—they laughed at her, and left her miserable and alone.

Stirred by this distress too strong for her mind to bear, I sang to her in the Second Language and the Inner Voice. "Be calm, my Little One."

She stopped, wonderment blossoming on her face. And she looked directly at me, her intense dark eyes meeting my multicolored leaves. The waves of Inner Voice that she projected changed pitch; distress receded and was replaced by gentle annoyance and rising awe. Hands on hips, she said, "Trees don't talk."

"Hlutr are not trees," I sang. And now a tinge of my own wonderment answered hers . . . for she understood.

Little eyes wide, Chiriga Ho sat at my roots, and begged me to tell her more of the Hlutr.

Artist that I am, even I cannot sing but a fraction of Hlutr history in a lazy Inse afternoon—and long before the afternoon was past, Chiriga had to depart. But she was back again before nightfall, and stayed until she was yawning. By the time the sun settled below the horizon, Chiriga and I had entwined our songs—the first of many such links we would make—and she could be with me even though her body was half a kilometer away in her bed. Her loneliness was over, and she clung to our narrow thread of contact like a vine to its nourishing host.

Chiriga Ho had at last found a friend.

Summer became autumn, as Inse retreated from the sun and the silvery bridge of the Galaxy began to rise later and later in the night. My fellow Hlutr were busy with the slow change of season, directing the migrations of winged animals and the shedding of leaves.

And in that long autumn, I came to love Chiriga Ho.

I loved her most for her strength. All Inse saw the determination that she brought to her schoolwork, to her daily exercises, to every corner of her life—but none saw the hidden strength that *I* could see within her mind. This was the strength that moved reluctant limbs despite constant pain, the courage that faced each new day of derision and humiliation with calm determination and impossible hope.

We Hlutr are strong by nature; but ours is the strength of time, the eternal gentle pressure by which plants crack solid stone. Chiriga did not have the luxury of centuries; her might was an indomitable will. Nothing could stand in her way: not pain, nor distance, nor even the disapproval of her fellow Humans. Through that autumn I saw more of Chiriga's strength than she had ever shown any living entity. This little Human taught me things I had never suspected, things that the Hlutr had never told me; I could not but love her.

It was a lonely time for Chiriga and her folk. Less than twenty seventies of them remained; the rest had long since moved to more hospitable worlds. The first snows buried a domed garden, and before it was dug out a second storm struck. Even from half a kilometer, the sound of the dome's cracking disturbed the animals that huddled around and within my roots for warmth.

Nearly a third of Chiriga's people left after the dome broke. Chiriga sat with me in the night, and we watched a few ancient shuttle ships taking the Humans away from Inse.

"One day," she said, "all of us will go. One day you'll see the last Human leave Inse."

"I hope that will never happen, Little One."

Yet the winter wore on, the hardest and coldest winter in Human centuries. Thick Hlutr bark and Hlutr inner warmth protected me and my brethren even as ice coated us; our roots went deep into boiling underground lakes and brought heat to the surface. We did what we could to shelter the other little lives around us: grubs and worms and tiny creatures burrowed between my roots, and I allowed the boring insects to enter my very body. Winged beasts huddled where they could, in crooks and elbows that offered some small protection from the wind. Even the lesser trees pulled close, turning themselves to the Hlutr the way they turned to follow the sun.

Plants went dormant, larger animals hibernated where they could and died where they could not. But for Chiriga's folk, there was no help.

I did what I could, and all of us helped. Confined to their settlement, hungry and lonely, the Humans were ripe for despair. We Hlutr could give them neither food nor warmth nor freedom—but we *could* sing to them in the Inner Voice, and give them back their will to live.

Chiriga helped. With a music sythesizer she found in an abandoned storeroom and her clear, strong voice, she sang and danced for her people. She could hear the Hlutr song, and she conveyed the quintessence of its meaning to her folk. And for a time, the song seemed to help them.

It did not last.

It was a few hours before Inse's slow dawn. Our sister planet, a great gas giant which the Humans call Eaun, was settling peacefully toward the western horizon. All at once the preternatural stillness was interrupted by a sullen groan deep in the rocks of the valley. Far below, relentless movements of Inse's crust had formed the valley; now rocks slipped against one another as balanced tensions were released. Mountains and valley shook, trees cracked and tumbled . . . and then the land was quiet again. For a time.

Chiriga's people woke in panic, and were just calming themselves when a slight skittering sound began at the north end of the valley. It continued, growing louder, and by the time the Humans managed to stumble to their observation screens, the sound had become an echoing roar that completely filled the night.

Half the mountainside, it seemed, came tumbling down upon the Human settlement, as irresistible as the onslaught of a summer storm.

In the end only a few lives were lost. The damage to the settlement was much greater.

"The avalanche buried our last deep-mining installation," Chiriga told me. "Without that . . . we have nothing to trade." She pressed her forehead against my frozen bark. Our shrunken sun was still climbing from the horizon. "In eighty hours it'll be night—the Manager wants everyone gone by then. Borshall is sending a transport, and it's supposed to be here by noon."

"Where will you go?"

"Mother says we have family on New Sardinia. The Manager's going to give us our shares of the Inse Company in Borshallan sols, so we won't have money problems for a while."

"It will be lonely without you, Chiriga Ho."

"I'll miss you very much." She stood for a long moment, hugging as much of my trunk as her little arms could embrace, shivering all the time. Then she said, "I'll try to sing with you, even when I'm on New Sardinia."

I shot her an encouraging note in the Inner Voice, but I had no hope that a Human, even one as talented as Chiriga, could make herself heard across parsecs of empty space. Only the Hlutr could do that.

So it came that as night approached, I lifted all my

leaves to heaven and watched the last of the shuttles sail upward, carrying the last Human to live on Inse. I followed Chiriga's mental song as long as I could, while night fell and her ship moved outward from the sun—then there was a distortion of the song as the ship passed into the mysterious tachyon phase, and she was gone.

That very night, at the depth of Inse's coldest winter in centuries, the Ice Dancers came out to play.

We know little about them; they appear only when the cold is so severe that even Hlutr find it difficult to live, when carbon dioxide snow falls on mountain slopes and water is hard as rock. Then, while airborne bacteria retreat into spores and even the viruses are crystallized, when the Hlutr live slowly just to survive the night—then the Ice Dancers frolic, moving through the night in their slow saraband. Listening hard, one can almost catch a hint of their stately song, one is within reach of the meaning of their odd, brief lives . . . then morning comes, and they are gone like the snows that evaporate upon the hillside.

Let me tell you about loneliness, my brothers and sisters.

You do not feel it, you in forests of Hlutr, who busy yourselves with watching and directing the ecology of whole worlds. You who sing with the rest of us whenever you wish, you who taste the very presence of life surrounding you . . . How can you know what it is like to be an Artist, to stand solitary in a valley with only the distant sight of a few hillside Hlutr to keep you company? How can you know what it is like to lack the power to change life?

Since the long-lost days of Paka Tel, there have been Hlutr like me—and since those days, the rest of you have shunned us. Even in your pity and compassion you set us apart, so that we can never completely enter the society of Hlutr. You rely on us to keep the tales of Hlutr history, you expect us to sustain the eternal Hlutr symphony in the Inner Voice.

And the Inner Voice gives us an escape from our loneliness. Worlds away, there are other Hlutr Artists, others who live as we do and understand the peculiar polyphony that we bring to the Universal Song.

I never expected to hear from Chiriga after she left Inse. And indeed, it took her more than half a revolution: on a late-summer evening I had cast my mind into endless space and was singing with my fellows, when I heard the trace of a melody recognized. Weak, distant and unpracticed, it was Chiriga nevertheless.

"Little One," I sang in delight, reaching forth toward her with all my will.

"Artist!" Her delight warmed me more than the midday sun on my widespread leaves. "It's been six years. I . . . I thought I'd never sing with you again."

"I am glad to find you. How fare you? What has happened in your life?"

"I am on New Sardinia. I've been training at the Ramatiad Conservatory."

"You are singing for Humans? The way you did during the Winter here on Inse?"

I felt her passion . . . and her distress, that she could not fulfill it. "I'm trying. I . . . I know I can sing better. Somehow I just haven't been able to capture the feeling I had then. Maybe I'm too old."

"Nonsense, Little One. My song, too, has been diminished since you left. Let us join our Inner Voices once more, and give the Universe the sweetest melodies it has ever heard."

So we sang, brothers and sisters, sang to the glory of the Universal Song and to the joy of finding one another again. And no matter what you believe about Human ability with the Inner Voice, our song was the sweetest heard in ages. Hlutr Artists on twice-seventy worlds heard us, and stopped their own songs to listen.

Under my tutelage, Chiriga soon left her Human teachers behind. New Sardinia is the world of art, of color and music and the poetry of life. My Little One sang for the Humans, and the best of them could merely sit astonished to hear such beauty.

Human art, my Elders, was suffused with the same despair that had struck their economy, their science and their politics. Death, pain, disease and disaster were the themes of Human song, Human drama, Human literature.

Now Chiriga stood before these men and women, singing the essential Hlutr theme of joy, of coexistence, of the wonder of the Universal Song. And for a moment, the Humans believed; I felt the glimmer in their minds.

Is *this* why you stopped us? Because together, Chiriga and I were bringing life back to Mankind? Then I weep for you, for you are truly deaf to the Universal Song.

In her thirtieth year, Chiriga returned to Inse.

She came in her own starship, purchased with the profits from her recent tour of the Sardinian League. Some Human buildings were still standing, and she set her crew to work refurbishing them. Then, wrapped in her warmest clothes, she came alone to see me.

"You have grown, Little One." In truth, Chiriga was barely over a meter tall, and would never be taller; her head was too large and her limbs too narrow. She had always been aware of her deformities, and they rose again in her consciousness . . . but now her voice and music had transcended them and made her a star on seventies of Human worlds.

"Thank you. You're looking well too, Artist." She hugged my trunk, and as usual her arms did not go even a fraction of the distance around. "It's so good to see you again."

It is late afternoon, and all around me trees have begun to shed their leaves. "Why have you come back here, Chiriga? Winter is coming on, you know."

"I know. I came back because Inse is my home." She sighed. "I'm a great success. I've toured the Sardinian League and the Metrinal Union, my recordings are selling as far away as Geled and Kertora. I can afford to live anywhere I want to . . . and Inse is where I want to live."

"I welcome you. We can sing together, and the forests will echo our—"

"Damn it!" She pounded her fist against my bark. "Why did I have to be born Human?"

"Whatever do you mean, Little One?"

Her mind seethed with anger and frustration. "You taught me to sing with the Inner Voice. And now I've gone about as far as a Human can. But I've *heard* the Hlutr song, and I know that I'll never be able to match it."

"You can. *We* can. If you wish, Chiriga, I will teach you."

"The other Hlutr say that I'll never be able to sing in your style. I've talked to them on every world I've visited."

"Then they are wrong. And we will prove them wrong."

As soon as her house was rebuilt, Chiriga sent her crew away. Then, through the long cold winter, she learned to sing in the Hlutr style.

No, my brethren, it was not easy. Not easy for me, and worse for Chiriga. A sapling Hlut learns the Inner Voice just as he drinks water from the ground or nutrients from the air. Chiriga had to work, and work hard. Yet she was not afraid to struggle, and her very alienness gave her insights foreign to the Hlutr.

The Hlutr song is the song of Life—and Life is the music of the Universe. Together, Chiriga and I explored the dimensions of the Universal Song. Pressure waves which gather the stuff of old, dead suns to make new third-, fourth- and fifth-generation stars and planets that will someday be home to new forms of life. The ceaseless progression of seasons on a millions worlds. Rain, which brings microscopic bits of meteoric dust from throughout the Galaxy. The soft soughing of Hlutr deep in thought, a soundless sound that permeates space. The sweep of Hlutr history itself, from our almost-forgotten origins on Paka Tel through our colonization of the Galactic Halo, and on to the Great Schism, the days of grand Avethell when the two branches of Hlutr were briefly united, and the present happy days when we stand peacefully dreaming in the suns of the Scattered Worlds.

The song of Life is one of endless variety and overwhelming intricacy. Everything, lifeless or not, is a part of everything else. The bacteria who drift in clouds around us, drawn by our body warmth and the scent of food, are as important to the Universal Song as the Ancients of Nephestal in congress together in their forever-dreams, as important as the Eldest herself in the Secluded Realm. Only Hlutr can appreciate how Earth's flowers called dandelions led to Mankind's expansion into the Galaxy, how tiny legless worms brought about the fall of the vast

Dorascan Empire, how the slightest breeze on a long-ago
hilltop on legendary Maela Gres brought about the Seed
Vessels that brought life into the Scattered Worlds.

Even at the present moment all the thoughts and emotions of all the living creatures in the Galaxy come together in the Universal Song—a Song which changes every
mind it touches, slightly or greatly, for good or ill. *This* is
the Song of the Hlutr, and this is the Song I learned with
Chiriga.

By the time spring came to frigid Inse, the time of
learning was over. Chiriga summoned her crew and her
starship, and she left. But this time she took me with her.
She took me in spirit, for the Inner Voice link between us
was now so strong that kiloparsecs of distance were no
barrier. And she took me in substance: a green-growing
sprig of my own body in a dish of rich Inse soil. This small
bit of myself, barely more than an ordinary nonsapient
plant, went with Chiriga to keep her company and remind
her of her true home.

She sang and danced on five hundred worlds. And everywhere she sang the Song—sang to the past glories of
Terra's sons and daughters, sang to the future they could
have. From New Sardinia she moved westward, in the
direction of lost Terra. Her ship, armed with powerful
weapons and escorted by a convoy of military vessels,
passed into the wild, lawless region known as the Transgeled. On planet after planet, settlement after settlement,
Chiriga gave her concerts. Worlds that had never heard of
New Sardinia welcomed her; settlements on which Terra
was a forgotten legend listened to her songs of the past.
And wherever she passed, she touched a few minds.

The Hlutr know, as no other creature does, that great
events spring from small actions. Each of us, from the
smallest saplings to the continent-spanning Eldest, grows
from the tiniest seed. Our power, our privilege and our
curse is that we change the destinies of races by adjusting
the atoms and molecules of heredity. So Chiriga brought
about change: with every mind she touched and every soul
she inspired, the decline of Humanity slowed in almost

imperceptible degree. She sang, she danced, and then she moved on to the next world.

Human starships travel at many times the speed of light; but Human politics create barriers even more firm than lightspeed, and a tour of five hundred worlds took Chiriga nearly ten Human years—five Inse seasons. She reached as far as Geled, a direct successor of the legendary Terran Empire, before she turned back.

Chiriga came home in high summer. Her dwellings needed repair, and as soon as that task was complete she sent her starship away. It would return when she wished it. Hardly had the ship left Inse than Chiriga was at my trunk.

"Time has not aged you at all," I said, after I had bent my limbs to take a good look at her and breathe the fragrance of her presence.

"Thank you. I don't know if it's the music, or if I'm actually learning to live more slowly as you Hlutr do."

For a moment we stood next to one another, Human and Hlut together in the warm sun. I was aware of grubs beneath my roots, insects in my branches and Chiriga's quiet melancholy. I had felt this sadness growing during her trip, but her silent emotions told me that we would not sing of it until she returned to Inse.

"I'm rich, you know," she said. "In trade goods alone we brought back a million sols, not to mention fees for my performances and reproductions." She shrugged. "I'm investing it all in Borshall's research labs. We need to get science moving again."

"You are sad, Little One."

"My people are dying. Th-they're turning their backs on life."

"This happens to all organisms, Chiriga. Growth is followed by stagnation."

"And I'm not sure there's ever going to be another growth cycle." She ran her hand lightly down my trunk. "Artist . . . I feel the Hlutr working against me."

"Against you?"

She sighed. "No. Not that. They just . . . don't care. I

cast my song out into the night, and it is all but swallowed up in the silence of the Great Ones. Why?"

"The Hlutr . . . feel that your folk have passed their prime. They feel, as you fear, that this stagnation is the end."

"It *isn't!*"

"I know, Little One. But my brothers and sisters do not listen to me."

"We must make them listen. Together."

"Little One, you do not know what you ask."

"I can sing the Hlutr Song. I've spent the last ten years doing that."

"Yes. And you have done things no Human ever tried. Were it not for the others, your songs would already have turned the tide." I quiver gently even though the sun is warm. "But you have sung to Humans. To join the councils of the Hlutr, you would have to sing across the space of Human decades."

She nodded, and the courage that radiated from that frail body could have lit stars, so powerful it was. "I can do it. Rest breaks and sleep periods won't matter—they'll be just momentary interruptions to the Great Ones. Between us, I *know* we can convince them to stop ignoring Humanity. All we need is the slightest bit of their attention, the barest notes of their song."

I did not have the strength of Chiriga, for I could not deny her this dream. She would die at this task, I was sure—yet she would spend her life no other way. "Yes, Chiriga. Go home and gather your strength. Tomorrow we sing."

The next day, we began. It started easily enough; Chiriga sat at my roots with a flower in her lap and breathed slowly. The fragrance filled her consciousness and mine, and together we raised our Inner Voices in the song. One day a flower, the next a stone, then perhaps just the gentle rush of air. Of such things is the Hlutr song made.

We developed a singing pattern that matched our different perceptions of time. Chiriga came to me every morning through the long lazy summer, and until late afternoon we sang together. Then for the rest of the day Chiriga was free while I continued the main melody of the song, building on whatever elements we'd added that day. This chopping up into daily segments was not at all the way a Hlut would sing—but the steady, leisurely progression of theme was not at all a Human method. The method worked for us, and worked so well that when winter finally came Chiriga was able to stay indoors without missing her daily contributions.

Humans will not credit what I say, and Hlutr will not understand: Chiriga spent the next three Inse years, over a quarter of a Human century, at work on our song. She did not sing *every* day, for what creature besides a Hlut could have such devotion—but she sang every moment she could, and when she missed days for illness, exhaustion or her increasingly-rare Human concerts, I kept up the song in her own voice. Three Inse winters passed, three lovely Inse summers. And in that time, brothers and sisters, you started to listen to us.

At first your attention was furtive: the Artists and the younger Hlutr listened, then turned to their own work. Soon I noticed a few Elders hearing our melodies, then a few more . . . and soon some spoke in the councils of the Hlutr, saying that perhaps we should cherish Humanity more.

Voices came from Amny, from Credix, from Sebya and Taglierre, from the very heart of the Secluded Realm. Mankind has always had his friends among the Hlutr, and now they dared to speak, dared to echo our song.

My brothers and sisters of Inse, you are a cold lot, cold as the carbon dioxide snows and the rock-hard ice. You are not cruel, but your souls have been touched by a frigid wind that froze whatever compassion you were born with. When you could no longer ignore me, when you could no longer discredit me or ridicule me, when you could no longer avoid answering my arguments—then you imprisoned me.

Chiriga was offworld, teaching a promising class of youngsters on New Sardinia, when you struck. You had contemplated your action well, you knew exactly what to do: the invisible curtain you spun about me was of impeccable weave. And now, brethren of Inse, I can sing only to you.

I know why you have done this to me: because Chiriga and I dared to defy your notions of propriety. That we create art together, fusing Human and Hlutr songs, disturbs you. That we defy the will of the Hlutr by attempting to renew the flagging spirits of the Human race, is the ultimate crime for which you cannot forgive me.

Chiriga's mind is closed to me. The other Hlutr do not hear my Inner Voice. And although I sing alone in the gathering dusk of another Inse winter, still I sing . . . for I can do nothing else.

You tell me that Chiriga will never come back, that your curtain will keep Humans away from Inse forever. I do not believe you. And so I wait, singing, for the deliverance that will surely come my way.

And yet . . . if Chiriga never arrives . . . I do not know what I will do then.

The Hlutr curtain is not an impenetrable barrier. It is only a device of persuasion, and a sufficiently strong mind can pass through it. This winter, I find out how strong Chiriga Ho's mind is. For the sound of her Inner Voice is carried on the wind, and even you, my brothers and sisters, cannot deny the strength of that song.

"Elders, hear me." Thus in Hlutr language Chiriga demands the attention of the Elders. Her Inner Voice is perfectly modulated, her emotions firmly under control. "I ask that this curtain be lifted."

Only now, brethren, must you confront Chiriga. Now you have no other choice, for suddenly the attention of all the Hlutr is upon you.

"By what right," asks one of you, "is a Human admitted to the council of the Hlutr?"

"Any Hlut can sing in council when he demonstrates mastery of the Inner Voice. Elders, the fact that you hear me gives me the right."

Through the softening curtain, undercurrents of the song reach me. *Travesty*, say some. *Admit her*, say others. Most wait, listening.

Chiriga continues, taking as granted her right to sing.

"The Artist of Inse is my friend and partner. Your curtain prevents me from singing with him. I challenge your wisdom."

From far away, the quiet Voice of an Elder sings, "Challenge offered. Brethren of Inse, defend your curtain."

"The Artist disrupts the consensus of Hlutr. It is the will of the song that Mankind shall be allowed to perish quietly and happily. The Artist demands that we reverse our consensus. Against the will of the Hlutr, he has taught the Inner Voice to this Human, has taken her far above her station."

Chiriga's ship has landed on the frozen ruins of the Human settlement. In a bulky thermal suit, she stumbles out onto the surface. "Let him speak for himself." I hear Chiriga's plea, but still she cannot hear me. Still my song is bound about me by my brothers and sisters.

"Child, the Artist has spoken in his own behalf." The Elder sounds almost compassionate. "Now it is your turn. He must have taught you so that you could plead for your own folk—now we will entertain your music."

No, this is not how I meant it to happen. Chiriga and I should be singing together. Instead, she is alone while Hlutr from all over the Scattered Worlds turn their attention upon her. Seventy times seventy thousand and more, they listen. What will the Human say?

She sings clearly. "You ignore us, and in doing so, you curtain us as surely as you have curtained my Artist. You say that we are a dying race—yet how can we fully live, when the Hlutr have cut us off from the world of nature?"

They do not understand, Chiriga. Sing it in terms that they can comprehend.

"I have learned the Hlutr song . . . and now I know that each living creature in the Scattered Worlds has a voice in that song. Aware or not, each sings. Yet with the Hlutr turning away from us, Humans cannot feel that song and cannot be fully a part of the Scattered Worlds."

There is a pause, then one of Inse raises his Voice. "Your people turned away from the Universal Song long before we closed our minds to them. The Hlutr will never

abandon any race that truly desires to hear the eternal
melody of life."

"Then do not turn away from us."

"Prove that you are worthy."

The wind whistles through my frozen branches, then
the night is silent. Pale Eaun, our sister world, shines
alone in a star-spattered sky, and carbon dioxide sleet falls
from the air. Go inside, Chiriga. This is no place for one of
your folk.

"Here is my proof," Chiriga says. She raises arms and
voice, and the music she sings is a strange, Human music—
yet a familiar one. It is a ghost of the music that the
Traveller heard from his Human friends, it recalls fragments of Alex Saburo's song of determination against the
Death. And it is wholly new, it is something that only
Chiriga Ho could sing.

It is a song of Inse.

Around me, on hillside and mountaintop, on valley floor
and even the frigid concrete and metal of the tumbled
Human settlement, the Ice Dancers blossom.

We Hlutr—even my brothers and sisters who doubt
Chiriga's ability—stand in amazement. For the Ice Dancers, whose mysterious dance carries a meaning always
hidden from us . . . the Ice Dancers are singing in response to Chiriga's melody.

They are wise and beautiful, these poor creatures who
live their whole lives in a stately ballet that lasts only until
dawn. In the heat of morning they will dissolve, their
molecules will sublime back into the air, perhaps to re-
form into their descendants on some distant wintry night.
They create an entire culture between midnight and sunrise, then pass on what they can in the echo of their song
and the inborn movements of their dance.

As we watch and listen, the Ice Dancers grow and
change. Children at first, they realize their doom and give
in to regret; then with an upward movement of the dance
they deny the triumph of time, and cast their voices out
into infinity. By the time Eaun touches the western horizon, these Ice Dancers have discovered other worlds,
have conversed with beings like themselves on a million

planets, have plumbed the mysteries of time and space that they will never visit.

Chiriga shivers, yet she keeps up her music . . . the music that enables us all to understand the Ice Dance. And now it is near dawn, the valley is heating and the Ice Dancers begin their futile retreat up the slopes. It is too late, for warm air currents bring death from Inse's dayside; yet still they struggle.

Their song is one of indomitable will. Stronger than Hlutr Elders, they face the extinction of their people with a courage and strength that I am sure we could never match. The structure of the Universe itself conspires against them, and still they fight to live.

In the last seconds, the peaks are alight with deadly sunshine and only a few Ice Dancers survive in still-frigid eddies. Only now do they give over to despair, and their cry is for succor in the face of an awful destiny. Tomorrow night the story will be played out again, and the night after, as it has been played every cold winter since Inse cooled; each generation starts where its predecessors started, and each ends the same way—with the inevitable genocide of sunrise.

Could Hlutr weep, we would cry for this catastrophe, for the loss of this race that could teach us so much.

"No."

The last Ice Dancers regard Chiriga, who bows her head. "I will remember your melody. I will sing it to those who come tomorrow night. They will start knowing what you know now." All curtains are down now, and I can feel the cold tracks of frozen tears on her face. "This tragedy will end. I promise you."

Sun creeps above the horizon, and the last Ice Dancers swirl away into nothingness. And the emotions they project are gratitude, hope and . . . at long last . . . peace.

Chiriga sighs, and all the Hlutr are still. Finally, one of the Elders says gently, "Hlutr of Inse, have you any statement to make?"

Waves of shame fill the atmosphere; the planet will smell of it for years. "Nothing, Elders."

The answer is quick and decisive as it must be. "Chiriga

Ho, you are the first Human ever to gain the right to sing with the Hlutr. This right is yours by your nature and your ability, and none may take it from you."

"And my people?"

The consensus of the Hlutr is a slippery thing, but for now it is clear enough for even Chiriga to read: any race that can produce a singer like her is deserving of Hlutr friendship.

The sun is higher in the sky, and Chiriga is beside me in her thermal suit. I have much work to do, repairing the damage that the cold night has wrought, but I will always have time for her. "Our work is not over, Little One. The Hlutr will hear your people and will support them, but Humans must want to live and grow. Times are still dark for your folk."

"No, Artist. Like the Ice Dancers, we have hope now." She bares her hand to the frigid air, lays it on my ice-coated trunk. "Like them, we have friends."

"Some of us, Little One, never left you."

She smiles, and her happiness is a gift. "Let's sing together."

And we do.

INTERLUDE 4

Kev was so excited that he couldn't sleep.

Tomorrow he was going to Credix. Not for vacation, not for a joyride: this time he was going permanently, or at least for the next few years.

All six families in the valley—nearly half the Human population of Amny—had come to his going-away party. It was the biggest bash since Dar left four years ago. Kev saw cousins, nieces and nephews whom he hadn't seen since he was little. For the first time, he joined the younger men in one of their drinking contests . . . until Mama Tiponya caught him at it.

"I don't care if you *are* going off to University; as long as you're under this roof you're my little boy and I don't want to see you getting drunk with the rest of those bums."

"Mama, I didn't mean to—"

"I know you're happy, Kev, and gods know there'll be enough drinking and carousing when you're on Credix. It's just . . . you make a woman feel old. Don't be in too much of a hurry to grow up."

"Besides," Father Alekos interjected with a wink, "you don't want to be too hung-over tomorrow."

Mama Tiponya hugged him. "I know I'm being silly. Just humor me, just tonight? I hate seeing my baby grow up."

"Aww, it's not like I'm going to the ends of the Galaxy.

I'll only be an hour away." Even as he said it, Kev knew that he spoke only part of the truth. University would change him, and inevitibly on his next visit to Amny he would find his home far different from his memories.

Then a cousin called to him and he raced off, hardly noticing the trace of hastily-concealed tears in Mama Tiponya's eyes.

The evening passed too quickly; by twenty-eight o'clock everyone had left and Kev's mothers and fathers went to sleep. But Kev couldn't sleep, and he stayed up in his room, looking at the stars and dreaming.

Perhaps it was the wine, perhaps he was more sensitive because he was leaving Amny tomorrow, perhaps it was simply a clear, calm night. In any case, he heard the old music calling, and saw the great tree silhouetted against the rising larger moon.

Music called, and Kev had no choice but to listen. He sat in his open window, head propped against a pillow, and closed his eyes.

"Tell me a story," he whispered.

PART FIVE:

Cadet

I am not old; I broke soil scarcely a few seventies of seasons before the Humans came here to Escen.

For all that I am young, I have been busy during my life, and I have lived far faster than Hlutr ordinarily do.

The other Hlutr call me Cadet, for I am one of a new breed decreed by the Elders: it is my duty and my pleasure to watch the Humans, to learn their ways. So well have I done my job that just a few seasons ago I was granted the rank of Elder myself. I am still surprised . . . and pleased . . . to have been selected for this great honor, and it is with trepidation still that I enter the councils of the Elders as they sing across space on the waves of the Inner Voice.

My major work is with the Human children, who are the future of the race. I began singing with these littlest of Little Ones even before their parents suspected that we Hlutr were sapient, more than five and a half of their millennia ago. I did not abandon them, as so many of my brothers and sisters did, during the deep winter of the Human Race; now that the fortunes of Mankind are again on the rise, I still pleasure in their company. Oh, I have my duties—it is not easy to co-ordinate Hlutr relations with Humans, throughout the fifty-world Escen Hegemony. However, I never allow those duties to prevent me from spending time with the Human children.

I love them all: the cheerful ones and the sad ones, the fussbudgets and the gigglers, the brain-damaged ones who only stare at the patterns of light in my trunk and leaves, and the bright ones who sing with me in the soundless melodies of the Inner Voice.

Something happens to Humans as they grow older, something that I do not completely understand. It is a look in their eyes, and it is a coldness in their hearts; and when it comes upon them, they lose the essence of their childhood.

For some this thing comes soon, in the winter of their tenth year when they first discover betrayal or the death of friendship. For some it comes slowly, over many seasons, and it is mainly concerned with the telling of time, and the ticking of clocks, and the meeting of deadlines. For many, the change is a deepening frost that comes when they begin to bury their own feelings under the cloak of their neighbors' opinions.

For some lucky ones the change never comes. Or it comes but does not take hold completely, so that later their hearts will thaw and they will regain what they were in childhood. These few are the most fortunate of Humans, and they are the ones I love nearly as much as I love the children.

Such a one is Sten Koleno, who serves now in the exalted post of Foreign Secretary for the Escen Hegemony. Those are strange words, Human words of diplomacy and government, and Sten Koleno sometimes laughs with me at the odd sound of them. We Hlutr have a simpler term for Sten's work of maintaining tranquility between the various Human and Nonhuman societies that surround Escen: we would call him Harmonizer, for he keeps his small part of the Universal Song free of discord.

Because part of my job is similar—I try to maintain harmony with the Humans, while doing what little I can to encourage them on the path to true maturity—I often have occasion to talk with Sten Koleno. Whenever he can escape from the Palace and his official duties, he comes to my grove with a bottle of wine and his guitar, and we sing. Always it is pleasure, to talk with him.

And because I love the children of Mankind, I often have occasion to sing with Sten's little daughter, Fenelia.

Fenelia Koleno was seven Terran years old this summer. This is a perfect age for Human children; they are on the verge of the great freedoms that will come with adulthood, yet most of them are still allowed to act immature when they must. I do not understand many of the things Fenelia tells me—the day-to-day events of study, games, holovideos and playmates are foreign to the Hlutr mind. However, I rejoice in Fenelia's energy, in her wonderment as she learns more of the marvelous world around her. Of all the Human children I have tended these many centuries, she is my favorite. In her, I see the direction that I would like all my Little Ones to follow.

Perhaps it is waiting for Fenelia, that nameless something that destroys Human innocence and brings an end to childhood. If so, I shall sing a mournful tune to the stars in the Inner Voice, for the loss of such great promise.

Today we play a game that we have played before: I visualize an object in the woods, and Fenelia finds it for me. It may be a rock, or a leaf, or even a small lizard or some manner of bug. This is a teaching game that we Hlutr play with the young of a billion different species, always with much success. For while they are distracted by the search, and their minds open to our mental pictures, we set the seeds that may grow into full-scale melodies in the Inner Voice.

This day, however, Fenelia's concentration is not on the game. When she brings a wiggling, furred insect instead of the rock I asked for, I turn my attention more carefully toward the tenor of her thoughts.

"What troubles you, Little One?" I ask in silent song. I know that Fenelia hears my meaning as a gentle voice in the breeze.

"Daddy doesn't love me," she says, putting the caterpillar on my trunk and turning away.

"Nonsense." I know this is not true: Sten and his mate cherish Fenelia deeply. "What makes you say that?"

"He and Mommy were mad at me yesterday. And this

morning he didn't say hello, and when I tried to kiss him h-he got up and left."

The pictures in her mind were distorted by anger and fear; I know that Sten Koleno would never run from his daughter the way Fenelia remembered. Human children often do not see things the way they actually occur. Many times they are swayed by their feelings, and some times they see a truth that is hidden from even the Inner Voice.

But not today.

"Where is your Daddy now?"

"Somewhere else. He went to the spaceport."

I am tall enough to see the spaceport from my woods behind the Palace, my senses acute enough to detect Sten Koleno's mind anywhere in the Capital. He is not here . . . probably not even on Escen. His job often takes him travelling.

Since I have the status of ambassador, the Humans have given me a few amenities not often granted to plants. A clever little Human computer system reads the changing colors of trunk and leaves that we Hlutr call the First Language, and replies to me in a pidgin form of the Second Language. Now I tell it to find Fenelia's mother and ask her to talk to me.

Sten's mate, Emele, is in the Palace; she answers quickly and now that I know where to look I can see her through the broad windows of Sten's office. "Koleno here."

I tell her that Fenelia is with me, and that the girl is feeling neglected and needs her mother. Before I am half done, however, Emele interrupts.

"It's wonderful that you're taking care of her, it helps Sten and me so much to know that Fenelia's in good . . . er . . . hands. If she's bothering you, I'll send a robot out to bring her back."

"No. It is my honor and my pleasure to care for Fenelia. But the child is distressed and needs one of her parents."

"But she loves being with you so much—it's all she talks about at dinner—and honestly, I can't take the time right now. It's this Fekrein thing, their economic minister is threatening embargo, and if that happens it could be war with Geled."

I consider the matter. Sten and Emele's work is vital—I who have seen Human wars appreciate fully the importance of preventing them. And Fenelia's distress, while real, is transitory. By tomorrow she will have forgotten it. "Continue with your work, Madame Koleno. I will send Fenelia home at dusk."

"Thank you."

I turn back to Fenelia. "Your Daddy is on another planet and your Mommy is very busy. I am lonely, Little One; would you stay to play with me?"

"Of course, silly," she answers. But her thoughts are elsewhere.

When the sun sets, I send Fenelia back to the Palace. I welcome the quiet of the night, the time of contemplation that comes when the creatures of the wood are asleep and Human minds become more tranquil.

With brilliant stars mounting the midsummer sky, I sing with my brothers and sisters scattered around Escen. We are not many on this globe, fewer than seventy seventies of us in all the forests of Escen. Before the Humans came this was a happy, quiet world without many large animals; a world that had known life for years numbering seventy-times-itself-five-times. Since Mankind arrived, our Elders have striven to maintain all that is best about our world: few though we are, we have kept Escen intact and kept her children happy and in balance.

There are always many decisions to be made and many things to discuss—and the presence of a spacefaring race like our dear friends the Humans only complicates matters. They have recently introduced a new strain of rice from Thunda Pol, a strain that disrupts the biochemistry of fen and paddy; we must decide how best to encourage slow change in the ecology of the northern plains. Our world continues its millennial slide into a cooler climate, and we discuss whether to ask the Humans to take control, or to allow another ice age to begin.

Deep in this conversation, the Human computer calls for my attention. "Emele Koleno here. Is Fenelia with you?"

"I sent her home at dusk."

"She's not here. I thought maybe you . . ." Emele stops, takes a breath. "I'll alert the Secret Service to look for her."

I broaden my senses, drinking in the quiet of the night and listening with the Inner Voice. The night is alive with dreams: the peaceful red dreams of plants, the more violent warm dreams that beat in the minds of the animals, the confusing visions that come from Humans. I know them all, I have heard their music before. Now I listen to them more closely.

This landscape of dreams is not something that we Hlutr explore often. I am searching for a gentle, pure song that I know well—Fenelia's simple mind. If she were in the wood or within the Capital, I would be able to tell.

She is not.

Now my brothers and sisters aid me, few though we are. Together we hear the fall of every twig and sparrow on Escen, the breath of every Human and the subtle growth of every plant. And nowhere, nowhere do we hear Fenelia Koleno.

Long before the morning comes, I know the truth that I will not say to her mother, the awful fact that Sten will discover when he returns at midafternoon: Fenelia is gone.

But where?

We Hlutr of Escen are rather insular; on our happy planet we do not have much need to commune with our brothers and sisters beyond the stars. Yes, we sing in the great Hlutr-song that fills space, and our Elders add what little they can to the councils of the Hlutr race. By and large, though, we keep to ourselves and our world.

Not so now. In my anxiety about Fenelia, I appeal to those Hlutr of other planets; I send my song forth to echo between the stars. And I listen, listen for any mention of a lost Human girl-child.

This is slow work, this blending with the Hlutr song. The Galaxy is a wide and varied place, an eternal forest filled with creatures of every description, and I am stunned at the mere glimpse of this complexity. I know that Sten Koleno has returned to Escen, that Secret Service agents are combing the planet and all its computers. To this work I pay little attention, and days slide past while I am lost in the grand song.

Stars above, what a delight the universe is! The Hlutr Song is a melody of millions of voices, each it seems singing in response to some other, each carrying meaning and information about their worlds. How, how can the Elders stand it?

Slowly I become accustomed to the Song. Slowly I learn from it, and the things the other Hlutr tell me make me afraid.

On Escen we have seen our share of wars, political coups, religious intolerance and even mass murders; but by and large, our Human friends have been well behaved throughout their history. We have cherished them the way we cherish the great forests and the sea-creatures, the way we cherished the magnificent colonies of one-celled beasts in times past. And our Humans have rewarded us with friendship and—most of the time—with peace.

Now I hear from the Hlutr of other worlds of the things that other Humans have done to their children. Beatings, assaults on privacy, destruction of dignity, even horrible and painful deaths: the abuses are beyond cataloging, almost beyond belief. How could any sapient race behave thus toward its own children?

Yet, the Elders beyond the stars tell me, there are those among every race—even the Hlutr—who will grow in the direction of evil. Humans are not unique; rather it is *Escen*, and other happy planets like it, which are the exception in this huge Galaxy.

Knowing now terrors that I had never conceived of before, I am even more frightened for Fenelia. The Escen Secret Service is hard at work tracking her, yet I know they will not find her. I listen with the senses of the Inner Voice, and what I hear is a soundless echo of a terrible distress. I ask the Human computer, and it searches its memory, then answers. It tells me of seventies-upon-seventies of cases like Fenelia, on seventies of worlds and settlements: children who have vanished from their families, never to reappear.

Those children are somewhere. Listen with the Inner Voice and you will hear it, that wail which darkens the pure light of the stars and spoils the freshness of the clean wind. Listen, and you will hear the sighs of loneliness, the tears of pain, the strangled moans of fear. They are out there, and they are making this fearful noise.

It is the sound of the Little Ones.

Crying.

I call upon the Human computer again. "I would speak with Sten Koleno."

"Koleno here."

"Sten, I must see you."

"Things are busy here, and—"

"It concerns Fenelia. She may have been taken deliberately."

There is an unaccountable flash of hope from the morass of despair that fills Sten's mind. "Don't say anything more. Not over an unsecured data line. I'll be right there."

He is breathless when he arrives; he sits at my roots and rests his head against my trunk. "Tell me."

I sing to him of what I have discovered, of the insanity of Human evil, of the mistreatment of children, of the sharp silent cry of the Human Little Ones far off in space.

"And wherever they are, my daughter is there too?"

"I do not know, Sten. I cannot pick Fenelia's song from the mixed cries of others." The pungent tang of disappointment sweeps through his mind. "Children have been disappearing; should we not seek Fenelia with the other Little Ones?"

He sighs, and I feel him struggling to consider despite the turmoil of his thoughts and feelings. "A little girl who might have been Fenelia was seen at the spaceport at about the same time a ship left for the Calmathis VI settlement. Secret Service agents are on their way."

I think of what I know of the Human settlements. Calmathis VI is on the edge of the wild area called Transgeled, far outside the border of the Escen Hegemony. I listen, and I sing questions to my brothers and sisters beyond the sky. It is difficult to make them think in Human terms of distance and borders and direction. "No.

The Little Ones are not at Calmathis. Farther. Deeper into the Transgeled, I think."

"Calmathis is our only clue. The agents may be able to find where she went."

I sing to my Elders, asking their advice on a thing that Hlutr seldom do. They are silent; the choice is mine. "Sten, I wish to accompany your agent and search for Fenelia."

"How can you do that?"

"Through the Inner Voice, a Hlutr mind can take root in the brain of an animal operative. It is not a process that we enjoy—but gladly will I do this thing, to help find Fenelia."

"Why? What's so important about my daughter, that you're willing to go to such lengths for her? I'm grateful, but . . . you've stood here the whole time my people have been on Escen, through wars and quakes and epidemics. And you've never involved yourself in our affairs. Why now, for one Human child?"

How can I explain to Sten? I broaden my Inner Voice, allowing him to hear the merest echo of the Hlutr Song. "Yours are a strange folk, Sten Koleno. For nearly six millennia we have been watching you, and the councils of the Hlutr have burned with the question of what to do with you. You have much to offer the Universal Song, but even the best of you are wild and uncivilized. The cause of this you carry in your genes and in your social heritage, and only the patience of seventies of generations will cure you." He struggles to understand; and he is one of few Humans I have known who *can* understand. "You and your daughter, and your children to be, are a major step along the way to Human maturity. We cherish you . . . and it would be a sad thing indeed for Fenelia to be lost."

"I . . . think I see what you're saying."

I peek at his emotions, and along with wonder there is a certain resentment. "No, Sten. You are *not* simply a piece in some great Hlutr game. Other races play that way—we cannot. You are truly my friend, Fenelia is my friend. The ways of the Hlutr are not the ways of your folk; through wars and plagues and disasters I have grieved that the ways of the Hlutr would not allow me to give aid. I rejoice that now I can allow myself to become involved."

He shakes his head. "It's beyond me. I hear what you're saying, but I can't comprehend it." He shivers. "Nonetheless, I thank you. Please find her."

I have been with the Humans too long, and have taken on too many of their ways. For now, I wish I could shed tears as they do.

My tears, as the notes of my song, leap forth for the stars.

I summon a host from among the tranquil, cultured folk of the planet Narbidra, which lies very near the Human settlements of Calmathis. The folk of Narbidra are small, furred creatures who live in the forests of their beautiful planet; long have we Hlutr had an affinity for their gentle ways and their sensitivity for the Inner Voice, and long have they served us as hosts and operatives.

My host's name is Shalit Kravito Ni, a young member of the same Kravito tribe that led the Narbidrans to enlightenment and maturity twice seventy million years ago. Shalit stands nearly as tall as a Human child, and to the sons and daughters of Terra who cannot hear the inner song of her mind, she resembles a rather shaggy pony with double-jointed limbs. This is her first trip into space, although she has hosted for Hlutr before at conferences on Narbidra. She comes to Calmathis VI on a ship of the Galactic Riders, and while the ship lays in port she opens her thoughts and her body to my Inner Voice.

"I thank you for this favor, Shalit Kravito Ni," I sing.

"I am honored, Elder. The Hlutr of Narbidra explained your mission to me: I am grateful for this chance to save the Little Ones of Mankind."

"I have not taken a host since my sapling days. You are most kind to accept me, and I hope the experience will be a rewarding one for you."

"Thank you, Elder." Now Shalit's mind closes in upon itself like a flower curling up for the night, and I take control of her strange yet graceful animal body.

I enter Calmathis VI.

I know that Humans have constructed small artificial worlds in space, and even that a few Hlutr volunteers live in some of these strange habitats. Yet I am not prepared for the reality of Calmathis that meets my borrowed senses when I step through the airlock.

Shalit's people have a very acute sense of smell, so it is the odors and fragrances that come to me first, in a vast cacophony of seventies upon seventies of different scents. Then I stop, amazed, as Shalit's eyes focus on the odd place I have entered.

A world rises around me, a world of forests and cities, of lakes and beaches, a world with all the smells and sounds of a real planet. At once I pick up the song of this world, its music composed and performed by trillions of creatures: tiny viruses, insects, Humans, trees, schools of fish and countless other living things. Calmathis is no sterile construct of metal and plastic; Calmathis is a *world*.

I stand, four feet firmly planted on the ground, and stare at the unimaginable beauty of Calmathis spinning its lonely way through the Galaxy. Then, too soon, my reverie is shattered by the voice of a robot: "Are you Shalit Kravito Ni?" The fluid Narbidran vowels sound flat in its toneless speech.

Shalit's mouth parts are extremely flexible and can easily handle the sounds of Human speech. "I am."

"Come this way, please." The robot leads me to a large building of glass and plastic; soon I am ushered into a small conference room where several Humans stand. All but one of them wear the uniform of the Escen Hegemony. My senses are drawn to the other.

Her body is small and her dark hair short; at first glance I would think her a child. Yet I am sensitive to the disciplined music of her mind, and I know that this is no Human sapling—she is an adult, and one who, like Sten Koleno, has not lost the essential innocence of childhood.

The others defer to her; I see in their eyes and in their minds that she is the leader. Showing no discomfort at talking to an alien being, she says, "I am Doku Tomich of Marcreni. I am a special agent in the Escen Secret Service. I bid you welcome."

"May your days be full and your future bright." It is a proverb of Shalit's folk, which springs unbidden to my lips. "Although my form is that of Shalit Kravito Ni, in essence I am the Hlut Elder who stands in the wood behind the Palace on Escen."

She smiles, yet her eyes are sad. "I remember you, Elder. I played in your woods as a child nearly thirty years ago. You taught me the music of the trees." She lowers her eyes. "I'm afraid that time hasn't given me much opportunity since to listen to that music. But occasionally I imagine that I can still hear it."

"It is there when you need it, Doku Tomich." I dimly remember her now, a younger playmate of Sten's who visited often when she was very young. "You departed Escen then, did you not?"

"My mother was ambassador from Marcreni. She returned home in my fifth year. I was at school when she died on a diplomatic mission to Fekrein."

Another Human interrupts her. "Madame, time is short."

She turns abruptly. "Quiet. Among civilized folk, it is the custom to exchange greetings." She looks back at me. "Excuse me, these louts know nothing of the customs of the Scattered Worlds."

"You were trained by the Galactic Riders," I guess.

"In part," she says with a sigh. "When I graduated, a Human Galactic Rider arranged for me to study with the Ancients in their academy on Ny. Once I even visited Nephestal itself." For just a moment, her thoughts sing with the eternal melody of life; then she quivers and the music is but a memory. "Those were happy times. But I decided I should serve my own folk, so I returned to the Hegemony."

"You have the form of a Human child, yet you are adult."

"Through reconstructive surgery and hormone treatments, I keep the appearance of a ten-year-old. I specialize in crimes against juveniles, so this disguise is very useful in my work." A fiery intensity underlies her words.

"Is there much . . . crime against juveniles?"

"*Too* much." Doku spreads her arms. "Drugs, kidnapping, abuse—and lately, worse each year." In her mind there is a flash of memory, quickly buried: a man who called himself her father, yet hurt her unceasingly until she was old enough to leave home. "And then there are the disappearances: over five hundred in the Hegemony alone just this year—and another six or eight hundred that we know of from nearby worlds."

"Where are the children going?"

"I wish I knew. We've been trying to find out. Three dozen were tracked here to Calmathis, but the trail ends. My people have taken this settlement apart, and the missing kids aren't here." She sighs. "That's why this case is so vital. Fenelia Koleno's father is important; we have full co-operation from the Hegemony government. Plus your aid. If you can help us find Fenelia, then I hope we'll locate the other children too."

"How can a thousand children be missing without the Humans finding them? Why do Humans permit this?"

"The Galaxy is huge, and even a thousand pairs of parents aren't much against that immensity. We need the resources of governments: authority to do computer searches, diplomatic immunity, military backup if we should need it. And we need the help of the Hlutr."

"You have it, Doku Tomich. What is our next step?"

She glances at a computer terminal. "We have one slender lead—one suspect: Nen Basilus. He's a solitary freighter pilot who makes an irregular run deep into the Transgeled. He's been very friendly with the children who hang around the port. He just might be our next link."

"What do you plan?"

"Now that you're here, we can get started." There is quiet determination in her mind . . . and just a trace of fear. "You see, I thought I could pretend to be a runaway child, and you my pet. Then we'll see if Nen Basilus will take us to wherever the other children have gone."

"And what then?"

"I wish I knew."

The spaceport smells of steel, old oil and electricity. It is an odd place, a domain of automata and machinery more than of living creatures. Yet there is a bizarre feeling in the air—almost as if the ships, the robots who tend them and the port equipment surrounding them, are struggling to be alive, yet forever doomed to remain inanimate.

Doku skips, and I follow at her heels. The machines sense her, and they move out of her path . . . in their own way, they are almost compassionately protective of their masters' children. Humans stand about the port, conversing or directing the machines; few of them take notice of Doku and me. We come to a corner, turn it—and a young Human man is before us, lounging next to the cargo dock that opens into the hold of his ship.

He is dark as Elders' sienna bark, dark as the good soil of Escen forests, dark from feet to head and clothed in fabric blacker still. His scent is heady, pleasant and rich; and his eyes are like bright twin stars in winter skies.

Doku nods to me. This is Nen Basilus. This is the man, perhaps, who took Fenelia away. The man, perhaps, who took all the rest of the Little Ones.

Where?

Nen Basilus smiles. "Hi."

Doku stops her skipping and grins back at him. "Hello. I'm Doku; who are you?"

"My name's Nen. Where are you off to in such a hurry?"

"No place special."

"Say, that's a swell pet you have there. What is it?"

Doku drops to her knees and puts her arms around me. "This is my Narbid. I'll bet you've never seen one of these before."

"You're right about that. Where'd you get her?"

"It's a *him*."

"Oh. Sorry. Where'd you get *him*?"

"I don't know. Daddy brought him home once." She peers around Nen at his ship. "Daddy brings home all kinds of animals."

"Where's your Daddy now?"

"I'm going to see him. He's . . ." she frowns. "Someplace far away. I forget the name." She waves in the direction of the settlement. "He sent a robot to take me there, but I got away from it."

Doku's performance is amazing. Even in the Inner Voice of her mind she has become a child; the sophisticated adult I spoke with is completely buried now under her childish persona, just as Shalit Kravito Ni's personality is submerged under mine.

Nen stretches, then crouches next to Doku and I. He runs his hand over my head, and I force myself not to start. "He's very pretty." He smiles. "Why did you run away from the robot?"

"I hate it. It won't let me see *anything*. And it won't let me reprogram it." Again she cranes her neck, looking into Nen's ship.

"Would you like to come inside for a little while?" he asks. "Just to look around?"

"Sure."

"Then come on." Nen stands and moves toward his ship; Doku slips one of her hands into his, and gestures at me with the other. "Come, Shalit."

I follow.

Inside the ship, I am lost. This is a place of plastic, metal and winking lights, a place of computers and viewscreens that project an unreal image of the stars. No Hlut can ever feel at home where there is no soil to anchor roots, no wind to carry the smells and sounds of the world. The stardrive field, even at minimum power, distorts the song of the Inner Voice that springs from my brothers and sisters beyond the stars. And Nen, who smiles so sweetly and smells so nice, is suddenly very menacing.

Doku is not afraid—or if she is, she hides her fear well. "This is a great ship!"

"You know . . . I could take you to see your daddy." Nen's offer, so like the courtesy of a Galactic Rider or the gentility of one plant to another in a large garden, is something altogether more sinister. Human society has its rules, and what Nen says is a transgression.

Doku pretends not to notice, and instead says, "My daddy doesn't want me there anyway."

"What makes you think that?"

"He said so to Mommy, on the ultrawave. They thought I couldn't hear. But she said she was sending me no matter what he wanted." She lowered her voice. "Mommy doesn't want me either. I get in her way too much."

"That's ridiculous. If I had a little girl like you, I wouldn't send her away." Nen glances at a display screen. "It's almost time for me to shove off. I guess I'll have to send you back to your robot."

Doku frowns. "I don't want to go. Take me with you."

This is the crucial moment. If Nen Basilus is not the man we are looking for, then he will put Doku off his ship. If he *is* . . .

Tension is thick in the enclosed air of the ship, and I almost choke on it. Then, slowly, Nen Basilus gives a small smile.

"If you want, Doku . . . if you *really* want . . . I can take you to a place where you'll be wanted. It's a secret place, and only kids can go there. Is that what you want?"

"That's what I want."

"All right." He takes her hand and leads her toward a closed door. "I'm going to have to put you to sleep, Doku. In hibernation."

"Like the old astronauts in the stories?"

"Exactly like that. And when you wake up, we'll be in that place I told you about."

She turns her head in my direction. "What about Shalit?"

For an instant Nen's mind projects turmoil; but he is trapped, just as Doku planned. "I'll put Shalit in hibernation with you. Is that okay?"

She turns wide eyes upon him. "Okay."

Soon, we sleep.

In hibernation, Shalit's metabolism is seventy times slower than its waking rate. Animal consciousness cannot function so slowly, so Shalit sleeps. We Hlutr, who change the rate of our metabolism to suit our needs, have no such problems. As Shalit and Doku doze, I use Shalit's senses and my own mind to learn what I can of the ship.

A dozen other children lie around us in hibernation chambers; Nen Basilus has been busy this trip. Scattered visions escape from dreaming minds, discordant images of the simple hurts and quiet anger that drove them to Basilus's ship.

The trip is long and slow; it takes nearly three Human weeks before we reach our ultimate destination. In the meantime, Nen makes three stops at Human settlements along the way. In the first, he picks up a pair of children from the docks the way he picked up Doku. The second is a large, rich complex of settlements circling a bloated gas giant—here Nen loads ten hibernating children like cargo while sour men and women watch, their minds burning with one single feeling: relief that they are rid of a problem. These Humans consign their Little Ones to Nen's care in much the same way as an animal voids itself of waste products, or a plant gratefully exudes noxious oxygen.

As Nen's ship slowly plies the great dusty gulfs of the Galaxy, I have time for pondering . . . and for what the Humans call research. Hlutr Elders do not have the limitations of Humans: even as I keep my attention firmly fixed in Shalit's sleeping mind, I am also on Escen and can talk with the robot who attends me. With its help, I examine Human records of missing children . . .and as I learn, the chill of space touches my very soul.

On the final settlement we touch, five older children board gleefully, eyes burning with the intensity of happy expectation: they are setting forth on a holiday, with the blessings of their parents who watch with pride and a little sadness.

From my research, I know the end of their story: their children will not return, and as weeks become months and then years, pain will grow within these parental hearts, a killing pain that will never ebb. For animals, and especially for those who bear their young alive, there is no pain greater.

Doku dreams, and her slow visions are cloudy and filled with dread.

She dreams of childhood, and I see two little girls: Doku and another. They are Fenelia's age, or less. I draw dream-knowledge from Doku's mind: this girl's name is Mari, and she has a new game. Mari's uncle plays this game with her, and when it's over he gives Mari things, like toys and money.

So Doku plays the game too, in darkness and secrecy. And Doku gets money, too. She buys a new doll.

They play for a long time, Mari and Doku, several evenings each tenday over the course of a long summer. Doku likes Mari's uncle; he is a tall, strong man, and he doesn't treat the girls like children.

Then the game changes.

Doku thrashes in her sleep, and in her dream there is the memory of a sudden difference. All at once, without warning, the game *hurts*. And Doku doesn't want to play any more.

Mari laughs at her. Mari waves money at her, Mari shows off her new earrings and a bright red jacket that Uncle bought her. You're a fool, Doku, she says. Look what you're missing, if you don't play.

But it *hurts*.

Don't be such a baby.

Mari and her uncle continue to play, but Doku does not join in. She has had enough. Until the day she wants a new toy, and does not have the money to buy it. Her mother will not get it for her—so she agrees to the game.

She doesn't like the way Mari's uncle looks at her, she doesn't like the smell on his breath or the look in his eyes. But she needs the money, so she joins Mari.

Alone in her hibernation chamber, Doku cries out with remembered pain. This wasn't the way the game was supposed to go! He was holding her too tightly, he was squishing her with his heavy body, he was tearing her apart . . . no!

She twists, and bites, and Mari's uncle lets her go, laughing. *You'll* play with me, Mari, won't you? You're not a scaredy-cat like Doku?

Mari nods, and takes off her pretty red jacket. And she laughs.

Then, too soon, she cries out. But before Doku can help, before she can force herself to move against fear and pain, crimson mingles with red cloth, and Mari says nothing more . . .

I have seen too much; I sing a peaceful melody and Doku's mind calms. This nightmare, which her conscious mind dares not face, has haunted her for a dozen Human years and more. Yet even as she settles into a more tranquil sleep, I see that her dream has no end.

Mari's uncle left the planet before he could be arrested, and in all the years since Doku had never found him again.

While we fly, I also keep special watch on Nen Basilus— through Shalit's slowed senses and through my own command of the Inner Voice. What drives this young man to go from place to place, stealing children? Where he is taking them we will know soon enough; for now I wonder only *why*.

Nen's mind does not tell me much; his thoughts are deeply buried and confused. Only once, while he sleeps and I lead his dreams in the direction I seek, do I get a glimpse of what Nen Basilus dreads: a strong, faceless man with great power . . . and the doom this man holds over the heads of a shy, aged couple whom Nen once called Mama and Papa. But even this vision has been thrust deeply into Nen's unconscious, buried and forgotten. A few Human months with Hlutr masters, and Nen might be healed. At the moment, nothing can be done for him.

And the mysterious figure who gives Nen his orders? Of *him* there is but a name: Avidore. Beyond that, not a glimpse, only a feeling of fear and the certainty of obedience.

Of Avidore, we will know soon enough.

As our ship emerges from tachyon phase into the shadow of a small cloud-shrouded world, I know our journey is at an end. I know from the reflections of Nen's emotions; but more, I know from the subtle swell of a soundless wail I have followed across space . . . the cry of seventy thousand Little Ones . . . a cry of rage and despair so powerful that surely, I think, it must turn the faces of the very stars themselves.

Unbelieving, my mindsong reeling, I reach forth for the comforting music of my brothers and sisters. Now I receive the rudest shock of all. For this planet answers my timid song with nothing but silence. There are no Hlutr here.

I broaden my appeal, reaching out with all the power I can muster. From far away I hear answering songs: from Velladhen, from Etile-viedel, from the Human world Kag'Jafr—but nearby, nothing. Nowhere within a hundred parsecs in any direction is there a trace of the Hlutr mind.

We round the planet as I ponder this problem, singing my question to my Elders on Escen. Through gaps in brilliant white cloud I see the blue of an oxygen-nitrogen atmosphere; odd that this world does not know the touch of Hlutr roots and Hlutr song.

My Elders answer. Few are the worlds known to us which we Hlutr have not adopted. Terra, Metrin, Credix, Phuctra, Cambolinee, Nobedila, Ymfrex, Digant . . . but we know only one world that swims in a sea of space which Hlutr spores have not crossed: a world both legend and nightmare. Karphos.

It was a Human world once, and because of its isolation, of great strategic importance to the Terran Empire. Karphos stood as way-station along the best trade route out of the Transgeled. When the Human empire dissolved in a series of ignoble wars, it was inevitable that Karphos would be a target.

The battle lasted but half a day—brief for Humans, and far briefer for my folk. When it was over fire had scoured the face of the world, and Karphos hid from the stars beneath a cloak of soot and ash. For Humans and Hlutr alike, it was too late. Karphos settled into an age-long winter . . . but there were no survivors of either race to feel the chill.

Shalit's body moves, and my time-sense is suddenly distorted; Nen has ordered the hibernation chambers to begin waking their sleepers. By the time I can match my song to Shalit's thawing brain, the winds of Karphos are whistling against the ship's defense fields.

There are clouds and bright sunlight, then a panorama of green—jungles such as any Hlut would rejoice to see. Before I even begin to hear the life-song of this strange new world, a mountain bulks on the horizon . . . then we circle it once, and are down on a bright landing field. Even as Shalit, Doku and the other children are stirring, Nen shuts off his ship's drive and Karphos's gravity hits, a quarter again of Escen's gentle pull. We have arrived at the place we seek.

May we survive to leave.

We fall.

This is terrifying to Shalit, whose people have lived for ages with complete control of gravity. It is slightly less frightening for Doku, and a positive delight to some of the other children, who shout with joy as we tumble downward.

We land in a heap at the foot of the mountain. To the right is the jungle; to the left, a series of rough caves and some brick buildings. Further up the mountainside I see a metal wall, and beyond it streets, houses and taller buildings.

Doku picks herself up, sniffs and shakes her head. "Pyew!"

The air is rank with the smells of blood, waste and death. A Hlut is accustomed to these odors; they are part of the life of the forest. But Doku is disturbed, and Shalit's hackles rise.

"Where are we?"

One of the other girls knows an answer. Picking herself up, she tosses her head and says, "Didn't you listen? This is kid's land. We can do anything we want, and nobody can stop us." She dances giddily for a moment.

A small boy looks about nervously. "I don't like it here. I want to go home. When can we go home?"

The dancing girl waves a hand. "Silly. Have fun. When you want to go home, they'll take you."

"Who?"

She indicates the mountain, whose slopes are lost in low mist. "Go to the top. They'll take you home. Me, I'm going to explore." She starts toward the nearest buildings, then stops and regards the rest of us, daring. "Well? Anybody coming with me?"

One by one the other children follow, until Doku and I are left alone at jungle's edge.

"What do you think?" Doku asks quietly.

"I do not know." The distance is great and Shalit's mind, while sensitive to the Inner Voice, is befuddled by the fall, the smell and the lingering effects of hibernation. Still, I sense the anguish of children around me. "I do not believe that the way home is as easy as she would have us believe. Otherwise more children would have returned."

"Maybe they have, and we just don't know it." She peers into the mist. "How many children would you say are in this settlement?"

I listen to the Inner Voice. "I hear them, Doku, but their cries are not subject to calculation in the Human style. There are *too* many."

"I agree." She shrugs. "Let's go take a look, eh?"

I keep close to Doku as we walk toward the nearest buildings.

The voices of children are audible before we enter. The nearest structure is a mud-brick building huddled against the side of the mountain; Doku and I enter through a wide doorway. The heat, the sound and the smell are oppressive.

This is a slaughterhouse—half seventy children are at work in a large cave, while ten times that many beasts squeal and thrash, waiting their turn. Some of the children make a game of their work—all but naked, covered with blood, they jump and shout and sing as they strike with knives and axes.

Doku turns away and steadies herself with a hand on my back. "Mother Meletia," she swears, "this is awful."

I lead her out. Doku's folk, accustomed to food from synthesizers and growth tanks, find distasteful the sight and smell of natural food. We Hlutr, who absorb nutrition from the soil, the air and the sweet rain, find nothing disturbing about the practice of eating and the rituals that surround it. It is merely another curiosity of animal life.

Besides, this slaughterhouse is not the source of the Little Ones' cries. Those who labor here enjoy their work.

We pass other children, but they pay us no attention. Doku is a bit more interested in the hydroponic gardens, many seventies of square meters of green algae and other simple plants. Their song is plain but it refreshes me; I close Shalit's eyes and listen inside, listen to a billion happy voices crooning softly in sunlight.

A scream—raw, anguished—splits the afternoon and makes mockery of quiet vegetable song. I look at Doku, and her face tells me that this scream was not just of the Inner Voice: she has heard it too.

"Come on," she urges, and we set off at a run.

My centuries with Humans have given me an understanding of their notions of distance, direction and other unfamiliar concepts; I am able to guide Doku toward the still-screaming Little One. We push past children crowded about a small cave, until Doku is face to face with the source of the psychic scream.

He is a tall lad, rather pudgy and dressed in tatters. His dirt-smudged face twists in alarm. When I touch his mind, I am amazed at his sensitivity to the Inner Voice. Not since the time of the great Human artist Chiriga Ho, six centuries ago, have I sung with a Human who could match him. Then I am drawn deeper into his thoughts, and I am saddened.

Sensitivity and talent are there; alas, the intellect is not. This boy is a defective, born with a brain barely complex enough for Human speech. When we can, the Hlutr help Humans like him to realize their potentials; when we cannot, we make their short lives happy with the music of the Inner Voice.

Two older boys are holding the lad, although he struggles to get free. Before Doku can say anything, they thrust him into the little stone house and slam a sturdy wooden door behind him. Laughing, they ignore his screams and his pounding, and throw a strong bolt.

Fear, shame, dark and alone—can they not hear the emotions he sends forth? Can they not set him free? The place they have thrown him is hot and stuffy, smelly and cramped. There are worms, insects and worse. Children have died there, and their ghosts haunt the place yet. Can they have no pity?

Although Doku does not realize it, his screams are like those of her friend Mari.

"Let him go," Doku says.

Surprised, the bullies turn to her and one of them laughs. "You want to go in the Hole with him, maybe?"

"Let him out."

"Make me."

"Fine."

I do not know much about fighting. When the Hlutr fight, we do it with song and the slow, inexorable power of genetics. Doku fights in the animal style, with movement and speed. For her size and features, she is still an adult, and trained; experience succeeds where strength and numbers might fail. Very quickly she has defeated the bullies, and they flee along with a large portion of the crowd.

Panting, Doku opens the door. The boy creeps hesitantly out, meets Doku's eyes, and smiles.

"What's your name?" she asks in a gentle voice.

"R-R-R-Robbie."

Doku extends a hand to him. "Come on, Robbie. You can't stay here. Let's see if we can't get you someplace safe."

The children of the Lower City make their homes wherever they can find a dry and secluded spot. As slow Karphos dusk settles, Doku and I follow Robbie to a makeshift tent on the roof of a small building near the slaughterhouse. Here we crouch together, sharing Doku's compressed rations and a few handfuls of nuts and fruit that Robbie had hidden in his pockets. I eat, wondering if Human food is nutritious to Shalit's folk.

Robbie is quickly confused and it is difficult for him to speak. Still, he attempts to answer our questions.

First, where are we?

"The m-m-m-mountain is Corella. This," he waves unsteadily, indicating the buildings and caves, "is the L-l-l-lower City." He frowns, concentrating; I hear discord in his mental song, and I do what I can to strengthen his inner melodies. He points upslope. "Middle City. Then Upper. Walls around them. Only special k-k-k-kids can go there. The Peak is at the t-t-t-top. Ships take off and l-l-l-land there." He scans the sky, then points. A bright star is visible at zenith through a break in the clouds.

"Heaven. Mister Avidore lives in Heaven. Good kids go there."

"What happens to bad kids?"

Robbie shakes his head. "The hunt. The Hole. W-w-worse places."

"How do *we* get to Heaven, Robbie?"

The child shrugs and turns his attention to his food.

I have attuned my own song to Robbie's, and he does not seem surprised when I speak. "Robbie, how did you come here?"

"M-m-m-my friend brought me. In a big sp-sp-sp-space ship. I don't remember his name. He told me all about Mister Avidore. He told me that I would be happy here."

"Are you happy, Robbie?"

He considers the question, while the song of his mind is alive with raucous discord—images of casual cruelties intertwined, some from his past life and some from this place. Then he nods. "I'm happy. It's good to be happy." A little wistful, he adds, "Some of the kids say that there are happier places in the jungle, far away from here. I've never been in the jungle. M-m-m-maybe someday I'll got there, to see."

"Do you want to go home?"

Robbie quivers with fear. "They were b-b-bad to me there. I don't want to go back." He lies back on the slate roof. "I like it here."

"Go to sleep, Robbie." I have worked with Humans like Robbie before, and it is simplicity itself to blend my song with his Inner Voice, to subtly persuade him to drop into a temporary, healing sleep.

Staring at the mountain looming above us, Doku shakes her head. "All right, what next?"

"We have found the children."

"I suppose so." She sighs. "I couldn't bring much equipment along, but I have one implant: an ultrawave set that should be able to reach civilization. But without knowing what planet we're on, I can't tell anyone how to find us. Can the Hlutr help?"

"You forget that I am on Escen as well as here. I can give information to Sten Koleno. Or I can summon a

Galactic Rider to fetch us. These things I will not do until our mission is complete."

"Well, can't your people help us find Fenelia?"

"My friend, this is Karphos. There are no Hlutr here."

"Karphos? I thought that was a myth."

"It is too real."

"No Hlutr?" She shivers, and I understand her distaste. The lower orders of life are accustomed to the presence of my folk on all the Scattered Worlds; it disturbs them to be without us. In honesty, it disturbs *me* as well. "Can you find Fenelia?"

I listen deeply to the song of the planet, to the voices of ten thousand sleeping Little Ones. "She is here. I do not know where."

"Let's find her, then get off this rock and go home."

"No, Doku."

"What?"

"Finding Fenelia is not our only task here."

"What do you mean?"

"Someone named Avidore has stolen Human children, brought them here at great expense and risk. I must know why. The Hlutr must know why." I can no longer deny it, to Doku or to myself: my inquiries have drawn the attention of my Elders beyond the stars, and there is growing Hlutr concern with this matter. As yet, the Elders merely listen—but they are interested.

"This place makes me sick. Once we get home, the Hegemony Navy can come back and settle accounts."

"Will they? According to your records, children have been coming here for nearly two of your decades. Why have the Humans in authority done nothing in all that time?"

She does not reply, for she knows that there is no answer. Karphos, once a world of death, is now a living planet of mystery; surely Doku is not the only Human ever to care?

"What is this bright star that Robbie calls 'Heaven'?" I ask.

"It must be a settlement or station in synchronous orbit. He said Avidore lived there."

"I think we must go to Heaven, my friend. Answers may await us there."

"Did Robbie say that ships take off and land on the peak?" She leans back, regarding the mountainside. "Any idea how we're supposed to get there?"

"Robbie may know. I will awaken him."

Our young comrade is ready with his answer. "To get to the P-P-P-Peak we have to go past the walls. It w-w-won't be easy." He frowns, and his will sings with the effort of disciplining recalcitrant thoughts. "I know a way through the f-f-f-first wall. There's a nice lady in the Middle City who m-m-might help us."

"Can you take us there?"

He nods, but his eyes are wild and his body tense.

I touch him with Shalit's gentle hands, the hands of a healer and a musician. "Do not be afraid, Robbie. The Hlutr are with you, and we will not allow you to come to harm." So the Universal Song repeats its constant refrain, as once again a Hlut vows to cherish and protect a Little One.

We three move silently through the night of the Lower City; and moving around us are the ghosts, for seventies upon seventies of Human children have died upon this mountain.

All races have stories of ghosts. Even we Hlutr know them, for our departed ones are ever with us . . . the taste of their memories in the sweet soil and the silver rains, the echo of their Inner Voice that rebounds through the Galaxy, the influence they have had upon the shape of the Universal Song. Standing here in the tranquil midnight of Escen, I can hear the song of the first of our folk to grow upon this globe, when spaceborne seeds found sparse nourishment in the primitive organic molecules and simple cells that thrived in primordial seas. I remember the acrid touch of methane and ammonia winds on hardened bark, the ever-so-careful manipulations to encourage that photosynthesis which would make Escen a fit home for life.

As the voices of these ancient ancestors sing within me, I hear echoes in *their* minds—echoes of a still earlier era, three billion years ago, when the Eldest of All was young and Hlutr spores first left the security of the Galactic Core to venture into the night of the Scattered Worlds. Still older voices sing, telling of a time before the Pylistroph, when the Seven Races lived in turmoil beneath the seventy billion suns of the Core, and even the Elder Gods were unknown.

There is no end to Hlutr ghosts, and not a few foolish saplings have lost their way in the song of ages gone by, returning to themselves only to find half a billion years passed and their worlds changed beyond recognition. I have no ambition to suffer such a fate; yet the ghosts call, beckoning me to remember a time before my home Escen was yet formed, when the Five Animal Races were unborn and the Hlutr sang their lonely song from the good soil of lost Paka Tel. Even then, four billion years ago as Humans count time, my folk had a long history; our bodies were different and our minds a bit strange, but still we sang the Universal Song and dreamed of our place in its melody. We regarded the skies, and knew that it was our destiny to bring life and diversity to all those distant, lovely stars.

And before the first Hlut sang with the touch of the Inner Voice? Before we gained our command of biological evolution, and structured our own natures to fit our purposes? Our ghosts do not tell. Perhaps the Talebba know, those crystalline intellects whose slow song awaited the first true Hlutr who cast their minds toward space. Hlutr legend tells that some of the Talebba were formed from light and matter in the very birth throes of the universe; perhaps *their* ghosts know of the beginning of my folk. For myself, I have presumed enough for one night, enough perhaps for one lifetime. Gratefully, I return my attention to Doku, Robbie and the children of Karphos.

The high wall separating Lower and Middle Cities is not impassable. In places stone and metal have been severely weathered, or broken by rockslides; in other locations the deliberate work of Human tools is evident. Robbie leads us over the rubble, then pauses, thinking.

In the Middle City structures are more elaborate and more numerous than below; buildings are laid out along unpaved streets in an arrangement that resembles the plan of Moulmein, Nerang or the other cities of Escen. We follow Robbie up one narrow street to a large brick building where a single flickering light burns in one corner window.

"T-T-T-There's a nice lady here, she'll help you." Robbie taps on the wooden door, which swings open after a second. A little girl, perhaps eight Escen years old, peers out.

"Go away," she hisses. "It's the middle of the night."

"Please l-l-l-let us in."

The girl looks up and down the street. "You I know . . . what about *her*?" She indicates Doku.

"She's my f-f-friend. Please."

"Come in." I follow Doku, but the Human girl bars my way with a foot. "Leave the animal outside. What *is* that thing?"

Before Doku can answer, I rise up on my hind legs and look the Human girl directly in the eyes. "I beg your pardon. I am not a 'thing.' "

She backs off, and I cross the threshold behind Robbie and Doku. The door slams; in dim, reflected light I see that we are in a small entryway. Doorways lead into other rooms.

The girl faces Robbie. "You should have known better than to bring them here. Especially an alien. They're probably from the Peak. I ought to throw you all out in the street—"

"Elly, what's going on out here?"

The new voice comes from a young woman, no longer a child and yet not fully adult, who stands in a doorway. She is twice Doku's height, and her long dark hair falls down her back like a luxurious mane. Although her voice is calm and quiet, it fascinates like the cry of a nightbird. With wide, friendly eyes she examines us, then smiles.

"Welcome. I am Lusela Holic, and this is my school. Robbie, will you and your friends come with me? Elly, that's all."

"But—"

"Good night, Elly." When the girl has withdrawn, Lusela

Holic beckons us to follow her into the corner room, where she sits before a computer terminal. "Make yourselves comfortable. Elly didn't mean any harm; it's just that everyone has been jumpy lately."

Doku, apparently completely at ease, takes a chair. "You're the first grownup we've run into."

"I'm hardly a grownup. You're right, though—I'm nineteen, and I'm the oldest person you're likely to see outside the Peak." She lowers her eyes. "That's part of the problem."

"What problem?"

"I've been here for fifteen years, and I'm getting too old. So far, the Peak hasn't been able to do anything to me—I've helped a lot of kids, and I have friends." She spreads her hands. "Sooner or later, that won't help me."

Wrinkling her nose, Doku says, "I don't understand."

"You're new. Corella is a place for children. Once you get too old, if you're not one of those on the Peak, then it's the Hunt, or the slaughterhouse . . . or maybe one night you get a visit, and you're not around the next morning." Lusela Holic sighs. "That's my problem, not yours. You must need help, or you wouldn't have come to me. What can I do for you?"

"They w-w-w-want to go to the Peak," Robbie says.

"I'm Doku Tomich and this is Shalit, my friend. We're looking for a particular child. Robbie says we need to go to the Peak."

Lusela narrows her eyes. "You're from the Outside?"

"We are."

"And you're not a child."

"Does it show?"

"Only to me." She shakes her head. "Others have come through before, wanting to rescue a particular child. Avidore always finds out. You're in danger, you know that?"

"Who *is* Avidore? What kind of power does he have?"

"Mr. Avidore runs Corella, and he knows everything that goes on here. You're just going to get caught. And he doesn't like people from Outside. You should leave this planet, now." Her voice and her inner song both are firm.

"You make it sound like it's easy to leave."

"I assume you have a way to get offworld. If not, I can arrange something. I still have friends on the Peak."

Doku is surprised. "You've helped others to get away?"

"Some. Over the years."

My friend's voice is filled with puzzlement. "Then why hasn't this place been investigated before?"

"Now I know for sure that you are not truly a child. Some who went home told of Corella. They were not believed. Adults don't credit what children tell them. They say that we're pretending, or that we don't know what we're talking about. Many children were even sent back."

"I don't believe any parent would do that."

Lusela shrugs. "You see?" She shakes her head and turns to the terminal. "Never mind. Who is the child you're looking for? Maybe I can find some reference to him."

I look at her, and I can tell that she is captivated by Shalit's deep eyes. "*I* believe you, Lusela Holic. Now believe me—changes will come to this world. Humans may ignore what happens here; but now the Hlutr are interested, and I promise you that something will be done."

For a second, she does not react; then her face changes and the melody of her inner song alters. Lusela Holic is sensitive enough to the Inner Voice that she feels the truth of what I say.

"Thank you." She brushes a hand across her eyes, then smiles. "What is the child's name?"

Ten minutes later, we have an answer.

"This girl you're looking for must be awfully cute, or terribly smart. She's on the Peak."

"What's that mean?"

"Depends. She might be there temporarily. A lot of the cute ones go from the Peak to Heaven. A lot of the smart ones stay to help manage. A few of the older kids are trustees—they have the guns, and they watch what goes on below. Avidore picks some to be recruiters. My guess is that your Fenelia is on her way to Heaven."

"What's going to happen to her there?"

Lusela shakes her head. "You don't want to know." She

consults the computer again. "I can get you into the Upper City; a friend of mine there will help you reach the Peak. From there you're on your own."

Doku nods. "Thank you."

"It's late, and we'll have to get you into the Upper City before morning. Robbie, take your friends to the kitchen and tell Cassie to find you something to eat. I have a few contacts to make, then you're on your way."

I touch Lusela, softly, with Shalit's right hand. "Do not fear, Little One. The Hlutr will set things right."

"I-I thank you."

The Upper City is haphazard, its dwellings nothing more than prefabricated shelters and hastily-erected wooden huts. Robbie, who has insisted on coming with us, trembles as we drop from the top of the wall; his mind seethes with anxiety. I do what I can to quiet him.

It is somewhat easier than before. More of my brethren pay attention to events here upon Karphos; the planet is surrounded by tenuous eddies of Hlut-song, and I draw power from the concentration of my folk. As yet the Hlutr are only mildly interested . . . yet there is a hint of a stronger fascination to come.

Why? What is one world to the Hlutr Elders, one world dead so long it is but a legend, one world populated only by seventy seventies of Human children?

The Elders are concerned to know *everything* about Humans. And when the matter concerns Human children, it is that much more vital. Two hundred Human generations ago the Elders recognized Human youngsters as the hope of this strange race; for five millennia only the children have consistently spoken in the voice which needs no sound, the true voice of the soul. If that voice is encouraged, nurtured and cherished, then the child grows into a truly mature adult.

As child is the key to the development of adult, perhaps Karphos is a key to the development of the race. Of course the Elders listen and watch. Learning of Karphos, they can do no less.

But will they do *more*?

And although I quiet Robbie's apprehension, I can do nothing to ease Doku's mounting distress. Her mind, far more developed than Robbie's and yet far less sensitive to the Inner Voice, is all but closed to me. Doku is disturbed by Karphos, and she broods as we walk.

Soon enough, following Lusela Holic's precise instructions, we have made our way to a certain building which perches on an outcropping and overlooks the grid of the Middle City as well as the slaughterhouses of the Lower. Before Doku can knock upon the door, it opens to reveal a tall, dark Human male whose face I know well: Nen Basilus.

His eyes widen and he shakes his head. "Get inside," he hisses, and we obey.

Inside, a large darkened room is crowded with sleeping children. Nen closes the door, then solemnly puts a finger to his lips. He beckons, and we silently follow him past slumbering bodies.

It is dark, but not too dark for Shalit's gifted eyes. Not a few of the sleeping children clutch dolls, most just stuffed rags sewn together . . . but all the dolls, disturbingly, have the same painted face. And some of those blank faces turn to follow us as we pass, almost as if the dolls are awake while their owners rest.

Nen lets us into a small office where a half-dozen terminals supply a pale, eerie light. With the office door shut behind us, Nen sighs heavily.

"I didn't expect *you*," he says to Doku. "You must be in some trouble, to need help from Lusela this soon."

Doku straightens and looks him in the eye. "You might as well know the truth—"

"Keep your voice down." He looks toward the door. "Don't you know anything?"

Before she can reply, I touch her on the shoulder. "The dolls, Doku."

"You talk!" Nen draws back.

I face him. "Are you surprised to hear an unfamiliar organism speak, in a world where dolls watch and listen? They *do*, don't they?"

"You're right. Everything they monitor winds up in

Avidore's files. So watch out." He nods at Doku. "Finish what you were saying. Tell me what's going on."

Quietly, Doku explains: her identity, our homes, our mission to find Fenelia. All through her story, Robbie keeps his eyes on her, even though I know he does not comprehend what she says. "So Lusela sent us to see you," she finishes. "She seemed to think that you could help us."

"Oh, she did, did she? We'll see about that." He reaches to a terminal, taps on the keyboard, and in a second Lusela Holic's image appears in the screen.

"Are you scrambled?" she hisses.

"Of course. I've got some kids here who say that I'm going to help them find some other brat. What do you know about it?"

"I sent them," Lusela answers.

"Are you insane? I told you, I've had it with this. Last time Avidore almost caught me. I'm not going to take a chance like that again."

"Trust me, Nen. Please. This one is important."

"No." His Inner Voice sings with an awful dread . . . Avidore will find out what he's doing, and Avidore will punish him. "I *mean* it, Lusey. I can't do this, not even for you."

She sighs. "All right. Send them back to me."

"What are you going to do?"

"You haven't left me with much choice, have you? I'll take them to the Peak myself."

Now a new fear strikes Nen. "You can't. You're safe in the city, but if Avidore gets ahold of you on the Peak, it'll be the hunt for sure."

"That's a chance I'll have to take, won't I?"

"Don't *do* this to me!" Fear battles fear within Nen Basilus. "Damn it, Lusey, I can't let you walk up there to get killed. What would I do without you? Don't force me into this."

"I'm not forcing you. I believe that these kids can really make a difference. I'm willing to take chances for that. If you're not, then it's my choice."

For long moments Nen sits paralyzed between dread

and terror . . . then he pounds his fist on the desk. "All right, damn it, I'll do what I can to help them. Better that than . . ."

Lusela Holic smiles. "Thank you, Nen. I didn't want to do it alone." She lowers her head. "Please be careful."

"Count on it."

"I love you."

"You too." He punches the terminal, and Lusela's image fades into darkness. Then Nen turns to us.

"You'd better sit down. This isn't going to be easy." With a deep breath, Nen begins. "I don't remember your friend—I bring in too many kids, and they all look the same in hibernation. If she's on the Peak this soon after arrival, chances are that she's waiting for transfer to Heaven."

"What does that mean?"

His skin, dark as night, flushes. "Avidore has a lot of customers. People pay him to take care of their kids—they don't know what goes on here, they think it's just a vacation for the children. People also pay him for . . . other things. Some folks come to the Peak, or here to the Upper City, and make selections among the kids. Those they pick get sent up to Heaven."

"And what happens to them then?" I can feel the stress in Doku's voice, the tension in her mind, as she asks this question. Whatever answer she expects, she does not want to hear it.

Nen shakes his head. "There are some sick people in this Galaxy. I've seen things that I still don't believe. Things that little kids shouldn't know about, much less—"

"I get the idea," Doku said. "So you think Fenelia has been picked to go to Heaven?"

"Most likely."

"What do we do about that?"

"What do you *think*? Give up. Leave. Summon whatever transportation you have, and get off this planet. When Avidore finds spies, he kills them. No trial, no appeal—just suddenly you're breathing vacuum."

"What's *your* part in this, Basilus? You bring him more kids? What else do you do for Avidore?"

Tight-lipped, Nen answers, "I fly a ship. That's all. He tells me to make a recruiting run, I do it. He tells me to fly shuttle between Heaven and the ground, I do. He tells to me bring hunters down, or bring kids to be inspected, I do it."

"Real heroic of you." She turns away.

Nen takes a deep breath and looks at one of his terminals. "Listen, little lady, I don't have to justify myself to you or anybody. I owe Lusela, so when she asks me to help I do it. But that doesn't give you the right to act superior to me. All I have to do is touch one key, and Avidore will know all about you—and then you can be sure that Fenelia will be killed along with you. I know how this place works, you don't . . . so why don't you listen to me when I tell you what to do?"

He is tense, she is angry—and Robbie, looking from one to the other, is frightened. Slowly, doing what little I can to ease the swirling emotions in this tiny room, I speak: "Nen, we cannot leave without making an attempt to save Fenelia. Believe me, Doku is prepared to die in this mission." And Shalit, who gave her body for Hlutr use—do I have the right to risk *her* life?

At least she is a volunteer. Fenelia, and the other children here, are not.

"What do you want from me?"

"Tell us how we can get to Heaven. Then we'll take over."

He sighs. "You can't take a shuttle unless you've been approved. Heaven is for Avidore and his friends, not for kids."

"There must be a way."

"There is, but you're not going to like it."

Doku turns back, her anger ebbing. "Tell us."

"All right." He gestures at the rest of the building. "I've gathered some kids here for inspection."

"What does that mean, inspection?"

"Adults from Heaven are going to look the kids over and choose the ones they want. Then I send the rejects down the slide, pack the others into my ship, and fly up to Heaven." He spreads his hands. "I'll make sure you're picked—that'll get you into Heaven. Fenelia will be on the same flight, I'm sure. From there it's up to you."

Doku shakes her head. "I need to know where Avidore is. Plans of Heaven. Schedules. What sort of ships are available."

He nods toward the terminal. "I can get you all that."

Doku looks in my direction. "Shalit? This seems our best chance."

"Then let us take it, Doku."

"I just wanted to make sure. Okay, Nen, let's see the plans . . ."

We never see the adults who inspect us through a holographic link with Heaven; nor do we read the comments that Nen punches into his terminal. Whatever he says about us, it works—Doku and I, as well as Robbie, are chosen with fourteen others to go to Heaven.

There has been much argument about Robbie. Nen and Doku were agreed on one point: they did not want to risk Robbie's life by taking him to Heaven. Robbie and I were equally firm . . . he will not leave Doku's side, and I will not allow someone so gifted with the Inner Voice to wither in the dead soil of Karphos. If the Hlutr cannot help him, perhaps the psychologists of the Daamin on Nephestal can bring him peace.

In the end, of course, we win.

Under the watchful eyes of the dolls, Nen cannot admit that he knows us—with the others we are taken to the Peak and herded into his ship without comment. Not long after, another group of children enters . . . and Fenelia is not among them.

In fact she does not board the ship until just a few moments before liftoff; she is accompanied by three older children, all in clean, well-cut clothing.

Robbie is afraid of spaceflight; he holds Doku's hand tightly, and I sing with the Hlutr to calm his seething mind. The liftoff is so smooth that I do not feel the actual instant we leave the ground.

Our journey to Heaven is not long: less than a half-hour after launch we are approaching a great silver wheel, a wheel ablaze with the dazzling gleam of captured sunlight. With a dozen dolls watching us, Doku does not dare contact Fenelia; we make the trip in silence.

As for myself, I spend the time pondering the mysteries of Karphos. How do Humans allow such a place to exist? What causes Nen Basilus, free with a starship, to bring more children back here, knowing the life to which he carries them?

And what drives Avidore, the enigma at the center of all other mysteries of this world?

I have no answers when we approach Heaven: only the sure knowledge that in order to understand, I must meet Avidore.

Heaven. How do I describe a place that is so Human, and yet so oddly familiar?

Like Calmathis and other Human settlements in space, Heaven is a self-contained ecological unit and does not depend on Karphos for nutrients, water or air. Even before we enter, I know that Heaven is a complete world, though a very small one: the song of that many living beings, perched on the edge of space twenty thousand kilometers from the ground, cannot be ignored.

As soon as Nen opens the hatch and I smell the air of Heaven, I am aware of its life: invisible micro-organisms happily floating in the air, hibernating fungus and plant spores moving instinctively toward warmth and water, tiny mites to whom dust grains are worlds, even a few visible insects that escape the notice of Nen and the children. Ship's atmosphere mixes with Heaven's—and before any of us reach the hatch, seventy thousand new organisms are born in the roiling interface of air. This is the way of life, in Heaven as much as on the planet below.

To a greater or lesser degree, all of the children are aware of the lifeforms of Heaven—and none more aware than Robbie, whose mind hums in tune with the ineffable melody surrounding him. I feel, reflected in his thoughts and emotions, the touch of distinct, nearby awareness: hectares of quiet green plants lazily following the slow-spinning sun, insects and worms burrowing in cool tasty soil, domestic animals in seventies of varieties . . . and

Human minds, not only the wondering consciousness of childen but the cold, closed minds of adults.

And somewhere—Avidore.

I know that Doku wants to follow Fenelia, but almost as soon as the door is open Fenelia and her three comrades depart, moving quickly. We must follow our plan. Nen will meet us at the designated spot, and then together we will determine Fenelia's whereabouts.

It is not difficult for us to slip away; the main docking bay is honeycombed with passages and Doku simply gestures for us to stray behind the main group until we can slip down an alternate path. Nen gives no sign of noticing when we leave, and none of the other children are watching.

"Wh-wh-wh-what if one of the d-d-d-dolls saw us go?"

Doku hardly pauses, simply muttering, "We'll just have to hope they didn't. And if they did—I guess we'll see Avidore sooner than we expect."

Silently, Robbie and I follow Doku, and artificial gravity slowly gives way to centrifugal force as we approach the rim of the station. Ramps, stairs and ladders take us downward, and at each bend in the passage Doku stops, listening for any sign that we have been detected. Every now and again she glances at her portable computer, where she has stored maps of the station.

At last Doku stops before a pressure door and points to the words on its surface. "Agricultural section ten," she reads—for neither Shalit's eyes nor my mind are trained to comprehend Human writing, and Robbie has never been taught how to read. "This is the place." Gently, Doku touches the door in a careful sequence, and it opens to reveal a wonderful land, a forest in the sky.

I cannot stop myself. Enchanted, I step forward, gladly greeting the happy plants and animals that grow under the eternal sunlight that shines through broad windows high above.

There are of course no Hlutr in this forest, but the mixture of lifeforms is delightful and amazing: Terran-life oaks alongside the soaring fronds of Dorascan star-trees, rabbits and squirrels living in harmony with their smaller cousins from across the stars, the whispering mosses of

Bendaplida and the tiny, peaceful crawlers and grubs of Marpethtal. And all these lifeforms live in harmony, existing in a complex ever-changing ecology that comes as a complete surprise to me.

"How does a forest like this come to be?" I ask Doku.

She shakes her head. "Heaven is a big station with a small population; not all of the agricultural sections are needed for food, so some have been allowed to go wild."

"And going wild, have developed their own infinitely varied world. Heaven is a treasure, Doku, for here life blooms where it never existed before."

She frowns. "Don't get too excited about it. We still have to get Fenelia and deal with Avidore."

I wish I could ignore the awful determination that burns in Doku's mind when she gives voice to that simple phrase: "Deal with Avidore." For I know what she intends: before leaving Heaven, Doku wishes to see Avidore dead. And I do not know if I can allow such a thing.

"We have to get to the meeting place," Doku tells me. "This forest is just a short cut."

"Go without me, Doku Tomich. I will catch up. I must have some time with this new forest we have discovered. I must have time to commune with my brethren." She looks into my eyes, impatient. "I must summon a ship of the Galactic Riders, if we are to escape from Heaven safely."

"All right. How will you find us?"

"I have seen your map . . . and I can follow Robbie's song. Go await Nen; I will come after you."

She is reluctant, but she has no answer for my arguments. "All right." She takes Robbie by the hand, and then they are gone.

I sit, and turn my attention to the glorious forest all around. Its music, the concert of living things, swirls like a fragrant mist about me and carries me upon its melody. In another instant, I have touched the minds of the Hlutr who watch events here at Karphos, and I am part of the grand communion of my people.

My first task is to call upon the Hlutr of Nephestal, who will in turn send a ship of the Galactic Riders to Karphos. Doku has planned for that ship to dock at Heaven so we can make a quick getaway with Fenelia . . . but I give instructions for the ship to wait in orbit nearby until I call.

For thrice seventy generations I have lived with Humans, cherished them and their children, spoken their language and sung their songs. Suddenly, I find that I do not understand them. Have they grown stranger, or have I? Before I came to Karphos in Shalit's borrowed body, I thought only of my Human friends on Escen and never concerned myself with the councils of the Hlutr which debated the fate of this race.

Now I am none too sure.

Brothers and sisters, guide me. These Humans are an odd people, an alien race that we may never know completely. What other peoples visit such atrocity upon their young . . . and what other young rise above their despair to find happiness?

The memory of the Hlutr is long, and our ghosts are always with us. We have seen much, on seventy times seventy times seventy times seventy worlds; worse than Karphos, worse than any perversion dreamed by Terra's sons and daughters. Worlds where intelligent creatures consume their young, publicly and with great ceremony, in order to prolong their lives. Planets on which breeding is happenstance and co-operation unheard of, where evisceration is the mildest of social interactions. There are societies based on degrees of pain and suffering, and others in which pity and compassion are perversions punishable by death.

What, then, are we to make of Karphos? Doku, I know, wishes that the Hlutr will destroy the world, send all its children back to their homes. Karphos is a bit unusual, but certainly not a crime that would warrant Hlutr action.

The key, however, is Avidore. While a world must be left alone unless its evil is too compelling, the Hlutr have acted to eliminate particular beings who are too warped to live in the civilized Galaxy—and will act again, whenever the need arises.

Mankind, the consensus of the Hlutr has decreed, must be spared. And I applaud that decision. Yet we have also taken it upon ourselves to help Man improve himself. If this means that Avidore must be eliminated from the Universal Song, so be it.

But help me, Brothers and Sisters, for I have never killed a Human before. . . .

The dark of space and the cool sound of the Hlutr song surround me; even on peaceful Escen, where my body stands in golden sunlight, I feel the refreshing coolness like the first breezes of winter. What must be done, will be done.

I am ready to face Avidore.

With the Inner Voice of seventy times seventy Hlutr concentrated in the space around Karphos, Robbie's song becomes ever easier to detect; now I hear his call, relayed from Doku. *Come, Elder, for Nen is here.*

Bidding the magnificent forest farewell, I pass through a durasteel-framed door and follow the scent and music of Robbie's passage.

They are waiting for me in a storage room just outside the aricultural region. Doku is anxious, Robbie placid . . . and Nen radiates a strange mixture of fear and elation.

"About time you showed up," Doku says.

"I was in deep communion with my folk."

Nen grunts. "I'm a spacer, and I learned respect for the Hlutr—but you'll have to forgive me if I say that there isn't time for that now. I managed to get in contact with Fenelia Koleno." He narrows his eyes. "You didn't tell me that she's so important."

"I did not know, friend."

"Yeah, well, she's moving up—way up. I think Mr. Avidore has taken a shine to her. She's got a session with him this afternoon."

His thoughts are confused and shadowed. "What does that mean, Nen Basilus?"

He looks away. "Avidore is going to have some fun with your girl . . . then she'll probably be sent down to the city to be a section leader or something. If Avidore likes you, you're set until you grow up."

With a sneer, Doku says, "Is that what happened to you? Did Avidore like you?"

"As it happens," Nen answers without feeling, "it did."

"And that's why you're a pilot . . . and a recruiter?" Doku's derision flys outward in waves of the Inner Voice, making Robbie cringe.

Nen responds with cool anger. "We can talk about that later. I told Fenelia to meet me here, and she'll be along in a few minutes. I thought you might want to plan what you're going to do."

"Shalit, is that ship going to be here?"

I listen to the song of the Hlutr. "A Galactic Rider of Raemkhar-Tapt is approaching the Karphos system even now."

"Good. I say we grab Fenelia and take her to the port. Then when we're on our way back to the Hegemony we can send the Navy to take care of this place."

"You don't know what you're doing," Nen protests.

Then it is too late to argue, for the door snaps open and my little Fenelia stands framed against the light of the corridor outside.

She is a little taller, a bit more filthy, and the light of the stars shines less intensely in her eyes. Yet from her innocent song alone, I would know Fenelia anywhere. Karphos has not touched that part of her that keeps her still a child.

I cannot restrain myself; on Escen I lift my branches and call for Sten Koleno. He answers in an instant, and weeps when I tell him his child is found.

"Bring her back safely, Elder," he pleads.

"We do our best, my friend."

"Who are you?" Fenelia asks.

Doku holds out her hands. "Your father sent me, Fenelia. We've come to take you home."

Then the pitch of Fenelia's inner song changes, teetering on the edge of that mysterious transformation that robs most Humans of their youth. "I'm not going," she says.

"Don't be silly."

"I'm not going, and you can't make me. I like it here." She takes a step back. "I'm going to tell Mr. Avidore on you."

"You don't want to see your Daddy again?"

Fenelia spins, in her eyes and mind the quick anger of childhood. "My Mummy and Daddy don't want me."

"How can you say such a thing? They love you."

"You don't know my Mummy and Daddy. They don't want me. They never wanted me. They were happy when I went away." She points to Nen. "*He* knows. He told me."

The look that Doku gives Nen speaks eloquently of her wish to do him harm. But she cannot see the turmoil inside him, the guilt and pain.

"Fenelia, you must come back with us."

"I don't even know who you are. I'm telling!"

This has gone too far, and I must act. I step forward, raising Shalit's body upon her hind feet and looking straight into Fenelia's eyes. "Child, do you know who *I* am?"

"I don't—"

Her eyes cloud, as deep within her she hears the melodies that I have sung her time and again on Escen's peaceful soil. "Elder!"

I nod. "Return with us, Fenelia."

"I . . . I can't." She turns away—frightened, ashamed, sniffing back a tear. "Mummy and Daddy . . ."

Clear is my song to Sten Koleno, who stands beneath my spreading limbs, eyes cast to the skies in a hope he dares not feel: *Sing with me, Sten Koleno. Your daughter needs you.*

I could not accomplish this thing I do next, were it not for the massed minds of the Hlutr and the nearness of Robbie's sensitive song. Across eight thousand parsecs, past a million living worlds, I carry Sten Koleno's image from Escen to a tiny storeroom in Heaven, far above the clouds of lonely Karphos.

He regards Fenelia, and for long frozen moments there is tension between father and daughter, between two entities just learning to be distinct from one another. Then Sten opens his arms, and Fenelia rushes into them crying. He is only an image, a phantom of the mind—but he is real enough to Fenelia and she buries her face against him. Then she turns and looks back toward me with real love shining through her tears.

"Take me home."

I lower Shalit's body and cast thanks outward through the Inner Voice. "Soon, Little One. Soon." I am tired, but there is still much to do. Reluctantly I let Sten Koleno's image fade. Fenelia comes to me and sits at my side, her arms around my neck.

Nen clears his throat. "I don't know what kind of ship you have waiting, but it probably can't get through Heaven's defenses. Come on, I'll take you to my ship and see if I can't smuggle you out."

Doku frowns. "Basilus, you're a decent sort . . . why do you help Avidore? How can you bring more children to this place, knowing what's in store for them?"

"What *should* I do?"

"You have a ship, man. Run for it. There are ten thousand Human planets out there for you to get lost among."

Storms lash the music of Nen's mind, and something dark is hidden beneath their violence. With Robbie's help I could lay bare this secret . . . but I stay my effort.

"Most of the kids I bring," he says, backing away, "are better off here. You don't know some of the things I've seen on those ten thousand Human planets—cruel things that make the mountain Corella or Heaven look like kindness. Here . . . here kids have a chance to *be* something, to make something of themselves."

"Oh, right, and then to die in the Hunt when they're old enough. I didn't see any adults on Karphos . . . that's why, isn't it?"

Nen hangs his head. "I do it because . . . because if I don't, Avidore's going to kill my folks." He turns away, while his thoughts ring with embarrassment and humiliation. In his mind is the image of a Human man and woman, gentle-faced and loving. "There, now you know, okay?"

"I'm sorry . . ."

Again with Robbie's aid, I sing the inner melodies that help calm Nen. "Little One, he cannot know where your parents are. His threat is empty."

"I can't take that chance." He shrugs. "Come on, let's get you to my ship. We'll figure out what to do then."

I exchange glances with Doku, and the same thought is in both our minds. "Not yet, Nen," I say. "We must first settle the matter of Avidore."

Nen's eyes open wide. "Now wait a *minute*. No. Never. What do you think you're going to do with him?"

Doku shakes her head sadly. "I don't think there's any question. Shalit, you take the others and get to the ship. I'll take care of Avidore."

The blood lust within her is as strong as any hunting animal's, and it pains me a bit to usurp her claim. "No, friend. Avidore is mine to confront." Elders, must I do this thing?

Nen shivers, torn between fear and shame. "You'll never get in to see him alone."

"Somehow, I must."

I do not know what Fenelia has been thinking, but she has listened intently. "I know what to do." She lowers her head. "Mr. Avidore is waiting for me—I'll take you to see him."

"No!" Doku shouts. "I won't allow—"

"You can't stop me." Fenelia looks at me, her eyes revealing the depths that Karphos has uncovered. "It's what I have to do, Elder, isn't it?"

"You choose your own course, Fenelia. It will help, but I cannot compel you to do this thing."

"I'll do it. But we'd better go, we're going to be late."

"One moment. Doku, you and Nen must make ready for departure. Go to Nen's ship and wait for us there." I take a breath, and the scents of Heaven fill Shalit's lungs. How many more times will I breathe in this borrowed body? "Robbie, I need you. I cannot compel . . ." Without Robbie to strengthen the song of my Inner Voice, I might fail.

"D-d-d-d-don't worry, you can c-c-count on me."

"Go, then."

"Gods be with you." A quick touch, then Doku and Nen depart.

I nod, and the three of us—little girl, retarded boy, and Hlut in a loaned form—set off to do what none could do alone.

* * *

Avidore's receptionist whirrs to itself for a moment, then flashes a soothing pattern on its screen. "Mr. Avidore will see you all." A door opens, and we pass through.

One wall of Avidore's office is a great window; the starry sky wheels past as Heaven spins. Some Human-style chairs, a couch and a table are grouped in front of the window, and as we enter a computer terminal is obediently tucking itself into its alcove. But my attention is drawn instantly to the man who stands before us, arms spread in welcome.

Avidore is slender, muscular and taller than most adult Humans. His hair is the color of sandy beaches, his eyes the deep blue of twilight. He wears a fine embroidered business gown, such as I have often seen Sten Koleno wear. On his face is a disarming smile.

"Hello, my dear Fenelia. How good to see you again. Who is your friend?" He gestures to Robbie.

This man's words are fair, his manner suave—yet Robbie shrinks back from him. When I touch his mind to read the unconscious melody there, I am shocked.

This is no innocent, no dilettante with unusually decadent tastes. Avidore looks at Fenelia, at Robbie, and within him is only the desire to *hurt* . . . the cloying anticipation of delightful pain. Such depravity I have not felt except in the evil denizens of the Gathered Worlds.

Human ghosts dance . . . the room reeks with the fear of those whom Avidore has tormented. And stars help me, I must face this wickedness.

Avidore advances toward Fenelia and Robbie, reaches out with deceptively-gentle hands. "Let's play a game. You like games, don't you?"

This has gone on far enough. Now it must end.

My Elders and my brethren are with me, and I know that they support whatever action I take. Robbie's mind is close—and through his sensitivity I draw my power and the power of the Hlutr like a whirlpool around Heaven. As Avidore touches Fenelia, he stands closer to death than he will ever know.

No. For I am of the Hlutr, and I cannot destroy a thing—individual or race—until I understand it. And I do not understand Avidore.

"Stop." Shalit's mouth parts produce Human words perfectly well, and Avidore starts, surprised. "Fenelia, stand by the door." Quickly, she obeys.

"Well, now, what are you?" Avidore bends over me, cocking his head slightly. The shadows I see in his imagination are frightening.

I raise myself to Shalit's full height. "I am an Elder of the Hlutr, Avidore. And I am your judge." My Inner Voice swells along with the chorus of Hlutr that surrounds us . . . and I think even Avidore hears that ethereal music, for a touch of fear appears in his mind.

"Get out of here." He raises his eyes. "Computer, send in—"

"No, Avidore." He struggles to speak, but for the moment he is paralyzed by the swelling song of the Hlutr. "Face me." Slowly, against his will, Avidore turns his eyes toward me. They are cold as the ice that orbits in distant space between the stars.

I reach out: one of Shalit's hands touches Avidore, the other meets Robbie's outstretched arm. The Galaxy spins around me as seventy times seventy thousand Hlutr focus their attention on this place, this moment.

Who are you, Avidore?

"I am . . ."

Sing with me.

And sing he does, reluctantly, yielding to the persuasion of the massed Hlutr minds. He sings of Heaven, and the vile things he has done there—of the years before he came to Karphos, when he ruled an inherited mercantile empire by day and tormented helpless Little Ones in the dark of night. And gods help us, he sings *pleasure* in those things he has done.

Avidore sings of his early adulthood, of financial successes and conquests of quite another sort. Even then his taste was for violence, for domination; even then he tasted the pleasure of the prostrate victim, the joys of conquering the unsuspecting prey.

Why?

"I hated them . . ."

Who?

Seventy times seventy faces swim before us, ghosts given form by the song of the Hlutr—this man is full of hatred.

"They hurt me."

Adolescent games, the thrill of discovery, the awful feeling of satisfaction when, at last, he was first enraptured by the sight of pain and humiliation in another's eyes.

When first he discovered power . . .

Who had been powerless so long.

"Mommy, it hurts!" The child, taken by forces he did not understand, betrayed . . .

"No, Daddy, not the Game. I don't want to play. Please. *Please.*"

The secret . . . the filthy little secret that he must keep within, never revealing. Why?

"I loved you! Why do you do this? Mommy, Daddy, I love you . . ."

The Galaxy spins about us, and the circle has swung full around—the master is the victim, the vicious adult is a child once more.

"I hate you. *Hate you!!* Don't touch me, don't you . . . ever . . . touch me." Avidore looks up, and his face is wet with a lifetime's unshed tears. "I love you," he whispers. "I just want you to love me."

Robbie's grip is strong, his mind completely attuned to my song. He has a great future ahead of him as an operative, this one.

Now I must save another.

Sten Koleno, I need you again.

Sten answers, faithful as ever . . . but when Avidore lifts his face, what he sees is the ghost of his *own* father, that long-dead man who set his son on this course to evil.

"Daddy . . ."

With a single nod, Sten steps forward. He does not know all that Avidore has done—all he knows is that here is a Little One in need. And Sten has enough of the Little One within him yet, that he gives of himself without hesitation.

"Come here, my child."

"No, Daddy. Not the Game."

Sten shakes his head. "Not that. Never again." He holds out his hands. "I love you. Come to me."

The Hlutr love you too, Little One. Your nightmare is over. Awaken.

"Daddy!" Avidore twists, and his mind desperately seeks some escape—but the Song is strong about him, and he cannot close his ears to it.

Sten steps forward, and closes his arms around Avidore, then lifts his face and brushes his lips against Avidore's forehead. "Come home, son. We love you. We will *always* love you."

Then it is as if the Song reaches a crescendo, and something snaps within Avidore. For a moment I am afraid that we will lose him altogether—but Robbie's song and Sten's arms stay strong. The Song subsides like the passing of a great storm, and again I am conscious of the stars wheeling peacefully beyond the window.

Avidore, sprawled on the floor, looks up at me. Whatever the thing is that happens to Human adults, that which robs them of their childhood—it is no longer mirrored in Avidore's face. His mind is like Robbie's now . . . but his soul has regained something priceless.

I let go of Robbie's hand and Avidore's, and turn to Fenelia. "Can you run down to Nen's ship and bring the two of them back here? We no longer need worry about escape."

Six thousand years have I stood in the good soil of Escen; thrice seventy generations have I lived with the fair Humans of my world. Yet these past few days I have learned more of them—and of myself—than in all my life.

Fenelia is asleep in her room and Shalit has gone back to her folk. Doku will soon return to her world and other cases; Nen will soon take Robbie to Nephestal so that he can be trained in his abilities. Yet this last night we are all together with Sten Koleno, while the eternal stars watch from black skies above.

"Avidore has been admitted to the Psych-care Institute," Sten tells us. "They don't know if he'll ever progress beyond the level of a four-year-old."

"My brethren will help him as we can." The Human computer sounds flat and unemotional as it translates my words; but all can feel my gladness on the cool night breeze. "In whatever case, he is happy now."

"I've talked to my folks," Nen says. "Elder, I can't begin to thank you for finding them. After I drop Robbie off at Nephestal I'm going to visit them."

"The Hlutr rejoice that you are reunited with them, my friend."

"I still don't understand," Sten says, "why you won't let us send a fleet to Karphos. I'm sure I can work out an interstellar agreement . . ."

"The children of Karphos have no place to go, friend Sten. Those who were taken against their will are being returned to their homes—but seventies upon seventies *have* no homes. Who will take them in? Your house is too small. Karphos is where they live now."

"Besides," Doku says, "they aren't being abandoned. People like Lusela Holic are there already—and as more kids grow up, some will care for the others."

Robbie's eyes glow. "And the EL-El-Elders haven't f-forgotten us."

"The Little Ones of Karphos will be cared for, Sten." Even now, Galactic Riders are landing on that tortured globe with the greatest gift they could bring: Hlutr seeds, primed for quick growth and early maturity. In less than a decade as Humans count time, Karphos will once again be home to full-grown Hlutr.

With Robbie's help I broaden my song and my awareness, until all can see the same ghostly image, the same tender shoots and many-colored leaves reaching for the distant sun . . . the same hopeful song of new life emerging into the warmth.

"The Little Ones of Karphos will be cherished. So pledge the Elders of the Hlutr." The pale glow of approaching dawn touches the eastern horizon here on Escen, and the world begins to settle down for that peace that comes just before sunrise, when the night and the day dance together with all the happy ghosts.

Little Ones of Karphos, you need never cry again.

We love you, now and always.

Happy ghosts dance, and the Song goes ever on . . .

INTERLUDE 5

Father Nnamdi met him at the spaceport. "Kev, you didn't have to come home from school for this. The autodoctor will take care of everything."

Kev took the man's hand. "Thanks. But I-I have to be here. I'm glad you called."

"I understand."

Immanuel was waiting for him in his old room; when he heard Kev enter he thumped his tail once or twice and lifted his head. An autodoctor hovered over the dog, its display showing a composite of life signs.

The adults left him alone, and he was grateful to them for that. There are some things that a boy has to face on his own.

"How ya doin', boy?" Kev knelt and scritched Immanuel behind the ears. Struggling to keep his voice level through the sudden, awful pain in his throat, he said, "Don't worry, it'll all be over soon. You've been a very, very good boy."

That got another wag of the tail, and Kev had to force himself not to look away. He kept his hand steady on the dog's head.

"Sir, we've done everything we can." The autodoctor's voice was programmed to be soothing, but Kev found no comfort in it.

"I know," he answered.

"You may wish to wait outside. The process is quick and painless."

Kev shook his head. "N-no. I can't l-leave him alone. He was always there when I . . . when I needed him."

"I understand." The doctor started to settle, and Kev stopped it with a hand, as if postponing the act might yet allow some sort of reprieve. "Wait," he said helplessly.

"Immanuel." What to say? Thank you for all the great times? I wish I hadn't left you for these last two years? There was nothing he could say, nothing that could in any way increase or diminish the love that shone in those wide brown eyes. "I love you."

A warm, dry tongue touched his hand, and Kev could stand it no more. With hot tears rolling unregarded down his cheeks, he said convulsively, "Do it," and the doctor obeyed.

Slowly, the display changed: one by one, glowing lines started flattening out. "Body functions will continue for a while, sir. The patient is unconscious; there is no need for your presence."

"Yes there is." That strong, loyal heart was still beating . . . suppose Immanuel awoke, without Kev there? Kev couldn't face such a betrayal. "Can't you end it quickly?"

"As you wish, sir. You must remove your hand."

"No."

"There will be momentary discomfort."

There was pain, but Kev welcomed it. Then it passed, and Immanuel was gone.

Kev dug the grave in the shadow of his treehouse tree. "I hope you don't mind," he said aloud. "It's the only place."

The wind and the leaves whispered to him, and he knew that the Hlut was in agreement.

It took Kev several minutes to steel himself to the next

task—then with one motion he lifted the burden from his flier and settled it in the trench. "Rest there, good friend," he whispered. "Remember, I love you."

As he shoveled, filling the grave, the leaves and the wind sang to him of other graves, far away and once upon a time . . .

PART SIX:

Caretaker

The Secluded Realm is the hidden heart of the Scattered Worlds. In this sacred refuge built with the skills of the vanished Pylistroph, the old ways still survive from the times before the Schism of the Hlutr, before the Gathered Worlds were lost to us. Here the Eldest of All abides, filling space with Her song and Her wisdom. Here is a home to all who are weary of the worlds outside, or who wish to honor the memory of times gone by.

Here, I tend the honored dead.

This is an animal tradition, to bury the dead and raise monuments to them; we Hlutr stand where we have died, our substance gradually to enrich our world. But it pleases the Eldest to go along with this practice, and so I and a few of my brethren grow in this luxuriant soil to ensure that no harm comes to those who lie here. Three times seventy Caretakers have proudly served before me; my own tenure began recently in the days of the Dorascan Empire, a mere million and a half years ago as Humans count time.

What do I know of Humans?

None of them rest here. Few have even visited, of the small numbers who have come to the Secluded Realm. This place is for the dead of mature races who are long past the times of Galactic domination; according to the Wise Ones of Nephestal and some Elders of the Hlutr, Humans have yet to realize their time of greatest glory.

181

True, some few have come, to pay their respects to the warriors and leaders of past ages. Fewer still have come to honor the others—poets, scientists, philosophers—who have enriched the life of the Scattered Worlds and the Universal Song.

And now, one stands before me, totally unsupervised.

His skin is the color of dry Hlutr leaves and his hair like webs that hang from long-untouched branches. He leans heavily on a tall looped staff of dull metal, and next to him is a shaggy, four-footed animal creature whose small mind is filled with devotion to its master.

When I touch the Human's mind, I am surprised at the depth and the firmness of control that I find there. Others of his race sing mental discord; this man's thoughts are like the complex, precise harmonies of the Daamin, or the slow-changing songs of the long-dead Kareffi aquatics who sang of old in the Pylistroph.

He bows before me and speaks in perfectly-accented Coruman, "Greetings, Elder."

Who is this creature, who speaks the ancient tongue of the Pylistroph as well as any who abide here in the Secluded Realm?

In this world, the youngest Hlutr seedling knows the quiverings of leaf and twig that make Coruman words . . . and I was taught this skill by the Eldest Herself. "I am Caretaker," I say. "May joy be yours. How may I serve you?"

For long moments the Human stares out across the land, where green-covered hillocks, mounds and knolls mark the barrows and monuments of a billion and a half years. We seek to preserve the newer monuments—but as entropy runs its course, we encourage the lesser plants to overgrow crumbling gravesites. In the end, it is all the same: and all, in time, goes into the soil to enrich the life of all.

"I seek," the man says at last, "to pay homage to one who lies here."

"Some hero of the past, perhaps?" Many of the Scattered Worlds' fallen have found their final rest here: Ashli Sicne, leader in the Migration of the Daamin; Batydded, great Queen of the Iaranor; Kylvan delv Minatan of Avethell; the fabled Galactic Rider Dareenten; and Halkinardda of the Kreen.

Here also lie Jel Haran and Lirith of the Asthoki, whose love still inspires all in the Scattered Worlds. And here is buried a golden brooch, all that remains of Aemallana, the legendary queen who ruled the empire of Avethell for seventy Human millennia—the longest time of peace and prosperity known in the Scattered Worlds.

"She whom I seek was no hero, Elder. She was a minor scholar of the Wise Ones: Diav Trnas." He smiles. "She was a teacher of mine."

A Human taught by the Daamin? Stranger things have occurred in the Scattered Worlds. But not often. "Directly behind you, up the hill and twice seventy times the length of your upper limb. Yon bitterwood sapling shades the monument."

"I thank you, Elder. I will return." He gestures to the beast at his side, and together they walk to Diav Trnas's resting place. The man kneels, then all is silent in this eternal afternoon.

The horizon of the Secluded Realm curves upward as it falls away into distance, ever so slowly, until at last it closes upon itself in bluewhite splendor nearly twenty light-minutes away. Directly above is the sun, an almost-identical twin of that which shone upon Paka Tel, the long-lost Hlutr homeworld.

The horizon surrounds and encloses us, but a stronger power protects us. If the Secluded Realm is the secret heart of the Scattered Worlds, then the Eldest is its hidden soul. Her curtain of song encompasses the Realm, and none may pass within but by leave of Her Warders.

This island—which itself is as large as whole worlds—is the home of the Eldest; Her roots pervade the soil as Her gentle song pervades the air. As far beyond us as we Hlutr are beyond the lesser orders, She knows all that transpires here. This Human, whoever he is, must have come with Her blessing.

I spread my song outward, seeking the eternal communion of the Hlutr. I must sing with my brothers and sisters. For little news has come to the Secluded Realm of these poor children of Terra; I had thought them a rude and uncultured race. *This* one, however, is as civilized as any creature I have met. Perhaps some change has come upon the Humans, while I tend the honored dead. Time can slip away, here in this realm where time stands still and the old days still live.

Brothers and sisters, tell me of Humans.

Slowly, answers come back from beyond the stars, led by the song of Humanity's current champion, the Artist of Inse. In the millennium since the Long Winter of Mankind, great changes have taken place. Political upheavals and expansion, cultural and scientific advances—and now a new religion is beginning to sweep through the Human Galaxy.

Lorecanism is a movement that shows much influence of the Daamin and other races of the Scattered Worlds. The central mystery of the faith is *kedankat*: a mental state of awareness that resembles the Forever Dreams of the Daamin. Lorecanism has spread through most of the Credixian Imperium, which is the largest and most influential of Humanity's states.

My brothers and sisters tell me the tenents of Lorecanism: inner peace, harmony with all living beings, the joy that sustains the stars and informs the melodies of the Universal Song.

Is it possible, I wonder, that Humans are maturing? Some of them—this Loreca, at least, who founded the movement—seem fully developed sapient beings, at least on a level with the Daamin, the Wise Ones of Nephestal.

The pilgrim has returned, and he bows before me. "I thank you, Caretaker. Now if I may beg your assistance once more, could you direct me to the Eldest?"

"The Eldest is all about, pilgrim. The sward, the trees . . . I myself . . . all are part of Her substance." A slight chill passes through me, and I feel the remote, indifferent attention of the Eldest Herself. As yet, only the most minor portion of Her being attends. "Who are you, that you wish audience with the Venerable?"

He lowers his head. "I am but a seeker of truth; aptly

have you called me pilgrim. I am Grigor Haentil . . . who is sometimes called Loreca."

If this Human feels my surprise, he does not show it; but the Eldest does, and suddenly I feel Her powerful Inner Voice under my mental song. "Welcome to the Secluded Realm, Loreca. You honor me; among your people you are a great teacher and a wise leader."

"Please." He strokes his companion's fur. "I am an old man. To the Galaxy outside, Loreca is dead—let him remain so. I am merely Grigor Haentil, in search of God."

"God?"

"Call it what you will. Long have my folk believed that there is something beyond us, a guiding principle, a Prime Mover, a benevolent consciousness to the Universe." A warm breeze stirs my uppermost leaves, and my visitor's inner melody falters a little. "I used to believe that too. I used to preach it." He spreads his arms. "In a long life, I've seen nothing to support such a notion. Before I die, I would like to *know*."

"So you come to the Hlutr?"

"I have asked my teachers, the Daamin. I have visited them deep in their Forever Dreams, and they cannot help me. Wise as they are, still they suffer pain, death, war—and still without knowing why."

"The ways of the Universal Song are not easy to understand."

He stares ahead, his inner sight looking far beyond the Secluded Realm. "I've visited the Watchers on Nephestal, the great Iaranori philosophers on Ismallia, even the immortal Talebba who swim on the edges of intergalactic space. None have offered me any comfort."

"What can we give you, Grigor Haentil, that no other race can offer?"

"The Hlutr are near perfection. In wisdom and power, none can match you. And the Eldest is the epitome of the Hlutr. Three billion years of life! What She must know. What She must be able to tell me . . ."

The Eldest sings Her slow song, and it touches the very root of my being. Memories swirl about me and within me, the sum of all Her great long life. She was nurtured in the soil of Paka Tel, beneath the billion stars of night and the bright sun of day, when life was but a slumbering potential in the Scattered Worlds. Under Her tutelage, seventy times seventy thousand races have lived and grown since the Schism of the Hlutr.

I AM NOT A GOD, GRIGOR.

The voice of the Eldest is like the incoming tide, like the lightness of air when a storm departs. It sings in the soul without disturbing the inner music.

My pilgrim bows. "None in the Scattered Worlds is more fit to wear the name."

The Eldest's song is alive within me. And also, for the moment, is Her understanding of the Galaxy outside the Secluded Realm. From the movement of stars to the twisting of a single worm in distant, rich soil, She knows the meaning of all. And that knowledge is mine.

"Grigor, your followers think that you have found what you search for . . . that you have transcended this world and moved on to the next level of existence."

He nods. "So they preach. So I agreed they should believe."

"The movement you started shall become the greatest and most powerful religion ever known to your people."

"That, too, was planned. I have left writings and programs that chart the course of my church for as many generations as I can foresee through the Forever Dreams. I have named all the Grand Primates for the next six centuries. My followers know what to do, and with the help of the *kedankat* discipline they will succeed. Only this way can we bring enlightenment to the greatest number."

"You have helped your people shed the legacy of their great winter and move forward into a new season of growth. Perhaps you have given them the means to take a few more steps on the path to true racial maturity. You have won for your people the respect of the Scattered Worlds."

"This is all true. But irrelevant. I am an old man. All my friends are dead, I am nearly at the end of life myself. Before it ends, I must know . . . I must know that it all matters. That there was a reason, to do all the things I have done."

"No one knows the reasons, friend. We strive, because that is our place in the Universal Song."

"Why?"

WHY, INDEED? ATTEND, LITTLE ONES. HEAR MY STORY:

Red, gold and orange beneath the starbright sky of Paka Tel, the Elders are decided . . .

The Animal Races, sprung from the oceans of their various worlds and nurtured by the Hlutr, have passed Hlutr understanding. The Daamin, Coruma and Evellan have discovered space travel, and with it have invented war. The universe is on the brink of a new type of order. The Gathered Worlds will never be the same . . .

"Sapling, you are the vanguard of the new Hlutr. Seventy times seventy generations have gone into your making. You will live longer, grow larger, and sing more strongly than we your teachers. Honor us always, Little One."

Barely able to understand this song, the little sapling shivers in the gentle wind that presages dawn. "What shall I do, Elders?"

"We cannot tell you, Little One. You must see what we cannot, sing the melodies that we cannot imagine."

Another voice breathes quiet peace, stills the quavering music of the frightened seedling. "Look to the night, Little One. Look beyond the stars, beyond the worlds we know. Out in the dark, where the gulfs are great and the soil bare of life."

"Where, Teacher?"

"In the Scattered Worlds is your destiny. There, perhaps you may right the mistakes we have made."

"Grow, Little One. Grow strong and sing heartily to the stars. All too soon, your time will come . . ."

Green and brown beneath the billion stars of Paka Tel; from the valleys of Messilinia to the islands of Daarsa, and even upon the high mountains of Verkorra; the Elders debate.

"The Seven Races are united in the Pylistroph," sings one of Messilinia. "Never before has there been such harmony in the Universal Song."

"Yet all races are still immature," argues one from crystalline Brennis. "Only the Hlutr and the Talebba, who do not share the passions of animal flesh, can see the danger of unbridled expansion."

"The animal races have sent their ships throughout the Gathered Worlds, sailing upon the light of the stars. Some carry Hlutr spores and seeds; thus we benefit from this exploration. But growth must be slow, supervised. I fear that the Coruma have gone too far."

The one of Messilinia answers in strong Inner Voice: "You are wrong, Teacher. The Coruma will send their Seed Vessels into the Scattered Worlds, thus bringing life to those dead planets. They should have the blessing of the Hlutr in this endeavor."

From Paka Tel's verdant plains, one who was once a timid seedling sings a firm and powerful song. With her is the memory of the teachers she has long outlived. "It is not the Hlutr way to let Little Ones grow without benefit of our guidance." She flexes her great limbs, touches the beasts around her with the strength of a song she has never sung before. "Let them send their seed vessels. But let the Hlutr go with them. We will send our spores into the void of night, to be driven by the light of the massed suns of the Gathered Worlds." She feels the warmth of sunlight on her leaves, but shivers for the eternal cold of the black night. "When the seed vessels arrive and the animal races begin to grow on strange orbs, they will find the Hlutr there to greet them."

Assent spreads through the communion of the Hlutr. "This is the will of the Elders; so it shall be done."

On Paka Tel, the sapling sings a satisfied melody to herself and the happy, quiet stars.

In the latter days of the Pylistroph, there is no debate of the Elders. The Council of the Wise—a few beings from

*each of the Seven Races—makes all decisions. And the
Wise enforce their decisions with their great war machines.*

*On Paka Tel, one whose memory spans the long history
of the Pylistroph consults with those few she trusts: the
Senior of the Daamin race, the Warders of the Talebba
. . . and the ever-growing multitudes of the Hlutr of the
Scattered Worlds. From one edge of the Galaxy to the
other, her song beats in the minds of those who bother to
listen:*

"The Wise have grown foolish, friends, and times are
dark. The noble aims of the Pylistroph are perverted. Life
has become regimented, and the Universal Song diminished."

"What are we to do, Elder? The Wise are powerful,
their legions numerous. And to fight is not our way." The
Senior bows her head, turning away from her Forever
Dreams to face the present with fear-filled eyes.

The Hlut of Paka Tel remembers the words of her first
teachers, and trembles. "Long have I known this time
would come, Ashli Sicne, but loathe am I to give the
counsel I must."

"Say what you will, Elder."

She sings, and replies come back to her from all the
scattered Hlutr kindred. And she knows that it is time to
do what she must. "The future of life is no longer in the
Gathered Worlds. We must leave our beloved billion stars
behind, and go into the night of the Scattered Worlds.
There, mayhap, will we find peace."

Shock and disbelief echo from the minds around her.
"In the Scattered Worlds there is naught but primitive
life. No culture, save that which we bring with us."

"Would you have us abandon our homes, the very worlds
upon which our people developed?"

"Do as you wish." She closes her leaves, bidding farewell to the bright night of her home. "The Hlutr have
made their choice."

The Senior nods. "Then those of the Daamin who still
love life and freedom, who still seek a better future, shall
come with you."

*   *   *

This was the Schism of the Hlutr, when the race itself was split asunder like a tree struck by lightning. And about the Gathered Worlds, we erected the Curtain of the Hlutr. For many millions of years it served to contain the so-called Wise and their successors.

Now there are not Seven Races, but seventy times seventy thousand. Each goes its own way, and the Hlutr can but try to guide all in the direction of maturity.

The struggle has been long and tiresome, with many setbacks. Empires rise and fall; the cultures of the Gathered Worlds attempt conquest and are beaten back—and each time the cycle repeats, we lose a little of our progress.

And here in the Secluded Realm, we keep the old ways, sing the old melodies for those who are not too busy, or too foolish, to listen . . .

I shiver, although it is warm here in the eternal afternoon of the Secluded Realm. Grigor Haentil shakes himself, as if waking from a dream; his furred companion sleeps on at his feet.

"Do you see, friend? The Eldest is no God. I am sorry, but there are no answers for you here. Perhaps there is no answer. Perhaps what you seek cannot be found."

NO, LITTLE ONE.

Grigor Haentil raises his head toward me . . . but I know he addresses the Eldest. "Enlighten me, Eldest."

"I, too, need enlightenment," I sing within.

YOUR TASK IS FINISHED, GRIGOR. YOU HAVE CHANGED THE COURSE OF YOUR RACE'S HISTORY. NOW YOU WILL HAVE A DESERVED REST.

"But *why?*"

THE STRUGGLE, GRIGOR—THE STRUGGLE IS THE ANSWER. EACH OF US DOES OUR BEST . . . AND WHEN DONE, GOES ON TO THAT REST WHICH NOW BECKONS YOU. REST CONTENTEDLY, LITTLE ONE, FOR YOU HAVE SERVED WELL.

A revelation fills my inner song, and I strain to fit it into unfamiliar and confining language. "You came looking for God, Grigor, so that you could be blessed and gain release from your life's struggle. Only *you* can give that blessing, friend. Release yourself, and be happy in a job well done."

There is no need now for Lorecanist *kedankat* or the Forever Dreams. True harmony sings from Grigor Haentil's mind, and I know he has found peace.

He looks to the sky, then back at me. "And what," he whispers, "of the Eldest?"

YOU HAVE GROWN BEYOND ME, MY FRIEND. THREE BILLION YEARS, AND STILL I CANNOT FOLLOW WHERE YOU LEAD. MY TASK IS NOT DONE, GRIGOR. GO, NOW, AND TAKE YOUR REST.

The remainder is but an echo on the wind, a dream: *Mayhap, one day, I will follow . . .*

Joy crests, and for just an instant I glimpse a song whose perfection I have never begun to imagine.

Farewell, little pilgrim. Thank you for this lesson.

The dog mourns for a time, but eventually I am able to turn its mind away from its loss, and it goes off to find another master.

Later in the eternal afternoon, I call a work crew and instruct them to erect a monument. There is no need to carve a name upon it.

The Eldest knows . . .

INTERLUDE 6

An old proverb of the Scattered Worlds said "See Nephestal before you die—for until then, you have not truly lived."

It wasn't quite that easy. Nephestal's planetary defenses were legendary. Any of the nonhuman Free Peoples could visit the planet without trouble . . . but politeness dictated that any Human tourist should have some kind of official sponsor.

Kev, of course, had a ready-made sponsor: his friend Dar, now a full-fledged member of the brotherhood of Galactic Riders. Dar had been urging Kev to come to Nephestal since he got his piloting license; only now, after six years of advanced schooling on Credix, Escen and Sedante, did he feel prepared to accept the invitation.

Kev wasn't disappointed. Dar had to drag him away from the Museum of Worlds in order to eat.

"Are other races treated this well?" Kev's temporary apartment in the Visitors' Quarter was spacious and full-featured; the meal was spectacular and the strawberry pie a delight.

"Yes," Dar answered. "The Llala-pili are in charge of cuisine on Nephestal, and they don't believe in doing things halfway. The food-synth for Humans comes from Haussner's Ramatiad restaurant on New Sardinia."

In the end, Kev spent three tendays on Nephestal. Just

before he left, Dar gave him a hug and said, "I've registered you with the defense network—from now on you're welcome here whether or not I'm around. Don't wait for an invitation."

"I won't. Thanks, Dar. It's been good seeing you."

"You too. Take care." They kissed, then Kev boarded his ship, a regular shuttle from the ancient Avethellan world Nantilla.

In five days he was back on Amny, filled with stories of all the things he'd seen.

He was happy to see the family again. Mama Tiponya seemed shorter and fatter than ever; Mama Cho was much less intimidating than he remembered her. Even Great-Grandma Aponi came out of her room to see him; her eyes sparkled as she talked about her own volunteer work on Nephestal over a century ago.

Kev helped Mama Cho argue with the farm machinery and Father Nnamdi with the robot cleaning staff, just like old times—but there was a difference. At twenty-two standard years (thirty-six short Amny years) he was no longer a kid, and the family didn't treat him like one. Father Alekos made it clear that Kev was welcome to stay as long as he wanted, as a guest or a junior member of the family.

"Thank you, sir. I think I'm going to go to Deletia to help with the First Empire dig. When that's over, maybe I'll have a little better idea what I want to do."

"Nevertheless, you always have a home here. Remember that."

"I'll remember."

He had one task to take care of before departing. In the bright summer late-afternoon, he mounted the old ladder and climbed up to his treehouse.

On Nephestal he had stood within a forest of Hlutr, listening to their soundless, profound music—it was even more delightful to him than the melody of the famous Singing Crystals. Now, sitting within the branches of the treehouse tree, he tried to recall that music.

I bring you greetings, he tried to sing, from your fellow Hlutr on Nephestal.

He didn't know if the message got through; there was

no reply but the swish of leaves. Finally, with a sigh he turned to go . . . and once again the old music blossomed within his mind.

Smiling, Kev settled to the platform and fell into a dream . . .

PART SEVEN:

Ambassador

The throne chamber here on Terra-Prime is thrice the height of a mature Hlut and the length and breadth of a small forest. It was built that large as a gesture of respect, that a Hlutr ambassador might grow comfortably here. Yet in all that vast space, I have no trouble hearing Emperor Demattar's bellow: "Damn it, they're at it again!"

I broke soil on Amny, ten thousand human years and thirteen kiloparsecs distant. I am the third Hlut from that world to be uprooted and taken to a Human capital. The first was my brother, the Traveller; the second was my sister, who followed in his wake as Hlutr ambassador to New York. And now I stand on this brand-new world in the fourth century of the Second Terran Empire, intermediary between my folk and the children of vanished Terra.

I have worked with each of the seventeen Emperors, from Rowena I to Demattar t'Kalis the First—and the blustery, quick-tempered present wearer of the Tortile Crown is by far my favorite yet. He does his people proud; and unwittingly, he does *Humans* proud as well.

The Metrinaire are as old a race as Humans, though perhaps a bit less advanced in culture and technology. Their first spaceflights came twenty-five centuries after their distant cousins of Earth had left their own world, and it wasn't until two centuries later that the Metrinaire discovered the tachyon drive.

It is rare in the history of the Scattered Worlds that two animal races have coincided so well, and many of the Council of the Free Peoples predicted serious rivalry when the two met. Indeed there were skirmishes, but for the most part Metrinaire and Human became fast friends. During the Long Winter of Humanity, when the fortunes of Mankind were at the lowest, the co-operative Metrinal Union retained its culture and its optimism.

Now, nearly seventy times seventy years later, the Second Terran Empire rules thirty thousand worlds and twenty-five trillion sapient beings: and it is a Metrinaire, not a Human, who stands at the axis of that great Galactic state.

These children have done well for themselves, indeed.

Yet not all Humans are pleased.

Emperor Demattar and I are alone in the throne chamber, so I assume his outburst is meant for me. I am not as skilled as the Elders, so a watchful Human computer translates my First Language color-changes into Imperial speech: "Who is at *what*, your Majesty?"

"Those madmen in Fulmeni. Look." He gestures with the leftmost of his three arms and a holographic image occurs, a dozen times life-size and horrifying in its reality.

Twice seventy Metrinaire and Humans stand together, some holding tightly to others, some defiantly alone. All wear prominent green crescents—the symbol of the Metrinal Union.

A cold voice says, "Tried and convicted of high treason against the most sacred Empire, your lives are forfeit. May the gods forgive you." Then, as one, the poor wretches lurch and fall like a whole forest struck down at once by bolts from the sky.

"Thus," says the voice, "is the fate of all traitors."

Demattar gestures, and the hologram fades to nothing.

"Well?" he demands.

"I felt their deaths on the waves of the Inner Voice this morning. I thought nothing of it. Certainly I was not aware that they were executed."

"Executed? Murdered! For no crime other than being Metrinaire, or Human friends of Metrinaire. For speaking with a Metrinaire accent, for having grown up on worlds of the Metrinal Union. For being different, in a way that offends the sensibilities of the so-called 'patriots' of Fulmeni." With a disgusted wave, the Emperor turns toward the throne. "Patriots who want only to see my dynasty toppled and my people destroyed."

"All wear the green crescent?"

He nods. "The proud symbol of our civilization for over five millennia—now become a mark of damnation."

Demattar snarls. "I don't know how you put up with us at all." He settles on the throne, which has been altered to fit the large hips and three legs of the Metrinaire. "No other race has problems like this Party for Purity."

"Your folk and the Humans have come far, friend. Some of my brothers and sisters have argued that both your races are hopeless, but I know better." I wait a moment, but it is never safe to remain silent very long around Demattar. Before he can start another rage, I say, "Why can you not simply outlaw this Party for Purity? You are Sovereign of Fulmeni."

"Yes, and Credixian Imperator, Duke of Geled, Hegemon of Escen and the whole endless list. I *have* outlawed the Puritists. But they have the sympathy of the population, and they act under cover." He sighs deeply. "For all their talk of punishing traitors, they hate my folk and they want my dynasty off the throne."

Demattar touches the throne, and the haunting music of his people fills the chamber. "I suppose this makes Imperials seem like barbarians to you."

"Hate is an emotion known to us, Demattar. We have seen it destroy other races. At least some among you deny its power."

"My advisors want me to take military action. Admiral Altamira and Navii Imperiale stand ready for the mission; but I don't want a bloodbath. I'll be damned if I'll start the first war in three and a half centuries."

"Your enemies would only use a war to hasten your downfall, your Majesty. Yours is not a position I envy, friend."

Demattar nods. "Summon the Cabinet," he says. In

only a few moments, it is done: from hidden doorways, the Imperial Cabinet converges.

Metrinaire may rule the Empire; but there are only a hundred billion of them to twenty-four trillion Humans, so it is not surprising that the Children of Terra overwhelm the Cabinet. Counting myself, the Emperor has nine trusted advisors—five are Human. The Consort, of course, is Metrinaire; I am a Hlut; Nulli Secundus is the Imperial computer. And Santa Vina represents the Aakad da'Estra, whose true race and form is known only to the Elders, the Wise Ones of the Free Peoples and the Elder Gods.

Nine stand in the chamber with Demattar and I, for Prince Calinteb attends this session as well.

"What do you wish, my Lord?" Nilapta k'Marish, Imperial Consort, is a poet and philosopher such as her folk have only rarely produced; it argues well for Demattar that he never makes a major decision without her advice.

"The Puritists have gone too far. Something must be done."

Tsheila Altamira bows, the braid on her uniform glinting in the sun. "Give me the word, Majesty, and we shall sweep over Fulmeni and avenge the folk who have so unfairly died."

"No, Admiral. That is not the way. Paal?"

Paal Larmant turns unseeing eyes toward the Emperor. He is the Grand Primate's Legate, yet he is also a Prelate of Circe Mater and quite adept in the practice of Lorecanism. His mind sings with the peculiar song of *kedankat*, the Human Forever Dream by which a mind is cast adrift in time. "Your Highness, the Church is doing what it can. These beasts . . . these who call themselves the Party of Purity . . . do not heed my ministers."

"Chen of Chen?"

"Demattar, the Puritists have sympathizers in Konfederum Galacta. Many have their own reasons for seeing your dynasty toppled. I cannot promise you much support."

"What you have given me so far is enough, old friend." He raises his eyes to the cloaked figure who sits passive beneath my trunk. "Santa Vina, can you not offer me any aid? These madmen are set on destroying all Metrinaire and their sympathizers. On the thousand planets of Fulmeni, millions are marked with the green crescent. All those millions are subject to instant arrest, torture, even death. Yet my hands are tied politically."

"Would that I could help, Emperor. Short of overwhelming force, or mind control, the Aakad da'Estra can do nothing for you."

"Nulli Secundus?"

The great computer's voice whispers like gentle breeze through the chamber. "I have dispatched agents to infiltrate the Puritist ranks. They are more extensive than I dreamed. And they gain converts daily. To destroy their sympathizers is to destroy one-third of Fulmeni's people."

"And when they're strong enough, they'll kill all my people." With desparation keening in his mental song, Demattar turns to me. "Ambassador, once again we must plead for Hlutr aid. You are on all our worlds. You can calm the minds that sing of hatred, and bring peace to this suffering land."

Brothers and sisters, would that I could give him what he wants. These Little Ones have come so far, both Human and Metrinaire—the clear notes of true enlightenment sing in their minds, and I do not wish to see them fail now.

But I cannot.

"Demattar, the Elders have spoken. This is not the Death, when your folk have no hope but Hlutr intervention. This is not the Long Winter, when Hlutr song helped keep your spirits alive. This is the time of the Second Terran Empire, when you Little Ones are at the height of your greatness."

"But you've changed Humans *and* my people. You've spent eight thousand years changing us. You have the power . . ."

"We give you the opportunity; in eight thousand years we have watched you change yourselves, and encouraged you when we could." I shiver, for the will of the Elders is cold. "I said before that we have watched races destroy themselves with hatred such as breeds in Fulmeni—and with great sadness, we would watch *you* destroy yourselves, if that is your way. Then we would mourn you forever."

Santa Vina laughs. "Bleak comfort from the Hlutr." In her mind she sings to me alone, *Yet you are right. They must do it for themselves. Otherwise they will not grow.*

Bleak comfort, I answer her.

Nilapta lowers her head. "My Lord and my love, there is but one way to stop this bloodshed."

"Which is?"

"Resign. Give the Puritists what they want: a Human Emperor to rule over Humans alone. Our people can withdraw to our own planets."

Before Demattar can answer, Chen of Chen speaks. "No, my Queen. Not only would the Puritists win, but they would take your action as a mandate to keep killing Metrinaire and their friends. Soon, none would be safe. You and your family would be the first targets, and everyone in this room would follow quickly."

"Wait." Paal Larmant stands, his eyes clearing as he emerges from *kedankat.* "I have six hundred thousand Alphitates and ministers in Fulmeni. Tsheila, how many Naval officers?"

She blinks. "Eighty thousand on regular duty."

"Nulli Secundus, how many Civil Service Competents presently in Fulmeni?"

"Sixty-two thousand four hundred nineteen."

Paal nods at the others. "Chen of Chen?"

"Perhaps thirty thousand in the Zone owe allegiance to House Chen."

"Between us, then, we command the loyalties of nearly eight hundred thousand in Fulmeni, and billions throughout the Empire." Paal glances at a newly-arrived servbot, which produces for him a scrap of green velvet. "Suppose all those billions wear this?" Two folds, and then Legate Paal Larmant wears the green crescent which is the sign of the Metrinal Union. "Suppose the Grand Primate of the Church dons it, and the Supreme Admiral, and half the Noble Families in Konfederum Galacta?"

Prince Calinteb laughs. "Within a tenday the whole

Empire would be wearing the crescent. It would lose its menace."

His Majesty nods. "And the Puritists will become objects of laughter."

"Their organization will lose its strength, its converts— then Nulli Secundus's agents would be able to track down the leaders and eliminate them, one by one."

Demattar looks up into my leaves. "Well, Ambassador, what do you think of our solution?"

I let him feel the waves of joy that sing within me. "You may not solve the problem . . . but you will keep it from destroying you until time solves it for you. Demattar t'Kalis, you may be remembered as the greatest Emperor of them all."

I doubt that, says Santa Vina.

I, too. Greater ones will surely come. But Demattar has done his job well, and now at least Humans and Metrinaire have a future again.

Aye. Whatever they make of it . . .

The throne chamber is thrice the height of a mature Hlut and the length and breadth of a small forest, and I stand alone in its empty immensity. Yet I am *not* alone, for the song of the Hlutr always surrounds me. And, occasionally, there is the laughter of my Little Ones.

They will have their future, and make of it what they will. For now, I and the Elders are content. Their laughter is enough.

Whatever tomorrow may bring.

INTERLUDE 7

Kev and Dar insisted that the ceremony be held on Amny, and the others didn't object. It was a beautiful world, and close enough to Credix that it was convenient for everyone.

Robots had been at work for a tenday, making a clearing in the forest into a chapel. As the sun rose on the last morning, its warm golden light opened ten thousand brilliant blossoms and soft music echoed through the glen. Kev looked over the site with approval, then shook hands with Dar. "Looks great, kid. I can't believe the day is actually here."

"It's here."

Elyene smiled, her eyes reflecting all the colors of the flowers. "It's been long enough coming. I think you three still don't realize that Miai and I have been courting you for more than three whole years."

Tim, perched on a fallen log with a terminal unrolled next to him, laughed. "Give *us* some credit too. Remember, Dar is the one who first popped the question."

"After Miai spent a whole night convincing him."

"I hope she doesn't mind staying at home," Kev said. After all, *someone* had to keep Mama Tiponya calm . . . and Miai was the calmest person he knew. She had to be, to balance Tim's manic moods and his own enthusiastic days-long work sessions.

Elyene stretched. "I think I'll get back to help her. Kev, Dar, it's great of your folks to let us stay here. *My* parents love me and everything, but they've made it obvious that they really don't want anybody else living in the settlement with them."

"Well, Amny's a nice central location . . . and there's plenty of room in the valley." Kev chuckled. "Of course, I doubt we'll be home often. It was hard enough to get us all together today for the wedding."

Tim shut down his terminal and hopped off the log. "I'll go back with you, Elyene. I have to call my fathers and make sure they're on the way."

"And I ought to check in with my folks," Dar said. "Are you coming, Kev?"

"I'll be along in a while."

"Okay. See you."

When the others were gone, Kev took a seat on Tim's log and surveyed the clearing. Everything was right, better than he had expected: some robots were setting out floating tables of food and drink, others had built up a platform where Dar's Galactic Rider friends would sing. And above lesser trees rose the multicolored leaves of Kev's treehouse tree.

He closed his eyes, listening. There was soft, ancient Human music . . . and under it, a song yet softer and more ancient. On this happiest day of Kev's life, the forest and the Hlutr were singing joy for him.

He sighed. It had been a long time—nearly twenty standard years—since he first heard the music of the Hlutr; still it had the power to return him to those careless days of eternal summer.

Dream, Little One.

PART EIGHT:

Explorers

The glorious Song of the Hlutr is but a faraway murmur, all but lost in the empty vastness that surrounds us. The Human-built artificial sun pains my sister, and it hurts my leaves as well. And there is no sapient life here, no higher order than simple mosses and blind worms. *That*, my friends, is the worst thing to bear—for the Universal Song is life, and without life there is only sterile silence.

My sister reminds me:

[We agreed to come.]

And so we did. Thus were we torn from the sweet soil of Kell, thus do we stand in the lofty mid-decks of *Virgo Mariner*, a vessel whose name will be legend for all time.

Thus are we come a million times seventy lightyears, to a dead galaxy once home to a splendid and cultured race. Thus are we here, to feel a civilization's ruin.

It is the fault of Little Ones that we are here. Of the Council of Free Peoples of the Scattered Worlds, who approved and encouraged the participation of half-seventy Free Folk in this journey—including we two Hlutr.

The fault of Humans and Metrinaire, who built this vessel as large as a city and sent her out into gulfs no one has crossed for thrice-seventy million Human years.

The fault of one Human: our Captain, the young historian Mal Arin, whose scholarship, curiosity and intellect have brought him fame throughout the Scattered Worlds, though his Human years number just half seventy.

What some of the Elders whisper is true: there is no end to Human arrogance.

[Arrogance indeed. Yet a strange arrogance, which brings along the greatest scholars of the Empire and the Scattered worlds. A rare arrogance, and one for which we should be grateful.]

How so, Sister?

[Since long before you or I broke soil, the Elders and the Free Peoples have wondered of the fate of the Virgo Culture. Once they filled a whole cluster of galaxies; their civilization was older by far than our own. Once the Hlutr could harmonize with a distant echo of the lifesong of these folks; yet for twenty million years and more they have been but a memory in the Scattered Worlds. Only the humans, only our arrogant Captain, found the courage to pursue that mystery.]

Of us two, I am a bit older . . . but my sister is accorded wiser by the Elders, and so I listen to her. For now.

We grew together on lush Kell, she and I, until our trunks touched and merged, and our substance became united. These millennia of our little lives, we have spoken to one another not through the First or Second Language, nor through the Inner Voice; our thoughts are joined like our bodies, and not even the wisest of the Wise can tell where one ends and the other begins.

Our Captain addresses his crew. Clever Human machines carry his voice and image throughout our great ship.

Mal Arin is tall for a Human, over two meters: his limbs are narrow, his fingers and toes delicate and gentle. In his mind is the song of ocean deeps: at surface his thoughts move from one topic to another as the wind, but under that surface are fathomless chasms wherein dwell strange and unexpected creatures. Mal Arin's inner song is among the strongest we have heard in Humans.

He speaks in Coruman, the ancient tongue of the Pylistroph which is the language of science and culture in the Scattered Worlds. The alert machines translate his words for those who do not understand the primogenial speech.

"My friends and loyal crew, we must confer. For eighteen days we have abided here, and probed this vast galactic cloud from rim to core; and yet we find no life. You all have seen the glorious ruins of the vanished race who once were masters here: the ghostly orbiting forts, forsaken cities and the lifeless dust of planets long forlorn. Our Avethellan telepaths have scanned, and find no trace of sapient life about. The Hlutr both concur. This galaxy is barren and its folk have long since fled. The Chief Astronomer will now report."

The Chief Astronomer, a Dorascan who has spent his life studying the galaxies of what Humans call the Virgo Cluster, appears next to Mal Arin. Behind him a holographic image looks out onto a violent sky.

We are thrice seventy kiloparsecs from the great galaxy's core, just within its halo. Here there are no clouds of gas and dust to hide stars and core, as in our own Galaxy: orange-red stars fall away into a blurred nebulosity that fills a seventh of the sky. The core itself bulks larger than Kell's setting sun in the sky of our homeworld, and glows with a cold bluewhite fury that is painful for my leaves to contemplate too long. From the core stretch twin, opposing jets of white-hot plasma, while the hidden heart of the galaxy screams with the anguish of dying suns.

It is as if we look into the crown of a great tree, one whose leaves glow with the colors of autumn—and the burning jets are like a bolt of lightning that pierces the tree's heart, killing it.

They tell us that half seventy galaxies the size of our own would fit within that great tree.

[Brother, we are far from home, and I am very small and lonely.]

How must the Little Ones feel, then?

The Chief Astronomer's backfin twitches. "Before we left the Home Stars, I extensively surveyed this galaxy with the Empire's Quite Enormous Array as well as Nephestalan instruments. My team and I have seen nothing to change our conclusions: the core contains a collapsar with the mass of approximately five billion G-type stars. The plasma jets are the remains of stars torn apart by tidal forces."

"My friend, could you attempt to summarize?"

"Of course, Captain. From most of the Scattered Worlds, twenty-one million parsecs away, this galaxy is characteristically the third- or fourth-brightest X-ray source in the sky. Interstellar space in this region blazes with X-rays and harder radiation; within dozens of parsecs of the plasma jet, the radiation level is well above the lethal threshold. It is the opinion of my whole team that no civilization could survive long in this environment." The astronomer bows, then his image fades.

"A million score of years have passed and more, ere the Scattered Worlds have heard from Virgo's race. Yet our legends do confirm that Virgan folk did flee this awful place, this isle of stars which gave their race its birth, and which became nought but a site of death." Mal Arin gestures, and galaxies appear before him like stars in our own night sky.

"Within the Virgo Cluster we have mapped five thousand galaxies of every type. Our legends say the Virgans ruled them all. Their probes reached out beyond the Scattered Worlds; they trod on soil throughout our Local Group, and Avethellan exploration ships found relics of the Virgans out as far as Pavo-Indus and the Cetus Clouds." He pauses, then sighs. "With twenty million years in which to move, and fifty hundred galaxies to choose—where might the Virgans hide? How can we know?"

The telepaths—two Avethellans, both quite mad—appear. Their talent is like the Hlutr Inner Voice, but only in the way that speech is like symphony. "Good Captain, we find traces of thought far away . . . yet not as far as the Home Stars. Alien, perplexing, but thought."

"Might these perplexing thoughts be Virgan folk?"

"They might be *anything*, Honored Captain. We must needs be closer to find out."

Mal Arin nods. "My faithful crew, you've heard all arguments. Ought we within this space unhealthy bide, or should we follow telepathic tracks and seek the hidden home of Virgo's breed?"

There is no question; we have come so far already to find the Virgo Culture. Yet the Captain will have his vote, according to the custom of his people. When it is done and tabulated by the machines, no one is surprised that the crew wishes to continue.

"Telepaths and Chief Astronomer, Navigator and Drive Specialist, please gather in the starboard briefing hall. Secure for tachyon drive; we fly at once." A single smile, then Mal Arin's image vanishes.

[What do you think, Brother?]

The Elders counselled us to accompany this expedition, both to lend our abilities and for another purpose: to observe Humans in this greatest of adventures. Now we are beyond the counsel of the Elders, and I do not know what to think, Sister.

[Do you still believe that humans must be prodded along the road to racial maturity?]

How can it be otherwise, Sister? I have watched Mankind since first his ships touched fair Kell; I have lived through his First Empire, his tragic Interregnum, and the bright days of his Second Empire. I have watched him grow toward maturity—his first hesitant steps, his retreats, his great leaps forward. But still he has a long way to go. The Hlutr must do for Man what we have done for other folk, and help him along his path.

[Look at this vessel, Brother. It is a shining triumph of curiosity, of knowledge . . . and of wisdom. Man co-operates now not only with Metrinaire and Dolphin and Dog, but also with the teeming races of the Scattered Worlds, without thought of conquest or competition. He would never have done that during the foolish days of his First Empire.]

Man has changed, yes. Humanity has begun to control its own aggressiveness. Now we can accelerate that change, and bring Man to maturity in half seventy short generations.

[Change has begun, yes. The Second Empire has reached a stable population, war is a thing of the past, spiritual enlightenment has touched every human world and settlement. When other races reached this stage, we Hlutr took over their genetic development and bred them into maturity. Brother, suppose we were wrong to do so?]

You gainsay the will of the Elders?

[As you have observed, we are beyond the will of the Elders. Even in the Home Stars, the councils of the Hlutr are divided. Humans have begun to change, begun to mature—why not allow that change to proceed at its own rate, and to its own unique destination?]

And delay Man's maturity for thrice seventy generations, or more?

[Brother, have we any lack of time? You are a dozen millennia old, I am younger—are you afraid we will perish before the goal arrives? Let it take thrice seventy *times* seventy generations, and we will still witness the adulthood of Humanity.]

And those generations will suffer . . .

[Do Humans suffer now? You have sung with our Captain's Inner Voice . . . do you hear therein the chords of anguish and sadness?]

One of the cabin boys, a genetically-advanced collie pup, bounds onto the mid-decks and stands panting before us. "Great Ones, I bring greetings from the Captain. The telepaths report interference from the living minds aboard this ship. Mal Arin begs that you join your Inner Voice with the crew's minds and help us all observe some moments of mental harmony."

[You see, Brother? What did Humans know of mental harmony, in the times when we first met them?]

Some knew, Sister. Some have always known. Now as then, never enough . . .

Together, we sing the melodious, peaceful song of the Inner Voice. And one by one, each as far as his ability will carry him, the crew sing with us.

Legends of the Virgo Culture abound in the Scattered Worlds, most of them pleasant fancies with no basis in fact. One tale we *do* credit is that of Lirith and Jel Haran. She was a singer, daughter of the Scattered Worlds; he was a great warrior from the Virgo Culture. Their love and their heroic deeds have inspired the folk of the Scattered Worlds for twenty million Human years.

We believe this tale because the Eldest, who was there, assures us of its veracity. Lirith spoke little and Jel Haran even less—but their words are all preserved on Nephestal and in the memory banks of our ship.

The pair returned to Jel Haran's native galaxy in the Virgo Cluster, and remained there for a long while. Tales give precious few details, but they agree that Jel Haran's homeworld was in a great ring of stars.

We have found that ring.

For ten Human days and across two and a half million parsecs, we have followed telepathic traces of sapience. Now we are come to an astonishing object: a single galaxy that is not a spiral nor ellipse, nor even an irregular cloud. Instead, it is a bright ring of starlight surrounding a small, hot core. A few wispy plumes trail inward, the ghostly spokes of a celestial wheel.

Our telepaths are certain: the Virgans are there.

The Chief Astronomer is suddenly very popular. Mal Arin schedules him for a number of lectures here on the mid-decks where the whole crew can gather to listen.

"Ring galaxies are uncommon, but not unheard of. This was once a normal spiral," he says, waving his limbs around a holographic projection of the strange object. "Do you see the small irregular galaxy fifty kiloparsecs to the south? Three hundred million years ago it collided dead-center with the Ring—the gravitational fields did the rest. In another hundred megayears the damage will be undone, and the Ring will have regained its spiral structure."

"I can't help but imagine, Doctor na-Pekah, that this sounds like a rather catastrophic event." This is Osteva Rul, a young Human woman who is the expedition's leading geneticist. My sister and I have tried talking shop with her, but our methods, our scope and our vocabularies are so different that we cannot communicate.

"Catastrophic? Only to the galaxy as a whole. Remember that galaxies are mostly empty space, even in their cores. To be sure, turbulence in gas and dust clouds gave birth to many new stars, so the Ring is brighter than a usual galaxy its age . . . but in time those stars spread out. I assure you, in a billion years the Ring will seem a perfectly ordinary spiral."

"Scant comfort," says one of the Iaranori, "except to the Hlutr."

"Not even to *us*," my sister quips. "None on this vessel need worry about living another ten million centuries."

"So where are the Virgans?"

The astronomer briefly lowers his nictitating membranes, the equivalent of a Human shrug. "The telepaths are at work on it. Certainly we find none of the traditional evidence of sapient life: no patterned neutrino emissions, no flashes of Cerenkov radiation, no large engineering projects—"

"Unless you count the Ring itself."

Doctor na-Pekah projects a brief note of psychic unease, then shakes his head. "The possibility has been considered. Nonetheless, the telepaths offer our best hope of finding Virgans. When they succeed, you will know as soon as I."

And the Hlutr will know sooner.

Even now my sister and I sing in mental concert with the two Avethellan telepaths, the Kreen, and the few Humans who show any sensitivity to the Inner Voice.

Somewhere in this galaxy, there is life. Its song pervades space, utterly unmistakable, a slow symphony of deep wisdom and quiet joy. But where are they?

Mal Arin makes an announcement. "Galactic Riders, please prepare your ships. The exploration teams shall each include a telepathic sensitive as well as empaths and a Hlutr operative. The Chief Astronomer will designate three members of his team to go along."

This is the sort of problem which animal races find irresistible: to locate something that is missing. We Hlutr would bide our time, learning more and finally communicating with the Virgans; but animals do not have our patience.

Virgo Mariner's crew includes three Galactic Riders: members of the age-old Scattered Worlds brotherhood who have dedicated themselves to serving the cause of universal harmony. Their star vessels, products of Nephestal's finest shipwrights, are the fastest, most maneuverable and most loyal available in our Galaxy.

• Also aboard are three brain-damaged Humans who have an extraordinary sensitivity to the Inner Voice; these creatures are intended to serve as hosts for Hlutr minds. My sister and I are practiced at animating operatives, and it is the work of but a moment to transfer a part of our awareness to each sleeping Human body.

The exploration ships are launched, and for five Human days we weave among the stars of the Ring galaxy, searching for Virgo's lost race. Everywhere we find their ruins: great space-cities, now dark and frozen; huge tracts of arable land planted with wild vegetation that shows the remnant of cultivated patterns; once-terraformed moons leaking the last of their atmospheres into space. In some areas there are indications of vast battles, shattering catastrophes and long-ago upheavals of land and water. Other spots are completely undamaged, as if waiting for the return of their masters.

Everywhere we go, there is much to learn . . . yet we pass on, allowing computers to gather what information they can during brief fly-bys and even briefer landings. If we do not find the Virgans, we can come back to study the treasures they left behind; for now our task is to locate the living beings themselves.

It is the Human Galactic Rider, a man called Fadil Tormity, who finally finds the Virgans' hiding place . . . although he is aided by one of the Avethellan telepaths, Doctor na-Pekah and an operative whom my sister controls. Even as the Captain gives the order to move *Virgo Mariner* into the planetary system, though, we wonder at what we have found.

The planet—which Tormity names "Metaneira"—is the second of its system, and somewhat larger and more massive than Terra-Prime or Kell. It orbits, however, a red dwarf star only five-seventieths as bright as Kell's fine sun and less than one-seventieth as massive. Metaneira's orbit is small, yet still the world takes over thirteen Human centuries to complete one swing around its sun.

Instruments, however, show that the planet is habitable; indeed, it is a bit warmer than Kell. And the chorus of happy thoughts that emanate from that cloud-wrapped globe cannot be ignored. If the Virgans still exist, they are below.

When *Virgo Mariner* and the other Galactic Riders arrive, there is some confusion; everyone wishes to be part of the first landing party. Finally the Captain decrees that the party will consist entirely of department heads, and that it will travel on Fadil Tormity's ship *Mary Ellen Carter*.

Twenty-three crewmembers—including the Captain and his current romantic companion, geneticist Osteva Rul—take their places in the ship. My sister and I, of course, share the senses of our operative. During descent to Metaneira, our seat-mate is a female Human biologist named Tila Zakodny: a woman of advanced age, whose scientific career has been like the steady shine of a constant star. She has twice been awarded the Imperial Science Medal, and holds the Teresa Hoister Chair of Biology at Akademii de Savoire.

Tila Zakodny is also sensitive to the Inner Voice, and has great appreciation of Hlutr biology and sociology. Through both her gentle studies and her fair friendship, she has won the approval of the Elders. We sang with Zakodny on the voyage to Virgo, and we have grown fond of her.

Since her inner song is ripped with tension, I attempt to draw her into conversation. "What do you expect to find below, Madame Zakodny?"

"I frankly don't know. I wish the xenopologists had had more time to examine Virgan ruins. We don't even know what kind of beings to expect: animal, vegetable, mineral . . . or something completely beyond our experience." Her thoughts are calming. "Jel Haran is the only Virgan on record as having visited the Scattered Worlds—and as far as we can tell, *he* was mostly cyborg with only a little organic tissue left." She smiles, appreciating history's joke on herself and her colleagues. "I don't suppose their mental patterns tell you anything?"

"They are sapient, their metabolic rate is roughly equivalent to your own, and their mental song is . . . disciplined and strong. I cannot tell anything else about them."

"I imagine we'll know soon enough."

"Yes, friend Zakodny. That we will."

The forests of Metaneira are among the most lovely in the entire Universal Song. They cover two-thirds of the land with a living carpet of simple-minded trees who sing not only with the Inner Voice but also with sound, so that every breeze wafts a gentle harmony through the warm air.

We ground in a large clearing atop a squat hill; Fadil Tormity's landing is so gentle that it does not snap even the smallest branch. Each of us steps out of the ship, then we stand together, transfixed by the music and the rich earthy smells of a brand-new world.

"Where do we find the Virgans?" whispers the geneticist, Osteva Rul.

"They," a telepath answers, "will find us."

My sister and I are content to stand, feeling the infinite subtlety of alien soil beneath and around bare feet, hearing the eternal pulse of life's inner song beat around us. After the long journey in *Virgo Mariner*'s hold, it is a relief once again to see real sunlight and feel unfettered wind. If only, I think, my sister and I could root ourselves here! Metaneira is a completely unfamiliar world, with an ecology and biosphere totally strange to us; it would take a forest of Hlutr and Human millennia to come to an understanding and appreciation of the planet's myriad subtleties.

The longer we stand, the more we see. These soaring trees, these thick vines and airy filaments that stretch between them, the just-glimpsed movement of shy creatures as in endless columned halls—all begin to resolve themselves into a greater pattern. I feel surprise and awe blossom in the minds of my companions, as one by one they come to the same realization: the forest follows some ancient pattern, interleaved ovals ranged around the hill on which we stand, as if grown on the ruins of some even more ancient architecture.

The trees sing of lost times, and just for an instant I

glimpse a great city of eons past, itself built up from structures even older.

There is movement in the forest, a quick and almost-imperceptible movement that blends with shifting shadows and the rustle of leaves; were I present in my Hlutr body I could not miss it, but it takes Human senses longer to notice the massing of dozens of strange, alien forms in the wood.

"They are arrived," whispers the telepath.

In the Scattered Worlds, the different types of life are nearly numberless: nine times seventy times itself and more. And we Hlutr are familiar with all these kinds of Little Ones. This familiarity is bred in our genes, it is sung in concert across the Galaxy, it follows us wherever we go. Even when a lifeform is unknown to us, at first sight and smell, instantly and effortlessly, we know its place in the scheme of life.

Not so on Metaneira.

The Virgans move toward us in a slow polonaise, accompanied by the hushed music of the trees, and I do not know what they are. Faintly vegetable yet animate, all dissimilar, they are a mystery to my senses. Some are like Hlutr saplings, some like the small predators of Tcherlatha, others like the Dawn People of Sebya. Most are like all these, and more.

What shape is the wind, or the stream? What form has the inexorable creep of time, or the heart of the summer storm? *These* were the Virgans . . . these and many others beside.

One of them approaches, one who perhaps is somewhat less strange than its companions. It stands before us, then speaks in perfectly accented, though slightly archaic, Coruman: "The Twilight Dancers bid fair welcome to our friends and cousins of the Scattered Worlds."

Mal Arin answers, speaker for us all. "Fair welcome bid indeed, to speak our tongue. Where hast thou learned the language of our folk?"

"A child of ours, Jel Haran, once did fly and sojourn long amid your distant stars. When briefly he returned unto his home, he told us of your ways and of your tales.

His love, fair Lirith, did instruct a few to speak your tongue, that we might understand the databanks that they had brought along."

"We are grateful for your friendship and your words—for we have traveled far through lonely space, and are refreshed by kindly fellowship."

One or two among our team are not versed in the Ancient Speech; the machines have been translating for them. A tall, slender Virgan listens, then says, "Perhaps not all among you comprehend our words. Might we invoke another tongue?"

"Our current speech is ceremonial; I fear you do not know our common tongue." Mal Arin lifts one of the small translaters. "These cast our words into Imperial."

The first Virgan reaches forth a limb, at the same time exuding a pungent scent of curiosity. "Permission to examine this device?"

The Captain hands it over instantly. Two Virgans converge on the one who holds the device, and together the three of them raise it high.

Music, which has whispered constantly in the background, rises now and for a few instants I almost feel that I am listening to the concert of the Hlutr—but listening from outside, as a Little One would, hearing the melody but missing the meaning. Before my sister and I can but grasp the barest seeds of that marvelous song, it is over.

The Virgan returns the machine to Mal Arin, then speaks in the flat tones of Human language. "If this mode of speech will make you feel more welcome, then we shall use it."

Zakodny shakes her head. "How did you do that?"

"We consulted the translater's dictionary. It contains full definitions and linguistic equivalents for the Imperial standard vocabulary, plus grammar and usage guides."

Osteva Rul, the youngest of us here, glances at her own translater. "You're trying to tell us that you absorbed over two gigabits in the space of a few seconds?"

"Child, it required but a thousandth of a second for us to read the dictionary. Fully understanding its information took far longer."

"But you did that without instruments—"

Mal Arin raises a hand, silencing her. "I'm sure we can discuss information retrieval later. First, there is much else to learn."

"Indeed." The Virgan folds in upon himself, then expands to his full size. "In your language, we call ourselves the Twilight Dancers. My own name means 'Song of the Eventide Wind.' Your vessel was detected in the central galaxy, and I received the message; so it is my happy duty to be your host. Any of my fellows can help you as well as I—but should you wish to see me directly, simply speak my name on the breeze. I will hear, and come to you." He laughs, and his laugh is the sweet taste of spring rain. "Now tell me your names, and of your interests."

We go from one to the other, and my sister and I go last. "We are the Hlutr, and we bring greetings from the Eldest of us all to Her cousins in the Great Ring of Stars." Unexpected and unbidden, a tremendous song blossoms within us, and we cast it forth on the waves of the Inner Voice. Until this moment, neither of us knew that we carried this message from the Eldest—even now we do not know exactly what it says.

The being called Song of the Eventide Wind laughs again, and answers in a song that is both like and unlike the Hlutr Inner Voice: "Brother and Sister, you gladden us, that once again we hear the song of this youth, this cousin, whom we feared lost forever."

Youth? The *Eldest*?

"I see that you are all perplexed. Osteva, so many questions beat in your mind that you cannot decide which to ask. Even my friends the Hlutr are disconcerted."

"No easy feat," mutters Fadil Tormity.

Song of the Eventide Wind shows no sign of hearing. "We have made ready to answer your questions. Will you come with us?"

Mal Arin nods.

We walk in the direction of the pale red sun, and the Twilight Dancers walk with us. They move elegantly, in great patterns whose complexity is lost on us. At first, nothing changes . . . then slowly, gently, the wind rises and stirs the trees about us.

The wind is the music, and the music is the dance. And the dance . . . the dance is that which alters the forest itself. First only a flicker on the edge of sight, a leaf changing color or the swift blossoming of a bright bloom— then a shift of limbs, a movement of roots, a slow descent of ground or the swelling of a hillock. Soon the entire forest is in flux, and the Twilight Dancers move in, out and around us as if unconscious in the progression of a stately gavotte. Only Song of the Eventide Wind remains constant, a few steps before Mal Arin.

The dance slows, the music diminishes, and the wind becomes the merest touch of breeze. And we are within a temple.

I cannot call it else. For all that we are surrounded by sky, trees and the living folk of the forest, we are within a sacred place—there can be no doubt that each of us feels the solemnity of this sudden grove.

Song of the Eventide Wind faces us, and raises his many limbs. "I must beg your indulgence for a bit of a story. When it is over, each of you may accompany some of my folk to learn more, or you may return to your vessel, or you may stay and tell us your own stories. But I think you will find these essentials interesting enough to justify your great journey."

He waves, and suddenly we are swimming in the dark of endless space. Shocked, I withdraw for an instant to my place on *Virgo Mariner's* mid-decks. All is well, the Humans' artificial sun burns bright. What occurs on Metaneira, then, is but illusion.

The dark is lit by tiny, intense points of light—we approach one of them and it swells, burning with a fierce inner fire.

"Fifteen billion years ago was the age of the quasars. Instruments have shown us a frightening hell of radiation, and few elements beyond simple hydrogen and helium; no life of our sort could have existed then. Only when the quasars cooled, becoming galaxies, would our kind of life be possible."

The bright spot fades, expands, and takes on a familiar spiral structure. From nowhere, I hear Doctor na-Pekah gasp in delight.

"Five billion years passed—the lifetimes of generations of hot blue stars—before third- and fourth-generation planetary systems formed with enough carbon, oxygen and nitrogen for the chemistry of life. Larger, more violent galaxies were favored spots."

Now the spiral became more cloudy, developing a larger nucleus and more scattered stars in the periphery. "Our home galaxy was both large and violent. Life began on our homeworld ten eons ago . . . long before most of your planets had even formed."

The galaxy expands, clouds resolve into single stars, and then a lovely yellow sun swims in crowded space before us. Around it is a tiny, dark world.

"The million dying suns in our galaxy's core drove biological evolution at a frantic pace. False starts abounded, but finally replicating molecules grew strong enough to resist destruction, while flexible enough to change. You are all familiar with the progress of simple compounds to cells to photosynthesis to oxygen-breathing life—the process which alters forever the very atmosphere of a world."

The dark planet turns the achingly beautiful blue of winter dawn. "Three billion years passed before intelligence touched my planet. In one-thousandth that time, we had left our planetary cradle."

Too fast to comprehend, impressions rush by: a strange evolution, forms part animal and part plant, strange technologies and stranger customs. Then the first leap into space, which many believe is the first note in the symphony of racial maturity.

"We were not the Twilight Dancers then . . . we were Aurora's Children, and we delighted in the wonderful universe around us. We explored our galaxy, on lovely ships that sailed the winds of space, and watched ten thousand races re-create our story. They became one with us. Together we searched nearby galaxies, eventually probed the entirety of what you call the Virgo Cluster . . . and nowhere else did we find life. There had not been enough time."

Images fade; we had never left the glade. Song of the Eventide Wind droops a little, and his voice carries the chill of almost-forgotten sadness. "We have charted two hundred thirty-seven billion galaxies in the Universe, each with potentially billions of worlds. We had not yet discovered the stardrive which moves your vessel so effortlessly through space: plainly, we could not explore each of those billions in search of fellow sapients. Any civilization we sought would be dead long before we reached it."

Osteva Rul opens her mouth, then shuts it. Again our host laughs.

"You are all ahead of me, of course. Why leave our home, when we could cast our inner senses out to find the song of life? But the distances are stupefying, the emanations of life so faint in a universe of quasars and million-sun collapsars. We would have to have delicate minds indeed. So we set about developing them, retreated into ourselves and allowed our galaxy-spanning empire to decline . . . the first of many such declines."

Sister, is what he says possible?

[The possibility is there, brother. We Hlutr have chosen a different path for our Little Ones.]

"I shan't bore you with the story of a billion years of mental evolution. Nor does it matter—for long before we reached our objective, we found life in a most unexpected place: a young dwarf spiral on the very fringes of our cluster, one we had given only cursory examination. Your own galaxy. This was six billion years ago as you count time."

Wu Plenr, who carries a store of information from the Temple of Worlds on Nephestal, and whose knowledge of Scattered Worlds history is legendary, gives a snort. "You are off by a million millennia. Sapient life did not appear on Paka Tel and Verkorra until—"

"Six billion years ago," Song of the Eventide Wind repeats. "In a lightsail ship, some eight hundred of Aurora's Children set out for your home stars."

"Seventy million lightyears? Ridiculous."

Debrettar, our quiet Iaranori Chief Engineer, nods his large round head. "Not so, my lord Wu Plenr. My own ancestors dispatched exploration vessels to other galaxies long before we found the tachyon drive. That was six hundred million years ago. Some have still not reached their destinations. I pray the Elder Gods that their crews sleep on forever, or have flown the path to eternal peace."

"I will not try to pretend that my folk endured the journey easily. They reached your galaxy only after great sacrifice, and with virtually no hope of returning to their homes. They were volunteers, and like Debrettar's people I believe they slept most of the way."

"That's still too early for sapient life in—oh."

"Exactly, Wu Plenr. We had not found sapient animals, nor the sapient plants who were to come. What we had heard was the endless, slow song of the crystalline intelligences who circle in the cold interstellar reaches of your Milky Way: the creatures you call Talebba."

I have sung with the Talebba, living so slowly that seasons race past like buzzing insects and the stars are solid bars of light in the turning sky. Their song is alien, and they do not often concern themselves with the dealings of we whom they call the Soft Ones. For Aurora's Children to have come so far, only to find the Talebba, was an ironic joke.

"I will spare you the anguish, the loneliness of those lost explorers. I am sorry, I do not know the name of the one who found a way to turn their defeat into victory. They had come to find sapient life, you see—and if they could not find it, they must needs *make* it."

I feel my sister's thought, as she carries Song of the Eventide Wind's story to its conclusion.

Stars above, no. It could not be.

But they called the Eldest a youth . . .

Do the Hlutr know?

"Our bodies were half vegetable already, and even then my folk had well-developed genetic skills. They found a world whose life had progressed to photosynthesis and beyond, where a number of plants had already blossomed in barren soil. From their own genes they gave the gift of the Inner Voice, and from the genius of desperation they gave an even greater gift: the ability to do as they had done, to alter the genetics of their world . . ."

Mal Arin is white, Osteva Rul quivers like a frightened infant, and even Zakodny reels. But none can close their eyes to the image that rises before them, the image of what Aurora's Children fashioned in the wastes of our early Galaxy.

The image of one of my ancestors. A primitive Hlut.

Metaneira's day is nearly fifty Human hours long. It is a convenient period for crew meetings, so the Captain has decreed a breakfast symposium on the mid-decks every Metaneiran morning. Not everyone attends every session; yet in the course of three tendays virtually every specialist has given some report of his discoveries.

One of our poets, a Human called LeMoine, is constructing an epic in Coruman, an epic which tells what we know of the story of the Twilight Dancers. This morning, LeMoine sings us the final verses of his work.

Song of the Eventide Wind left out much when he told us the history of his folk, and LeMoine's song skips quickly over the parts we do not know. "We cannot tell you everything that we found in this vast and glorious Universe," Song of the Eventide Wind explained, "else we would spoil your own fun." Some of the crew, I sense, would rather have had the fun spoiled.

We were told that the Virgans experienced sixteen great enlightenments, and suffered nine great collapses of their civilization. LeMoine sings of the last of these, which started eighty million years ago when the core of the central Virgan galaxy exploded, sending forth deadly bolts of dying starstuff that poisoned the whole starcloud. Leaving behind their ruins, the Virgans sought refuge on the far side of the cluster, and centered their realm in the Ring Galaxy.

The story of Jel Haran and Lirith, a long and powerful tale, is but a footnote to the ongoing decline of the Virgans. Twenty million years ago their power and majesty were far beyond anything Lirith had ever seen in the Scattered

Worlds. Five million years ago, when grand Avethell ruled our home stars, the Virgans had withdrawn to the Ring Galaxy alone.

By the time Doctor na-Pekah's people rose to their greatness and Dorasc was chief among the Scattered Worlds, the folk of Virgo had found their sixteenth enlightenment, and became the Twilight Dancers.

Abandoning most of the Ring, they moved onto a few planets of red dwarf stars—stars like Metaneira's sun, which would burn for thirty times seventy billion years. There they would stay, Song of the Eventide Wind told us, living ever slower as they pondered the Universe and dreamed of eternity.

The last notes of LeMoine's song still echo in this great chamber, when Osteva Rul steps out of the dropshaft. "Very nice," she says, "but I don't believe it for an instant."

She strides to an empty couch next to Mal Arin, stretches, and reclines. At once a Human robot glides to her side with a tray of foods. Belatedly, Osteva raises her eyes to the Captain. "Sorry I'm late. I've been in Genetics all night, testing samples."

Mal Arin smiles—and in his mind, his love for Osteva is mixed with the sort of indulgence one shows a bright child. "You're forgiven." They kiss, then Osteva bends her attention to her meal.

"Begging your pardon, Madame," LeMoine says, "But why do you say you don't believe my tale?"

"Oh, your *tale* is fine," Osteva mumbles around a sweetroll. "I just doubt that the Twilight Dancers are going to settle in and dream for the rest of infinity." She frowns. "I'm not even sure how much I trust the rest of their story."

"What do you mean?"

"We haven't been told everything. Far from it. You see, I've taken samples from the trees, the small animals, the Twilight Dancers themselves—and my instruments tell me that their biochemistry is a thousand times more complex than any we've experienced in the Milky Way."

My sister is interested; in Human language, she says, "What have you found, Little One?"

"For one thing, the Twilight Dancers don't have a single biological form as our races do. Everything—plants, animals, even the micro-organisms—are all types of what we think of as 'The Twilight Dancers.' "

"One visiting a Human world for the first time might come to the same conclusion. Life is intertwined."

"Not to *this* degree." With a studied calm, she finishes her last bite and then says, "Does anyone know that each of the Twilight Dancers can alter his own genetic structure at will?"

There is a sudden silence. Then Ximu Qin, a Daamin geneticist, rises. "I must your results see. This is unprecedented."

Osteva produces her computer, unrolls the terminal and spreads it flat on a table. Ximu Qin studies the display as Osteva taps silently on the keypad. Then she shakes her head. "The Human is right. I know not any race with this ability."

"The archives tell of none," says Wu Plenr. "Do the Hlutr know of any?"

My sister contemplates, then answers, "Some of the Aakad da'Estra have used their science to perform genetic alterations on themselves. The Dareta h'Lamoth and the Folk of the Thousand Suns could shape the development of their children to a certain extent. The Children of Lost Time, the Minstrel Fish of Jasenifora and the Grand Starwoods of Ziparque all managed species evolution by force of will. Humans, of course, have practiced gengineering on seventies upon seventies of species, including dogs and cats as well as nonsapient domestic animals and plants. The Hlutr retain the ability to alter our own genetics as well as that of other races."

Osteva dismisses all with a wave. "Pikers. I've seen a Twilight Dancer change from one form to another in the space of a tenday. That's far beyond the ability of any Scattered Worlds race."

Mal Arin nods, his inner song radiating satisfaction— with her, with himself. He drops into Coruman for a moment. "My friends and fellow seekers after truth, I counsel that we all investigate the consequences of this startling news." Then, back in Human language, he says, "During the next few symposia we'll share our results. Osteva, will you make your data available to all?"

"Of course." She touches his hand, then yawns. "I've been up all night, and I'm tired. Before I go to sleep, though, I want to submit the following for discussion: This revelation changes the nature of our mission. I propose that we establish a permanent research station on Metaneira, then send *Virgo Mariner* back to the Scattered Worlds with some of the Twilight Dancers. I know that many of my colleagues on Telorbat and Ptyra will want to study them, and I'm sure that most of you can say the same." She spreads her arms. "This is a shattering discovery. Think of what we might be able to do with such knowledge."

Osteva takes the Captain's hand. "You've been awake longer than I have. Can't you take a break?"

Mal Arin stands, and hands his rolled terminal like a wand to our second-in-command. "Kiryl, you're in charge. Genetics has top priority." Together, he and Osteva walk to the dropshaft.

Just before they step off the mid-deck, Zakodny whispers, "Suppose the Twilight Dancers don't want to come home with us?"

Her comment goes unanswered.

In the body of a Human operative, my sister and I are on Metaneira with Zakodny, Ximu Qin and Borinat t'Lemest, a Metrinaire economist who has offered his services to the biology section. We have spent the long morning studying beachfront ecology, and now are resting in warm air as we wait for Fadil Tormity to retrieve us. A few robots are in attendance, and one was thoughtful enough to bring simple food for our picnic.

"I can't support the notion," Zakodny says. "The Twilight Dancers have a history that spans eons—longer than even the Hlutr. All they want is to stay on Metaneira and live out their lives in peace. We don't have the right to drag them back to the Scattered Worlds, or to set up research stations so we can study them and learn how to exploit their abilities. They've been gracious enough to us already, giving us free run of their planet while we're here."

Borinat crosses his three legs and reclines on warm sand. "I don't think Madame Osteva has put herself in the place of our hosts. I've noticed that empathy is not her strongest quality."

"Don't blame her too much, friend. She's planet-born, remember."

"Your pardon I beg," says Ximu Qin. Somehow the short Daamin has managed to retain her dignity even though sand adheres to her fur in patches and her left leg is drenched. "I understand not what you have said."

Zakodny laughs gently. "I'm sorry, nui tarysh." She uses the Coruman honorific quite naturally. "I shouldn't have used the term without explanation."

My sister surprises me by saying, "May I attempt to explain, Madame Zakodny? Then we will know if we understand the concept as well."

"Please do."

"Ximu Qin, the Human race is really *two* races—those who were bred in space habitats and colonies, and those who were raised on planets. Only a scholar of Humanity can comprehend this distinction, of which Humans themselves are only unconsciously aware. Spacers, on average, are more civilized than the planet-born."

Zakodny frowns. "I don't know if I'd put it that strongly."

"Humans have not been the main thrust of my study. What is the purpose of such distinction?" Ximu Qin questions.

My sister answers at once, "It is a matter of evolutionary process, not of social forces. The distinction is quite simple, my friend. Small settlements in orbit are much more vulnerable than planets. Their smaller ecology and constrained sociology are much more threatened by an individual's uncontrolled aggressiveness. These individuals must either be removed or eliminated, else the settlement will fail and all will die. Humans have lived in such settlements for nearly half a thousand generations. Evolutionary change is inevitable. To a lesser degree, the Metrinaire have done the same."

"Are you saying," Zakodny asks, "That we Humans have been breeding out our own aggressiveness?"

"Not at all. Merely that *uncontrolled* aggression is vanishing from your species, as more and more of you are descended from spacers."

"I'll admit that there's a social distinction between spacers and the planet-born . . . but that's cultural, nothing more."

"How long has it been, Tila Zakodny, since Humanity's last large-scale war?"

"Two . . . no . . . three thousand years. A litte more. But the Empire . . ."

"Is a *consequence*, not a cause. Your population has remained steady at twenty-four trillion for two millennia—spacers do not reproduce with the abandon of the planet-born. Scholars among the Free Peoples estimate that your folk are now one-third spacer . . . and that fraction is increasing as more of the planet-born move to settlements."

Ximu Qin is satisfied. "We have watched this progression with other races: the Iaranori, the people of Avethell, even the Dorascans and the Kreen."

"In the terms of the Scattered Worlds, Zakodny, your people are becoming more mature."

My sister is right; for Human millennia the Hlutr have known these facts and have debated them. Still the question remains: how best to help Mankind reach true maturity? Should we accelerate the change, as we have with other races . . . or do as my sister believes, and allow it to proceed at its own rate in the hope that it will result in a different kind of maturity?

Zakodny shakes her head. "Whether or not that's true, the fact remains that the planet-born have a different culture than spacers. And that's why Osteva sometimes doesn't seem too empathetic. However, that shouldn't stop us from opposing what she wants to do to the Twilight Dancers."

"I imagine the Captain will take a vote of the crew," Borinat says.

"I'm not so sure. It would be a nova in his sky for sure, to return to Ptyra with a discovery like this. He's young yet, with his whole career resting on this voyage." Zakodny blushes and briefly turns her face away: in her swirling emotions my sister and I read deeper feelings. Mal Arin is the same age she was, when she won her first Imperial Science Medal. In our Captain, she sees herself . . . and she understands all too well the pressures that act on him. "Akademii de Savoire and the Emperor gave him full authority over the ship; maybe he'll decide that the final judgement is his."

"Then we must hope," says Borinat, "that he will judge correctly."

Just then a great wave comes far up the beach, and we all forget ourselves in laughing and scrambling for higher ground. We are barely dry when Fadil Tormity's ship appears from nowhere and makes a gentle landing on the beach near us.

The robots gather equipment, and just before we step onto the ship Ximu Qin stops for a last glance at the ocean. "Tell me," she asks, "What is Captain Mal Arin? Be he planet-born, or spacer?"

"Spacer," answers Zakodny.

"Then perhaps all will be well."

We are aboard the ship, and very gently my sister and I withdraw our presence from our operative. There is much else to do . . .

Virgo Mariner spins in polar orbit high above Metaneira, and on the mid-decks there is a council of the Free Peoples of the Scattered Worlds.

We are few: two Hlutr, three Daamin, four Iaranori, three Avethellans, sixteen Kreen and a Dorascan. The Metrinaire and dogs, subjects of the Second Terran Empire, are not strictly part of the Free Peoples, so they are excluded from our council. Fadil Tormity, as a Galactic Rider, is welcome and sits slightly apart from the others. We Hlutr have curtained the area; none will feel any desire to enter until we are done.

"Osteva Rul has spoken her intent, that we unto the Scattered Worlds return and that we bear some Twilight Dancers there." Doctor na-Pekah, who has no definite opinion on anything smaller than a large globular cluster, has agreed to act as an impartial moderator. "She wishes to establish on this globe a research station and to send her folk to study and exploit the Dancers' power. We here are met to now discuss this plan."

Tigath delv Napitsha, one of our Avethellan telepaths, speaks first. "The Peoples of the Scattered Worlds would gain in knowledge from Osteva Rul's research. Yet more than information do we win: with those abilities that the Dancers have, we may yet break the awful power of the Gathered Worlds and free our sundered brethren from that tyranny which holds them enslaved within the Galactic Core."

The Kreen speak with one voice. "We can do nought but listen and agree. The Curtain that the Hlutr once did weave around the Gathered Worlds has stood for more than twice six hundred million Human years. Only in the reign of Avethell was that fair Curtain parted for a time. The struggle to bring freedom to the Core demands that we must use what tools we can. Within the Dancers' genes is such a tool."

Wu Plenr rises, his eyes blank as he speaks from the distance of the Daamin Forever Dreams. "Not just the tyranny of Gathered Worlds is in consideration here today. The Twilight Dancers have achieved a thing which is beyond our poor imaginings. Genetics and the wisdom they have gained have led their folk to great enlightenment. If we can have their knowledge for our own, our possibilities are limitless."

I feel that I cannot listen any more, and I long to cast my mind loose on the waves of the Inner Voice, to seek the concert of souls that dance below. How arrogant these animals . . . all of whom *we* raised from nothing. Now we have found the Hlutr ancestors themselves, and all these animals can imagine is to steal the secrets of these wise ones.

My sister tempers my anger.

[Wait, brother. Listen to the others. Let the Galactic Riders speak.]

Mondappen, the ancient Iaranori who is the Scattered Worlds' most senior Galactic Rider, struggles to his feet.

His voice is faint, yet all are transfixed by its power. "All must alone by conscience guide themselves. Yet those who speak of freedom do not seem to understand the concept that they praise. The Twilight Dancers do not wish to leave the home to which at last they have retired. They chose to keep their secrets to themselves. We do not have the right to steal from them, nor to disturb their contemplative rest, no matter what potential gain we see."

"So you would have us leave at once, my friend?"

"I do not seek to make your mind for you. I beg you to recall the creed which rules Galactic Riders and Free Peoples both: Instruct and guide and cherish as ye may, but never shall Galactic Rider *force*."

I can no longer contain myself; my leaves and limbs tremble, faster than any but the Kreen can follow, and my words fill the mid-deck. At the same time, I project a sharp annoyance through the Inner Voice.

"You speak of many things beyond your ken. Do you suppose the Hlutr have not sought to build the powers that you envy so? Do you suppose your races are prepared to deal with such abilities as these? You speak of opening the Curtained Core, of seeking paths of bright enlightenment. And yet, Wu Plenr, even you do not yet comprehend the nature of these tasks. Still less our Human brothers understand. Would you bestow abilities that dwarf the Hlutr skills on Terra's wayward sons?"

My sister speaks before any other can say a word . . . and she speaks in the Human tongue which we all understand. "Mondappen is right. This decision is not ours to make. We all joined this mission agreed that Mal Arin was the final authority. *He* will decide; we can only offer counsel."

Wu Plenr stands again. "The Council of the Free will always be the final judge within the Scattered Worlds."

"My friend, we are not within the Scattered Worlds. If our Captain decides to take the Twilight Dancers hence, *then* let the Council make a judgment."

Mondappen closes his eyes. "The counsel of the Hlutr is a gift that no one wise would ever dare refuse—yet would you have us trust this matter to the judgement of a simple Human child?"

"This Human 'child,' my friends, has brought us to the Twilight Dancers when none, not even grand Avethell, dared to journey so far. Can we trust him on one matter, then withdraw our trust on the other? I propose that the Free Peoples should remain silent unless asked; that we allow Mal Arin to make up his own mind in his own time. Then if it is decided by the Council of the Free Peoples that reprisals should take place, let them."

Doctor na-Pekah raises a limb. "I ask for the consensus of the hall."

Each speaks, then, and when it is over my sister has won. The Free Peoples will wait for Mal Arin's decision.

If Mal Arin decides wrong, Sister, and the Council rules against him—we Hlutr may be asked to hurry our efforts to bring his people to maturity. Humans will be danger-ous, not only to themselves and the Free Peoples but to the Hlutr. The Eldest might agree.

[Then you will have what you want, Brother.]

You gamble much on a single man's decision.

[I gamble nothing, Brother.]

I hope you are right . . .

When Song of the Eventide Wind asked to visit *Virgo Mariner*, the Captain immediately sent Fadil Tormity to bring him up. Now he stands before my sister and I, alone on the mid-decks, and we both rejoice to meet him in the flesh for the first time.

Already we have learned more about the ecology and genetics of the Twilight Dancers than our Human friends will learn in a dozen of their years.

If they had that long.

Song of the Eventide Wind sings to us in the Inner Voice, his song pitched so that not even the Avethellan telepaths can detect it. My sister and I must strain to take meaning from his unfamiliar song. As he sings, his people sing with him, so the song is fathomless as deep space itself. Their minds have depths that even we Hlutr cannot begin to touch.

"Cousins, we know of the conflict that touches your vessel. The Human Zakodny has told us what is going on . . . and the Human Osteva has asked some of us to accompany your ship back to its home. We do not wish to do this thing."

"Our Captain must decide," my sister answers. "So we have agreed."

"We will not leave Metaneira. But if this ship does not return to its home, the Humans will send others. Even if the Humans agree to only leave a research team behind, more ships will come. We will not have our contemplation disturbed thus."

"Yet you have borne our presence this long. You opened Metaneira to us in the beginning. Surely your could have hidden so expertly that we would have concluded this galaxy lifeless."

The Twilight Dancer bows. "Indeed. We chose to let you find us. We chose to allow you onto our world. It is not fitting that you should go in ignorance of your true origins." He straightens, and his Inner Voice is like the voice of the ocean. *"Now it must stop."*

"Cousin . . . you must speak to Mal Arin. Tell him what you tell us."

"No. Gladly will we converse with you, for although you are children, your folk are the closest thing we have found to ourselves. The other races, whom you call Little Ones—they are too distant, too different. Mal Arin will perceive what we say as a threat . . . and he will answer that threat as all animals answer."

"Perhaps you misjudge him."

"Perhaps *you* do. Nevertheless, be assured that we will not hesitate to eliminate such minor irritants if they disturb us too far. We do not wish to do so, yet we will." His tone bears no menace, simply a statement of fact.

"We shall do what we can, Song of the Eventide Wind."

"Then you have our thanks. Sing with us, now, for we have not joined your folk in concert since before the Schism of the Hlutr two and a half eons ago. Soon you must go, and the distance to your home is too great for our song to cross."

We sing, then, and the music of the Twilight Dancers is far more beautiful than the vast Song of the Hlutr. It is wisdom, it is life, it is joy incarnate. While the song lasts, we are fulfilled—all our questions answered, all our dreams made real. The Twilight Dancers have conquered death and decay, have taken the very form of life into their hands and shaped it according to their will.

They are greater than Humans can begin to imagine, greater than Hlutr can hope to be. Their childhood is finally over, and now they wait on their eternal worlds circling eternal stars, taking the first steps on the road to an adulthood we can only glimpse.

The song ends, and I ache for its loss.

"Goodbye, cousins. I wish you well in your own quest for maturity."

It is a long time before my sister and I can trust ourselves to speak.

Zakodny meets with Mal Arin the next morning, on the mid-decks after the symposium is done. While robots clear away uneaten food, she fixes him with her clear, strong eyes.

"Captain, I've come to talk to you about Madame Rul's proposal."

"Sit down, Doctor."

"Please," she says. "don't be so formal. I wish you'd grace me by calling me by name."

He frowns. "I'm sorry. I . . . I just can't forget that I'm talking to a woman who has won the Imperial Science Medal twice. Your work on the populations of Tralanek L5 was stunning."

"That's a good beginning," she says with a smile.

"What do you want to say about Osteva?"

"I think she's wrong. I don't think we should exploit the Twilight Dancers. I . . . I don't think her findings should be published, and I think we should leave soon." She lowers her head. "We've learned everything we're going to on this voyage. More than we ever thought we would. Let's give up now, and go home."

"Doctor Zakodny—"

"Tila. Please."

"Tila, then. I've been wrestling with this decision. If the geneticists at Akademii de Savoire know what I refused to bring back to them, they'll have my innards on a plate."

"They don't need to know."

"Do you think Osteva will keep quiet? No, they'll know."

She considers this. "Then you'll have to go before the High Academy. Tell them *why* you made your decision. Convince them, and they'll censure Osteva. They won't approve any more expeditions."

"I went before the High Academy to convince them to give me *this* vessel. I don't know how well I'd fare against them again."

"I'll be with you. I know others of the crew who feel the same way."

"It may not come to that. Assuming that I decide to deny her proposal—and I haven't made that decision yet—Osteva knows that I could ruin her career. Maybe she'd keep quiet on her own." He sighs. "I just don't want to be forced to that."

"I know you love her."

"Then you know more than *I* do, Tila. I met Osteva when we attended seminars together at the University of Prakis. I kept in touch with her, and she was an obvious choice for geneticist when I was putting this crew together. She's brilliant, Doctor Zakodny, in her own way far more brilliant than I am."

"Don't underestimate yourself, Mal Arin. In thirty-six years you've done more than most scientists in a lifetime." She stands. "I have to get to my lab; I've left the poor computer running a population simulation, and it's probably halfway into the next eon. Think about what I said."

"I promise you, I will." He waits until she is gone, then settles back on his couch and raises his eyes to my sister and I.

"I know you've been watching, and that you're concerned. I've heard from everyone else on board—what do the Hlutr think?"

I am ready to answer, but my sister restrains me. "The

Hlutr," she says, "think that Mal Arin must make up his
own mind."

A grin. "Why do I have the feeling that more rests on
this decision than I'm aware? Wu Plenr made it sound like
a matter of cosmic importance, LeMoine keeps telling me
I'll wind up the subject of a thousand ballads, even the
cabin boy seems to think that the Twilight Dancers will
destroy the Human race if we don't leave them alone."

"If others want to make a moon out of a dust speck, my
friend, how can you stop them? They will whether you
wish it or not."

"So I should forget about whatever else hangs in the
balance, and simply decide?"

"You must do as you think best, Captain."

"I suppose so." He touches my sister's trunk, and both
of us are instantly aware of the conflict that rages within
Mal Arin.

[If he solves this dilemma, he will be much strength-
ened by the experience.]

*He is right. So much to rest on the actions of one man:
the fate of his race. Sister, can we find no better way to
make our own choice?*

[No, Brother. this is the best way.]

Quietly, Mal Arin steps into the dropshaft, and is gone.

Once every ten Nephestalan years, the Galactic Riders
hold a festival to honor their founder, Tenedden. *Virgo
Mariner*'s three Riders had made arrangements with Mal
Arin before leaving the Scattered Worlds, and now the
appointed day has come.

There is no work today. For the first time since our
arrival at Metaneira, the whole crew is aboard the ship.
The mid-decks resound with the music of the Galactic
Riders and their invited performers. For Mondappen this
day is a triumph—for his folk, like Humans, count by tens,
and this is his hundredth festival. He sings the Tale of
Tenedden in the original Iaranori language, and when he
finishes no eye is dry.

Mal Arin rises and stands before the crew. "My friends,
I ask for your attention please." He smiles for an instant.

"I hope you'll forgive me for dropping into Human speech: the announcement I'm about to make is being recorded for the folks at home and I don't want any translation problems."

In Mal Arin's mind there is no hesitation, no uncertainty. His inner song is clear and strong.

"This happy day, when we remember one of the greatest heroes of the Scattered Worlds, is an appropriate time for me to give the decision you've all been waiting for. Geneticist Osteva Rul has proposed that we set up a permanent research station on Metaneira, and that *Virgo Mariner* return to our home Galaxy so that we may tell what we've learned. Some of you support the plan, others oppose it."

He pauses for a breath, and there is no other sound. Even the song of the Twilight Dancers, which pervades space around Metaneira, seems strangely hushed. The Dancers are listening.

"I won't keep you in suspense. After much discussion and contemplation, I have decided that *Virgo Mariner* is going home. We will bear news of the Twilight Dancers— but I will ask each of you for your oath not to reveal the nature of their genetic abilities. After five billion years, these folk have earned their rest. Beside them, we are tiny, ephemeral creatures; let us go, and not disturb them further. Navigation will begin calculating flight plans. Departure will be no later than local noon tomorrow."

Mal Arin settles back onto his couch, and for a timeless instant there is silence.

[Well, Brother? He made the right decision. In the face of all pressures and all potential gain for his own people, he made a judgement worthy of a Hlut. Do you still say that this race is incapable of guiding its own development?]

"Wait!" Osteva Rul jumps to her feet, her eyes ablaze and her mental song casting angry discord toward the stars. "That's not all there is to it. You can't simply forbid us to talk, against our rights. On a matter this important, the High Academy should make the final decision, if not the Empress Herself."

Mal Arin looks toward her, and in his mind there is great weariness . . . and a touch of regret. "Appeal to them, Osteva. But I'll be there first; I and dozens from the crew. When the facts are known, I'm confident that the High Academy and the Empress will see things the same way I do."

"You . . ." She clenches her fists, and her mental song dissolves into a cacophony of discordant emotions. "You've ruined my career. Whichever way things fall, you've destroyed me."

"Enough!" His tone is sharp, carrying firmness and the unmistakable tenor of command. "With the discoveries we've made here, everyone is entitled to the Imperial Science Medal as well as a share of the glory. You can write your own ticket at any academy, university or institute in the Empire. Osteva, if your career is to be ruined, then it will be your own doing. Not mine."

Through the discord one emotion rises above all: the ugly, searing notes of hatred. Without a word, Osteva Rul turns and walks away.

Mal Arin sighs. "Well, that's done. We have many things to do before tomorrow. Mondappen, will you give us one last song?"

Mondappen sings, but I cannot keep my mind on the tale.

Sister, you see only Mal Arin; what of Osteva Rul and Humans like her? We have the ability to eliminate that branch from the Human tree—why should we restrain ourselves?

[She is planet-born, Brother. Leave humanity alone, and soon the excesses of her kind will be bred out of the Human strain. But could Mal Arin be what he is, *without* Osteva Rul? Remember, she alone of all discovered the Twilight Dancers' genetic secret. If Human evolution is allowed to proceed at its own pace, her best qualities may be preserved.]

Our brothers and sisters will heed us? They will decide as we have?

[They will listen, Brother. And we will convince them.]

Then I am agreed. We will let Humans find their own way to maturity, though it may take much longer.

I think on the Twilight Dancers, who face eternity with

patience and joy. We Hlutr can learn from these, our distant forbears.

We will wait . . .

We pause seventy kiloparsecs outside the Ring galaxy, allowing our navigators to make their final calculations and our pilots to tune the marvelous music of our engines. *Virgo Mariner* is going home.

Mal Arin stands before me, his eyes on a projection of the Ring as it appears now, a gloriously-bright loop of mist and smoke across a black sky strewn with tiny bits of light, the far-off galaxies of the Virgo Cluster. He is silent, but his inner song reveals many things: loneliness and regret, yes, but also the firm joy of *rightness*. And an echo, however faint, of the song of the Twilight Dancers.

In the last day I have come to know Mal Arin far better than ever before. Now his inner song is part of me, and mine of him. We have much in common, he and I, much that I never saw before.

"The Twilight Dancers revealed themselves to us, you know," he says suddenly.

"What do you mean?"

"With their abilities, they could have stayed hidden. But they let us find them. They let Osteva discover their genetic abilities. They set up this whole situation."

"Typical animal paranoia." But he is right. The Twilight Dancers knew we were coming, knew more about us than we know ourselves. "Why would they do such a thing?"

"I don't know. But then, I don't know everything about what's gone on. I just have a feeling that much greater decisions were made here than mine."

"I think you may be right, Mal Arin."

He is silent for a time, and both of us regard the Ring. Metaneira's sun is invisible at this distance, but its location is marked on my soul.

"We're both leaving a lot behind there," he says after a moment.

"We are, Mal Arin. My condolences on your loss."

He shrugs. "She wanted to stay. Song of the Eventide Wind promised he would take care of her. She ought to be happy—she'll never run out of things to learn." He shakes his head. "She would never be satisfied back in the Empire. There's nothing for her to go back to. On Metaneira she can achieve a kind of greatness she never thought possible."

The Ring trembles, just a little, as our pilots make some last-minute adjustments in the engines. Mal Arin chuckles. "Besides, maybe the Twilight Dancers can teach her to forget and forgive." Then, more serious, he says, "But *you've* lost a lot too."

If I could shrug, I would. "As you say, she wanted to stay."

And yet . . . stars above, will I ever become accustomed to the strange feeling in my trunk, where skillful Dancer surgeons cut her away? Will I ever become accustomed to the silence in my mind, where once she used to speak?

"One of us must return to the Scattered Worlds, friend Mal Arin. And she . . . she needs to stay here more than I."

The Dancers sing, and carried upon their song is another Voice, one I know all too well. *Farewell, Brother. I will listen for your song.*

And I for yours, Sister.

Thank you . . .

"Ready for tachyon phase, Captain."

Mal Arin gives one last glance to the Ring. "Execute," he says.

The engines surge, their unnatural music filling space— then the Ring falls behind us, and *Virgo Mariner* is on its way home. I can still hear my sister's song, but already . . . too soon . . . her meaning grows indistinct.

There is motion on the mid-decks, and Tila Zakodny steps from the dropshaft and walks to Mal Arin's side. "I waited until we were launched. I didn't want to distract you."

"What can I do for you, Doctor Zakodny?"

"Captain, I just wanted to say that I'm grateful for your decision. Even though it cost you a lot, it was the right thing to do. I . . . thank you."

She turns to go, but he stops her with a single touch. "Doct—Tila, I couldn't have decided the way I did without you. I kept asking myself what *you* would do in my place. And in the end, there was no choice to be made."

"You flatter me."

"It's true. Every word." He reaches out, hesitant, and she takes his hand in hers. "Do you . . . that is, do you think we might spend a little more time together during the trip back?"

She smiles. "When we return to the Empire, you're going to be the most famous scientist in Akademii de Savoire's history. Do you think I'd give up a chance to monopolize your attention for the next hundred days? That is, if you want to be seen with an ancient wreck like me."

"Eighty-eight isn't old. It's I who am too young for you. I'll bet you have children older than me."

"As a matter of fact, no. I've never had any. I guess . . . I guess I've just always been too busy. And I've never found anyone that I—"

Suddenly, clumsily, they kiss. It comes as a surprise to both of them, then they smile and do it again.

Hand in hand, radiating joy, they walk into the dropshaft and are gone.

The Ring falls away behind, and I turn my thoughts and my song to the future.

INTERLUDE 8

At four tendays, Kimee was old enough. Kev carried the little body carefully, as her nanny followed nervously behind, its cradle perched to catch her should she fall.

"Leave me alone, you stupid machine," Kev said, "I know how to carry a baby." The nanny fell back a meter or so, but still it followed.

It was very warm; Kimee cried and kicked until Kev took her blanket from her. Once they were outside she stopped crying and her little blue eyes darted this way and that as if they could track on the surroundings.

When they reached Kev's glade, the nanny insistently took Kimee from him and started changing her diaper. Kev smiled. "This is where your mommies and daddies were married, little girl," he said. "I don't expect that means much to you right now. Wait until you're a little older."

Kimee gurgled and waved her tiny hands.

The nurse finished quickly; Kev lifted Kimee to his shoulder and strode to the treehouse tree.

Was he becoming more sensitive to the Inner Voice, or did the Hlut sing more distinctly with Kimee's mind to focus upon? Kev didn't know . . . but he felt a welcome and delight that was almost in words.

"I brought her for you to see," he said to the tree. "I don't know exactly why, it just seemed the right thing to do."

I welcome you and your Little One, the music seemed to say.

"I-I don't know how often I'm going to be back. We're talking about moving the family to New Sardinia. It's more convenient for Miai's concerts, and I'm just dying to organize a study of the Iglesias memory cubes. Trelin Carnodip has a theory that they contain some hints as to the location of Old Earth, and I have an idea that he may be right."

There was no reply from the tree.

Kimee cooed, reaching her little arms toward the tree. Kev brought her closer, and she giggled as she touched the bark.

Kev shrugged. "I don't know exactly why I'm here. I guess—I guess I just want to know that it's okay for me to go offplanet. I know that's stupid . . . you're a Hlut, you have important concerns on your mind. Why should you care about me?"

We care, Little One.

Kev shivered. "Why? Why me in particular? What am I to you? Is it because I can hear your music, like Chiriga Ho?"

The tree did not answer.

Kev felt silly. "Anyway, I just wanted to show Kimee to you, and to tell you that we're all going away." He waited a moment, but there was no further response. To his surprise, he was disappointed.

Silently, he turned back toward the house. The nanny spun, following him. Then, out of nowhere, music sang.

Wait, Little One. Listen . . .

Kimee quieted, and Kev sat down with her to listen.

PART NINE:

Astronomer

My midnight sky is dark and empty. The walls of the material world are so far away that they seem less than the merest hazy backdrop for vast, unrelieved blackness.

And death spins toward us, a single filament of web drifting through eternal night, closer each passing instant.

There are not many of us here; this poor world will not support a large population and we must be careful to preserve the fragile ecology we have built up over the ages. Thus, less than half seventy Hlutr are rooted world-wide, surrounded by scrub and small starving beasts. The tiny creatures of the ocean are the most successful forms of life here; without them the atmosphere would soon be unbreathable, so we preserve them at all cost.

We are not near enough one another for the colors of the First Language, and the gentle susurrus of the Second Language is drowned in rolling surf and whispering breeze. When we must communicate, we do it through the song of the Inner Voice. In truth, we do not have much opportunity to converse; sometimes we sing merely for the joy of the singing.

Who can hear us, in this void that spans three hundred fifty million parsecs? The nearest galaxy is so far away that its light departed in the last days of the Pylistroph. Our own home stars are yet more distant, and could we see them we would observe the Gathered Worlds as they were at the height of the Pylistroph, before the Schism of the Hlutr and the colonization of the Scattered Worlds.

Yes, I know of the Schism. For even though we are sundered from the Home Stars by unimaginable gulfs, still we hear tales of the galaxy we left behind.

We live very slowly, and space is quite flat here in the Void. Now and again we can hear the song of the crystalline Talebba; now and again they bring us tidings, repeated over and over again, of the doings of our brethren. We know of the Schism, and the Little Ones of the Scattered Worlds, and the tyranny of the Core.

Once we might have cared.

Four of us remain, who came to this world with the original Coruman scientific expedition. A lone star, bearing three planets, had been ripped from its home galaxy and thrown into the void. Finding it, the Coruma could not resist exploring it. We are still not sure what happened to the vessel that bore us here; it was long ago and we Hlutr do not pretend to understand the mysteries of stardrive.

We were stranded, marooned on a barren world whose few metals were buried deep in the crust and whose atmosphere was all but poison.

Many Coruma died, but in dying they gave us the genetic and biological material we needed to tame this planet. Their companions survived a few seventies of generations, and built up a rather rich culture.

Even then, we did not care. We preserved what life we could, because that is the Hlutr way. But we did not concern ourselves deeply with the doings of the Little Ones. We had come all this distance to observe, to taste a different space, to sing in endless emptiness. We did all these things, and more.

In the end, the Coruma had become a dull, savage race who bordered on sapience. Later, none of us were quite certain when the last of them died. By the time we noticed, the ruins of their city were crumbled and not even skeletons remained.

Many of my brothers and sisters at home, I know, would view my thoughts as heresy—but many would agree.

I believe that the Hlutr have no business involving themselves in the trivial doings of a billion species of Little Ones. We have given them sapience . . . let them amuse and improve themselves. If they become irritants to us, they must be removed. Some few, like the Wise of the Daamin and the sagest of the Coruma, contribute to Hlutr life and can be conversed with in an intelligent fashion. Otherwise, they are not worthy of our attention.

Now, with death approaching, I wish we had some of those Little Ones about. The youngest of us have tried to evolve sapient creatures from the sea beasts and the root-gnawers; but there is not enough time.

Before they died, the Coruma solved the puzzle of the voids. Doing so, they uncovered new and greater mysteries.

The universe, they told us, is structured like a froth of bubbles: galaxies cluster in sheets surrounding vast empty voids. No one knew why, until our vessel made its journey. Now we know the reason, and it is a splendid and beautiful one that has captivated our attention through all the ages since. Now it spells our doom.

The Coruma called it *len-anyaar*, and we know it as the Web of Space. It is a strange and wonderful condition that dates to the very earliest times, and it carries within it the memory of Creation itself.

In the very beginning, the Universe was filled with energy—a blaze of something that was neither light nor heat but as far beyond them as the Hlutr are beyond the scrub—and all forces were one. Expanding space could not stand the strain, and within a few seconds the very fabric of space changed, like water freezing into ice. That ice was our current space, filled with all the particles and waves that make up matter and energy, space and time, gravity and life . . . even the song of the Hlutr itself.

In places, however, space did *not* change. Imperfections remained, like flaws within a crystal. These are strings: some infinitely long, some loops as big as galaxies, all very different from the space we know.

I do not begin to understand all the properties of strings: great mass, enormous tension, superconductivity, oscillations at near lightspeed. I know only what the Coruman scientists concluded: shorter strings evaporated early, producing great waves of energy only slightly less than those that spawned them. This energy swept the voids clean of matter—smashed together at the boundaries, hot gas and dust gathered around larger loops of string to form first quasars, then galaxies.

String still remains, endless loops of it in the great universal voids. And now, pitching in its wild gyrations, a section is approaching our peaceful world at just less than the speed of light.

None of us know for certain what it will do: the awful tides may tear our world apart, the energy may cook us where we stand, mayhap it will simply skim by and rip our world from its orbit and we will freeze in the eternal dark. But we are certain that we shall not survive the passage of the string.

We have called, half seventy of us, across the gulfs of space—but there is no answer. An age ago we began, when first we noticed the approaching string; with each passing turn of seasons we have sung more loudly still, and with each turn there is no one to hear. The Home Stars are too far, the Talebba can do nothing but carry dim rumors of our tragedy outward.

Still we sing, singly or together, for it is not in the nature of the Hlutr to face such catastrophe with equanimity.

Now we may have an answer.

The music of a single mind is very faint, very indistinct—it must be some species we have never encountered, far from home and alone. Still, we Hlutr bend our efforts toward making contact. As one, we sing with a focus and an intensity which we have seldom experienced before.

It hears.

The reply comes not in words, not in song, but in a strange combination of both: *I don't know who you are, but I'm coming.*

My fellow Hlutr are disturbed. What, they wonder, can a single entity do to help us? Approaching string will be here in less than ten times seventy of this world's quick years; will there be time to divert it? How, they want to know, will a mere Little One be able to conceive of our danger, much less deliver us?

Why should it *want* to?

We shall see, I tell them, when it arrives.

Soon enough, it is here. A small vessel, perhaps only seventy times as massive as an adult Hlut, suddenly appears above our world. Now that stardrive distortion is gone, the pilot's mental song is clear: *Where can I set down?*

I will sing, and you may follow my music. Here I am not only Elder, but Eldest; the other Hlutr recognize my right to deal with this visitor.

Right you are. Here I come.

Wind stirs, and the scream of its approach echoes long before the vessel is actually visible in my sky. It lands, and the pilot emerges.

It is an odd creature: obviously a distant cousin to the Coruma, but also quite different. Its limbs are stubby, its face like the nightmare of a Coruman child, and its inner music altogether bizarre. Is this what the Hlutr of the Scattered Worlds have been up to all these ages?

Still, we are fortunate in the chance that has brought us a creature from the Home Stars. It might have been any lifeform from this infinite universe.

It speaks in unintelligible grunts, but its inner song conveys meaning and I know that it has practiced communicating with Hlutr.

"My name is Daavyor Lenno. You've surprised me; I didn't expect to find a colony of Hlutr this far out." Concentration whirls in its mind, replaced almost at once by clarity. "I'll bet you're from the Masgath expedition."

I have not practiced speaking with Little Ones for seven ages and more; my ragged reply is in the Inner Voice. "The Coruman who commanded our expedition was of the tribe of Masgath. How did you know that?"

"On Nephestal the Daamin have preserved all the records of the Pylistroph. When I decided to come out this way, they told me of Limat Masgath's voyage. But that was—gods above, over a billion and a half years ago. How did you survive?"

It is not seemly that a Hlut should find himself answering the demands of one of the lesser orders; but it has been long since I conversed with anyone other than my fellow Hlutr and the Talebba. I sing to this Daavyor Lenno, sing of our survival on this world, of the long ages that have passed since we left the Home Stars.

He projects sympathy and wonder. "Four of the original crew still alive, and your descendants? And you've kept this planet habitable for all that time?"

"Our task has not been easy," I agree.

"I'll say." He looks up to the dark sky. "You're a long way from anywhere, you know that? Something tremendous must have ripped this planetary system out of its galaxy long time ago. You're zipping along at better than four percent of lightspeed." He laughs. "At this rate you'll be through the void in ten billion years."

"We will not, Daavyor Lenno. Soon we will meet doom." I sing to him of the approaching string, of death that comes out of the midnight black.

"String? Really?" He peers into space. "That's nasty stuff. You'd better get out of here."

"Would that we could, friend. However, we have no vessels and no way to summon help." When first this creature answered our summons, I felt hope—but now that has faded as the light of sunset fades. "And your ship is too small to carry even one of us."

"Ah, there's more power in that ship than you suspect. She carries a million metric tons of antimatter, and her engines can move small asteroids." He laughs. "I need that power, to zip around out here."

"Can you return home and get help from your folk?"

His thoughts turn somber. "Now, that might not be as easy as you'd think. Oh, I'm sure they have the technology to move your planet—we might not be as advanced as during the Second Empire, but we still have a few tricks up our sleeve. I'm just . . . er . . . not too sure that they want to see me again back in the Home Stars."

"I do not understand."

"See, the Council of the Free Peoples is helping us reduce our population gradually, without too much upset in the economy. It's not easy to dismantle an Empire of thirty thousand planets, you know. Our ancestors did some pretty strange things. I think we've made great progress, too: we're down to about two trillion in a little less than a thousand years."

"The Hlutr allowed your people to breed to such numbers? Madness!" Under the Pylistroph, we did not allow animals to overpopulate so drastically.

"Yeah, well, there have been a few political changes since you left, I understand."

"Yes, of course. What has this to do with your return to the Home Stars?"

"I was just getting to that. See, there's a lot of opportunities in the Milky Way. A shrewd trader can turn a profit in a dozen different ways." His mental song is filled with rueful amusement. "I guess I carried a cargo or two that I shouldn't have. My big mistake was landing on BDA Tr ska. I managed to . . . er . . . relieve a Tr skan Knight Economic of his holdings, and then I didn't leave quickly enough."

"I do not understand."

"It was an honest mistake. But the Assembly of Knights didn't view it that way. The Council of Free Peoples of the Scattered Worlds agreed with them."

"I do not understand what you are telling me."

"They . . . asked that I leave the Galaxy. They also . . . er . . . requested that I not return. Under pain of death."

"You are a criminal."

"Not really. They found out that I've traded with the Gathered Worlds. Purely accidental, I assure you: I didn't know that the Core was behind my buyer. Besides, the weapons weren't that good." His Inner Voice shivers. "The Council wanted to execute me. If it hadn't been for the Hlutr, I'd be dead. Your cousins argued for leniency, and eventually they settled on exile."

"So you cannot return to your folk."

"They let me keep my ship. And gave me all the information they had on extragalactic journeys." His thoughts become contemplative. "I've seen things that they can't even imagine. Galaxies bisected by rings of stars, habitable worlds sharing the same orbit, a giant planet whose clouds match the continents of Fulmeni Prime—and a million others. It hasn't been that bad, really."

His words are brave, but the song from his mind contradicts them. Loneliness runs deep, the loneliness of a social animal deprived of others of its race. Wonders he has seen, yes, but deep within Daavyor Lenno is tired of wonders, weary of wandering. Whatever his crime, the punishment is too extreme.

"So you cannot return to your home?"

"No, I'm afraid not. Even if I did, they wouldn't listen to me." For a moment he is subdued. Then his inner song brightens. "But what are we moping around for? You said there are less than thirty-five Hlutr on this planet? Hells, my ship has enough power to take you all to safety."

"But it is not large enough for even *one* Hlut."

He waves a limb. "No problem. I'll just zip to the outskirts of your system and bring back a small planetoid. My antigravs will tow it, and I have enough power to extend the tachyon field and defense screens to cover a couple of cubic kilometers. You might be a little crowded, but otherwise it'll be a comfy ride."

Depart our home? Leave this lovely world, this light in the void, never to return? Say farewell forever to the glorious balance of her ecology, the beauty of her sky?

"The alternative," Daavyor Lenno says, "is to die here. Do you want that?"

The answer is obvious, but I am loath to give music to it. Would there were another way.

"You'll see, it'll be over before you know."

"Our song goes with you, Daavyor Lenno."

"Thanks. I'll need it." Daavyor Lenno's mind has acquired a strange opacity; we Hlutr are not skilled in technical matters, and I suppose his thoughts of tachyon fields and power generators are blocking his song. He takes a deep breath of the chill midnight air, then re-enters his ship. "You might get your fellow Hlutr ready to depart; digging them up is going to be something of a shock. I'm glad I have a full complement of robots."

Without another word, he is gone.

Together, all the Hlutr of this world watch his progress. He is so close, and his mind so strong, that we have no difficulty singing with him.

Daavyor has no trouble locating a suitable planetoid; many thousands of them accompany our sun, and a few have even collided with our world in the past. He reports that he has the planetoid in tow, and we expect him to turn back to our world—but his song departs, and after a moment there is the distortion of the stardrive.

"Wait, Daavyor Lenno. What are you doing? You must return."

"Don't worry," comes his answer. "I'm just going to dash out and take a closer look at that loop of cosmic string. We won't have time later. It's only a quarter of a megaparsec. I'll be back before you know it."

I turn my senses to the midnight sky. The string is distant, but I know its location—it is like a sour note in the Universal Song, a minor discord that will keep growing over the time to come. I wish you well, Daavyor Lenno, in seeing this mysterious stuff from the beginning of time.

The night wears on, and our world turns its slow way through space. Dawn is far away, as Daavyor Lenno counts time; now that I am living at his rate I am reluctant to slow my metabolism again. Let this one night pass slowly.

Sooner than I expect, I hear from Daavyor Lenno again. His mental song is terribly distorted, and I find that I must live more slowly just to grasp his meaning.

"I hope you'll get this. I've come out of tachyon phase on the far side of the length of string. Now I'm building up my velocity—I'm at 99.8% of lightspeed now, and I'm hoping to shave at least another tenth of a percent off that. When I'm going fast enough, I'll drop the planetoid and go back into tachyon phase."

"Daavyor Lenno, what are you doing?"

"You'll see. This string is weird stuff. I tried throwing some small rocks at it—they went right through, but tidal effects cut them in half. The string wasn't damaged at all."

"There is no way to destroy it. String is the fossilized remnant of the Universe as it was in the first few seconds after Creation. You cannot break it, nor can you deflect it from its course."

"We'll see about that. Ninety-nine point nine five . . . my antigravs are starting to feel the strain. I'm just twenty light-minutes out from it. I'm going to release the planetoid now."

"I do not know why you are doing this . . . but our thoughts are with you."

Now his song returns to normal. "Well, that was easy. The planetoid will hit in just over twenty minutes. Now you'll have to excuse me for a minute, I have to get rid of this vector and accelerate in the opposite direction."

In all the ages we Hlutr have abided here, I have found nothing as difficult to comprehend as this strange creature. His presence is somehow refreshing.

It is not long before Daavyor Lenno calls. Once again his song is distorted, far slower than its usual rate. "There, that's done."

"You alter your metabolic rate, Daavyor Lenno. I did not know your species could do that."

"It's relativistic, not biological. Oh, never mind. I'm in the groove—I have my ship pointed toward the string at 99.9% lightspeed plus change. If my computer has done its work, we'll hit at the same time the asteroid impacts."

"What are you doing? If you destroy your ship, how will we leave this world?"

Feigned amusement covers fear. "With any luck, that won't be necessary. I'm going to let loose my fuel reserves at the instant we hit. When that much antimatter and matter meet at these speeds, there's got to be some big explosion."

"You will destroy yourself for nothing! String cannot be broken. So the Coruma scientists assured us, a billion and a half years ago."

"So maybe we've learned a thing or two since then."

"Return and take us off this world."

"Don't give me that. You don't want to leave . . . none of you do. We'd never find you another planet this far away from everything. And after all this time in the Void, you'd never be happy in a galaxy. Well, maybe I can give you what you want."

"You are a fool, Daavyor Lenno."

"So maybe I am. I'm a fool who's sick of being lonely. The Hlutr gave me life, back home; at least this way maybe I can balance accounts."

"You owe us nothing."

Astonishment fills his Inner Song. "We owe you *every-thing*. The Hlutr brought life to Earth, you created humans. You've saved us again and again from destruction. You've guided us toward maturity. Gods know, this is little enough payment." His song tenses. "Computer says impact is approaching. I just regret that the folks at home will never know—"

We cannot see the impact. Light is far too slow. But the waves of the Inner Voice are much faster, and they tell us all.

I do not know if this is what Daavyor Lenno expected, but it suffices. There is a burst of energy, as far beyond light and heat as the Hlutr are beyond the scrub.

What happens when that much energy is confined in such a small space, I will leave to the physicists and engineers of Daavyor Lenno's folk. To those of us who watch, it is clear: for an instant, conditions duplicate the energy levels of Creation itself.

Just as ice can be melted and re-frozen, the fabric of space itself can be returned to its primal state, then allowed to jump back to the reality we know.

And in the process, all defects are healed.

Where Daavyor Lenno died, there is a sudden gap in the loop.

String cannot have endpoints, and now, marvelously, the entire loop—as large as seventy times seventy planetary systems—unravels, dissolves, gives up its hidden energies and becomes as normal space.

Daavyor Lenno has plucked an infinite string . . . and the music is—the song of Creation itself.

Light, heat, gas. In instants, the history of the Universe is replayed on a minor scale. Eddies form, condensations, hot spots that may one day become stars with planets of their own. Someday, like a great vine strung across heaven itself, there will be a loop of worlds here in eternal night.

And we . . . we will be here, to bring life to those brand-new worlds.

I just regret, he said, *that the folks at home will never know.* Never know of his deeds? They will, Daavyor Lenno. The Talebba will carry the tale, and eventually it shall reach the Home Stars. All will know, my friend, that you are a hero.

Never know . . . that Little Ones can save the lives of Hlutr? That your folk, whoever they are, can be as selfless and compassionate as we who consider ourselves so far beyond you? That tale, too, will make its slow way to the Home Stars. If my distant brethren have misjudged your people, Daavyor, they will know.

Or did he mean that they will never know . . . how sorry he was, for the things he had done?

They will know, Daavyor. I pledge to you.

They will know.

INTERLUDE 9

It was a beautiful night, clear and cold under a black sky strewn with stars by the thousands. Until he went to New Sardinia, Kev had never known how much he treasured the starry sky of Amny.

They buried Great-Grandma Aponi in the old family cemetery, amid the heather that she loved and the birds she had always enjoyed so much. Everyone cried, but Mama Tiponya most of all. Still, it was a good funeral and a splendid wake.

Mama Cho was the one who comforted him most. She took him aside, looked up into his eyes and said, "She wanted you to know how proud she was of you. On Election Day morning she voted as soon as she could, then spent the rest of the day asking if the returns were in. It was almost as if she wouldn't let herself die until she knew the outcome." Mama Cho touched Kev's cheek tenderly. "When she found out that you won, she just smiled. The poor thing was too weak to talk, but she tapped on her terminal how happy she was. And then the next morning, she was gone."

Afterwards Kev made his way back over the hill, where his own house was waiting patiently for him, tended by robots and just as spotless as the day he'd last seen it. A robot had met him at the door with, "Greetings, Assemblyman Mathis."

Assemblyman. How odd it sounded. Kev supposed he would grow used to it over the next ten years.

The house was too lonely. Without Dar and Tim, Elyene and Miai, he just couldn't stand the silence. It was well past local midnight when he crawled out of his sleep cocoon stepped out into the cool darkness.

In no time at all, he stood beneath the treehouse tree. He stopped for a moment before Immanuel's grave, then stood looking up at stars framed by rustling leaves. Then with a great sigh he started up the old ladder.

The sixth rung was still loose; he'd never managed to remember the glue. He had to crouch to enter the treehouse. It was all so much smaller than he remembered.

One thing had not changed: the almost-soundless beat of whispering music that touched his soul.

"I'm an Assemblyman now," he said. "I didn't really think I'd win, historians seldom do. But the voters thought I can do the job, I guess."

No response. What did the Assembly of Humanity mean to the Hlutr? Just another group of animals sitting around chittering to one another.

Never that, Little One.

"Great-Grandma Aponi died. We buried her today. I think . . . I think she might be the one I got it from, my ability to understand your music." He shrugged. "I guess you can't tell me that, if you even know."

Sit down, friend.

Kev sat. "Another story?"

The Hlut's laugh was like a breath of floral fragrance. *You know me too well, Little One.*

Kev laughed too, then leaned back against the tree. Under a thousand stars, music swelled within his soul, and he fell into the dream once again.

PART TEN:

Biologist

Now Humans have gone too far.

It begins with the barest echoes of the Inner Voice; with a melody that is at once like Hlut-song, and yet terribly unlike. Few among us hear it, and fewer grasp the awful implications of that song.

Oddly, it is Humans themselves who alert us.

For Human millennia I have stood in the fair soil of Nephestal, not far from the Assembly Hall where meets the Council of the Free Peoples of the Scattered Worlds. My brothers and sisters stand behind me in their seventies, the greatest forest of my folk outside the Secluded Realm. Beyond the Assembly Hall stands the Temple of All Worlds, and beyond that the Singing Crystals. Here at the apex of the Scattered Worlds, we have stood for time uncounted; the first of us came as seedlings when the Daamin made this world their own after the Schism and their great migration.

The sons and daughters of forgotten Terra are seen more frequently here in the three and a half millennia since their Second (and last) Empire dissolved; as Galactic Riders, as volunteers in the schools and the temples, as performers in our theatre and concert halls—and most of all as tourists, craning at the Singing Crystals, kissing in the Lovers' Grove where Jel Haran and Lirith first plighted their troth, and swarming into the Temple of All Worlds to

gaze at the artifacts and precious treasures of their culture
on display for all to appreciate.

Still, it is seldom that we see Humans even on the edge
of our Forest, more seldom still that a group of them
approaches accompanied by three high officials of the Council. They stop beneath me in a pleasant grove that the
Daamin have constructed for visitors, and wait for me to
acknowledge their presence.

"Greetings, friends," I say after an interval that is short
even as Humans count time.

A single woman seems to be chief of the Humans; she
steps forward and bows. "I am Bandaranaike Thovold, and
I speak for the Assembly of Humanity." Mankind, like
most other races nearing maturity, has given up his childish experiments at "government"—yet still structure and
order are necessary. The Assembly, which meets on ancient New Sardinia, speaks for the billion-or-so Humans
who inhabit a few dozen worlds and countless settlements
in the Scattered Worlds.

"Welcome, Bandaranaike Thovold." I recognize the three
with her, but not any of her Human companions. "Welcome, my friends of the Council."

They nod in answer, and Clombortau Nor'Piqenn, an
overly-friendly giant lizard from Marpethal, wags his tail
with such intensity that the ground quivers.

"How may I serve you, Bandaranaike Thovold?"

"I will get right to the point, Elder. We feel that a
Human scientist is conducting dangerous research, and we
have come to the Council of the Free Peoples for advice
and aid. These three honored ones have agreed to investigate the matter with us. Friend Arhineal delv Trespidaan
here advised that we seek your opinion."

"What is the nature of this research?"

"Biological, Elder. Lately some strange creatures have
appeared, one at a time, in various Human settlements.
We do not recognize these creatures, and at least one
seemed particularly susceptible to Human diseases." She
shrugs. "Lacking knowledge, we are nonetheless disturbed
to see something which mimics our biochemistry. When
we communicated with the scientist involved, we were

told to mind our own business. Further communications have been refused."

"I do not know how the Hlutr may help you in this matter."

Sinlath Trnas, a Daamin scholar of Humans, raises her eyes toward me. "Elder, we have brought a specimen of the unknown lifeform. Will you grant us the courtesy of examining it?"

"Let it be brought here."

Sinlath Trnas gives an order, and in only a moment the strange beast is here, carried in a web of insubstantial forces projected by a tiny Daamin device floating above it. Suddenly the web collapses, and the creature stands before me, exhausted and frightened.

It is perhaps one-quarter the height of an adult Human, and it bears the same general shape. At first sight, I think it is one of their monkeys. Then the cool breeze of Nephestal brings me scent of its tissues, and I start at a taste so familiar and yet so unexpected.

Whimpering, it moves away . . . and the grove is filled with song, with the same freakish melody which has echoed through the stars of late on the waves of the Inner Voice.

My brothers and sisters speak to me in the First Language, sing to me in the Inner Voice, cry out with the sounds of the Second Language—all voicing their outrage, their disgust at what has appeared in our midst.

Sinlath Trnas acts quickly, and the beast is once more trussed. The Humans huddle together, frightened; even Clombortau Nor'Piqenn is still.

I sigh. "You know the scientist who has created this beast?"

Bandaranaike Thovold nods, but does not speak.

"What he has done is forbidden. We will go to him, and we will judge him."

Finally she finds her voice. "We?"

"I will join the panel of judgment; together the four of us will judge this scientist in accord with the laws and customs of the Free Peoples."

"Elder," Sinlath Trnas says, "*you* will accompany us in your own flesh?"

"It is not unheard of. Call a vessel, and summon a work crew. I will be uprooted by evening."

A drastic step, yes . . . but this time the Humans have gone too far. My brothers and sisters cry out for punishment, even for death—and I cannot blame them.

"What prompts this act, Elder? What has this Human scientist discovered?"

"You will know, my honored friends, when we arrive and I can confirm our suspicions. I ask your patience until that time."

I will go to this Human place, and I will be the senses of the Hlutr race. Then a decision will be made, and action will be taken.

Thus is the Hlutr way.

I am rooted in an artificial ecosystem: a huge, mobile device that simulates the soil, air and lifeforms of my Nephestalan wood. This pocket ecology is aboard a large star-vessel of Human manufacture; this vessel approaches the Human world of Phuctra.

Some few Hlutr live on Phuctra's inhospitable swampy surface, directing the course of life on a planet whose oceans are a salty, poisonous soup and whose air pressure is ten times that of Nephestal. They greet me, concerned with my mission but distracted by the constant struggle for existence.

Around Phuctra stretches the Ring, an inhabited loop of metal and plastic that glows with the light of a million captive stars. The Ring has expanded in the fifteen thousand years since its construction during the Human First Empire, but it is largely deserted now; a few thousand men and women live here, where once ten billion Humans thrived. If nothing else, Mankind has done well in bringing his numbers down to reasonable levels.

"The Human scientist is here?" I ask.

Clombortau Nor'Piqenn bleats an answer in the subtle language of Marpethtal: "One can only admire them. Where best to conduct possibly-dangerous biological experiments? If anything goes wrong, the scientist can evacuate his laboratory and open it to vacuum and radiation. Few organisms could withstand that treatment."

"Hlutr spores could," I say, leaving Clombortau to wonder.

We come closer, and I am suddenly aware of the same dissonant near-Hlutr song that I heard on Nephestal . . . but stronger, far stronger. The source is somewhere nearby.

"Who is this scientist?" Arhineal delv Trespidaan asks.

Bandaranaike answers at once, "His name is Saburo Imhotep. He's the son of Gregor Mendel Watson, a brilliant geneticist who left the University of Credix a few decades ago."

"Does Saburo Imhotep know we are coming?"

"He has been informed; we have received no answer from him." Bandaranaike's mind seethes with resentment, and also with a touch of anxiety. What terrible thing, she wonders, has this scientist done, that causes a Hlut to lift himself from the soil of his native world?

She will learn soon enough.

We approach the Ring, and in a terrifying instant of whirling, contradictory motions our vessel effortlessly mates with that great structure.

Arhineal delv Trespidaan raises an obvious question. "What if Doctor Imhotep doesn't receive us?"

"Don't worry," answers Bandaranaike. "We can force our way in."

Clombortau Nor'Piqenn pulls himself to his full height, which is nearly half my own. "I do not think we will have much trouble on that score," he says with a laugh.

"My robots can take care of anything," says Bandaranaike. "Wait here, and I will return with Imhotep."

We do not wait long. Bandaranaike returns in minutes, followed by a tall, pale Human male.

Indignantly, Saburo Imhotep says, "I understand that you want to talk to me about my research. What gives you the right—"

His eyes find my trunk, follow it upward, and then he stops abruptly.

"You speak of right?" All my life I have communicated with the lower orders in their own languages; it is simplicity for me to produce the raucous sounds of the Human tongue. "What gives *you* the right, Saburo Imhotep, to use what you have taken in defiance of the will of the Hlutr?"

"I might have known," he mutters. Then, hands on hips, he faces me with defiance singing in his Inner Voice. "The same thing that gives you Hlutr the right to direct the evolution of other lifeforms: I have the ability."

Bandaranaike stamps her foot. "*Someone*," she commands, "had better explain what's going on here."

Saburo Imhotep answers at once, "The Hlutr are upset because of my father's work—which I am continuing. It seems that we're using Hlutr genetic material without their permission."

"What you are doing is worse than casual use of genetic material. Your products and investigations are an insult to the Hlutr race, and a threat to the well-being of all the Scattered Worlds."

Clombortau Nor'Piqenn laughs. "One of you is right, one is wrong. A pretty dilemma, to decide which."

"With due respect, Elder," Bandaranaike says, "I must ask Doctor Imhotep to explain himself. Afterwards I will give you a chance to express your opinion." She takes my silence for assent, and gestures to Imhotep. "Well, Doctor?"

"I don't suppose any of you know the origin of the Human mitochondria? No, I didn't think so. Mitochondria are the structures within Human cells responsible for energy production. We can't live without them. The interesting thing is that our mitochondria are really independent organisms. They have their own genetic material, and they reproduce independently of the cells they inhabit."

"How can such a thing be possible?" asks Arhineal delv Trespidaan, with a feeling of repugnance.

"Billions of years ago the ancestors of mitochondria swam into the ancestors of Terran animal cells. They liked the environment, and became symbionts. Since then they've been passed down through the ovum, with perhaps a few contributed by the remnants of the sperm cell, for millions of generations."

"What does that have to do with—?"

"Everything, my dear Bandaranaike. Don't suppose for an instant that the mitochondria are the *only* such symbionts we know of. If you go back far enough, many structures in Human cells were independent. Chloroplasts are analogous symbionts in plant cells. The Metrinaire are *collections* of symbiotic organisms. Other races have similar structures."

"So Humans," chuckles Clombortau. "Despite your traditions, are not individuals at all. Each of you is a colony."

"The folk of Marpethtal are in the same boat, my friend."

"While this is fascinating, Doctor, it doesn't begin to explain—"

"Of course it does. Do you imagine that the Hlutr don't have their own little symbionts, hiding within their cells where they think we can never find them?"

I can stay quiet no longer. "You have said enough, Doctor Imhotep."

"Not nearly." He bows to the Free Peoples. "I assume you will want to fully understand this matter, before reaching a decision?"

Sinlath Trnas speaks for the three of them. "Continue, Doctor."

"Haven't you ever wondered about the Hlutr Inner Voice? You, honored daughter of Avethell: your folk have produced the most skilled telepaths of the Scattered Worlds, yet they do not comprehend the Inner Voice. Some individuals hear it, others do not; and nothing we can do seems to change that."

"And you think that some symbiont in Hlutr cells is responsible?"

"My father isolated the symbiont two decades ago. It is the sole source of the Hlutr Inner Song. Mutated versions of the organism live in the cells of some of us . . . but in vastly differing populations. Thus some hear the Inner Voice better than others."

"So what you've done is to inject these symbionts into the cells of your test animals? You've made creatures that can sing the Inner Voice as well as the Hlutr?"

He dismisses Bandaranaike's guess with a wave of his

hand. "Of course not. Unaltered, the symbiont will not survive outside Hlutr cells."

"No," I say. "What you have done is far more of a travesty."

"I've only done what the Hlutr could have done three billion years ago, if they'd wanted." He sighs. "Every form of life can evolve—but these cellular symbionts, perfectly adapted for what to them is an unchanging, beneficent environment, there is little evolutionary pressure. My father and I have simply removed them from their native environment and bred them into independent lifeforms again."

Bandaranaike shakes her head. "I'm afraid I don't understand. These monkey-things that you've made, they're grown from Hlutr cellular symbionts?"

"Not quite. My father took the symbionts to the stage of free-living organisms—something like algae or molds. After he . . . after he died, I merged the symbionts' genetic material with Human DNA. The result is a hybrid: what you call 'these monkey-things.' But I assure you, their biochemistry is vastly different from yours or mine." He shrugs. "In effect, I've created a new form of life. One that has full ability to use the Inner Voice."

"And this is the source of the strange music we Hlutr have been hearing lately."

"All right, Elder, I've kept you waiting long enough. Why do the Hlutr oppose Doctor Imhotep's research?"

"It is an abomination. Animals braying in the Inner Voice—already his creatures disturb the flow of Hlutr song throughout the Scattered Worlds. When there are more of them, their noise will drown out our song entirely."

"I'm sure that ways can be found to insulate—"

"Regardless, it is abomination. What Imhotep has done is the ultimate invasion of our being. What if the Hlutr reached within you and pulled out these mitochondria, made them into independent creatures? Even into your competitors?"

"Ah," says Imhotep. "Here's the real issue, isn't it? The Hlutr don't want any competition. That's why they've always discouraged advances in genetics. I wouldn't be surprised to find that part of the Hlutr song is an attempt to inhibit the study of genetics by other races."

"Imhotep, you know not what you embark upon. Will you control your own creation? Have you the power to deal with their lusts, their aggression, their murderous hates and their uncontrolled pain? Given the force of the Inner Voice, these things will destroy you . . . and in time, can destroy the whole of the Scattered Worlds."

The song of the Hlutr is strong around me. From the Secluded Realm to Nephestal, from Amny to Inse, from the plains of Avethell to the lonely mountains of Kree, my brothers and sisters sing with a unanimity seldom matched in our history.

Imhotep has gone too far.

WAIT, sings a Voice I have heard only in dreams: the Voice of the Eldest of us all.

Imhotep smiles. "I think you'd all better come with me. I have something to show you. Bandaranaike, if you'll take your ship to the cargo port I will point out, there will be room for both the Marpethtalan and the Hlut to follow."

The ship moves, while my mind seethes. This is a matter for the Hlutr race alone; I should never have agreed to involve the Council of the Free Peoples. However, one must move carefully when dealing with animals, even of the most mature races; having asked their advice, I cannot ignore it until it is given.

Then . . . the will of the Hlutr will be done.

Imhotep has done something whch is forbidden by the Hlutr, forbidden since long before we left fair Paka Tel: he has meddled with the tiny symbionts which give us the Inner Voice. Such meddling must be corrected.

We dock, and Bandaranaike opens the great cargo doors. We move slowly forward, and as we pass into the Ring I feel the Hlutr song fade around me. There is interference such as only great distance or great turmoil can create. Another mutation of the symbiont? Imhotep piles abomination atop abomination, sin atop sin.

We enter a new world.

My brothers and sisters have told me of the worlds that Humans create in their space settlements, but until now I did not believe it possible that a construct of metal and plastic could taste like a real planet. However, Imhotep has created such a world here, in a hollow only a few kilometers wide. There is soil, and water and air scented with the smell of life. There is gravity, light and warmth, and my roots itch to bury themselves in this rich ground, to experience this place and make it mine own.

There is song . . .

"Imhotep, what have you *done?*"

"Look around, damn you. You see what I've done. You, of all creatures in this Galaxy . . . you should see what I've done."

We stand at the top of a small rise, and my height lifts me far above the landscape. In a valley below us there are structures, small huts woven from leaves and fronds. Among them sit the monkey-creatures, these travesties that Imhotep has created by an unnatural fusion of genetic material. Some monkey-things move, some cuddle small ones, some merely sit.

All of them . . . sing . . .

As if one discovers a beloved symphony suddenly played on unknown instruments, so I hear the music that I love, the music of the Hlutr, carried by twice-seventy new and unsuspected voices, sung in an unprecedented key. I cannot help but answer; and in answering, I am drawn immediately into their world, I am become one with them.

The experience of beauty is one that I have not faced for half a lifetime: even the lovely vistas of Nephestal and the brilliant stars of night have become overly familiar to me. Now I hear beauty, now I experience something that is a rare delight for my people. Now I make contact with sapient minds that are the equal of my own, the equal of my brothers and sisters.

"You see?" Imhotep says.

"Will someone *please* tell me what's going on?"

"Do you want to tell her, Elder?"

I am ashamed, suddenly, of the things I have said to him, of the judgments I made before I knew reality. "You tell her, friend. Tell them all."

"I knew the Hlutr would be against it, so I had to keep

up my screen during the early stages of my experiments. Some of the first trials escaped; I'm sure that's what you found."

Sinlath Trnas is far ahead of him. "I did not think Human genetics was this advanced."

"My father was a genius. And I have access to Phuctra's Ragnarok Eight Thousand computer—the biggest and fastest model that the Second Empire ever produced."

Frustration explodes in Bandaranaike's mind. "What have you done?"

At last Imhotep takes pity on her, and on the other two who also have not realized the truth. "The Elder was right, of course. No one could control the emotions of dumb animals, especially when amplified through the Inner Voice. The solution was simple to enunciate, and it took two decades of computer time to find."

"What?"

"I had to make the monkey-things into a fully mature, sapient species from the very beginning. I doubt that they're really successful in evolutionary terms—they don't have much ambition or aggression. But they have some interesting ideas about the meaning of life."

"Do not be so sure that these folk are unsuccessful, Saburo Imhotep. They may outlast us all."

He smiles, and in his own rudimentary Inner Voice I sense the satisfaction of a job done well. "Now if you don't mind, could you move outside the screens and tell the rest of the Hlutr what you've found? I don't relish being under a death sentence."

"Let us take down your screen, Saburo Imhotep, and your creatures may tell the Hlutr themselves."

"It will take a while."

I spread my song outward, and it is answered by the monkey-things—by a profound melody that is joy itself. I wish nothing more than to lose myself in communion with these new minds. There is so much to learn. But first, I remind myself, I must answer Imhotep.

"I can wait."

Music calls, and I surrender.

PART ELEVEN:

Piper

Once more Hlutr roots drink deep of Terran soil.

I am third. The first was the Traveller, chosen by the Elders to live his strange life in exile. The second was our ambassador to New York, who spoke to the First Terran Empire and watched over the ruin of Earth.

I am third.

Since I broke soil a Terran century ago I have known what I am: the Elders bred me specially for life on this fair blue globe, and I would not feel at home on any other planet, not even lost Paka Tel.

It is time for Humans to come home.

Sixteen thousand years ago, Mankind lost his home world. It was in the time of the Death, when my Little Ones almost left the Universal Song. Hlutr intervention saved them; but the path to Earth was lost, and none would rediscover it in all the millennia since.

At first it was easy. My brothers and sisters on surrounding worlds had only to put forth the barest effort, and approaching travelers turned away from golden Sol without knowing they did so.

Later Humans were more sophisticated, and it was necessary to establish an actual curtain around the planet. In the high days of the Second Empire even that curtain could not serve, and the telepaths of Avethell moved in. The Aakad da'Estra, too, aided us.

Twice seventy centuries and more, my brothers and sisters labored to keep Mankind's home safe and undisturbed.

Daamin biologists worked slowly, healing the scars of this battered world. That work took half a thousand Human generations. By the time Man reached his true maturity, his native world had been reclaimed.

Then Iaranori craftsmen and Kreen historians rebuilt the monuments and cities of vanished ages; Dorascan scientists brought modern technology to the planet without disturbing its ecological balance; and finally, the Hlutr sent my seed to be planted in the fertile soil of this beautiful valley.

It is time for Humans to come home. And I must bring them here.

The Galactic Riders have been busy, restoring to Terra all the art treasures which have been held in trust in the Museum of Worlds on Nephestal. Yet there is sadness: for each wonderful creation saved from destruction, seventy are dust.

Still, we of the reclamation crew are happy with what remains. We have built a museum here in the valley, as much for the returning Humans as for ourselves. And I cannot help a small feeling of pride: even in their violent childhood, my adopted children created works of art that have delighted the Scattered Worlds. I understand that the Council had quite a struggle to get Lisa del Gioconda away from the Master of the Museum.

Everything is ready; it is time.

My brothers and sisters have been busy already, under my direction. For the last century we have sung a song of homecoming, and more often the thoughts of Humans have turned to lost Terra. Several major expeditions have set out to find the lost globe . . . but we have prevented them until everything was right.

Just over one million Humans live in the Scattered Worlds today. Many serve the Galaxy as Galactic Riders or in other capacities; more are independent souls on a thousand worlds and settlements throughout space. Such a throng could never make the pilgrimage to Terra without leadership, without someone to inspire them.

I have found the leader.

Now beneath the eternal stars, I sing out into the night. All Mankind will hear that song, but one soul will resonate with it, one soul will respond.

Seasons pass.

Around me the members of the reclamation team bid their farewells to Earth, and one by one they depart. Perhaps my Little Ones will choose to allow nonhuman visitors on their world, or perhaps like the Iaranori they will keep their world for themselves alone—either way, it will be their decision to make. Ours is the gift of Terra: afterwards, the gift is theirs alone.

I am alone, as sun and stars race past. Out in space, an incredible migration swells.

They feel the power of the leader's vision, and even folk who have sworn never to leave their homes find themselves moved by the leader's words and the song in their hearts. Some will return at once to space, some will abide here a while and then leave, others will stay forever—but *all* will walk on Terran soil before they die.

The leader must show the way.

From Credix to Borshall, from Prein to Lathyros, they gather in starliners, in individual ships, in family settlements . . . they gather around New Sardinia, where the Assembly of Humanity awaits their will.

Take us home, says the massed will of Mankind.

"I do not know the way," says the leader.

Here is the first and most important of the tasks for which I was born. I sing, and the leader's soul echoes that song. *Come to me, Little One.*

He comes. And the others, they cannot help but follow.

It is a glorious morning when they arrive. Ten thousand starships sing around Terra, a million wondering minds regard a single blue world . . . and they weep, in happiness for their long-delayed homecoming.

One ship breaks from the orbital formation, one vessel settles slowly toward me. *Welcome,* I sing, as it touches the grasses of this place called Oldavai.

For a moment it sits, inert, a silver seed alone beneath the sun. Then it opens, and the leader emerges. There is both irony and celebration in his ancient words as the first Human foot in sixteen thousand years touches Terran soil: "That's one small step for a man, one giant leap for Mankind."

It is done. My children are home. I sing thanks to the Elders who made me, to the teachers who taught me, to the Universal Song which has blessed me. Then, singing a song of joy and welcome, I turn to the waiting leader and speak in Human tongue.

"Welcome home, Kev Mathis."

The long story of Humankind has begun . . .

WHAT OUR READERS SAY ABOUT

LOIS McMASTER BUJOLD

"I read [THE WARRIOR'S APPRENTICE] very carefully with an eye on making criticisms based on my experiences as a former military officer, but each time I found something, you repaired it.... I could find nothing to fault in the story. It was well done and well written."
—Kevin D. Randle, Cedar Rapids, Iowa

"I am reading Lois Bujold's THE WARRIOR'S APPRENTICE for the third time.... The girl [sic!] plots intricately. I love her writing, and will buy anything she writes."
—R.C. Crenshaw, Eugene, Oregon

"You may be off on a new Space Patrol with the Dendarii Mercenaries. It will strain my purse, but I should cut my eating anyhow!"
—John P. Conlon, Newark, Ohio

"I have been recommending [SHARDS OF HONOR] to my friends, telling them that the book is about personal honor, love, duty, and the conflict between honor, love and duty. I am looking forward to your next novel."
—Radcliffe Cutshaw, Boca Raton, Florida

AND HERE'S WHAT THE CRITICS SAY:

SHARDS OF HONOR

"Bujold has written what may be the best first science fiction novel of the year."
—*Chicago Sun-Times*

"A strong debut, and Bujold is a writer to look for in the future."
—*Locus*

"An unusually good book."
—*Voice of Youth Advocates*

"Splendid ... This superb first novel integrates a believable romance into a science fiction tale of adventure and war."
—*Booklist*

THE WARRIOR'S APPRENTICE

"Highly recommended for any SF collection."
—*Booklist*

"Bujold continues to delight."
—*Locus*

"Bujold's first book, *Shards of Honor*, was called 'possibly the best first SF novel of the year,' by the *Chicago Sun-Times*. *The Warrior's Apprentice* is better."
—*Fantasy Review*

ETHAN OF ATHOS

"This is Ms. Bujold's third novel, and the consensus of opinion among those who enjoy watching the development of a new writer is that she just keeps getting better." —*Vandalia Drummer News*

"An entertaining, and out-of-the-ordinary, romp." —*Locus*

"I've read SHARDS OF HONOR about twenty times; THE WARRIOR'S APPRENTICE not so repeatedly but I'm working on it. If [Ms. Bujold] can maintain the quality she'll rank with Anne McCaffrey and C.J. Cherryh." —Aeronita C. Belle, Baltimore, Md.

"I just finished your book SHARDS OF HONOR. It was so good I almost don't want to take it back to the library.... Keep up the good work." —Jan Curtis, Delaware, Ohio

---

WILL *YOU* SURVIVE?

In addition to Dean Ing's powerful science fiction novels—*Systemic Shock, Wild Country, Blood of Eagles* and others—he has written cogently and inventively about the art of survival. **The Chernobyl Syndrome** is the result of his research into life after a possible nuclear exchange . . . because as our civilization gets bigger and better, we become more and more dependent on its products. What would *you* do if the machine stops—or blows up?

Some of the topics Dean Ing covers:
*   How to *make* a getaway airplane
*   Honing your "crisis skills"
*   Fleeing the firestorm: escape tactics for city-dwellers
*   How to build a homemade fallout meter
*   Civil defense, American style
*   "Microfarming"—survival in five acres
    And much, much more.

Also by Dean Ing, available through Baen Books:

ANASAZI
Why did the long-vanished Anasazi Indians retreat from their homes and gardens on the green mesa top to precarious cliffside cities? Were they afraid of someone—or some*thing*? "There's no evidence of warfare in the ruins of their earlier homes . . . but maybe the marauders they feared didn't wage war in the usual way," says Dean Ing. *Anasazi* postulates a race of alien beings who needed human bodies in order to survive on Earth—a race of aliens that *still* exists.

FIREFIGHT 2000
How do you integrate armies supplied with bayonets and ballistic missiles; citizens enjoying Volkswagens and Ferraris; cities drawing power from windmills and nuclear powerplants? Ing takes a look at these dichotomies, and more. This collection of fact and fiction serves as a metaphor for tomorrow: covering terror and hope, right guesses and wrong, high tech and thatched cottages.